PRAISE FOR
AN ARCANE INHERITANCE

"Unforgettable and unputdownable, *An Arcane Inheritance* is a visceral dream of a novel that will haunt you even in the daylight hours. Kamilah Cole has woven a genre-defining triumph."

—**Chelsea Abdullah**, award-winning author of *The Stardust Thief* and *The Ashfire King*

"An intriguing, atmospheric puzzle box of a novel that is both an alluring romantic thriller and an incisive takedown of all that haunts our most hallowed halls."

—**Olivie Blake**, *New York Times* bestselling author of *The Atlas Six*

"Old-world glamour meets the underbelly of modern academia in this ivy-wrought thriller about the magic and brutality of memory. Cole's voice is as deft and elegant as a fountain pen, sharp enough to draw blood."

—**S. T. Gibson**, #1 *Sunday Times* and *USA Today* bestselling author of *A Dowry of Blood*, *An Education in Malice*, and The Summoner's Circle

"A tautly paced, keenly observed thriller, set against an atmospherically rendered backdrop where questions of privilege and wealth haunt the narrative just as much as the literal ghosts. This is everything I adore in a dark academia book."

—**Ava Reid**, #1 *New York Times* bestselling author of *A Study in Drowning*

"*An Arcane Inheritance* reads like a stunning fever dream. With sizzling tension between academic rivals, chilling twists you won't see coming, and a narrative that seeks to dismantle privilege and those who abuse their power, this dark academia fantasy truly sets the standard for its genre. A must-read."

—**Pascale Lacelle**, *New York Times* bestselling author of *Curious Tides*

"Intriguing, skillful, and an interrogative mirror to ghosts that haunt—*An Arcane Inheritance* uncovers the dirty underbelly of academic institutions through a thrilling and propulsive mystery. This is dark academia at its finest."

—**Maddie Martinez**, author of *The Maiden and Her Monster*

"Kamilah Cole's foray into the world of dark academia is nothing short of masterful. From the very first page, readers are transported into an academic hellscape that is as outwardly alluring as it is deadly. Ellory Morgan's story is infused with a growing tension that kept me turning the pages well after midnight, and Cole does a remarkable job of peeling back the layers of glossy varnish and ivy-clad brick to expose the rot beneath. Romantic and meaningful and at times downright bone-chilling, *An Arcane Inheritance* is the sort of story that reminds us that all power comes with a cost."

—**Kelly Andrew**, *New York Times* bestselling author of *Your Blood, My Bones* and *The Gravewood*

"As twisting as it is relentless, Cole weaves a tale of power and sacrifice, ripping apart the ivory facade to reveal the rot that lies at the heart of our most honored institutions. A tour de force that centers the academia in dark academia, *An Arcane Inheritance* is a must-read!"

—**K. M. Enright**, *Sunday Times* bestselling author of *Mistress of Lies*

"A stunning meditation about what it means to belong within institutions built on foundations of exclusion. *An Arcane Inheritance* blends the occult and dark academia in a riveting narrative while also questioning what it means to be remembered—and who is or isn't given that privilege."

—**Liselle Sambury**, author of *Blood Like Magic* and *Delicious Monsters*

"A twisted, propulsive, and utterly captivating dark academia with magic and madness at its core, *An Arcane Inheritance* draws readers into its spell before asking readers to consider who pays the true price of power—and what it means to refuse to let the powerful win."

—**Laura R. Samotin**, author of *The Sins on Their Bones*

"Academic rivals to lovers at its absolute best, this twisty dark academia is a must-read! Kamilah Cole has become an instant one-click author for me!"

—**Katee Robert**, *New York Times* and *USA Today* bestselling author of *Tender Cruelty*

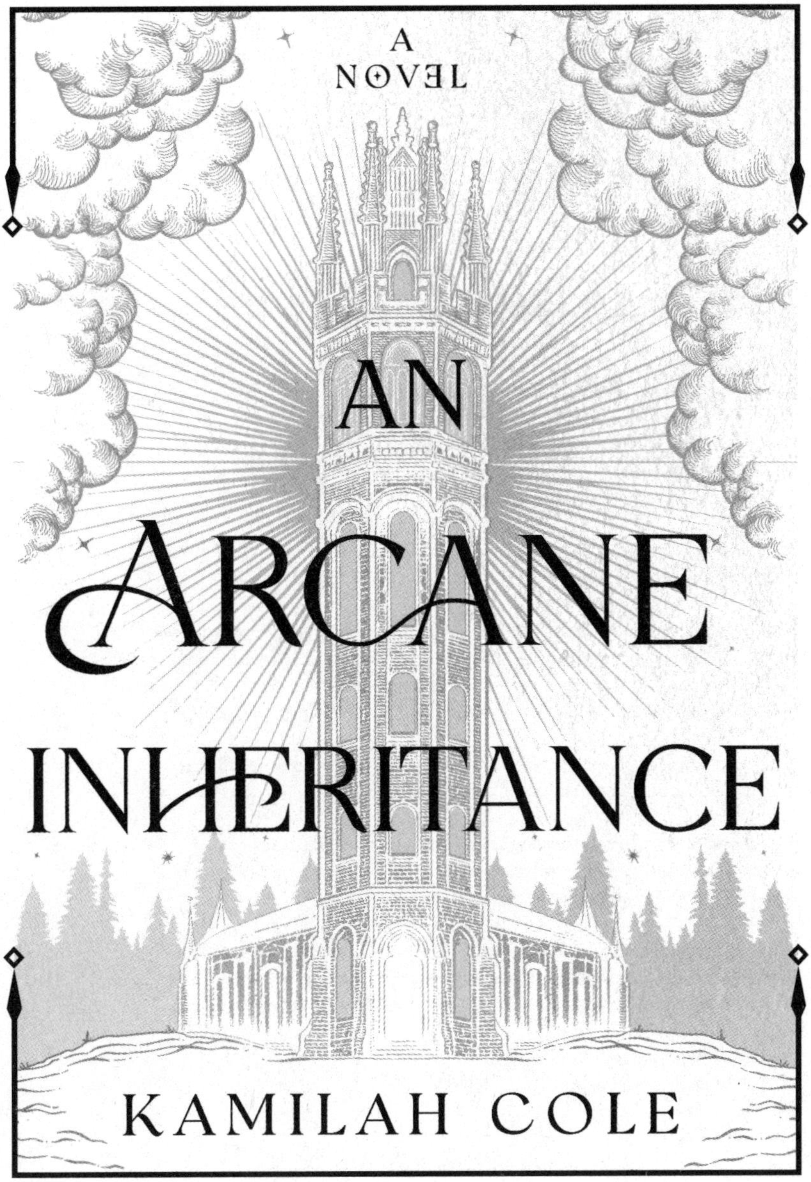

A NOVEL

AN ARCANE INHERITANCE

KAMILAH COLE

Copyright © 2026 by Kamilah Cole
Cover and internal design © 2026 by Sourcebooks
Cover design and illustration by Andrew Davis
Internal design by Tara Jaggers/Sourcebooks
Map art by Cho-hyun Kim, Illustrator (IG @nong247)
Spot illustrations by Ash Jon/Sourcebooks

Sourcebooks, Poisoned Pen Press, and the colophon
are registered trademarks of Sourcebooks.

All rights reserved. No part of this book may be reproduced in any form or by any electronic or mechanical means including information storage and retrieval systems—except in the case of brief quotations embodied in critical articles or reviews—without permission in writing from its publisher, Sourcebooks.

No part of this book may be used or reproduced in any manner for the purpose of training artificial intelligence technologies or systems.

The characters and events portrayed in this book are fictitious or are used fictitiously. Any similarity to real persons, living or dead, is purely coincidental and not intended by the author.

All brand names and product names used in this book are trademarks, registered trademarks, or trade names of their respective holders. Sourcebooks is not associated with any product or vendor in this book.

Published by Poisoned Pen Press, an imprint of Sourcebooks
1935 Brookdale RD, Naperville, IL 60563-2773
(630) 961-3900
sourcebooks.com

Cataloging-in-Publication Data is on file with the Library of Congress.

Printed and bound in the United States of America.
MA 10 9 8 7 6 5 4 3 2 1

To Lauren: It's you, it's you, it's all for you, everything I do.

And to Ebony, Jane, and Tyler, for going
to the college parties I didn't go to.

WARREN UNIVERSITY

CAMPUS MAP

An Arcane Inheritance contains racism, classism, elitism (all challenged), allusions to death, corpses, burials, anxiety and panic attacks (POV), closed-door sexual content, violence, attempted murder, and body horror.

They say magic moves in the shadows and writes its history in the memories of those lost along the way. Can you follow its trail through Warren University?

DIVINATION   EVOCATION   INCANTATION

PART I

A DANGEROUS ADMISSION

Their shadow dims the sunshine of our day,
As they go lumbering across the sky,
Squawking in joy of feeling safe on high,
Beating their heavy wings of owlish gray.

"Birds of Prey," Claude McKay

PRELUDE

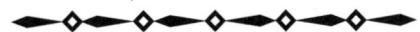

WARREN UNIVERSITY STARTED AS A joke. Not to the founders—three vainglorious men who had been born with the world in their hands and their futures glittering like gold coins eager to be spent—but to the people of Hartford.

Colonized in the 1600s by the Dutch—whose belief in European expansionism was matched only by their inability to believe that the Algonquian tribes already occupying the land could be considered people—Hartford was, at different points in history, one of the wealthiest and one of the poorest cities in the United States. When the university founders began buying acreage, it was well on its way to rock bottom, barely surviving a flood in 1909, a fire in 1944, and, worst of all, *immigration* in the postwar decades.

Suffice to say, building a prestigious university on the west bank of the Connecticut River, directly opposite the eventual industrial sprawl of East Hartford, was truly ridiculous.

Trinity College, though not yet coeducational, already smugly occupied its new campus in Gallows Hill. The University of Hartford would not be built for another three years, but the

University of Connecticut's School of Law was already there and housing the Hartford Seminary as a bonus. Warren University was expected to be a social experiment that swiftly closed or merged with a more prestigious school.

The doors opened in 1954. The inaugural class was coeducational *and* integrated, thanks to the *Brown v. Board of Education* ruling in May of that year. The first students walked a gorgeous three-hundred-acre campus of pristine lawns, curated parks, and neoclassical architecture, soundtracked by the distant yet ever-present chords of rushing river water, to learn social sciences and liberal arts from a university that would, by the end of the year, become the last member of the Ivy League.

And if some of those students disappeared before graduation, well…every college needs a ghost story.

1

THE POLITICAL SCIENCE MAJOR AT Warren University was a prestigious murder weapon.

Ellory Morgan had been staring in rising dismay at the dense pages of her con. law textbook for over two hours, and in that time, her mind, her soul, and her confidence had expired. In theory, these constitutional principles were her keys to unlocking a successful future. In practice, Ellory thought bludgeoning herself with the book would help her absorb roughly the same amount of information. It might even be less painful.

It was only three weeks into the first semester of her first year, and already stress flavored the stagnant air inside Graves Library. At every table, at least one student was about to break down, was in the process of breaking down, or had just come back from a breakdown in the bathroom, crimson-eyed and waxen-cheeked. Books were stacked like barriers to give people the illusion of privacy, but it was silent except for the turning of pages and the *tip-tap* of autumn rain against the windows. Ellory could hear someone weeping, but that could have been the Graves Ghost. According to the orientation walking tour, he'd *also* died studying.

The Graves, as the library was more often called, had been named for its donors and design. The Gardiners, a Connecticut old-money founding family, had married into the Graves line, whose members all came from Virginian post–Civil War new money, and they'd celebrated their union by gifting the library to Warren—because that was what people with fuck-you money did with it. Modeled after the Catacombs of Paris, the Graves consisted of an ornate one-story entrance, languishing beneath the sun like a king in repose, and eight more underground floors of book stacks and study rooms, tables with the world's most uncomfortable chairs, and vaulted stone ceilings with a round skylight that flickered every time someone walked across the levels above.

During her first week on campus, Ellory had gone to the basement and looked through the skylight, curious if she would be able to see all the way up to the painted ceiling that watched over the entrance. But it was too disconcerting. Even with the air conditioner at full blast, the permeating late-August heat made her feel as if she had been buried alive. The longer she stared through that quivering skylight, the more a scream built in her throat, one she knew without knowing would only echo around the stone walls of the ossuary-like basement, never bleeding through to anyone who could help her. Goose bumps had pebbled her arms until she'd made it back to the elevator.

Now, as a general rule, she never went lower than the second floor of the Graves. The memory made her tremble so violently that she almost dislodged her backpack from its precarious perch at the edge of the table. Papers spilled across the surface in swatches of cloud white, charcoal gray, and sandstone beige. Her eyes hooked on one in particular, thicker than the rest, emblazoned in black, green, and gold.

AN ARCANE INHERITANCE

Ellory made sure no one was paying attention to her and slipped the flyer into her textbook. It was a flyer she should never have taken, let alone carried around every day since, its edges so frayed from her frequent handling that it could be mistaken for scrap paper, but still she traced the fading letters like they spelled something holy. NEW YEAR, NEW REPORTERS: JOIN THE WARREN COMMUNIQUÉ, read the colorful advertisement—colorful and *pointless*, because she had no time for extracurriculars. Not when she had started so strong only to start slipping in her classes, even though her scholarship depended on her excelling every second of every day.

And yet the *Warren Communiqué* was the most well-respected student newspaper in the country, rivaled only by the *Yale Daily News*. She imagined seeing her byline below the emerald-and-onyx logo. An above-the-fold, front-page feature story with a glossy photograph that would earn them a Pulitzer. Maybe one day her very own beat or column, with readers who picked up the *Communiqué* to read *her* words...

Ellory crushed the seed of that dream before it could sprout into fresh disappointment. She had no time for writing, for hobbies, for clubs. Not if she wanted to pass this semester. She wedged the flyer back into her bag, shoved the bag closer to the center of the table, and yanked her textbook into her field of view. Constitutional law. She could do this. She could *do* this.

Laughter cracked the brittle quiet. Ellory glanced through the fingers she had buried in her curls, locating the place where people were actually having fun. Haloed by the fluorescent bulbs of the chandeliers and the natural skylight, the table was near the center of the room and bursting with students. Freshmen, she guessed from the fact that none of them looked dead inside. Some had taken chairs from another table and jammed them into every available space at the communal one, and they were unpacking their backpacks in a flurry of joyful energy.

She tilted her head to observe them better. Newly graduated from high school, probably. Many of them seemed to know one another in a way that ran deeper than orientation desperation.

Though she was also a freshman, at twenty-one, Ellory felt distant from recent high school graduates. To go to college, one had to have go-to-college money, and go-to-college money meant disposable income in the hundred thousands. Each of her university acceptances had come with a scholarship rejection. Predatory loans and strangely specific grants did not pan out. Odd jobs and freelance work paid pennies compared to the zeros at the end of each semester's tuition.

In the end, Ellory was forced to defer admission. Before Warren, before the Godwin Scholarship, she had resigned herself to taking classes online one at a time as she earned enough money to register for them.

Now she was here, but it was awkward to be so much older than most people in her core classes. Awkward to field questions about why it had *taken so long* for her to get into a school. Awkward to explain that somewhere between the lower-income population and the upper-income elite were people like Ellory, lost in the shrinking abyss of middle income, where living paycheck to paycheck didn't make her needy enough for a single needs-based grant.

Watching these freshmen now, so wealthy and carefree and full of potential, made her feel like a crone. It had taken her three years to get where they'd never once doubted they'd be. For them, college had been a guarantee. For her, it had been a gift—one that could be taken back at any moment.

"This is a library," said a voice colder than the air conditioner the school had yet to shut off, "not a comedy club."

Hudson Graves loomed over the freshmen like an angry god, swathed in a midnight peacoat and gripping a thick leather-bound book. His ombré fade had been freshly touched up since the weekend, his curls dyed white gold and cresting over his forehead like whitecaps frothing against a stormy sea. His full mouth was twisted into a frown, his body language haughty and unfriendly. Ellory bit the inside of her cheek to keep from scowling, especially when a swift hush fell over the once-bright table. One sheepish student murmured an apology, as though Hudson Graves were a librarian whose word alone would get them thrown out.

Since Hudson was the scion of the family that had purchased the building, that wasn't an *unreasonable* fear, but his ego was large enough without such unwarranted deference. He was no librarian, and he was no god. He was a bigger pain in her ass than con. law could ever be.

Hell, he was part of the reason con. law was such a pain in her ass. It was one of the few classes she shared with seniors like him.

During the first full day of classes, Ellory had made the mistake of sitting down next to Hudson Graves. She hadn't even been looking at him; she'd seen an empty seat and captured it before the embarrassment of trying to find a friendly face had time to kick in. The worst part was that it had been a good day up until then. The sky was an effervescent periwinkle, the sun sparkled from behind a wreath of cotton clouds, and the weather was a perfect marriage of summer and autumn that required nothing but a light jacket. She'd practiced walking the path to her classes so many times that she had arrived in Rousseau Hall with fifteen minutes to spare, a half-finished iced vanilla latte dangling from her fingers. Her work-study program had placed her at an on-campus café literally called Powers That Bean, and she'd scoped it out ahead of her shift mainly for the discount drinks.

And then Hudson Graves said, "Did you ask if you could sit there?"

"What?" she'd responded, more confused than offended. "I didn't realize I needed to ask permission to sit in an empty chair."

These days, it burned to remember that her first thought when Hudson Graves had fully turned to face her was an inane one: *What pretty eyelashes.* They were lush dark smudges curving upward from tan skin so golden, it took her a moment to realize he was Black. His Afro-textured hair had been dyed a light blond that was nearly silver, and his jaw was outlined with overnight stubble that this class had taken priority over shaving away. She thought him handsome, but in a boyish kind of way. Thick-browed and big-nosed and round-cheeked, he looked like he was still growing into his features and the final product would be breathtaking. His downturned eyes were the deep brown of an avocado seed, reminding her of something her aunt had once said:

The color brown has been associated with so many things that people would never call beautiful: Dirt. Mud. Shit. But we're copper and amber, tiger's-eye and smoky quartz. We're tawny and sepia, umber and russet. We're forest wood and fresh soil, warm coffee and sweet gingerbread, a spill of ink, a starless sky, a damn good glass of brandy. A person who sees that sees you.

Ellory opened her mouth to defuse the situation with a compliment, fascinated by the way the overhead lights brought new shades of brown to the fore of his intense gaze, but he spoke over her.

"The seat's not empty," he sneered, "and you'll have a tough time in this class if all you do is make assumptions."

AN ARCANE INHERITANCE

His expression was the only reasonable argument against climate change, so cold that it could single-handedly refreeze all the polar ice caps. Then Hudson glanced over her head, and a manicured hand landed on her desk. Seconds later, a hostile feminine voice said, "There's assigned seating. This one's mine."

Ellory scurried away so quickly that she probably left a trail of smoke, her cheeks burning. It all felt so juvenile, so *high school*, that she knew she should let it go. It was one man on a campus of people, and one class—she hoped—that she had to share with him. The mature thing would have been to ignore him... But his sheer fucking *dismissiveness*. The way he'd underestimated her. How he'd assumed that she could afford to struggle in this class or any other. It rankled more than his rudeness.

And so, when the professor strolled in five minutes late, Ellory's hand rocketed into the air at the first opportunity to answer a question from the reading she had done in full over the summer. Beneath the lazy inspection by her half asleep classmates—and one set of burning brown eyes—she analyzed the broad gray areas still inherent in the application and interpretation of constitutional law.

Shortly afterward, Hudson Graves answered a different question, expounding on his theories regarding why the American constitution was one of the hardest to update in the world.

She brought up six Supreme Court cases that had changed the interpretation of the same line in the constitution. He countered with the fact that the SCOTUS's power of judicial review was created through *Marbury v. Madison*, not the constitution, so wasn't it unconstitutional that the court had changed the interpretation at all?

The class fell away. The students disappeared. The professor might as well have never shown up. There was only her and Hudson

Graves and an hour-and-fifteen-minute-long chess match that never reached a checkmate.

Ellory left that class without a backward glance, her blood pumping and her enmity secured. And twice a week, for an hour and fifteen minutes, Hudson Graves had found new ways to rub it in her face that she was falling further and further behind.

Now he was harassing freshmen in the very library where she was studying. Though she was glad the dumpster fire that he called a personality was willing to burn people other than her, she didn't want to be in the blast radius. As the simpering students drew him into quiet conversation, Ellory packed up her things and found her umbrella.

The elevator spat her out into the street-level atrium, with its white stone floor, painted dome, and circular skylight. Rose-tipped clouds spanned the vibrant celestial mural that decorated the ceiling. Rain clattered against the glass, the real clouds a hazy purple gray that threatened lightning. Though it was early afternoon, the only light came from the lanterns in the wall sconces, electric in power but ancient in appearance. In her experience, most universities loved three things: money, tradition, and aesthetics.

"Morgan."

Ellory's shoulders tensed. She fiddled with her umbrella, desperate to get it open even though she was still several yards from the front doors.

"I know you hear me."

"Isn't it a little hubristic of you to study in the library named after you?" she muttered.

Hudson Graves caught up with her easily. He was only four inches taller than her, but those inches were mostly in leg, and his waterproof Timberlands gave him an added boost. Ellory didn't embarrass herself by trying to run, but her fingers dug into the folds of her umbrella.

"Isn't it a little masochistic of you," he drawled, "to study in the library named after me?"

His peacoat was open, flapping around his body like the wings of a bird in flight. Beneath, he wore a beige cable-knit sweater over a powder-blue button-down fastened all the way up his neck. The leather-bound book was gone, replaced by a smaller volume that he carried at his side, tucked against his black jeans.

This one he held out to her with an infuriating smirk. "However, I imagine you'll find it difficult to study at all without this."

It was her constitutional law textbook. Ellory's face flamed. She snatched it back, half expecting him to turn this into an adolescent game of keep-away to drag out her humiliation. His fingers brushed the inside of her wrist during the handoff, but he didn't call attention to it, and neither did she. Her skin tingling, she eased the book into her satchel, a thrifted steel-gray messenger bag covered in pins and patches that looked so silly next to his Montblanc sling. One pin read, MAYBE TOMORROW, SATAN. Hudson quirked an eyebrow at the sight of it.

"Well," she said before he could comment. "I'd love to stay and chat, but I'd rather sit on a cactus than look at you, so—bye."

The rain came down in sheets, wind tearing at the trees that lined the cobblestone square around the library. A sudden gust tried to suck her umbrella inside out, but she pushed her head closer to the nylon fabric and pressed on. Water welled from between the stones, turning the square into a muddy creek, levels perilously rising. Footsteps splashed behind her. Ellory swore under her breath, unsurprised to see Hudson Graves haunting her trail. His umbrella was black, and the white glow of his phone screen washed out his face until it looked like a skull, all sharp, gaunt angles and deep, dark eye sockets.

Behind him, Graves Library lurked, its limestone facade bathed in the golden light of the windows. Built in the style of the Barrière d'Enfer—the neoclassical tollhouses that marked the entrance to the Catacombs of Paris—the stone arch of the building entrance seemed, for a moment, like the gaping maw of some primordial creature sucking all the air out of the courtyard.

Then she blinked, and the library was just a library, the man just a man.

And she was tired of both of them.

Though her residence hall was to the left, Ellory cut a right on Powell Street. Moneta Hall also happened to be near the student parking lot, and she would much rather take the long way around than risk Hudson bumping into her with more unsolicited advice and unwanted commentary.

Without the trees to act as cover, the wind howled like a dying animal. Her heart kept time with the rain: *pitter-pat, pitter-pat, pitter-pat*. People clustered beneath the overhang next to the bus stop. Ellory thought she recognized one woman from her criminology class, but to take a hand off her umbrella even long enough to wave would be to lose it to the elements.

Everything looked different in the gray. As she walked the Loop, which was what students called the half-moon stretch of Archive Lane that cut around the back of Graves Square, the landmarks were slick and shadowed, her view hindered by the incessant rain. She should have waited in the lobby, Hudson or no Hudson. He had to walk no farther than the student parking lot down the street, where he'd take his fancy car to his fancy off-campus housing, while Ellory was stuck hoofing it through torrential rains to get back to the freshman dorms, where her eighteen-year-old roommate was probably streaming some incomprehensible reality show and wrinkling her nose at the amount of mixed-berry yogurt Ellory had managed to pack into the minifridge.

Stop letting him get to you when he's not even here.

Rain splattered the side of Ellory's face and dripped from the tight coils of her hair. She swore again, adjusting her umbrella to protect her twist out, and walked even faster. But instead of Ellory arriving at Moneta Hall in ten minutes, fifteen elapsed without any sign of the dorm. By the twenty-minute mark, she'd passed empty quads broken up by the occasional copse of trees, but she saw no road markers or statues, no other students or parked cars, no Warren buses or security booths. The storm had, if possible, gotten worse. Her phone said 5:00 p.m., but the sky said midnight. The clouds were so thick that she couldn't see the outline of the sun. Lightning cracked without thunder, the only illumination on a path whose streetlights had yet to turn on.

She stopped at an intersection. Was she even still on campus?

A passing car barely avoided splashing her with the grime of a puddle beyond the sidewalk. She jumped anyway, losing her grip on her umbrella. Water soaked into her hair, into her forest-green hoodie, into her newly polished thrifted high-tops. Her slate-gray messenger bag turned a deep charcoal. A single raindrop trailed down the face of her MAYBE TOMORROW, SATAN pin. Poetic fucking cinema.

Ellory fished her umbrella out of the sewer water and blinked the rain out of her eyes. But even after she dragged her damp sleeve over her damp face, clearing her vision enough to bring the world back into focus, she recognized nothing about this area. She had walked this campus from end to end that summer, refusing to broadcast her freshman status by lumbering around with a map in hand, and before this moment, she would have claimed there was no part of Warren she couldn't navigate. Twenty minutes was not enough to leave school grounds. Twenty minutes was not enough to lose landmarks. Twenty minutes was not enough to make her so disoriented that her surroundings ebbed and flowed as if she were caught in a riptide.

She wiped her eyes again, as if that would somehow cause her to wake up at Moneta Hall. Instead, thunder clapped above her and shadows reigned around her and brackish water rose below her—tiny natural disasters that shot her anxiety to new heights.

This wasn't possible. This wasn't *possible*.

Ellory's breath rattled out of her lungs in hitching pants. Through the hammering rain, she thought she heard a giggle, but when she whirled around, there was no one there. The path she had walked to get here had grown darker, unfamiliar, like an elongated black tongue. Trees twisted in the gale, branches splayed like the limbs of a broken puppet. Lightning snapped across a sky the dark purple of a fresh bruise.

Perhaps the laughter was only in her mind, her subconscious processing what she was so slow to accept.

Impossible or not, she was lost.

The storm had somehow swallowed her whole.

2

E LLORY HAD WORKED A DOUBLE shift the day the letter arrived. She might not have opened it at all if it hadn't been for Aunt Carol, who was the kind of gossip who sat in her lawn chair on the fire escape to watch the neighbors in the Hummer-sized cement block her building called a courtyard. Ellory had spent four hours at Midtown Comics being talked down to about Marvel by people who considered "Do you like *Blade*?" to be a form of flirting—the same people who sputtered when she fixed them with a dead-eyed stare and a "Why? Because I'm Black?" Then she'd spent another four hours at the Queens Public Library at Astoria, reshelving books from the endless supply of carts and trying not to get caught reading between the stacks.

Most of the mail that she got were bills or advertisements—for government candidates, colleges she couldn't afford to attend, and preapproved credit cards—and she kept them in a chaotic pile on her night table until she was in the mood to open them all at once. But when she got home that day, Carol was in the kitchen, sitting in front of a battlefield of torn envelopes and crumpled letters. The holiday popcorn tin they'd repurposed into a piggy bank was open in the center of the table, and Carol was carefully counting out money for each bill: Rent. Electricity. Wi-Fi. Hospital. She would take an envelope of cash to the bank to deposit into her savings account, then cut checks by the end of each month. It was the only way she could guarantee she wouldn't waste it all in a debit card swipe and end up short.

As soon as Ellory stepped into the kitchen, her shoes neatly discarded by the door and her jacket tossed over the half-empty barrel wedged into their narrow hallway, Aunt Carol looked up at her with a grin. "You got an envelope. A thick one."

"And it didn't fall open when you left it on the shelf over the kettle?"

"I have no idea what you're talking about," Carol sniffed. "But no, it didn't."

Ellory was tossed a brown envelope—as thick as described—that was still damp from the steam of the kettle. The return address was a sticker with an unfamiliar logo, the letters *W* and *U* in ink-black sans serif with forest-green ivy curled around the letters. Beneath, a scroll-like banner read, FOUNDED IN 1954. Her name was written neatly in the direct center of the envelope, ELLORY JESSICA MORGAN, as if they'd wanted to make sure there was no mistake about which Ellory Morgan they were writing to. Her aunt's eyes bored into her forehead as Ellory sank down in the chair across from hers and fiddled with the seal.

> *Dear Miss Morgan,*
> *We are reaching out to invite you to a four-year*
> *academic opportunity at Warren University*
> *in Hartford, Connecticut. Please find all*
> *informational materials enclosed.*

AN ARCANE INHERITANCE

As your academic records are three years old, we ask only that you sit for our free attendance exam at one of these hopefully convenient times. Should you pass, tuition, room, and board will be fully covered by the Godwin Scholarship in the amount of...

When she saw the numbers listed across from what that money would be covering, her hands started to shake. She read the letter twice before she managed to release her death grip on the paper and hand it over to Carol. She hadn't even applied to Warren University in her hopeful initial round, three years prior. Columbia and Cornell were in New York, Princeton closer, in New Jersey; *those* had been her reach schools, and she'd lost her place in Princeton after her deferral year.

Since then, each time she brought up the idea of going to community college, Aunt Carol looked like Ellory had slapped her.

"You want me to tell your parents that they entrusted you to my care so you could end up *at a community college?*" she'd said, her hand over her heart like a scandalized Puritan. Ellory's well-worn arguments that there was nothing wrong with community college, that it would give her the same degree with less debt, and that Carol's reaction was both elitist *and* classist had just made her aunt even more outraged. Community college was, in Carol's eyes, a curse capable of staining their bloodline for generations to come.

Ellory googled WARREN UNIVERSITY while Carol read the letter, soon landing on the Wikipedia page. As she'd known, it was an Ivy League, a member of the Ancient Nine, the last added and the last built. The list of notable alumni included ten congressmen, six diplomats, twenty actors, and one serial killer serving a life sentence in CSP-C. Their admissions process involved a terrifyingly high rejection rate, fleshed out by active outreach to marginalized and underrepresented communities and a robust financial aid program. And they wanted her. Not to apply, but to attend on a full-ride scholarship.

When she met Carol's gaze over her phone, she saw her own awe reflected at her. But there had also been a dawning hope, a fire not yet lit but flecked with embers. If this was real...if this was legal... it would be her second chance. Her almost-lost shot.

Her new beginning.

Bullshit. In three weeks, Ellory had made an enemy or two, cried in a third-floor bathroom after a lecture so confusing that it had made her question her grasp of the English language, and gotten troublingly addicted to the particular swirl of syrups and espresso in a Powers That Bean iced vanilla latte. Now she was hyperventilating in a hungry tempest, her sense of time and direction slipping through her shaking fingers.

If this was her beginning, she was going to hate the ending.

The rain formed a cage that blocked light and sound from the streets around her. Ellory fished her phone out of her wet bag to send Tai a text and let her GPS guide her back to her residence hall, only to find that it had no service—a feat she had not believed possible in the United States in this day and age. Two minutes later, when the tiny text remained the same, she turned around. A blue umbrella, its long rib jutting away from the canopy like an axe handle, skidded across the path and disappeared into the trees. Rain dripped from her shrunken hair and down the sides of her face. She shivered, her hoodie and T-shirt clinging to her clammy skin.

Wind giggled through the leaves. A strange scent hit her nose, making it wrinkle...and it wasn't petrichor like she expected. She smelled inert dust and rotting wood and stale air, as if she were not outside but inside a tomb long abandoned.

Ellory stepped forward but didn't sink into the gray water below the sidewalk. The ground beneath her fumbling feet was even, steady. She had *just* been on the side of the road, but she looked now and found nothing but gray-brown concrete spread forward and back, trees to one side and a darkness too complete to pierce on the other. The giggling returned, high and clear, as if to prove that this was nothing as mundane as the wind. Beneath that, she could make out a low metallic trill, like the vibration of a buzzing bee.

Hallucinations, delusions, paralogia…the sudden onset of all that seemed more likely than the testimony of her own senses. And yet…

And yet this had happened to her before.

As a child, her parents had let her go to the corner shop alone, money in hand for candy and scratch tickets. Halfway there, she got lost despite the shop being straight downhill. Her landmarks—the lavender house with the two dogs in the front yard, the cactus attempting to grow into a worn telephone pole, the stop sign that someone had drawn a curse word on—disappeared, leaving her on an endless dim street framed by thick foliage and twisted tree trunks. A doctor bird wove through the leaves above her, iridescent green wings a blur on either side of its round body, its long black tails stabbing the air like needles.

Just when Ellory was ready to sit on the sidewalk and wait to be found, she heard a familiar voice. "Mi closed," said Miss Claudette, the elderly woman who owned it. She stood at the end of the lane, right in the center of the road, her hair wrapped in a bronze scarf. Although it was a hot, windless day, the trees seemed to inch toward Claudette, waving back and forth in time with Ellory's breathing,

closer and closer every time. Even the doctor bird had disappeared. "Gwaan home."

"Zeen." But her stomach twisted with the sense that something was *off*. "Yuh good, miss?"

"Mi seh yuh fi gwaan home," Miss Claudette repeated, turning away.

Ellory went home. She stepped through the door and right into her panicked parents' arms, confused but delighted by the attention. Only later did she find out that the corner shop had caught fire shortly after she'd left.

Only later did she find out that Miss Claudette had been inside.

When she told her parents that she'd seen the old woman, even spoken to her, they had said the same thing she told herself now: *Hallucinations, delusions, paralogia.* Ellory learned to rationalize and ignore those moments when the world seemed to stretch beyond the boundaries of what was real, into a liminal space where she could see a dead woman in the street or hear phantom giggles on the wind. Eventually, they'd gotten fewer and further between.

So why was it happening again now?

Her hands tightened around her bag, pressed it to her chest. Her heart rattled around her chest cavity. Her cold limbs dripped colder water down her skin and over her ruined umbrella. She pressed her eyes shut. This wasn't real. This *wasn't* real. This wasn't *real*. Maybe she'd fallen asleep in the library. Maybe she'd slipped on a puddle in the courtyard and was unconscious on the stones where Hudson Graves no doubt would have left her. Maybe—

She peeked through her damp lashes. Her eyes flew open.

She...she knew this place.

Ellory was standing in the same tree-lined area, in the same storm that had so disoriented her, in the same darkness that had breathed and breathed around her, but she *knew* this place. Without a thought, her feet strolled confidently across the road, took a left, and kept going. She didn't check her phone again. She didn't need to. This strange déjà vu made connections snap into place like a rubber band.

She knew that if she walked five more blocks and took another left, she would come across Moneta Hall, shining bright against the gloomy evening. She knew that, if she went right instead, she would eventually hit Bancroft Field, where the soccer and lacrosse teams performed some kind of athletic alchemy that kept the school board happy. And she knew that this, right here, was Riverside Campus, where the neoclassical architecture of every carefully crafted academic building yielded to the parts of nature that weren't cleared to build Warren University, beginning with a footbridge that led across a pond and into a wooded area popular among on- and off-campus hikers. She knew that because she'd been here before; of course she had; this was where they'd—

No memory rushed to explain the sudden familiarity. Not even when she made the turn and realized she was correct.

There was Moneta, a ten-story building with large white pillars, a sloping, temple-style roof, and pale aloe-green walls that looked more like seaweed in the darkness. Her keys were so slick that she had to swipe the fob twice before the keypad let her drip inside. Her roommate, Stasie O'Connor (of the Irish royal house of O'Conor, at least according to the crest on the wall above her bed), was present but alone, watching a video while painting her toenails. Her only comment on Ellory's appearance was curt: "Keep all that on your side of the room."

But even after Ellory dumped her possessions on the windowsill to dry despite Stasie's judgmental nose crinkle, even after Ellory took such a long time in the communal bathrooms that someone knocked on the wall beside her curtain to make sure she was alive, even after she detangled and twisted her freshly washed hair over the course of an entire comedy special before tucking it under a satin bonnet, she still felt a chill. Her ears rang with adrenaline, and behind her eyes, she could see those trees that clawed at the sky in a darkness too all-encompassing to have happened anywhere on Warren's campus.

You were seeing things. It's a typical panic response. Once you calmed down, your brain reminded you of what you'd forgotten.

Stale air and rotting wood.

High-pitched giggling and low metallic trills.

Rainwater so cold, it froze her down to her marrow.

You were seeing things. Sometimes, you see things. That doesn't make them real.

It took Ellory a long time to fall asleep.

◆

It rained for three more days before the sun got out on parole. From the moment Ellory tied her apron on to the moment she yawned back to her dorm, Powers That Bean filled with students who bought a single chocolate croissant and then parked at a table by an outlet for six hours to stay out of the rain. Others loitered by the doors and walls, pretending to be waiting for friends until the manager forced them out into the deluge. Mopping the floor became an exercise in frustration as new packs of customers tracked mud and grass inside, and though they grimaced and whispered, "Sorry," when they saw the mess, not a single one left a tip.

Iced coffee sales remained steady. There was no weather that iced coffee didn't improve.

After her shift, Ellory took a walk in the restored sunlight, her drink in hand. The soccer team had claimed Bancroft, which she knew only because Hudson Graves was among them. Ellory refused to do anything more physically strenuous than squeeze into a packed train car on the N during rush hour, so athletes were an alien breed to her. They ran the length of the field (why?) back and forth, again and again (*why?*), shouting insults and encouragement to one another:

"Pick up the pace, Mendoza!"

"Looking sharp, Novak!"

"Wilson, you're falling behind!"

"Go! Go! Go! Go!"

No one jeered Hudson Graves, who was ahead of the pack of sweaty, grunting people by at least three yards. His long brown legs ate up the field with every stride, his moss-green jersey clinging to his muscled body. When she didn't actually have to talk to him, Ellory could admit to herself that Hudson Graves had a certain allure. He was clearly in his element, and that confidence translated to his elegant gait and focused mien. If he was even panting, she couldn't tell from here.

She needed to keep walking before he saw her and mistook her interest for something else. But she was rooted to the spot.

Luckily, Ellory wasn't the only one who couldn't take her eyes off him. On the other side of the field was a small crowd, also wearing jerseys, staring at Hudson like he was a two-for-one sale. Ellory had heard that the football and basketball teams were forever trying to recruit him, but this was the first time she'd actually seen their starving gazes in person. Maybe they meant it to be flattering, but it was dehumanizing, these covetous sentries longing for what they had been told repeatedly they could not have.

Ellory had been to Bancroft twice since she'd moved to campus. Tai liked to watch the soccer team play, especially in the humid summer days when the players would wrap their practice jerseys around their waists and let the sun turn their sweaty torsos gold and pink. But that was mostly because Tai's partner, Cody, had decided to play for the men's team. Cody waved when they saw Ellory, and Ellory waved back, admiring their new haircut: shaved on one side, flowing down to their chin in a wave of amber on the other. They were near the middle of the group, keeping pace but not showing off like Hudson Graves, even though, at well over six feet, they *could* have. Ellory knew a bit of what that was like—that innate fear of calling attention to herself in a place where it was safer to blend in.

"Hey, Morgan."

Oh no.

"Hello, Graves," she said evenly as he jogged toward her. "Keep a distance, please. I can smell you from here."

Behind him, Cody slowed, their eyebrows two thick lines of concern. Even if she *weren't* complaining to Tai all the time, Ellory's war with Hudson was infamous enough that Cody was probably considering whether to intervene.

Hudson stopped a few feet away, close enough that she could see the perspiration collecting at his temples but far enough that at least four people could link arms between them. She couldn't actually smell him, but she was sure he stank with the fetor of athleticism. His eyes were mockingbird black. His skin was golden brown in the caress of sunlight. His rose-pink lips held the raw ingredients of a smirk without quite finishing the recipe.

A bead of sweat traced the curve of his cheek, dripped onto his sloped shoulder, and disappeared into the fabric of his jersey. Ellory swallowed sharply.

Hudson tilted his head. "Did you hear there's going to be a pop quiz in con. law tomorrow?"

"What?" Surprise yanked the words from her dry throat. "How would you even know about a pop quiz?"

"*I* talked to the TA, but it's all over class."

Ellory bit the inside of her cheek to keep from saying something she'd regret. After the first day, she'd been afraid to talk to the rest of her classmates in case they were all members of Hudson's fan club. Her classmates seemed equally content to never speak to her. Occasionally, she checked the student message boards where they submitted assignments, but there was no casual chatter on there. Just CAN I GET AN EXTENSION and WHEN IS THIS DUE AGAIN and DOES ANYONE HAVE THE NOTES ON GIDEON V. WAINWRIGHT?

"Why are you even telling me this?" she asked around a thoughtful sip of her iced vanilla latte. Today she'd tried the oat milk that everyone was going wild for; so far, she was unimpressed. "If I fail, you have another opportunity to gloat."

Hudson snorted. "I don't want to be better than you because I have information you don't, Morgan. I want to be better than you because I'm obviously better than you." He began to jog backward, and—annoyingly—he didn't even trip. "Anyway, you have the information now. Study or don't study. It's up to you."

Ellory hated that he was right, that their petty academic rivalry meant nothing if they weren't on an even playing field. Hated that he *knew* that, believed that, which made her grudgingly respect him. She also hated the way his black shorts clung to his powerful thighs, and yes, she'd definitely been standing here for too long.

"Think fast, Graves!"

He thought fast, twisting out of the way of the soccer ball that had been hurled at him. It zipped toward Ellory's head, and she

locked up like a deer in headlights, too surprised to move. *Move, damn it. MOVE.*

A blinding flash swallowed the world.

Her skin went hot and then cold and then hot again, and sound swung back in like a punch: The shouting team running across the field toward her. The distant babble of the Connecticut River indifferently flowing southward to the Long Island Sound. The wind rustling every leaf on the surrounding trees until they loosened and joined the rising piles on the quad. Hudson was in the same place, but everyone else stopped abruptly to murmur among themselves, their gazes on her feet. Ellory glanced down, expecting to see her ankle boots and a pile of shit between them.

Instead, she was standing in a circle of dead soil.

The path that looped around Bancroft Field was a dirt trail, dark brown and packed tight. Now it was the color of wet sand, dusty and cracked. Fissures spider-webbed out from beneath her feet and stretched toward the grass before stopping mere inches from touching the vibrant green. It was like a target of ruptures, and she was the bull's-eye.

Between the field and the cracks, the soccer ball rested. She hadn't even seen it drop.

"Are you all right, Ellory?" called Cody. Like everyone else, they stared at the soccer ball like it was possessed. "I thought—well, I'm glad it didn't hit you."

"Autumn winds," Ellory heard herself say, and it was automatic, easy, like she'd said the words a thousand times before. Her hand wanted to fly to her throat, as if that would help her figure out whose script she was performing, but she *still couldn't move*. Only her lips remembered how, her mind steady in the certainty that this wasn't the first time she'd made these excuses. "Weird."

One of the team members—Novak, perhaps—chuckled. "One time, I swear the wind yanked my backpack halfway across the quad while I was napping."

"Oh, please," said another. "You're so fucking scrawny, you probably got dragged away from it."

"Who are you calling *scrawny*?"

The two began to play wrestle, and whatever spell had fallen over them all was broken. Someone, the captain probably, shouted at everyone to get back to their drills. Cody fetched the ball with the kind of friendly wave that promised a full interrogation later. The team jogged away to launch into their next round of exercises, leaving Hudson and Ellory behind in a ringing silence.

There was a wrinkle between Hudson's eyebrows, but even after he stopped staring at the ground, his gaze settled anywhere *but* on her. "I'm glad you're all right, Morgan," he said to a point over her shoulder. "Be careful when—just. Be careful."

Then he was gone before she could question his sudden and unprecedented concern for her welfare. Ellory stepped gingerly from the center of the blast radius, half expecting the cracks in the dirt to follow her. Instead, they remained as a monument to where she'd once stood, a serrated circle of death.

This time, she wasn't seeing things. Everyone else had seen it, too.

Ellory shuddered. What was going *on*?

The more distance she put between herself and that moment, the more her thoughts raced. She took a long sip of her watered-down latte in the fruitless hope of a brain freeze that would calm her mind.

For a moment, it had seemed like she had...

But that would be ridiculous. It was more likely that the *wind* had stopped that ball in its tracks. As for the path...she'd probably been too distracted to notice that dead patch. No one else had mentioned its sudden appearance, so maybe it had already been there. That was plausible. And plausible was better than the alternative. The alternative made it sound like she was hallucinating again, and Warren was the kind of place that would pull the Godwin Scholarship if she started claiming she could…what, stop a speeding soccer ball with her *mind* and crack the *very earth itself* in the process? Ridiculous.

But for a moment, it had seemed like…

No. *Ridiculous.*

Ellory threw her empty cup in the recycling bin, tossing her uneasiness out with it.

3

"Sometimes, you make me so sad," said Taiwo Daniels from her throne on the bed.

Her entire single was like a palace: one bed with sheets the rich blue of the Jamaican ocean; posters that advertised '90s anime like *Cowboy Bebop* and *Ghost in the Shell*, as well as the poetry of Wole Soyinka; a desk that doubled as a bookshelf featuring the works of Murasaki Shikibu, Chinua Achebe, Grant Morrison, and Agatha Christie; and framed family photos, the largest of which showed Tai beaming with an arm thrown around her sister, Kehinde, the two of them wedged between the more reserved Daniels parents. As the resident assistant of the sixth floor of Moneta Hall, Tai got a single room *and* a stipend. In exchange, she said, her residents gave her headaches.

Ellory, one such resident, glanced up from her textbook and blinked until Supreme Court cases stopped floating in front of her eyes. "Hm?"

She was stretched out on the plush geometric rug that added another pop of personality to the room. Her constitutional law textbook was open in front of her, the page bookmarked by her quiz. A big red *98* was circled in the top right, a matching slash by the one question she'd gotten wrong.

"You got a ninety-eight," Tai pointed out. "Why are you acting like you got an eighteen?"

"Hudson got a perfect score."

"So? You're not in high school anymore. You're not competing for valedictorian."

"I *know* that. This is personal."

Like Hudson Graves, Tai Daniels was a senior. Unlike Hudson Graves, Tai Daniels wasn't an asshole. They had met during Ellory's first night on campus, when Tai had called a floor meeting to introduce herself to all the residents. Ellory, quite frankly, thought Tai was the most beautiful woman she had ever seen. Tai wore a braided mohawk that met in a thick black-and-purple pony that fell to her mid-back, a gold septum piercing, and a cropped crochet tank top through which her gold bra peeked through. Reading from a speech written on papers she'd smoothed out on her slate-gray cargo pants, she told them the Moneta Hall rules, her hours, how best to contact her, and what would happen if they were caught drinking or smoking in the freshman dorms.

Two days later, Ellory worked up the courage to knock on Tai's door only to find Cody Flores lounging beneath her sheets, playing a handheld game, completely undressed and completely unconcerned about it. Tai shifted to block Cody from view, and Ellory stammered something about orientation, but before she could run back to her room and die from embarrassment, Tai invited her to go out to lunch with them. By the end of a meal at Lucky's, a café off campus, Tai and Cody had become Ellory's friends. Tai was a business major from an upper-class family, Cody was an art history major whose parents worked for the FBI, and both of them agreed that Ellory needed to make *two awesome friends her own age*.

In many ways, that awkward moment had been a blessing. Thanks to her instant attraction to Tai, Ellory was able to get something better than a girlfriend: a best friend.

But it had been only four weeks. There were things Tai still didn't understand, and Ellory's rivalry with Hudson Graves was one of the biggest. Tai's Nigerian American parents ran their own pharma company, which she was poised to take over, so, in her opinion, anything that happened in these four years didn't matter as long as she didn't get arrested. *I like to live my life with the confidence of a mediocre white man*, she often joked. *But I'm not a complete fucking idiot.*

Meanwhile, Ellory still struggled to explain her wildly different upbringing, where her future was not guaranteed and part of her was relieved when her parents' calls from Jamaica had slowed down because she didn't want to be a disappointment. Their precious baby, sent abroad for a better life, excelling only up until America put a snowballing price tag on excellence. She struggled to explain how low Hudson Graves had made her feel in only a few sharp words, how he saw her and dismissed her like her struggles, her hard work, and her *existence* didn't matter. How it was about Hudson Graves, but it wasn't about Hudson Graves, not really—it was about how there were a million men like Hudson Graves everywhere, who took one look at her skin or her gender or her address or her accent, still present in the way she pronounced certain words she'd only ever read, and assumed she was nothing. That she was lazy or angry or sassy or emotional or a *problem*.

And Hudson Graves might have had light-skin privilege, but he was just as Black as she was, so his contempt hurt in a different way. Like missing a step on a familiar staircase at night, that brief moment of shocked betrayal that something you'd thought would be there had rejected you instead.

She refused to lose against someone like that. Her desire to beat him was like an addiction, and instead of detoxing when they didn't have class together, she would do this: Study. Obsess. Prep for the next round.

Tai looked like she wanted to say something else, but there was a knock on the door. A student Ellory faintly recognized from one of the rooms at the end of the hall—maybe the one with the Halloween decorations up even though it was mid-September—stood on Tai's welcome mat, mumbling about smelling weed through the vents. Tai stepped outside to continue the conversation, leaving Ellory alone with her textbook and resentment. The crimson 98 continued to mock her, but she rolled onto her back to stare at the ceiling instead. There was a crack near the light bulb that kind of looked like a centipede—at least, she hoped it was a crack. If it moved, she would run.

Bzzt. Bzzt.

Ellory found her phone; AUNTIE flashed across the screen along with a picture of Carol posing with a head of lettuce as if it were a crystal ball. "Waa gwaan?"

"Mi deh yah," Carol responded brightly. She always got a kick out of Ellory reaching for the little patois she could still speak without sounding like she was *from foreign*. "How's school?"

"How's your heart?"

It was an unspoken fact that half the reason they were so often strapped for cash was because of Carol's frequent trips to the hospital. The congenital heart defect she'd been born with had evolved into hypertension and cardiovascular disease, and though her aunt hadn't had a stroke in months, Ellory had read far too many articles about heart disease being the biggest killer of Black women in America to truly rest easily. She would work *four* jobs without complaint if it meant they had enough money for Carol to get the care she needed when she needed it, without having to wonder if this stroke was "bad enough" to risk the deductible.

"Mi gud, mi gud," said Carol before switching back to English. "You worry too much, Lor. Tell me about school."

"Not until you tell me about your heart."

Carol sighed as though *Ellory* were the one being childish. "I'm taking the pills. I'm eating healthy. I'm doing my little yoga. I'm as well as you left me, okay? *Now* can I hear about school?"

Ellory watched the centipede crack for signs of movement and caught her aunt up on the week since her last phone call: The endless assignments and the pop quiz. The sleepless nights and the breathing boil that was Hudson Graves. The friends she'd spent time with and the walks she'd taken. She and Carol didn't have a *Gilmore Girls*–like closeness that had them swapping secrets over coffee, but the more she spilled her problems into the phone, the lighter she felt.

Maybe that was why she made the mistake of bringing up the *Warren Communiqué*.

"Do you even have time for something like that?" Aunt Carol's voice took on an edge that made apologies rise in Ellory's throat. "You're struggling in your classes. The newspaper would take away from the time you should spend studying."

"I know." Ellory forced herself to laugh. "It was just a silly idea—"

"And since when are you even interested in journalism? You never want to watch TMZ with me."

Ellory thought of the decorations in her bedroom, colorful posters of Lois Lane and Iris West, black-and-white photos of Ida B. Wells and Marvel Cooke. She thought of her high school promise to herself that if she loaded up on AP classes, she could turn her participation in Newspaper Club from a hobby into something more legitimate at community college. She thought of the battered Moleskine notebook in which she'd practiced her bylines and signature: *Ellory Morgan. Ellory J. Morgan. EJ Morgan.*

"You're right. I don't have the time."

"Good girl. You've been given such a huge opportunity at Warren, and I'd hate to see you waste it. Reporters don't make money. Lawyers do. Imagine being the first lawyer in the family!"

Ellory once again found it hard to swallow. What had she been thinking? The average salary for a reporter was nowhere near the lowest average salary for a lawyer. She couldn't very well leave Aunt Carol—who had fed her and housed her, spoiling Ellory whenever she could—to pay for her own medical bills. A free ride to college, and Ellory fantasized about wasting it on *that*? On a stupid childhood dream with no money or job security?

It was selfish. It was too selfish, when her parents and aunt had given up so much for her.

"Have you heard from Mom and Dad?" she managed to say around the lump in her throat. "Did they call or...?"

"Not since you left," Carol said. "I'll probably call them this weekend. Desmond has been late on the payments."

Ellory hated when Aunt Carol called them *payments*, like Ellory was a job worth however much money her parents were able to wire every month. But all she said was "Well, let me know. In the meantime, I should probably get back to studying. I didn't score as high as I wanted to on that quiz, and..."

"Say no more, my little academic. I'll call you next week."

"Mi gone den."

"Likkle more."

The phone screen went black. Ellory shoved it into her bag and then rolled back onto her stomach. A circle of liquid distorted one of the sentences in her textbook. She touched her face. At some point, she'd started to cry.

"Sorry about that," Tai said, reentering the room and knocking the door closed with her hip. "You won't believe the—Lor? Is everything okay?"

Ellory swiped at her damp cheeks. They felt hot under her fingers. She didn't usually cry in front of other people. "I'm good. I'm fine. Maybe a little stressed."

Her throat still felt as congested as Midtown traffic. Worse, she felt that chill again, that odd sense of familiarity but with a melancholic twist. This wasn't the instinctive knowledge that would clear her a path through the campus; this was a wound that had scabbed over until she'd picked at it again—though she was certain she'd never brought up her journalistic aspirations with her aunt before. Not that she could remember anyway. It must have been more of a symbolic wound, the knowledge every immigrant kid had that there were only about four career paths that would make their parents and guardians proud. Journalism would never be one of them.

Ellory sniffled and then jumped when a tissue appeared before her.

Tai, kneeling on the other side of her textbook, wiggled the tissue. "Take it. And then go back to your room and get dressed up. We are going out."

"Oh, I'm not really in the mood to—"

"Did I ask you?" Tai wiggled the tissue again. "You're so

stressed out that you're crying, Lor. That's not good. There's a party tonight. I wasn't going to go because—well. Look, I think you need to socialize. To have fun. To take a *break*. You're not going to learn anything this way."

Ellory took the tissue. Her con. law textbook suddenly looked as if it had been written in Russian. A headache was building behind her eyes, the same one she always got when she cried, the same one that would eventually crest into a migraine if she didn't take something for it now. Tai was right. Yet the thought of seeing anyone else tonight made Ellory want to scream.

"Come on," said Tai, closing the textbook. "You need this. If I'm wrong, we can leave, whether it's been five hours or five minutes."

"You promise?"

"I *promise*."

"Is Cody going?"

"I can text them if you want."

Tai was less likely to abandon Ellory if her partner wasn't there to distract her. Ellory shook her head. "Just you and me, please. I'll change. I'll go. But if I'm not feeling it, you're bringing me right back here."

Tai brandished her pinky, and, laughing, Ellory hooked hers around it. She packed up her things and headed back to her room, where Stasie and several of her freshman friends were bundled like sardines on her bed, watching a reality show. The only light was from the laptop screen and the silvery moon stretching through the hole in the blackout curtains. None of them looked Ellory's way, which was good, because she was pretty sure her eyes were bloodshot and her cheeks were sallow. It would take a lot of makeup and maybe a late-night coffee to get her in the partying spirit.

Then again, she hadn't been to *any* parties since classes had started. Her nights off were spent studying, and casual invitations had dried up after orientation week had ended with core groups and friendship circles clearly delineated. Maybe Tai was right. Maybe this was exactly what Ellory needed. And if it wasn't, then at least she had a guaranteed ride home and could probably sneak some snacks out in her purse.

4

"I'D LIKE TO GO BACK now," Ellory said, her arms folded. "This is a waste of a dress, and you damn well knew what you were doing."

She couldn't believe that she'd worn her most club outfit—a long-sleeved metallic-black minidress with sheer mesh between the bust and the skirt, and a pair of black heels she could kill a man with—only for Tai to drive her off campus to a house that belonged to none other than Hudson Graves. Ellory hadn't known that Hudson was somewhere inside by looking at it, of course. Her obsession—and in the dark of the car with only the stars to witness, she could admit it *was* a bit of an obsession—didn't extend that far. Tai had instead shut off the engine and admitted this little proviso in quick, jumbled words, and Ellory was having none of it.

On top of all that, she was clearly overdressed. The house was a flat-topped two-story redbrick building with five white columns that held up a gray box gable roof over the porch. People spilled out onto that porch and the dying lawn beyond, chatting over the pounding of music with a lot of bass. Everyone was carrying soda bottles that clearly did not contain soda, or narrow-necked flasks in crumpled paper bags, and they were dressed like extras on a teen drama, all flannel shirts and crewnecks, ripped jeans and ankle boots.

"Let's go inside," said Tai, affecting a pout. "Just for like five minutes."

"You promised you'd take me home if I wasn't having fun."

"We're *in the car*."

"And I'm not having fun!"

Tai's pout grew even more exaggerated. "It's a big house, Lor. You probably won't even see him."

"Oh, I will," Ellory said darkly. "I'm unlucky like that."

Sometimes Ellory imagined herself and Hudson as magnets with opposing ends, but the universe seemed to think them more like nuclear fusion, binding together with explosive results. The house could be two stories or ten, the yard could be ten acres or twenty, and she and Hudson Graves would find each other. The only real question was when.

"At least give me your flannel," she finally relented, after five long minutes of Tai sulking in the driver's seat without turning on the car. "I can still make this work."

It was oversize and plaid, the deep red of Baldwin apples. Ellory slipped it over her shoulders and tied it in a knot beneath her breasts, making her look less like she was standing in line at a nightclub and more like an actual person. Her heels and cat's-eye makeup, she could do nothing about, but she finally got out of the car.

Music drowned out the New England night, so loud that Ellory was shocked the neighbors hadn't complained. A light wind stirred her halo of curls, but it was a warm breeze like the dying breath of summer. Yellow-green bushes clustered in front of the building, some tall enough to partially cover the ground-floor windows. Between their stems, she could see crowds gyrating in flickering neon color.

In the corners of the house, shadows bubbled like fresh tar. Ellory blinked once, twice, three times, but she could still see that teeming darkness spilling across the lawn, flooding every inch that wasn't illuminated by porch lights. It oozed closer and closer to where she was standing, indifferent to her racing heart. She was outside a house party, but it was like she was in a painting and someone was taking varnish to the colorful details, leaving her alone in the void. The music had been replaced by the buzzing of a thousand bees, and she couldn't see anything but the wicked dark and the crouching building that now seemed farther away.

Hands grabbed her shoulders. A scream tore from her throat.

"Whoa, whoa," said Tai, raising those same hands in surrender. "I didn't mean to scare you. You zoned out on me for a second there."

When Ellory looked back, the shadows were harmless and still. The only sound she could hear was the pulsing music.

It had all been in her head.

It had all been in her head.

Breathing hard, she dragged her gaze back to her confused friend. "Sorry, I thought I saw—sorry."

"Sounds like *somebody* needs a drink."

Tai linked their arms and dragged her through the front door. The walls were baby blue. The spacious floor was gray wood. That was all the detail Ellory managed to gather around all the *people*. Either the students of Warren were starved for entertainment, or Hudson Graves really knew how to throw a party, because there was hardly any room to navigate the living area. People were tucked into corners, talking, laughing, or making out. Others were swaying to the music, half of them too drunk to remain on beat. A group cheered one another on as they took turns chugging cups of who knew what. Someone was fast asleep on the long side of an L-shaped couch. On the other side, someone else—a friend?—texted, pausing only to glare at anyone who came too close.

Ellory's first and last college party had been during orientation week, in one of the residence halls with a dining hall on the first floor, and it had involved mild property damage and a warning from the resident manager. By comparison, this was wildly boring. Too loud to think, too crowded to stand out, too tame to worry.

She loved it. In this chaos, she could breathe again.

Tai took her to the kitchen, where they found two unopened Coronas in a cooler on the kitchen island. The fridge was stainless steel, sitting alongside white cupboards and black marble-top counters. Half-full bowls of colorful snacks were everywhere: tortilla chips and spinach dip, pretzels and dried fruit, popcorn and carrot sticks. Tai rooted through the cupboards until she found a clipped bag of barbecue potato chips. "What?" she asked in the wake of Ellory's judgmental stare. "I don't know where all these grubby hands have been, and that dip already looks funky."

Ellory grabbed a fistful of chips. The spinach *did* look funky.

They ended up in the backyard, a wide expanse of flattened grass protected from the other buildings and houses by trees on three corners and a listless chain-link fence on the fourth. The party had spilled out here, too, but it felt more intentional. Fairy lights were threaded through the tree branches. Someone was fiddling with a keg. Folding tables were set up, and flip cup and beer pong were in full swing. A Bluetooth speaker duct-taped to the side of the house made sure the music was still an invisible guest.

Tai was immediately sucked into a game of flip cup; Ellory wouldn't cross her mind again until she'd made everyone else at the table cry. Ellory wandered over to a small circle of people playing hacky sack and watched them kick the glow-in-the-dark footbag back and forth. It looked like a confused meteor, an ever-moving orb of phosphorescent light in the dimness of the yard.

One of the players caught sight of her and, after knocking the footbag across the circle, broke rank to come over. She had never seen him before, but he was catalog-model handsome, the kind of white man who looked like he answered to the name *Tripp* or *Digby*. His carefully coiffed chestnut hair swooped back from his broad forehead *just so*, his clean-shaven square jaw gave him an approachably masculine appearance, and his thick biceps screamed *crew team* or *tennis club* or both. He was over six feet tall, wearing a black-and-white-striped polo, loose blue jeans, and black plimsolls—a type of shoe Ellory had had no reason to know the name of before she'd come to Warren. Now she didn't dare confuse them with loafers or oxfords.

"Hey," said Possibly Tripp, pushing a hand through his hair. His smile was relaxed, open, and practiced. Not toothy or overstretched, but a tool that only enhanced his natural good looks. "I don't think I've seen you at one of these before."

"I've never been to one of these before," Ellory confirmed. "My friend brought me."

She pointed over at Tai, then saw the light of recognition in his chocolate-brown eyes. Which was no surprise. Tai definitely knew the Tripps and Digbys of the world—or at least all the ones in New England. "Well, if you came with Tai, then you must be good people! Can I get you anything to drink?"

"I'm still working on this."

"The Corona? It's empty."

"Because I'm working on it." His pencil-thin eyebrows knitted together. Ellory decided to have mercy on him. "I could maybe use some more chips."

The smile returned, this one like the spill of morning sunshine through a window. He left Ellory standing there blinking, wondering what exactly she'd done to earn a smile like that. Shame flared within her at how quickly she'd judged him, cutting him down to stereotypes that justified her sarcasm. That feeling only increased when he returned less than five minutes later with a plate of individual snack packs of several different kinds.

"I didn't know what you like," he explained, "so I got the basics."

The basics turned out to be potato chips, cheese puffs, pretzels, onion rings, cheesy tortilla chips, and graham crackers. Guilt softened her tone. "Thanks. This is great. I'm Ellory, by the way. Ellory Morgan."

"Liam Blackwood," he said, plucking the graham crackers from the plate with a wink. "Delivery fee." The wink must have been practiced, too. It turned him from handsome to devastating. There was no way he didn't know it. "So, Ellory Morgan, what's your story? I would remember if I'd seen you around campus before now."

"I'm a freshman," she began. Then, at the flash of alarm on his face, she quickly added, "I'm twenty-one. I started late."

"Ah. Godwin Scholarship?"

"The school has other scholarships," Ellory said, her grip tightening on the plate. "But yeah."

"Oh, I didn't mean it…however you're taking it. I know plenty of Godwin Scholars. Come here a sec."

Liam's large hand pressed against her shoulder blades and steered her back into the house. Tai was still at the flip-cup table, knocking back a plastic cup of beer and then positioning it at the edge of the table. She flicked the base, which sent it tumbling through the air before it landed upside down in the center of the table. Cheers erupted from her team. Her opponents looked pained but not yet defeated. Ellory felt sorry for them already. Tai's scorched-earth, kiss-the-ring, bend-the-knee approach to every drinking game would crush their spirits one way or another.

To the left of the living room was a staircase with white balustrades. An actual velvet rope was attached to one, barring the way upstairs in a way that made the second story of the house seem like some exclusive nightclub and thus would stop absolutely no one. Liam led her to a group of four loitering in front of the stairs, most of them people of color, most of them women. A pale redhead with glittering pastel-pink lip gloss. A russet-skinned woman in a sour-apple-green hair wrap. A spiky-haired man with golden skin, wearing a Manchester United T-shirt. A freckled woman with her hair drawn up into a frizzy bun and a black cherry White Claw in her hand.

They all stared at her, making Ellory feel like a kindergartener on the first day of school. All she needed was a Bluey lunch box to clutch to her chest or maybe a box of Crayola crayons—the good shit, the sixty-four pack with the built-in sharpener—to trade in exchange for friendship.

Liam's hand slithered to her shoulder. "I found another one. This is Ellory. She's new."

"Hey," the man said first. "I'm David Chang Vargas." His smile, when he turned it on Liam, stopped shy of friendly. "Blackwood's been collecting as many of us as he can find tonight. Have you checked off your bingo card yet?"

Liam laughed obliviously. "Not yet, but I'll keep you posted."

Everyone else made their introductions. The Black woman was Imani Khalif. The redhead was Addison Sullivan, "but you can call me *Red*." The final woman was Ximena Moreno, an introduction she followed up by offering Ellory a White Claw from her oversize purse. Imani and David were nineteen-year-old poli-sci majors, while twenty-one-year-old Ximena was suffering through biochem, and Red, twenty, was here for electrical engineering. All of them apologized when Ellory said she was majoring in poli-sci, too.

"We're still mostly doing core classes," said David, assuming, like everyone did, that Ellory was a senior. "But even those are soul crushing. Something about the atmosphere here is so..."

"*Serious*," Red finished, "in a super-pretentious way. Like, we get it, you're a future hedge fund manager with an inheritance you can't wait to snort your way through. There's no need to wear a fucking suit to the student center."

"That was *one time*," Liam said. "And I had a networking event."

"It was twice," said Imani. "And you wore different suits each time."

"I had *multiple* networking events!"

His hand was still on Ellory's shoulder. She reached up to pat it. She didn't know how to explain to him that the problem was probably that he owned a full suit in the first place, let alone more than one. If he wasn't aware that they were expensive, that most people rented them for prom or thrifted them for interviews, then there was nothing she could do to save him from the undercurrent of resentment this group was sending his way.

He didn't seem to notice it, at least. She wondered what that was like. Did elevator music play in his head when someone didn't like him, drowning out the barbs and the side-eyes? Or did he notice the barbs and take the high road, the road that money allowed him the luxury of taking?

The conversation turned to coursework, professors who made them want to give their best and professors who made them want to drop out, and the general lack of time for anything resembling a life thanks to the demands of the Godwin Scholarship. Ellory ate her pretzels and let the words wash over her, trying to stay engaged. But the more they spoke, the more she thought about her constitutional law textbook and the quiz she'd come to the party to escape. So far, she hadn't seen Hudson Graves anywhere. Maybe he hadn't deigned to attend his own house party. Maybe that was why he'd scored higher than her.

The pretzels tasted like lead. She handed her plate and empty Corona bottle to Liam. "Is there a bathroom?"

"There's…" Liam pointed to a door a few feet to their left that had a couple enthusiastically making out against it. One groped for the doorknob behind them, and they tumbled inside, only two hands visible. "Well, there's another one upstairs, to the right. Oi!"

Ellory left him to deal with that. Upstairs was quieter, cleaner, emptier. The walls were painted a peaceful blue, and the bathroom was white brick and tile with a sunset-orange shower curtain hiding the tub from view. Ellory peed and examined herself in the mirror over the sink as she washed her hands. Her mascara was still impeccable, her dark lipstick only slightly smudged from the beer. She touched it up and then took several deep breaths, shoving con. law to the back of her brain where it belonged. She was at a party. She was having fun. She could talk about schoolwork and make new friends without having a breakdown. It wasn't even obvious that she'd been crying earlier this very night.

Back in the hallway, she paused. The stairs were ahead to the left, but there was another door between them and the bathroom that she'd ignored in her haste to empty her bladder. It was half-open, and she could see bookshelves. Did these people actually have a home library?

No, it was a bedroom, albeit one that seemed stuck in the transitional stage between that and a library. There was a queen-size bed wedged in the corner. There was a desk underneath a window with short cherry-red curtains. There was another door opposite the bed that she assumed led to a closet. Almost every other inch of space was full of bookshelves or books that couldn't fit on the bookshelves and had instead been stacked unsteadily over the black carpet. There were books on top of the shelves, books in front of the shelves, books on the desk, and books under the desk. There were books on the bed, fanned out across the pillow as if they'd fallen asleep.

It was a literary wonderland.

Ellory forgot about the party, instead losing herself in the cracked and well-loved spines. These books weren't for decoration. They had all been read, some of them many times. Nonfiction biographies and memoirs. Crime novels and fantasy epics. Essay collections and leather-bound classics. Romance novels piled next to a single self-help book. She gasped and reached for one of the tomes on the desk, a copy of *Reel to Real* by bell hooks that had been read so many times that the cover had been taped back on. It was her favorite of the author's works, a series of essays on the influential nature of films—whether they meant to teach a certain lesson or not.

During those first few years after she'd moved to America, television had been Ellory's gateway to culture. She couldn't speak like her classmates, and she didn't grow up with the same references, but she kept a list of the things she overhead so she could diligently catch up. Then Aunt Carol bought her a copy of *Reel to Real: Race, Sex, and Class at the Movies* from the bargain bin at the Strand, and Ellory devoured the analysis, pored over the highlighted stereotypes, and took a more critical eye to all the media she consumed from then on.

It was as if she'd been asleep, and bell hooks had been her gentle awakening to a world that said so much more than she had been picking up.

She traced the cover with loving fingers, a small smile on her face. The pages were dog-eared and annotated with thoughtful comments and questions that made it clear the owner had really engaged with the text. She flipped to the chapter on *Crooklyn*, her favorite of the essays, almost eager to get their thoughts.

"Of course," said a bored voice behind her. "With an entire floor of food and festivities, why *wouldn't* you instead break into my bedroom?"

Ellory dropped the book. Her smile went with it.

Standing in the doorway was Hudson Graves.

5

Hudson was dressed like he had come from the party: loose black jeans and a slate-gray crewneck sweater, black high-tops, and a Natty Ice. It was the kind of frat boy beverage she would have thought was beneath him, but then again, she would have thought that crime novels were beneath him, that romances were beneath him, that bell hooks's film criticism was beneath him… If she hadn't held the evidence of a book read over and over, full of written notes and taped edges, she might have still thought that. The callous, condescending reality of him usually shattered whatever soft illusion she pieced together in his absence.

"The door was open," Ellory said. "I'd hardly call it *breaking in*."

"There was a rope blocking off the second floor."

"Has that literally ever worked?"

His lips twitched like he wanted to smile. "No."

"Well, you can blame Liam Blackwood. He said I could use the upstairs bathroom."

"This isn't a bathroom." Hudson's eyes fell to the book at her feet. An expression bolted across his face, there and gone too quickly to read. "But you seem to have made yourself comfortable."

"I love this book," she gushed as she retrieved it. "I love bell hooks, but *this* book—" It took all she had to stop herself from being vulnerable in front of someone who had consistently preyed on her weaknesses. He was staring at the battered paperback, a frown heavy on his face. Ellory had the sudden strange feeling that she was the one who had caught him in a weak moment, but that was ridiculous. "I mean, when she talked about *Tarzan* as a white savior fantasy…"

It was a test, one she didn't feel good about but needed him to pass. She thought she knew his handwriting as well as she knew her own by now, but this could be someone else's copy. Liam's, perhaps, or maybe a paramour had left it behind. Maybe it had come with the room, and he'd simply been inspired to create a great wall of other books around it.

"I thought she stretched the white-daddy metaphor a little too far in that chapter, but yeah." Hudson stepped farther into the room. "She made really interesting points about the way society—and we ourselves—view Black and white masculinity, and how it's further colored by an unfair portrayal across film and television."

"What, did your film and media studies major fall through so you had to settle for poli-sci?"

"Hilarious." Hudson joined her at the desk, setting his can of Natural Ice on the only free area he could find. The stacks around it wobbled but ultimately remained standing. "I actually want to be a lawyer, but that doesn't mean I can't have other interests."

"Like"—she nudged a book on top of a nearby pile with her free hand—"Nora Roberts?"

"Did you go through my closet, too? Should I call the campus police?"

"We're not on campus."

"They like me more than you do."

"Complete strangers on the street like you more than I do. An anthill you'd smash likes you more than I do. A baby you'd kick likes—"

"Your point has been assiduously made, thank you."

Her mouth moved before her brain signed off on it. "Why do you always talk like you swallowed a textbook?"

Familiarity shivered through her. The words, the almost-playful way in which they'd come out...it felt old, common, *routine*, and yet this was the longest conversation they'd had in the four weeks since she'd started at Warren. Wasn't it?

"Hey," Ellory murmured. "Do you ever feel like...? Have we had this discussion before?"

"About bell hooks or about my elocution?"

"Okay, Encyclopedia Brown." That nickname. It felt unnaturally natural, even though she'd never used it before. "Seriously, have we...?"

"I have no idea what you're asking me, Morgan," Hudson deadpanned. "You'll have to use your words."

Ellory realized for the first time that the space between them had disappeared. Hudson leaned against the desk, gazing at her like he was searching for something. She clutched *Reel to Real* between them, but that was all that was between them. If she breathed too deeply, her knuckles would brush his sweater. Their height difference had evaporated, thanks to her heels. When she didn't have to tilt her head to meet his eyes, they felt more equal. It startled her, how intense the brown of them was from so close.

Strong and earthy, deep and dark. The kind of brown that buried people alive.

The kind they wanted to be buried in.

"Morgan," he said, and it sounded louder than usual. The distant sounds of the party trickled in slowly, a light drizzle too insubstantial to register. "What exactly are you doing in my room? Even with the door open, you couldn't possibly have seen that book from the hallway."

Ellory sighed, setting bell hooks back on the desk. She cleaned imaginary dust from the cover to buy herself some time. There was nowhere to sit but the bed, and she refused to sit on the bed. Bass rattled the carpet beneath their feet. Cheers filtered in from the backyard. The conversation she'd fled echoed in her ears all the same, shriller now thanks to his reminder.

"I got tired of the party," she said. "It's a party, but all anyone wants to talk about is homework."

"Talking about homework isn't your idea of fun?"

"I actually want to be a lawyer, but that doesn't mean I can't have other interests," she parroted back at him, eyebrows raised.

Hudson made a noise she chose to believe was a chuckle, though it was more breath than sound. "*Do* you want to be a lawyer?"

Her pulse skipped. "What kind of question is that? Of course I do."

"Not everyone has the passion. And there are plenty of things you can do with a degree in political science besides taking the bar—"

"*I want to be a lawyer.*" It came out like a bark, too quick and defensive to be believed. Ellory realized her shoulders had inched up toward her ears and forced herself to relax. "You don't know me, Graves. If you're trying to intimidate me away from law because you know I'll be better at it than you, it's not going to work. And, quite frankly, it's beneath you."

Hudson's expression was carefully blank. Ellory almost wanted to take the words back, but she was tired of doubting herself. She didn't need to hear her midnight thoughts from his sneering mouth. It didn't matter what she wanted. She had her family to think about, their sacrifices to get her here. Everything else—this conversation and this party, her hallucinations and this unrelenting sense of déjà vu—was a distraction.

And, unlike Hudson, she could not afford distraction.

"Have you heard of Professor Colt?"

Of all the things Hudson could have said next, Ellory had not expected that. Preston Colt was one of Warren University's most prestigious instructors; he taught political theory to the upperclassmen, but he had also written several award-winning books and been on almost every talk show. Finding out that he taught here had eased the last of Aunt Carol's concerns about the impromptu scholarship offer. If Ellory could walk the same halls as Preston Colt, it was worth ignoring a few red flags.

"He hosts a monthly salon at his house," Hudson continued when she didn't answer. "It's a select group, but we're each allowed a guest. I've never taken advantage of that particular clause, but...how would you like to be mine for the one in October?"

"What?" Ellory blinked. "Why me?"

"I—"

"*There* you are." Tai appeared, beaming, her eyes bright with obvious drunkenness. She wore a colorful medal that, upon closer inspection, appeared to be several beer-bottle caps welded together. Her car keys dangled from a finger. "You need to drive us home, because I am *fuuuuuuucked upppppp*." Her grin dimmed into more of a puzzled curve. "Am I interrupting something?"

"No," Ellory said quickly. "Of course not. Are you ready to go now?"

"Are *you*?"

Ellory glanced at Hudson. He was still leaning against the desk, but now he was staring out the window as if to let them have some privacy. If Hudson had been about to give her an explanation less shocking than the initial invitation, the moment had clearly passed. She wasn't sure there *was* an explanation less shocking than the initial invitation. She was afraid that if she lingered, he would realize the absurdity of extending her this opportunity and snatch it back.

She cleared her throat. "Yeah, I'm ready." And then, to him: "I'll go. But if this is some sort of prank—"

"I'll text you the details. Give me your phone."

Ellory held out her hand. With another puff of amusement, Hudson handed his over. His background was blank, factory settings, but when she inputted her number, sent herself a text, and closed it up, she saw that his lock screen was Luke Fox in the Batwing suit. She didn't comment, even though she desperately wanted to smile.

"All right, Flip Cup Queen," she said, stepping forward so Tai could throw an arm around her shoulders. "Let's get you back to Moneta without your residents seeing."

"I'm an adult," Tai sniffed. "Please don't let me puke in my car. I just cleaned it."

"I'll pull over."

Ellory could feel the prickling weight of Hudson's gaze as she shuffle-dragged Tai to the stairs, but she forced herself not to look back.

◆

Instead of returning to her room after putting Tai to bed, Ellory camped out on the floor in case she was needed. She'd forced Tai to down an entire bottle of water before falling asleep, and now her friend snored on her side from between the pillow barricades Ellory had erected to keep her from rolling onto her back. There was a bottle of ibuprofen on Tai's side table. The trash bin had been emptied and placed by the bed in case she couldn't make it to the bathroom. She was sleeping deeply, but Ellory found it hard to do the same.

Adrenaline chased away her exhaustion. She replayed her interaction with Hudson a thousand different ways. It was an oddity in a month of oddities, and she couldn't shake it off as easily as the others.

Ellory was familiar with déjà vu in the same way most people were: it was a French loanword, a cliché, something children picked up from pop culture to describe a universal feeling. She had been on campus since the last week of August, and instead of a fleeting moment once or twice in her life, déjà vu had become a presence as constant as her shadow. And every time she tried to rationalize it, to ignore it, it returned more insidiously than before.

Then there were the things she couldn't explain: the way her surroundings had twice blurred around her like watercolors, the discordant giggling that appeared to have no source, the soccer ball that had dropped to the ground in front of her when all science, all logic, indicated it would've slammed into her face. Reality always seemed to reaffirm itself afterward: *Of course, this is Riverside Campus. Of course, I was panicked and seeing things in the gloom. Of course, that strong wind was capable of stopping a ball in its tracks.* When she thought about it, *really* thought about it, she was uncomfortably unsure if these were her own desperate excuses or the placating hand of something she couldn't remember once her breathing calmed and her world made sense again.

Maybe she had always been haunted, and her body was begging her to finally *do* something about it.

After a long stretch of time spent staring at the same crack in the ceiling, Ellory reached for her laptop. She had no idea what she expected to find, but some of the tension sloughed from her shoulders when she opened a blank Word document.

Riverside Campus. Miss Claudette. Teeming shadows. The *Warren Communiqué*. Encyclopedia Brown. Everything poured out until she had a chaotic wall of disjointed sentences, a bullet point list of weirdness in Times New Roman twelve-point font. Then she wasted a half hour adjusting the borders of the document, adding and formatting the dictionary definition of déjà vu, and organizing the information under headings, afraid to look directly at what she'd written.

But she was too well trained from her long days and longer nights in Newspaper Club. Her mind began to see patterns in the fractured memories, ghostly illusions, and visceral dread that swept over her in those moments. If places she'd never been and conversations she'd never had felt familiar, there *had* to be a reason, even if that reason was that she was under so much stress from the workload that she was starting to crack.

Aunt Carol had once said that déjà vu was past lives reasserting themselves. "I read on Facebook the other day—don't make that face; it wasn't that anti-vaxxer or flat-earther crap—but apparently Plato said that human beings used to be androgynous. Zeus thought we were too powerful like that, so he split us in half, and now we spend our lives searching for our missing piece. Our soulmates."

She'd taken another sip of brandy and continued: "It's

heteronormative bullshit, *but* there's something to the concept of people who feel like you knew them in another life. Maybe you did. Our brains can store only so many memories, and we're already losing the earliest ones from *this* life before we're even halfway through it. Who's to say this is the only life we've ever had?"

Feeling silly, Ellory plugged her own name into Google, pulled up her genetic-testing results, and fell down a Wikipedia rabbit hole for a page that felt a little too close to home. But if she'd had a past life, it didn't reveal itself to her before the sun crept over the horizon.

There was something here. She knew there was, even if it wasn't coming together as quickly as she'd hoped. She saved the document and emailed it to herself as a backup. Her eyes felt strained, and her temples pounded in a searing ache.

Yet she also felt accomplished. Like she was off to a strong start. Like she had more control.

Maybe she couldn't secure her own invitation to Professor Colt's mysterious salons, and maybe college had been an impossibility without the sudden benevolence of total strangers. Maybe she hadn't scored as high as she'd wanted on her con. law quiz, and maybe she couldn't handle a simple conversation about school without fleeing. But her instincts were still sharp enough to find a narrative where others might have seen nothing, and that was enough.

She slid her laptop back into her bag, her fingers catching on the flyer. For once, it didn't cause a pit to grow in her stomach. Instead, she traced its edges lovingly, a reassuring touch from one friend to another. She didn't need the *Warren Communiqué*. She was starring in her own story, weird and frustrating though it might be. Figuring out what was going on with her life suddenly felt more pressing than interviewing locals about neighborhood crimes or her fellow classmates about curriculum changes.

Above her, Tai snorted herself awake with "Buh? Oh, god. Oh, fuck."

"The trash is to your left," Ellory said. "Ibuprofen is to your right."

"Fuck."

"You're welcome."

6

OCTOBER ENTERED LIKE A BULLDOZER, demolishing any hope of a slow transition to autumn. One minute, the days were warm enough for Ellory's lace-white classmates to stretch out on the quad in bikini tops, sunglasses on their faces and suntan oil glinting on their stomachs. The next, Ellory was wearing a sweater to every class and carrying a light jacket in case it got colder when the sun went down.

The trees had grown red with warning, those that had leaves left to change, and she was already contemplating going home for her winter clothes. Though the two states converged at the southwest border, Connecticut cold was *nothing* like New York cold. Ellory's *soul* needed a hoodie, or it would freeze to death inside her.

It had been two weeks since the party, and the weather wasn't the only thing that chilled her. Acknowledging the strangeness of her school year seemed to have given that strangeness more power.

Once, Ellory had been behind the counter at Powers That Bean during a shift so slow that she hadn't had a customer in hours. She was taking advantage of the quiet to read a book, one of the

few times she could read for leisure, and she turned the page, only for the words to swim before her eyes. The lighting over the page changed from late afternoon to early morning, and her nails were painted rather than plain, and it felt like she had read this book before, except that she had never read this book before. When she blinked, she was breathing hard and the book was on the floor, her hands still curved as if holding it.

Another time, the sharp *honk* of a car horn narrowly saved her from being struck by the speeding vehicle as she stepped into the road, lost in a memory that had unfurled and dissipated like incense. In her mind's eye, she hadn't been on a sidewalk; she had been outside an ornate yet somehow nondescript house at nighttime, seconds away from pressing her face against the lit glass to see who was inside. Her stomach dropped, and she leaped back onto the sidewalk, gasping for breath as a man cursed at her through the car's open window. She stood there, frozen and blinking rapidly, until her brain reoriented itself, until she could remember nothing of the daydream that had distracted her except that golden light in the darkness.

And then there was the time Ellory crossed campus, only to find out that her class had been canceled, freeing her to take a walk to the greenhouses. She didn't even make it inside; the second she touched the doorknob, she saw not the plants on the other side of the shaded glass but bodies, rows of corpses with unseeing eyes and unrecognizable brown faces. The greenhouse was no longer a greenhouse but a mausoleum, and all the graves were open to reveal husks that withered from brown to black, curling in on themselves like a newborn's fist. Maybe it had been a dream or a vision, maybe she'd been exhausted from the walk or blinded by the sun, but it had scared her so much that she hadn't gone inside.

AN ARCANE INHERITANCE

It was like being a child again, talking to people who weren't there and hearing murmurs in the trees that no one else could and lying awake while straining to hear her parents' quiet conversations about what was wrong with her.

Still, after two weeks, all she had was a too-long Word document and a too-short list of resources. Her mind had become an unreliable thing, an Etch A Sketch that shook itself clean at random, and she never knew when she would lose her grip on reality next. Around her investigation, she still had university to drown her in weeks of homework and studying, quizzes and the occasional argument about refrigerator space with her roommate. By the time the day of the salon arrived, she was almost relieved to be anxious about something else for once.

Ellory checked herself over one last time in Stasie's full-length mirror with a sigh. She had no idea what a salon was, let alone how to dress for one at an award-winning professor's house. For her, the word *salon* conjured images of Astoria hairdressers, Black women with press-on nails and all the best gossip, metal chairs that needed to be pumped up so she could see her untamed Afro in the vanity mirror, the miserable pain of getting fresh box braids put in and knowing she'd be taking ibuprofen to sleep. Apparently, a salon was also a gathering of the noblesse, and she didn't have the money to dress like someone who used the word *noblesse*.

Instead, she'd let Cody dress her in business casual. A long-sleeved off-white silk shirt tucked into a pair of high-rise black skinny jeans. An oversize double-breasted check coat in brown and black, and a cherry-red scarf would keep her warm. She wore the same black heels that she'd worn to the party, mostly because she didn't want to learn to walk in a pair of ill-fitting ones on such short notice. Who would be paying attention to her shoes anyway?

After his initial text with the date, time, and address, Hudson Graves had resumed treating her like her existence was inconvenient. Classes were still a battlefield. Comments were still bladed. Gazes were still cold. Ellory wound up checking her phone every day, making sure his text was still there, that their conversation at the party hadn't been the result of spiked Corona. Even now, part of her doubted he would actually show up. Or, if he did, maybe it would be with the rest of his friends in tow to laugh at her before they pulled away to the salon from which she was definitely excluded.

graves: outside moneta

She sent back coming! and eyed herself in the mirror one last time. She looked good. She felt good. If she could impress Professor Colt tonight, she could score her own invitation to future salons, and she wouldn't need to rely on Hudson Graves. She couldn't mess this up. She *wouldn't* mess this up. She could do this.

graves: hurry up

Then again, making it through the night without strangling Hudson Graves in front of a crowd of witnesses would be enough of a miracle.

As promised, he was right outside the lobby doors, playing a game on his phone. He wore a dark brown cashmere turtleneck, a storm-gray chesterfield coat, and brown loafers. His slacks were black, his scarf was tartan wool, and his hair was curlier than usual. The platinum blond of it seemed to glow beneath the fading sunlight.

"Nice," he said, when he finally looked up at her. Ellory might have taken this as an insult if it weren't for the way his eyes lingered on her, not dismissive but not considering either. *Appreciative* was the best word she could come up with for how his gaze traced her lines and curves. He slid his phone into his coat pocket. "Come on, then. We don't want to be late."

The walk to the student parking lot was a silent one. Ellory didn't want to ask questions until it was too late for Hudson to take her back to her residence hall. The sky was dimming from clear blue to hazy gray, the foliage dusted pink and orange by the sun. Dusk was when the campus caught a second wind after the marathon of classes drained the energy of their morning coffees. Students traveled in packs to the dining halls, to off-campus bars, to the library to get ahead on their homework, and to night classes they didn't regret until it was actually time to go.

When it wasn't stressing her out, Ellory could admit that Warren was beautiful, with its endless green lawns and trimmed elm trees, its dramatic columns and French-inspired grandeur, its iron gates and the creeping ivy that twisted around each spire like sleeping serpents. It wasn't welcoming, it wasn't homey, and it wasn't at all accessible, but it *was* beautiful. It flaunted the same beauty of national parks and private islands: established by wealth and nurtured by exclusivity.

"Holy shit," Ellory said, stopping in the middle of the parking lot. "Is that—"

"A '71 Plymouth Barracuda?" Hudson smoothed his hands over a sleek black muscle car that looked like the sort of thing the private detectives would drive in a monochrome movie. "Sure is."

Ellory blinked. She had been staring at the silver Lamborghini parked in front of whatever the hell that was. Hudson, a man who owned cuff links and an alarmingly large collection of five-hundred-dollar sweaters, struck her as a Lamborghini type. She needed a moment to process the fact that there was someone else around here who would believe a Lamborghini was an appropriate car to drive around a college campus.

"It's been in the family since it came off the assembly line. They stopped making the convertible that same year," he continued. "It can be a nightmare in terms of upkeep, but Boone does all the repairs and modifications for me. In exchange, he doesn't have to pay rent."

Ellory blinked again. Was it her imagination, or did he sound quietly proud? "I...see. You like old cars?"

"I like things that tell a story."

The inside of the car was black vinyl and smelled like citrus. The steering wheel was bronze, and the cassette tape deck and radio had been replaced with a more modern setup. She watched him place his phone in the dashboard mount and flick through for a song, apparently less concerned about being late than he was about finding the right soundtrack. It was such a small intimate thing for them to have in common. She turned to the window, pulling her coat up around her shoulders.

"Isn't She Lovely" by Stevie Wonder crooned from the speakers as Hudson backed out of the parking space. She loved Stevie Wonder—and this song in particular. Aunt Carol had used to sing it as a lullaby to get her to sleep, used to tell her about Motown and Diana Ross, Marvin Gaye and the Temptations. Her shoulders relaxed automatically. "You like bell hooks and *Songs in the Key of Life*? This is starting to feel performative."

Hudson snorted. "Who in this car am I performing for, exactly? I don't need to impress you. You hate me."

"I do," she confirmed, "so you understand why I have to ask again why you're bringing *me* as your guest. Is this a *Most Dangerous Game* situation? Are you and your friends going to hunt me for sport?"

"These people aren't my friends. And trust me, I'm not doing you a favor. This is a punishment, Morgan, not a gift."

His jaw was clenched tight, and his fingers were tense on the steering wheel. He really believed that. Ellory had even more questions, but she swallowed them down for now. Hudson was probably trying to psych her out. Everyone knew that even juniors with exemplary grades found it nearly impossible to get into Professor Colt's classes. His waiting list was extensive, and his connections were legendary. No matter what Hudson Graves said, this *was* a huge opportunity. He had the privilege of deciding whether he liked these salons. Ellory didn't care if they *did* hunt her for sport as long as she got a recommendation from Professor Colt at the end of it.

It was a twenty-minute drive to the house. Professor Colt lived in the kind of neighborhood that was more trees than people, where the residences had acreage and driveways that curved away from the main road to hide them from view. But when Hudson turned up the drive for this one, Ellory didn't see a house—she saw a mansion. The three-floor cottage had a slate roof, white stone at the top and red brick at the bottom, and two different chimneys, as well as a sunroom attached to one side and a garage attached to the other. There was a stone deck littered with chairs, a firepit, a grill, and glass-top tables. There was a sprawling view of what looked like a golf course across the way. There was a backyard so wide that Ellory couldn't guess at where it ended and the neighboring property began.

Hudson slotted the Barracuda behind a BMW and an SUV, both diagonally parked in front of the closed garage doors. If he noticed Ellory's awe, or even found it amusing, it didn't show. Instead, he swept toward the front door, leaving her stumbling to catch up with him. There was a skull plastered at eye level, spitting a black door knocker out of its open mouth. It was for the holiday; she knew it was for the holiday, knew she should find it fun and quirky. Instead, her heart pounded a little faster as Hudson rang the doorbell.

The skull watched them both, unfathomable.

When the door swung open, Ellory froze like a rabbit within view of a wolf. Perhaps she'd stared at the door knocker for too long, but for a moment, all she saw was death: A bleached face with sunken cheeks and gaping eye sockets. Teeth bared at her in a predatory warning.

"You're late," said Preston Colt. "But now I can understand why. Who is this lovely young woman?"

His voice was a soothing balm to Ellory's anxiety. It was no skeletal corpse that stood before her, but a handsome white man in his early to midsixties, his graying dishwater-blond hair combed back from his broad forehead and almost-nonexistent eyebrows. His smile was kind, not sinister, and his sunken blue eyes were framed by crow's feet that implied a lifetime of laughter. He wore all black—black suit jacket, black collared shirt, black slacks, black oxfords—which only drew attention to those few spots of color: The salt-and-pepper beard that lined his jaw. The silver glint of a Rolex. The lavender square curving from his left breast pocket.

"—Morgan," Hudson was saying when her ears stopped ringing. "We're in con. law together, and she's a great admirer of yours."

"She also speaks for herself," Ellory managed. She reached out a hand. *Firm handshake. Maintain eye contact. Smile, but not too much.* "It's such an honor to meet you, Professor. Thank you for having me."

They shook. "It's nice to meet you, Miss Morgan. *Colt* is fine during these little salons. Come in, come in. May I take your coats?"

The inside of the house was as lavish as the outside. They stepped through an arched doorway into a tasteful land of hardwood floors with neutral throw rugs, leaded windows that gazed out onto a beautiful verdant lawn, carved wainscoting, and a mahogany grand stairwell that twisted out of view. Colt led them to a carpeted first-floor study that had a lit fireplace and inlaid bookshelves housing fancy editions of books without visible titles. More windows lined the right wall, but in here the curtains were drawn, lending it a more intimate feel. Cushioned armchairs and a silver couch surrounded a glass table laden with hors d'oeuvres, including a charcuterie board.

Another thing that Ellory had thought was made up before she'd come to Warren.

There were already seven people present, four men and three women. Aside from one of the women, everyone was white, which meant that she and Hudson single-handedly brought the nonwhite population of the room up to a third. Their faces brightened at the sight of Hudson and then pinched at the sight of her, as if they were unused to new people and wondered if she might be a threat. Ellory straightened her shoulders and met their confused gazes head-on. The only person who didn't immediately look away was the brown woman, but she also didn't return Ellory's answering smile.

"Tough crowd," she whispered to Hudson.

"Oh, you just wait," he whispered back.

He carted her around the room, opening and then facilitating conversation until she was stitched into the tapestry of the salon. Ellory expected to feel like a showpiece, the starving artist to

Hudson's smug patron, but he was so different here. If he had been performing in the car, he was putting on an Oscar-winning routine for these people. He asked about parents and cousins, weddings and stock market prices. He used words like *summering* and *authenticated*, referenced artists like Modigliani and Flinck. He laughed at jokes that weren't funny and smiled like he'd never known what it was to do anything else. She tried to keep track of names, but several times she found herself simply gaping at his transformation. This was code-switching on such a grand scale that she felt out of her depth, unsure which parts of him were genuine.

Eventually, Hudson abandoned her to have a whispered conversation with Colt while the scent of butter rolls wafted in from the kitchen.

"The food at these things is always legendary," said a model-tall blond woman with severe bangs whose name was possibly Greer. "I heard that his chef is poached from a restaurant with *two* Michelin stars."

Ellory, who had no idea what that was supposed to mean, nodded sagely. "Are you in his political theory class?"

"I took it last semester. Worst few months of my fucking *life*." Greer wrinkled her nose. "He doesn't even teach the same curriculum twice, so I paid for a set of useless notes from some guy who took it in the fall. Asshole."

Ellory, unsure if she was talking about the guy or Colt, nodded again.

"I'm surprised I've never seen you before," Greer continued. "I always go to those rallies and everything. Is that not the best way to support anymore?"

"Support what?"

"Black Lives Matter." She turned her clutch to reveal that there was a pin advertising the movement affixed to the front of it. "I've been seeing fewer people there. Are we staying home and just donating again? Because I have dates and stuff."

"I, uh." Ellory blinked. "I've never gone to a Black Lives Matter rally."

"I fucking knew it. A waste of time, right? Like—"

Ellory excused herself before she had to hear the end of that sentence, her eyebrows nearly one with her hair. But the rest of the conversations only gave her further whiplash. For every person who showed an interest in her life in Astoria, where she'd sourced her outfit, or what classes she was taking, there was another who dismissed her outright for being a freshman, or expressed shock that she'd never been on a yacht, or led her over by the fireplace to ask, unironically, if she had any international weed connections because they wanted that *strong Bob Marley shit*. By the time Colt reappeared to call everyone to dinner, Ellory was genuinely considering opening the window and making a run for it.

"You do this *every* month?" she asked when Hudson reappeared at her side. *"Why?"*

Hudson smiled, and it looked so bleak that Ellory almost begged him to stop. It made her feel sorry for him, that he was capable of smiling like that. And yet it made a perverse kind of sense. He made her so miserable sometimes that he had to be well acquainted with the feeling.

"Dinner will be better," he promised. "Not by much, mind you, but there's wine."

The untouched hors d'oeuvres would haunt her all night, but all Ellory said was "Okay."

7

Dinner was served in the dining room, a separate space from the kitchen, with a long wooden table decorated by exactly ten chairs, ten place settings, ten wineglasses, and an intimidating number of utensils. The dishes spread out in the center had little cards before their silver trays, helping Ellory to identify them: TRUFFLE CHICKEN AND POTATO GRATIN, ROASTED PHEASANT WITH PEARL BARLEY, SMOKED SALMON AND LEMON RISOTTO, DUCK BREASTS WITH A MAPLE SYRUP VINAIGRETTE, PEAR AND SHALLOT TARTE TATIN WITH WHIPPED GOAT'S CHEESE. It was like the food was speaking its own opulent language, one that Ellory wanted to learn. No wonder the wealthy looked so full of themselves all the time, if they got to eat like this.

She and Hudson ended up in the two seats to the right of Colt. Her desire to fill her plate like it was Thanksgiving was checked solely by her desire not to make a fool of herself in front of the professor. She kept one eye on him and Hudson, reaching for everything they reached for, using the same forks they used, pouring as much wine as they poured. She seemed to be the only one who expected to eat dinner at this dinner party. For everyone else, the food was a decoration for their plates, to be ignored as they talked and went through the decanter.

"My mother is thinking of investing in some California vineyards," said Quentin Yardley, one of the few names Ellory had retained because she couldn't believe someone had named their child that. "Napa Valley has a billion-dollar economy that only increases with every passing year."

"Their business is also enduring and practically self-sustaining," said a woman whom Ellory was pretty sure was Kendall Rhodes. "Between the vineyards and their annual tourism, wouldn't it be near impossible to make any sort of mark, let alone a profit?"

"Overseas investments are definitely more lucrative right now," Greer added. "The American economy is a joke."

After every statement, the speaker would glance over at Colt as though expecting a pat on the head. The professor was smiling politely, indulgently, the kind of smile that offered nothing and took everything. He looked like a Roman noble watching a gladiator fight, picking through a plate of grapes and assorted cheeses while people died for his entertainment.

Ellory almost flinched when he turned his attention to her.

"Miss Morgan," he began, "tell us a bit about yourself. It's not often we have guests, even though they've always been welcome."

Ellory imagined telling a table full of people who had overseas investments that she lived in a two-bedroom in Astoria and kept cash in a cookie tin. She said, "I was born in Jamaica. Mandeville, to be specific."

"Oh, really? You barely have an accent!"

"I mean, I've lived here since I was four, so…"

"We went on a cruise to Montego Bay once," said Duncan

Something-or-Other, a man with bronze hair and a beauty mark by his straight nose. "Have you ever been to the Tryall?"

"Um, no." The Tryall was a private-members club, and Ellory was fairly certain he knew that. "Anyway, I live with my aunt in Astoria, so I don't really—"

"Are your parents dead?" Greer gasped, a hand coming up to cover her mouth. "Was it gun violence?"

"*Hey*," Hudson snapped. "Can you let her speak before you hurt yourself jumping to conclusions?"

The edge to his voice felt personal. Ellory wondered if this was how his first dinner had gone, the color of his skin painting such a violent image for these sheltered people that he had to learn to aggressively assimilate. Still, she was grateful enough to shoot him a smile. If Hudson Graves hated these people more than he hated her, that made them a united front. For now.

"My parents are in Mandeville." She considered telling them that it was common, in Jamaica, to consider schools in North America to be somehow better, to believe that the opportunities in the United States and Canada were more plentiful than the ones the island had to offer. The American dream's hold on some Jamaicans had never faded, even after *The Great Gatsby*, *Death of a Salesman*, and *Between the World and Me*. In the United States, they flocked to Florida, New York, and California. In Canada, they gathered in Toronto, Vancouver, and Montreal. For many of her countrymen, the devil they didn't know was better than the devil they did. "They sent me up alone so I could go to school."

"Sorry," Greer murmured, as if Ellory hadn't spoken. "I didn't mean to be rude or anything. I'm not racist."

"No one who isn't racist has ever needed to say they aren't racist," said Sofia Aston, the only other woman of color in the room. Ellory had learned, earlier, that she was Filipina, and that her parents worked in tourism. (*And that's all you need to know about that*, she'd said in a clipped tone.) But even though she was beautiful, round-cheeked and dewy-skinned and wavy-haired, she had been so standoffish that Ellory hadn't pushed for more conversation. "Especially when no one called them that in the first place."

Greer's pale cheeks went red. "That's not what I—why are you—it's that—*Professor*."

"Miss Aston, leave Miss Hammond alone," Colt said, though his crow's feet had deepened and his eyes glittered as if at some private joke. "We gather together to have productive discussions, not to accuse one another of groundless isms."

It wasn't groundless, Ellory almost said but didn't.

"Miss Morgan, would you like to continue? I'm especially interested in this aunt of yours. Does she have any children of her own?"

"No, she's never been married." Aunt Carol considered marriage and children something for other people, people who didn't know how to enjoy their lives and needed a distraction. Ellory assumed she was aromantic and asexual, because she'd never even seen her go on a date, but Carol had very strong opinions about the expectation of women to be *maternal* and to be only half formed without romance to make them whole. "She used to be a teacher until—um, now she kind of does freelance tutoring."

Colt tilted his head like he wanted to ask her about everything she wasn't saying. Thankfully, he just nodded. "A woman after my own heart. There's nothing more important than education and the bright future it creates for the minds of tomorrow."

"I agree. That's why she wanted me to go here. Aunt Carol is all about bright futures."

"Is it true you're a freshman?" one of the men—Miles

Clairborne—asked, leaning forward with sharp green eyes. "On scholarship? What's that like?"

"Fine? How did you—"

"My father's opposed to the Godwin Scholarships," Miles continued. "He hates handouts since he pulled himself up by his bootstraps."

Hudson gave Miles a bored look. "By his bootstraps with nothing but a half-a-billion-dollar loan from your grandfather to start his business, isn't that right?"

"What's *that* supposed to mean?"

"Can I use the bathroom?" Ellory asked, before the inevitable fight could get underway. Greer and Sofia were still arguing with each other about what was or wasn't racist, while the final guest, Percy, shrank between them like he wanted to go home. Kendall, Duncan, and Quentin were talking about cruises they'd taken and where they considered the best place to grab some winter sun. Hudson was looking at Miles the way that he looked at the whiteboard during class sometimes, like this was a war and he was already making plans to win the first two battles. It was a lot.

It was too much.

"Down the hall," Colt said absently, without taking his gleaming gaze off Miles and Hudson. "Past the sunroom."

Down the hall and past the sunroom, Ellory opened the door to a short mirror-lined hallway. There were chairs and majesty palms, like someone might have a meeting in here. Beyond that was a second door that led to the actual bathroom. English ivy spilled from baskets hung from the ceiling, and the floor was lined with oversize tiles with a wooden finish. The sink was a white marble vessel with gray veining, the bathtub was a freestanding matte-black pool with no curtain, and the toilet was a wall-mounted contraption with a built-in bidet and a gold stripe. It was almost a crime to pee in it.

How many times was she going to hide in bathrooms? This couldn't be her entire life at Warren, accepting invitations to social gatherings only to break down next to the nearest available toilet. It wasn't as though she had never experienced things like this. In job interviews, there had always been that brief moment of surprise when she'd shown up, as if Ellory Morgan were too normal a name for a woman who looked like her. Once, she hadn't unfrozen fast enough to hold the elevator for a man running toward her, and she had heard him call her a slur through the closed doors. She'd been asked if this was her real hair, she'd been told by friends' parents that they had made chicken for her, and she had seen stifled smiles if she chose watermelon-flavored anything.

Like most Black women, she had a lifetime of microaggressions to prepare her for Warren University.

But they had been spread out over seventeen years, humiliation that built and burned but could then be rationalized and forgotten. This was a night designed to remind her that progress would always be slow when there were whole classes of people who thought like this, surrounded by other people who thought like this, who never—by choice or by coincidence—had to engage with the fact that they might be doing anything wrong at all.

Trust me, I'm not doing you a favor.

This is a punishment, Morgan, not a gift.

At least Colt seemed to like her so far—or didn't actively dislike her, which was good enough. It was even more important that she went home with his goodwill, because she was leaving her dignity in tatters across his wooden floors. This was not the time or place to call people out on their shit, she knew that, but fuck if it didn't make her feel *small* to swallow her thoughts and force her smiles.

Her stomach rumbled, reminding her that her thoughts were the only things she'd swallowed tonight. All that food going to waste while they gorged on self-indulgence.

"Morgan?" The knock on the door sounded so distant that she would have thought she had imagined it if not for Hudson's voice. She'd never heard concern in it before, and she wouldn't have known how to make it up. It softened the way he said her last name, until it sounded more like a nickname. "You've been gone for twenty minutes. It's disrupting dinner. Do I need to drive you to the hospital?"

That was more along the lines of what she'd expected.

Ellory wiped her damp hands on a small towel and stuffed it in the laundry hamper. "I'm all right," she said as she returned to the mirror-lined hallway. "Go back to the dining room. I'm coming."

There was a pause. "Are you certain? If this has been too much—"

"I'm fine. Go away, Graves."

Somehow, without opening the second door, she knew he was still standing there. She could picture him leaning against the wall, his arms folded, his eyes downcast while he tried to think of some witty rejoinder that she didn't want to hear. The night wasn't over, and Ellory was not in the mood to be comforted. A part of her yearned to ask him again why he put himself through this once a month, but the rest of her refused to show that weakness. Not because it was him, but because if he could do it alone all this time, then she could certainly make it through this single event with him looking out for her.

And in the quiet of the bathroom, she could admit that he had been doing that. Looking out for her. Curbing the worst of what he'd dealt with, leaving only the echoes for her to handle. She didn't know what to do with that knowledge. That kindness.

"Colt's asking for you," Hudson added. He rapped his knuckles against the wall in a nervous *rat-tat*. "We're actually eating now, so things should be more fun from here."

"I'm okay," she said more softly. There was a smile that wanted to inch onto her face, a smile that she fought back. If she didn't know any better, she would think he was trying to cheer her up. "Really. Tell Colt I'll be there soon."

She waited until she heard him shuffle away before she stepped closer to the mirror. Though her makeup had held up well, she reapplied her mascara and brushed her thumb across the corner of her mouth to make sure her lipstick hadn't migrated toward her cheek. She'd figured there would be wine, so she'd gone for a long-lasting brand that was, so far, living up to its name. Finally, she dragged a hand through her curls to give them a bit more bounce, like maybe that would give her the confidence she'd need for whatever *fun* entailed.

Ellory stilled with her fingers near the crown of her head.

The mirrors faced each other, allowing her to see herself from the front and back. With her hair still half smooshed by her hand, she could see something on her neck, deep black like an ink stain. She walked backward until she was in front of the other mirror, but no matter how she contorted her body, she couldn't get a better look. The longer she tried, the more her heart attempted to gallop out of her chest—and not from the exertion. That nameless dread had returned with a vengeance, and it would choke her if she didn't do something. Already, the overhead lights felt too bright, and goose bumps crept up her arms like baby spiders erupting from Charlotte's posthumous egg sac.

Ellory fished a scrunchie out of her pocket and pulled her hair up into a messy bun, baring her neck to the aloe-scented room. Her phone was unearthed next. She used the mirrors to line up the camera as best she could and took several pictures. Black spots danced before her vision, and her fingers shook around the phone. She nearly dropped it twice trying to look at the results. It was as if her body was protecting her from what she was about to see by completely shutting down.

"What the fuck," she whispered, leaning against the mirror in case her legs decided to give out. "What the *fuck*."

It wasn't an ink stain but a tattoo, one that didn't even look recent. Her skin wasn't puffy or red; there was no bandage or pain that would have alerted her to its existence. There was only black text, a single word with a backward capital *E* in the center of it, permanently scrawled in her own handwriting:

RemƎmber.

8

Ellory left the bathroom in a daze, shrouded not in numbness but in triumph. Her fingers traced the lines of the tattoo—or where she guessed the lines were, as her skin felt smooth to the touch beneath her tangled hair. Part of her wanted to stay in that hallway, studying the impossible from every angle, but the rest of her was energized. Finally, she had more than feelings without facts. How could she have forgotten *getting a tattoo*, let alone one in her own handwriting? Something was wrong with her memories, and this was tangible proof. Tangible and terrific and terrifying.

"—if you can believe it!"

Ellory jumped as laughter echoed down the long corridor, reminding her that there were other people in the world. Sterling-silver utensils clinked against porcelain plates. Muffled conversation fused individual voices. She turned toward the foyer, freeing her coat from the hall closet before freeing herself from the house. Outside, an argent moon stared her down, half hidden by the smudged shadows of the surrounding trees.

The chill wind kept her grounded, focused. Without the autumn cold slicing bladed air into every gap between her coat collar and bare skin, her mind would have been stuck in that incredulous moment—a moment that already felt like it was slipping away the longer it took her Uber driver to arrive. She flipped between the photo and the app, the app and the photo, *Rem℈mber* and Your driver is 5 minutes away. Neither felt real.

"Morgan, what the hell are you doing?" Hudson Graves stood in the doorway, one hand struggling into the sleeve of his peacoat and the other resting on the skull door knocker. "You've chosen a fine time to get some air."

Ellory looked back at her phone. "I'm going to campus."

"What? Why?"

For a moment, she considered telling him—about the tattoo and about the peculiarity of her school year, her expanding document of notes at the dorm, and her rising sense that something was not right with her head. But they were not friends just because he had finally buttoned up his coat and was now joining her on the gravel, his face tight with concern. They were not friends just because he had noticed her being missing from the salon within minutes. This night held them as close as a secret, but the sun would soon rise to illuminate the truth: She and Hudson Graves would *never* be friends.

"Tell Professor Colt I wasn't feeling well," she said. The Uber had missed the turn up the drive and was now looping around the massive block. "I'd love to come next month if he'll have me."

"Morgan, you can't—" Ellory watched him visibly think better of telling her what she could and could not do. "Please come inside. I know this group is...a lot, but I promise you're meant to be here."

There was a gravity to the way he said it that made her pause. Darkness painted the fiery fall foliage in black and gray, making the trees appear like monsters circling their prey. Hudson, too, seemed monstrous by moonlight, the pewter rays making the angles of his face more severe. His eyes were in shadow, his lustrous mouth set in a familiar frown. The wind swirled around them, toying with the ends of her curls, the tops of her ears, the unprotected line of her chin. It was as if they existed in a world divorced from reality.

Meanwhile, her Uber circled and circled and circled the block, getting no closer to whisking her away. She would have to walk down the drive to meet the car, navigating the thick gloom of a yard that was, by now, as dark as a tomb. There would be nothing but the watery light of her phone, nothing but the slide of her shoes through the grass, nothing but the puffs of her breath and the hope that there was a driver waiting for her at the end of a too-long walk. She'd seen far too many horror movies with a scene like that.

Ellory canceled the car.

"Fine," she said, putting her phone back into her pocket. "But only because these people waste so much food, it physically pains me."

Hudson's lips twitched into something resembling a smile. "Shall I get you a to-go box?"

"Shut up," Ellory muttered, sliding past him. The salon waited, and the house would be a welcome haven from the crisp breeze.

His hand curled around her forearm, then slid down before she could take another step.

Ellory was so surprised by the contact that she allowed it. His fingers were soft when they settled at her wrist, loose enough for her to pull free if she wanted to. His thumb traced the fragile lines of her veins. She still wasn't used to being this near to him or to the electric charge that his touch incited across her nerve endings, shocking and grounding all at once. Her mind told her to step away, but her body swayed closer to him, weak to his gravitational pull. In turn, he bent toward her like a flower to the sun, his dark eyes open and searching. Sometimes, they were compulsively intersecting lines, but other times, times like right now, they were a tangled knot whose interwoven threads were impossible to unravel.

"Thank you," he said, "for coming."

"Thank you," she replied, "for inviting me."

Behind Hudson, the front door opened. He dropped her hand as if her skin were suddenly slicked with acid. Professor Colt squinted at them in the halo of the porch light. He held a silver lighter in one hand and a cigarette between his lips. The look on his face made Ellory's cheeks heat, even though there was nothing going on but a temporary ceasefire. "We'll be having after-dinner drinks in the study soon. Will you be joining us?"

Hudson's moon-kissed face was turned away, so it was Ellory who answered, "Yes."

"In you go, then."

Colt stepped out onto the gravel. The flame of his lighter glowed like a firefly against the night, there and gone. By the time Ellory dragged her eyes away, Hudson had disappeared into the house, leaving her with the sense that she'd lost something vital.

◆

Stasie was awake when Ellory returned to the residence hall, and for the first time, that was a blessing. Tai hadn't responded to repeated knocks or curses at her door; instead, her answering text was delayed by fifteen minutes and had apparently been sent from Cody's bed. Ellory loved romance as much as the next single person, but her friends had chosen the *worst* possible time to get laid.

With no other options, she changed into her pajamas with her back to her roommate, trying to think of the best way to broach the subject of a mysterious tattoo without sounding like she needed to visit the Student Health Center. She had a complicated relationship with therapy, something her aunt believed in even less than she believed in community college. *Those pills aren't natural*, Carol always said. *If you're feeling bad, you can always come home. That will set you right.* Added to the fact that Ellory couldn't afford it without the guaranteed health insurance of a full-time job—if even then—and it all meant that therapy was a stigmatized luxury she'd always gone without. No matter how badly she might have needed it.

But if the tattoo was a sign that she was losing her mind, Ellory was sure Stasie would tell her.

It helped to have other things to distract her. At Professor Colt's house, the cloud of conversation—increasingly inappropriate the more wine was consumed—had faded into background noise as Ellory had studied Hudson Graves. After stopping her from disappearing into the night, he went out of his way to avoid being near her, even if it meant talking to Greer while his entire body stayed tight with the obvious desire to tell her to shut up. Ellory drank and spoke little, trying to pierce his head with her gaze and read his confounding thoughts. She had spent more time with him tonight than in the last three months, and she had never felt less like she understood him.

"Did you forget how to get dressed," Stasie asked, "or is this you coming on to me?"

Ellory realized she was standing in front of her bed, still wearing nothing but a pair of pajama bottoms. She'd gotten her head through her threadbare band T-shirt, but then she'd stopped there, lost in her own thoughts, her lower back and stomach bared to the room. Over her shoulder, Stasie was reclining with her phone in hand, a smirk on her face that suggested she wanted to laugh at her own joke but couldn't allow herself to be that uncool.

"Can I ask you something?" Ellory asked once she was fully dressed. Stasie didn't look at her, but she also didn't say no. That would have to be good enough. "Have you ever noticed that I have a tattoo?"

"No, but I'm not surprised. Aren't you from Queens?"

Stasie said *Queens* the way some people might say *maximum security prison*.

"What does that—anyway, it's on the back of my neck. You've never seen it?"

At this, Stasie finally looked up. Her threaded honey-brown eyebrows drew together. "You don't have a tattoo on the back of your neck."

"Yes, I do."

"No, you really don't." Stasie wrinkled her pert nose. "Or are you trying to tell me that you got one tonight?"

"No, I—no." Ellory bit back the story of her night, well aware that it would only make Stasie's nose wrinkle deeper until it concaved back into her skull. "It's right here. Come and look."

Instead of providing an argument or a snide remark, Stasie came to her side. They were the same height, so Ellory stooped a little to make it easier for Stasie to examine her neck. Her hands clenched and unclenched, brimming with restless energy. But Stasie was silent as one second turned into ten and ten into twenty.

AN ARCANE INHERITANCE

Finally, Stasie said, "There's nothing there. *Like I said*."

Ellory turned to see that her roommate had brought her phone with her, and she was already texting—likely telling her friends about the latest weird thing Ellory had done. She frowned, wondering if Stasie had even *looked* or had simply stood there long enough to seem like she had.

She nodded toward Stasie's phone. "Show me."

"Okaaaaaay."

Ellory's heart dropped as she stared at the subsequent photo, and then it began to beat at a dangerous speed. Because Stasie was right. There was no longer a tattoo on the back of her neck. Unblemished skin stared back at her, slightly lighter than the brown of the rest of her body, framed by curls barely held out of the shot by her fingers. Stasie had taken four bright pictures, and not a single one of them showed the tattoo.

"This doesn't make any sense," Ellory said, digging around for her own phone. "I just *saw*—"

Nothing. The photos she had taken were still on her phone, different angles and lighting as she contorted herself in that mirror-lined hallway, but, where they had once shown a tattoo Ellory didn't recall getting, they now proved…nothing. Because her skin was blank in them, too, and Stasie was staring at her like she might call the Student Health Center herself, and Ellory's heart was thumping in her chest like a drum.

Her fingers touched the back of her neck where the tattoo was. Where the tattoo had been. Where the tattoo was no longer.

RemƎmber.

Remember what?

"If you're done being weird," said Stasie, retreating to her bed, "can you find somewhere else to be? My friends are coming over."

"It's one in the morning."

"Please don't make it my problem that you don't have friends."

"It's *one* in the *morning*."

Stasie rolled her eyes and returned to texting. Ellory realized her hand was shaking around her phone and tossed it back on the mattress. She had seen the tattoo. She was sure she had. First in the mirror and then in the photos she'd studied in Professor Colt's front yard. She was sure of it. She was *sure*.

Yet her instinct was to doubt herself. What if it had been stress? What if it had been a strange angle? What if it had been a defect in the lens?

But, a stubborn voice roared from within her, how many things could she write off as the product of an overactive imagination? She had a document full of the unexplained, a month's worth of haunting inconsistencies, and still she doubted herself. She had worked since the moment she'd gotten her driver's license, sometimes three jobs at a time. She had crafted a well-researched nutritional guide for Aunt Carol after her first stroke, learned to cook heart-healthy meals, memorized medication times and dosages, filled out hospital forms, and done her homework by her aunt's bedside. She had been an honors student, an AP student, a fucking valedictorian with near-perfect SAT scores.

One month in this place had hollowed her out until she no longer trusted her own screaming instincts.

She imagined trying on the moneyed confidence of her classmates, the aggressive hubris of Stasie O'Connor and Hudson Graves, the passive sangfroid of Taiwo Daniels and Liam Blackwood. If she could wear that self-assurance like a costume, maybe she would finally feel like she belonged here—and maybe she could actually figure out what was wrong with her.

"Hey," Stasie snapped as there was a knock on the door. "Are you leaving or what? My friends are here."

"No," Ellory said decisively, climbing into her bed and putting her back to her sputtering roommate. Her exultant smile followed her down into the darkness of her dreams. A little confidence felt good.

INTERLUDE

I T WAS A COMMON MISCONCEPTION that Warren University had no evidence of secret societies.

Most knew of Skull and Bones, the infamous underbelly of Yale University. Fewer could name the Porcellian Club at Harvard, the Quill and Dagger at Cornell, or the Ivy Club at Princeton, a university that banned *secret* societies but allowed for *senior* societies, so-called eating clubs, with even stricter membership. But none could name a single society, public or otherwise, at Warren University, despite their robust annual Club Festival, which added new booths every year.

Like every member of the Ivy League, Warren produced politicians and actors, CEOs and lawyers, famous faces from families well acquainted with the Fortune 500. But unlike every Ivy League, there was nothing to unify the illustrious alumni beyond the same prestigious degree, no complicated handshakes or coded greetings, no engraved rings or exclusive clubhouses, no typed invitations on vellum paper or Deer Island retreats.

That was because Warren University knew what all the other universities, with their media references and society Wikipedia pages, did not: how to actually keep a secret.

9

ELLORY HAD SPENT HER FIRST month in Hartford exploring the area in search of the perfect bookstore, and she had found it in Cover Story. Located ten minutes away from campus—twenty-five if she was walking—it was an independent bookstore up a short flight of stairs painted to look like classic books: *Persuasion* and *Moby-Dick*, *The Age of Innocence* and *Things Fall Apart*, *Les Misérables* and *The Count of Monte Cristo*. Beyond the mint-green-and-pearl-white awning, rustic cedar bookshelves were packed with titles, all sorted by category. The armchairs scattered throughout the space were also bookshelves, lined with tomes in the arms and base. Plants atop the shelves kept the open room smelling like a garden, and the front windows allowed a steady stream of sunlight inside to help them grow.

From the moment Ellory had first stepped inside, she'd felt comfortable. Safe. When she wasn't on shift at Powers That Bean or pulling her hair out over homework at the Graves, she was here in this cozy harbor, tracing the spines of beloved stories or buying one of the ever-changing homemade bookmarks that decorated the front counter. It was like Cover Story had an enchantment within its walls that forced her shoulders to relax and her anxieties to fade.

"We can have lunch after this," Tai said as she led Ellory inside the stacks, her braids decorated by a powder-blue crochet turban-beanie. "But clearly you're under way too much pressure right now and need some chill vibes."

Music was playing in the bookstore, a classical song Ellory didn't recognize but knew was from a *Looney Tunes* rerun. Bubblegum-pink hydrangeas and silver-lavender Russian sage glanced down at them from the pots, adding extra flashes of color. Ellory's hand was in her pocket, brushing against her phone, and her mind was fixed on the pictures that still waited in her camera roll to unbalance her again. When Tai had heard the whole story, she had insisted on this trip before Ellory could even suggest it, diagnosing Ellory with an acute case of stress brought about by *spending too much time in the presence of that shit stick, Graves.*

Meanwhile, that shit stick Graves hadn't contacted Ellory since dropping her off at Moneta the night before. That was normal, and yet she could still feel the echoes of their time together: His fingers around her wrist, palm kissing her pulse point. His eyes on her face like she was the answer to a question he had yet to ask. His pointed absence for the rest of the night. Every time she forced these snapshots of midnight delirium to the back of her mind, they pinballed to the forefront, gliding through the lateral fissure of her brain to attack her. And she couldn't tell if it was stressful or frustrating or even meaningful, this unexpected shift in her understanding of Hudson Graves, but the chasmal potential of it sent restless energy zinging through her body.

She exhaled slowly, pushing herself to focus. She had bigger problems than Hudson Graves right now.

AN ARCANE INHERITANCE

Tai disappeared into the graphic novels section, and Ellory walked on. The store was filled but not overcrowded; every so often she would pass someone tucked into an armchair or sitting on the floor between shelves, reading or having hushed conversations with a companion. A bulletin board half her size spanned one wall, brimming with colorful advertisements for tutoring and babysitting services, for local bands and comedy shows, for African hair braiding and psychic readings. Someone was blocking the right-hand side, adding a new graphic poster to the noise. It took her a moment to recognize that fluffy brown hair, those broad shoulders, those thick biceps.

Liam Blackwood turned at the sound of his name. His face lit up when he caught sight of her, that model smile firmly in place. He wore a thick cream cardigan with oversize brown buttons over a coffee-colored polo shirt with off-white stripes. A pair of relaxed-fit khakis in the same shade as his shirt completed the outfit. She half expected a pair of sunglasses to be hanging from his collar and artificial wind to tousle his chestnut waves, but he instead had a slate-gray jacket thrown over his arm and white tennis shoes on his feet. No wind. No pretense. Just Liam, as chipper as a puppy.

"Ellory Morgan," he exclaimed, "how the hell are you?"

She had no idea how to answer that question, so she nodded toward the bulletin board instead. "What are you doing?"

Liam turned back to the board as if he'd forgotten that it was there, even though his hand was still on the flyer he'd pinned to it. It appeared, Ellory gathered from squinting around his thick fingers, to be an advertisement for an upcoming lacrosse game. "My duty as captain," he answered. His brown eyes twinkled as he watched her. "I don't suppose you're interested in coming to one of our games?"

"I'm not really a sports person."

"Are you a dinner person?"

Ellory raised her eyebrows. "They eat dinner during lacrosse?"

"Afterward, you and I could grab some." Liam's charm was like a physical touch, sending a pleasant shiver down her spine. He was a hard man to dislike, and he clearly knew it. "I'm interested in figuring out what kind of person you are."

"I'll think about it," she managed. "Right now, the only thing I'm interested in is books."

Liam accepted this answer easily. "Well, you're in a great place for it. How did you find this bookstore?"

Ellory lost track of how long they stood there, talking about Cover Story and the first time they'd each stumbled inside. That turned into a conversation about favorite books, which dissolved into a playful argument about which Jane Austen novel had the best film adaptation, which somehow swung into a debate on whether dogs or cats were superior. She laughed harder than she could remember laughing in a while, and she did not miss her apprehension at all. This close to Liam Blackwood's inherent light, there was no room for shadows.

"I have to hit up the rest of the businesses on this block." Liam sighed. When he checked his watch, a quick glance at the face told Ellory they'd been talking for a little over an hour. "But can I at least get your number? You know, so you can share more of your wrong Sherlock Holmes opinions."

"Smooth," Ellory said, but she still gave it to him. A smile tugged at her lips. "*Elementary* was a masterful Sherlock Holmes adaptation, and I will die on that hill."

"I can't believe I wanted to have dinner with you," Liam said in mock offense. Then he winked. *That wink.* She shivered again. "See you around, Morgan."

Once he was gone, Ellory tried to stop smiling, if only because he clearly knew the effect he had on people and was delighted that it worked on her. She failed hard until she remembered that she had not come here for Liam Blackwood.

She grabbed a slip for African hair braiding and moved on.

Ellory started in the psychology section, wading through Jung and Vygotsky and Thorndike until she found titles on repressed memories and auditory hallucinations and general cognitive psychology. Next, she pulled books on neurophysiology in the medicine section, books on past lives in the occult section, and a Moleskine notebook from the writing section. Finally, she spread her haul across one of the tables near the back of the store, many of which were already bursting with people taking advantage of the outlets and Wi-Fi, and prepared to take detailed notes that she could copy into her Word document later. She only had the money to leave the store with the Moleskine, but each book came with an index that helped her focus her skimming to relevant paragraphs only.

That familiar rush energized her, the sense of rightness that came with chasing down a lead like a golden retriever in pursuit of a ball. It was a high she couldn't replicate with quantitative political research or social choice theory, though she'd spent the last month and a half trying. She wanted to become Elle Woods or Annalise Keating, getting her thrills from picking the scorched remains of her opponents' arguments out of her teeth as she won another case, but she wasn't even in law school yet and she could feel herself fumbling.

Investigative journalism—though itself inherently political—felt like wading through the muck to unearth a clean nugget of truth. It was shining a light down a dark hallway. It was giving a voice to the voiceless. Politics felt like reaching into the grime to find another, filthier layer underneath. It was the slow erosion of long-held morals for short-term gains. It was constantly choosing the *least awful option* until there were none left.

But political science would keep the lights on in her apartment. Journalism would only give her four roommates all sharing the same fork over the last bowl of ramen for years before she had a spare dime to put in her savings account.

Do *you want to be a lawyer?*

Annoyed by the direction of her thoughts and the intrusion of Hudson Graves, Ellory gathered up the books to return them to the shelves. She had to pay for the Moleskine, and she had to find Tai. Her stomach growled, a reminder that she'd had nothing but overnight oats for breakfast, and though she could still taste faint traces of the honey and Greek yogurt she had mixed in, that was no substitute for a full meal.

But as she passed the local-interest section, she slowed in consideration. Here, the shelves boasted books about Warren University and Connecticut as a whole. It was a long shot, but maybe she would find something about Warren being built behind a deadfall or in the center of a fairy circle—something that turned it into the kind of liminal space where she could slip more easily into a shadow world. It sounded ridiculous even as she thought it, but the sound of that incessant buzzing and the sight of those teeming shadows drove her deeper into the stacks. Dread pooled in her stomach, but she clenched and unclenched her fingers as if she could massage the terror from her epithelium.

Ellory froze when something caught her eye.

J.

On the otherwise-empty spine of a book, the letter was written in gold and surrounded by a circle of silver ivy leaves—the same stylized ivy that surrounded the Warren University crest. She tugged the volume from the shelf, frowning when she saw it was another reference book about the school's founding. Her fingers ran over the symbol before she flipped it open, searching for something she didn't have words for yet. Whatever it was, she reached the end without finding any sign of it.

Ellory went to put the book back and paused. The hole it had left on the shelf was shadowed, but there was a flash of something corpse pale within. Switching the book to her nondominant hand, she reached inside, her fingertips catching on a torn edge of paper. She tugged it free of the tape keeping it affixed to the back panel of the shelf. Only a quick fumble kept her from dropping the book when she saw her own handwriting on the paper, which was nondescript and lined like she'd torn it from a notebook.

She didn't remember writing this. She couldn't even remember a time she'd come down this aisle before.

hudson will hǝlp, the note read. The single *e*, like the one on the book, like the one that had been on her neck, was backward.

Ellory crumpled the paper in her fist as her rising unease was swallowed by furious disbelief. This *had* to be a joke. Of all the absurd things that had come to define this school year, leaving herself the advice to rely on Hudson Graves for any kind of help had taken this one step too far. He obviously wrote it. Maybe the entire salon was in on it. There was an optical illusion on the mirror that made her see ink where there was none. He'd learned to forge her handwriting and left this note in her favorite store.

And all the rest? Coincidences and a stubborn need to see beyond the veil. She'd created a story out of nothing.

She was such an *idiot*.

"Ready to go?" Tai asked, appearing at the mouth of the aisle holding no fewer than three graphic novels. "Or are you buying that first?"

Ellory realized she was still clutching the book. She switched it to her other hand to hide the paper and moved away from the shelf as casually as she could. Her wrath—at herself, at Hudson Graves, at herself again—built like a storm, and her body coiled like lightning about to strike.

Tai lifted an eyebrow. "You look even less chill than you were before we got here," she observed. "Maybe we should have had lunch first."

"I'm fine."

"*Okay*, snappy. Come on, then."

Ellory glanced back at the hollow in the shelf where the book had once been and felt another hot rush of anger at Hudson Graves. She would get her answers, one way or another. Whether he survived the questioning was a different story.

10

For someone so popular, Hudson Graves was often alone. He disdained company the same way he disdained everything else, stalking around the campus like a tiger with his fitted peacoats and pointed stares. Trying to find him at first proved an exercise in frustration. Every professor claimed he'd just left. Every teammate claimed he'd called out of practice. Every so-called friend told her to mind her own business.

Ellory wasn't desperate enough to show up at his house uninvited, so she kept prowling his usual hangouts and glowering at the unanswered text she'd sent him that morning. He'd left her on READ, as if she'd broken some unspoken etiquette rule by using his number for anything other than its designated purpose. The mass of contradictions that was Hudson Graves made it even more unlikely that she had truly been the author of the note claiming he could help her. He was as helpful as a match was to an oil spill.

Ellory had once thought him to be everywhere—especially places she didn't want him to be—but it was almost dark when she stumbled over him in the bowels of the Graves, surrounded by books that lined his lone table like an electric fence. He was on the second floor, or the seventh floor, depending on how she decided to count. Here, only one level up from the basement she avoided, there were so few students that it was almost like a private stadium. The entire space smelled faintly of decaying flowers, a stench both musty and saccharine that burned the back of her throat and the inside of her nose. And it was silent, the hollow kind, a lack of sound that made sure its absence was felt. The carpeting even swallowed any noise from her heeled ankle boots.

A chill caressed her spine. She kept walking.

But when Ellory pushed a column of books to the side to reveal Hudson, she had to stop and stare. He wore a lemon-yellow knit sweater that was the loudest thing in the building. Perhaps the loudest thing she'd ever witnessed.

"Surely," Hudson said without glancing up from the book he was reading, "you have better things to do than follow me around."

"How many rubber duckies had to die to make this outfit?"

"What—"

"One million? Two million?"

"—do you want?"

"You look like Arthur Read," Ellory finished with a flourish. Hudson rubbed his temples, which filled her with a particular sense of satisfaction. The anger was still there, writhing like a nest of wasps, but she was never above this level of pettiness where he was concerned. "But I do actually want something, yeah."

He gestured for her to sit down, but she ignored him to set the note on top of the book he still hadn't closed. While he examined it, she examined him. He'd paired the sweater with neutral colors: a gray button-down and beige slacks. Dark crescents sagged beneath his eyes, and his light-brown skin was sallow with exhaustion.

From a distance, he'd seemed intimidatingly put together, wrapped in the caution tape that was his personality and his book barrier. Now that she could see the cracks in his performance, it dulled the edges of her displeasure.

Hudson's eyebrows were pinched as he flicked the note away. "Help with what?"

"Why don't *you* tell *me*?"

Her tone made his brows pinch further. "It sounds like you're accusing me of something, but I didn't buy tickets to this circus. Can you translate the clownery into words I can understand?"

Ellory sat down. The crumpled note now hung off one of the cleared edges of the table, and she grabbed it before it could fall. She spread it out between them, but Hudson didn't even bother to look at it this time.

"You've been playing tricks on me all year," she snapped, "and I want it to stop. This isn't—"

"I didn't write this," said Hudson. "And I have no idea what you're talking about."

His face and tone held no hint of deception. Ellory narrowed her eyes.

"Morgan, I have to do research for my thesis, so—"

Ellory snatched the book out from in front of him before he could use it to ignore her again. She heard him call her *unfathomably juvenile* as she left the table, but he still followed her all the way to a study room. As she stepped across the threshold of the one closest to the elevators, she felt it: the sense that she'd been in this room before, even though she couldn't remember studying on this floor at all. The lighting shifted from midafternoon to late night and back again, as if another version of the room were trying to press in on her. Resigned to his fate, Hudson had closed the glass door behind them, leaving them in a space empty of anything but a round table and enough chairs for a small group. Alabaster walls enclosed them on three sides.

It was all so suddenly familiar that Ellory thought she might be sick.

"All right, Morgan," Hudson said, folding his arms over his bright yellow sweater. "You have my attention. What is going with you?"

The story burst out of her like she'd been waiting to tell it to him, a geyser of not-quite-coincidences and glitches in the Matrix, of déjà vu and dread and disappearing tattoos. Halfway through, Hudson's posture loosened, his arms falling to his sides and that focused stare turning sharp with concentration. He didn't interrupt. He didn't laugh. He didn't run. *She* would have run.

Ellory set his stolen book down on the table. "…and if it hasn't been you messing with me, then I don't know what to do or what's going on. It's too early in the school year for a psychotic break, don't you think?"

Hudson said nothing for such a long time that Ellory grew self-conscious.

"You don't believe me," she sighed. "Why would you believe me? I barely believe me."

"No, I do," Hudson finally said. "I believe you."

Ellory's mouth opened, but no sound emerged. Hudson was looking at one of the walls, rubbing his chin like a cartoon villain stroking an imaginary beard. The sight almost made her smile, but shock had numbed her to anything but her own breathing.

"You're one of the few on this campus whom I would consider my intellectual equal," Hudson continued. "Imagine what it would say about me if you needed to be committed."

That sounded more like him. Ellory scowled.

"Besides, you forgot that I was there that day. When you stopped that ball from hitting you in the face. The wind alone couldn't do that." Now Hudson was looking at her, his eyes the deep brown of burning firewood. "True, I'm approaching this with a healthy amount of scientific skepticism, but paranormal phenomena have been researched at all levels of society for centuries. And I've yet to find a rational explanation for...that."

Ellory's mouth remembered to form words: "Okay."

She could think of nothing to add. She'd expected a longer fight. She'd expected to have to cite her notes. She'd expected...anything other than easy acceptance. His faith in her made it all feel real. That sour tang of dread returned. When it had been a thesis, it had felt almost like a game. Now she didn't think she was wrong, but she suddenly, desperately wanted to be.

"Maybe this is all a mistake—"

"Come now, Morgan." Hudson stepped close enough to back her into the table. But all he did was take his book and move away, leaving behind the faint scent of shea butter. "It's worth looking into. At the very least, this might make for a more interesting subject for my thesis."

"Magic? That hardly seems compatible with a degree in political science."

"Divine right of kings. Occult sciences. Western esotericism. The bloody history of belief in preternatural forces that shape political systems and justify who gets to wield power within them is more novel than my original pitch."

"Are you single-handedly trying to prove the myth that human beings use only ten percent of their brain by making sure ninety percent of yours is made up of pure bullshit?" But she was smiling, and not even against her will. Him getting something out of her misery was more acceptable than his belief, the kind of belief she hadn't even been able to get from her parents as a kid or her best friend as an adult. "But fine. What do we do now?"

"I," he said, lifting his book, "am going back to work. You can meet me at my house this weekend. My roommates are going to a matinee, so if you come around eleven in the morning, we should have some privacy."

He left without waiting for her response, assuming—arrogantly but correctly—that she would agree. After all, it wasn't as though she had a choice.

11

SATURDAY WAS A RARE WARM day, one where the sun chased away the glacial autumn wind. Ellory had a jacket folded into her backpack, but she wore nothing heavier than an oversize hoodie and a pair of turquoise leggings. Sleep had eluded her since they'd made their plans. Every night, she lay in bed for hours while the compendium of horrors she'd witnessed played out in startling detail behind her eyelids. Every day, she moved through classes and shifts like a wraith, jumping at shadows and waiting for her reality to tilt once more. Now that she was finally on her way to get some answers, or so she hoped, she was glad for the unseasonable heat to give her something else to think about.

A tray with two coffees from Powers That Bean rocked in Ellory's lap as the Uber carried her through Hudson Graves's neighborhood, which looked like an entirely different place in the light of day. The streets weren't clogged with parked cars, and the air wasn't thick with loud music. Without the marks of a college party in progress, it was a normal suburb with clipped lawns and reddening trees. Two children played catch on a sun-gilded sidewalk. A woman pushed a lawn mower through her overgrown grass. A stray cat weaved between the empty garbage bins in someone's driveway.

She felt like she was in a sinister suburban drama. She half expected to see a single drop of blood slowly *drip-drip-drip* down a pristine window.

Hudson's precious '71 Barracuda was parked as close to the house as it could get without entering the living room, a literal orange traffic cone behind the bumper to warn people away from approaching it. The lawn was more yellow than green now, and the bushes that huddled beneath the front windows were more branch than leaf. But the porch had been newly cleaned, each beam of wood shining in the morning light. To the left of the stairs rested a lopsided jack-o'-lantern with a cell phone wedged inside.

The door swung open after a single knock. Hudson yawned out a greeting, more dressed down than she'd ever seen him: loose white T-shirt, black sweatpants, and white socks with yellow ducks on them.

Ellory grinned. "Is that for me?"

"Is *that* for me?" Hudson replied, eyeing the coffee tray with longing. His roots were growing out, night black tipped with sun gold. "Boone broke the fucking espresso machine."

"There's a phone in your pumpkin."

Hudson yawned again. "That's Liam's problem. Come in."

She handed him the coffee, and he stepped out of her way. In front of the silver L-shaped couch rested a black walnut coffee table that hadn't been there during the party. Books were stacked in a neat pile on top of it. A sage-green rug—also new—was beneath it, lending the room a calming sort of elegance. From the kitchen, she could hear the tinny sound of R & B playing through laptop speakers.

Hudson padded in that direction, and Ellory slipped off her shoes and laid them neatly in the shoe rack before following him.

His laptop was on the kitchen island, open and surrounded by papers. She'd expected more books, yet there was nothing here but an empty plate smeared with the remnants of maple syrup and a black pen that dangled over the edge of the sink.

Hudson settled onto a barstool and drained half his coffee. His eyes opened a little wider. "A cinnamon roast? How'd you know?"

Ellory opened her mouth to answer and then closed it. Because she realized, right then, that she had no way of knowing he preferred a cinnamon roast. Hudson Graves had never been in the Powers That Bean, at least never while Ellory had been on shift, but she had ordered it for him without even thinking about it. It hadn't seemed strange until now.

hudson will həlp

She cleared her throat. "You're welcome."

Hudson watched her for a moment over the rim of his cup and then took another sip. "There are eggs on the stove if you haven't had breakfast yet. Bread's on top of the fridge, apricot jam inside. I trust you can find the toaster by yourself."

Once Ellory had fixed herself a plate of scrambled eggs, toast, and jam, she settled on a barstool beside Hudson. His screen saver was the word of the day: MAGNILOQUENT. He pulled the laptop closer to himself and scrolled through news sites while she ate. There were no windows in the kitchen, but petal-shaped glass pendant lights hung over the island, casting a golden glow over the countertop. It was almost noon, yet the house was as sleepy as the man beside her, soft and open in a way it hadn't been at the party.

The music played on. The aroma of coffee filled her nose. It was peaceful.

"I looked up the symbol in your note," Hudson said, after he'd washed up and refused to let her help dry. "The backward *e* has a lot of meanings, but the most relevant one is its status as an existential quantifier. In mathematical logic, that symbol essentially means, 'There is at least one,' or 'There exists.' And that's—"

"The Warren University motto," Ellory finished for him. "But why would I tattoo that on my neck?"

"School spirit, clearly."

Ellory glared at him.

"Rah-rah," Hudson snarked, adding a little fist pump.

Ellory ignored that to dig through her bag until she found her notebook. By now, it was half-full with data and decorated with small multicolored page flags and neon Post-it notes scribbled with her handwriting. She'd returned to Cover Story several times as every detail she recorded only created more mysteries. Psychology had been swiftly abandoned for the esoteric, especially as she'd pried deeper into the history of the school.

Hudson closed his laptop and pushed it to the corner of the kitchen island, making room for her to set the notebook between them. Then he pulled his chair closer, close enough that she could feel the warmth of his body. Even though they weren't touching, Ellory knew how easily they could, and it brought her thoughts to a screeching halt. His scent enveloped her, citrus and earth and *man*, and was she really so starved for sex that her body was having a chemical reaction to a guy with the temperament of an open sore?

She stared at the countertop. "I've been doing research, and I found out something interesting. Did you know Warren University has a supernatural history?"

Hudson snorted.

"Apparently, the founders of the school were former members of the New England Society for Psychic Research, and their initial goal was to open an academy to educate people about the arcane. Warren was originally registered as the School for the Unseen Arts for about a month before the change. Even now, several books claim that occultism and witchcraft is still baked into the stones of this place—especially since it was given Ivy status the same year it was founded. Prior to Warren, the most recently founded college was Princeton in 1865."

"Weren't *all* the Ivies officially given Ivy status that year?" Hudson pointed to one of her page flags. "This says the Ivy Group Agreement happened at an athletic conference in 1954."

"And you don't find that strange? That Warren started as a laughingstock and became an Ivy within *months*?"

Hudson frowned. "I guess that is a little strange."

"There used to be rumors about demonic bargains and dark magic, especially when students began disappearing. Letitia Rose in the 1960s, Manuel Sharp and Angel Mclaughlin in the 1970s, Olivia Holloway, Tasha Butler, and Eugene Kang in the 1980s, and Kristopher Douglas and Joel Carroll in the 1990s." Ellory turned to another page, where she had summarized a paragraph from a book that referred to the disappearing students as *the Lost Eight*. "They were never found, and to this day, no one knows what happened to them. There isn't a lot of information on it that I could find. But maybe that's why all this is happening to me again. Maybe I'm haunted because the school is haunted."

"Your theory is that you're experiencing strange phenomena because the dead founders kidnapped eight people and, what, fed them to a demon for power?"

Ellory slammed the Moleskine shut. "Listen, if you're not going to take this seriously—"

"I'm not seeing what any of this has to do with what's happening *now*. Even if the founders did make some sort of infernal pact to join the Ivy League, who cares? It seems like they got what they wanted in 1954."

"You're relating this back to political systems for your thesis, right? Well, when have people in power ever stopped when they've gotten what they wanted? If you knew magic existed—if you could manipulate it to change the world—would you stop? Would you *ever* stop?"

Hudson was now frowning *at her*. They were so close that she could see the line of stubble he'd missed during his morning shave. His leg brushed hers when he turned to face her, their knees grazing. Without the music in the background, Ellory became overly aware of their breathing synching up.

"You think magic exists?" he asked.

"I don't know." She was trapped in the melted chocolate of his eyes. His attention was a heady thing. When he wasn't making her angry, the intensity with which he studied her bolstered her confidence that she knew what she was talking about. "I think it depends on your definition of magic. We don't even know everything there is to know about the ocean. How can we claim to know everything there is to know about the world?"

"But...*magic*."

"I don't know if it's magic! Let's stick with the word *haunting*. That's how the New England Society for Psychic Research got started. It was established by Ed and Lorraine Warren, a demonologist and a trance medium who traveled the country investigating supposedly haunted sites. There are loads of movies about their cases." Ellory managed to free herself from Hudson's gaze and pulled her notebook protectively against her chest. "Maybe the things I keep seeing are...a death echo from the Lost Eight. Because I'm—I don't know—spiritually sensitive. Or maybe I've seen one too many movies. But the one thing we know for sure is that no one knows what happened when those students went missing. And they deserve justice, don't they?"

Before Hudson could respond, the front door opened. Ellory shoved the Moleskine into her bag and zipped it shut while Hudson scooted his barstool away from her and opened his laptop. Her cheeks were burning, though they had been doing nothing more illicit than talking about ghosts. She chalked it up to the hot kitchen.

Ellory heard the duo before they actually appeared in the doorway. The first to enter was Liam Blackwood, today wearing an aquamarine polo and black jeans. Though he wore long sleeves, Ellory could see that his ringed hands were also tattooed and that more ink inched under the fabric. Bird wings, she thought from a quick glance. Behind him was another man, with almond skin, thick black hair, and tattoos on his neck that disappeared beneath his black shirt.

The man dressed in black was the first to react to the scene. "I fucking told you he wanted us out of the house for a reason."

"Don't be rude," said Liam, beaming. "This is Ellory Morgan. She was at our last party. Ellory, this is my other roommate, Boone Priestley."

"What're you two up to?" asked Boone, whose onyx eyes had not shifted from the scene in front of him. "Study date?"

"It's not a date, but yes," said Hudson. "I thought you were going to see a movie."

"It sucked ass. We left early." Boone seemed to sense that Hudson didn't want them here and found this amusing. He grabbed one of the other two barstools, dragged it around to their side of the kitchen island, and perched beside Ellory with his head propped up on his arm. His sleeve slunk down enough for her to see that another one of his tattoos was a sun with a random line through the center. "What'd you say your name was? Emory?"

"Ellory."

"Hud's never brought a woman home before. How long have you two been together?"

"*Never?*" Ellory asked with feigned shock. Hudson looked like he would have tried to strangle them both if there weren't a witness in the room, and that made Ellory add an exaggerated gasp. "What a nerd."

"Don't encourage him, Morgan," Hudson grumbled. "You'll regret it."

"Not that long, then," said Boone, "if I've never come up before now."

"Like the rest of the world, I don't think of you when you're not actively annoying me."

Boone blew Hudson a kiss that served only to make Hudson even more murderous. Ellory had to bite her lip to keep from smiling. Usually, when Hudson was spewing poison at someone other than her, it was cold and short and made her uncomfortable to even be in the room. But he and Boone acted like belligerent siblings, bickering without blades. There was something endearing about seeing him like this, dressed down and unguarded, fond and fighting a smile. He was so different here, in the heart of his home—or perhaps he was different in public, surrounded by strangers and sycophants.

Liam grabbed Boone by the back of his shirt and yanked him off the barstool. Ellory half expected Boone to fight, but it seemed this was more normalcy. He let Liam manhandle him out of the room and toward the stairs, laughing all the while at a joke only he seemed to get.

The kitchen was too quiet with them gone. Hudson's softness had left with them. When she looked at him now, the wall he erected between himself and other people was firmly back in place, with her on the outside. His expression was as distant as the Talcott Mountain peaks, his eyes as hard as winter soil. It was again like looking at a different person, but in a worse way. Hudson's previous openness no longer felt like a sign that he was capable of being tender. Instead, it was further proof that he would never be that way *with her*. That he chose not to be that way with her.

"I should probably leave, too," Ellory said into the silence. "I don't think we're going to get anything else done with everyone here."

"We need an action plan," Hudson pointed out. "Unless you're hoping that you stumble upon more books."

"You have my number." Ellory hopped down from the barstool and grabbed her bag. "Learn how to use it."

She made it out of the kitchen before being stopped, this time by crashing nose first into a firm chest and a sea of aquamarine. Liam Blackwood blinked down at her. "Leaving so soon? I was hoping we could hang out a little."

"I'm going to the bus stop," Ellory said, sidestepping him. Her shoes were still arranged neatly on the shoe rack, but they'd been half buried in other shoes: combat boots and white sneakers. "It was nice to see you again."

"Do you want a ride back to campus?"

"You have a car?"

"Of course I have a car." Liam laughed. "How else would I get to class?"

Ellory decided to let that one go and put on her shoes instead. She'd been spending too much money on travel lately anyway. "If you're not busy, I'd love a ride."

Liam's smile was warm and cozy, like a campfire on a crisp autumn night. "I'm never too busy for you, Ellory. I'll meet you outside."

12

During the next week, Ellory and Liam started texting from sunrise to sunset. True to Hudson's word, the phone in the jack-o'-lantern had indeed belonged to Liam (*Boone*, he'd explained with a roll of his eyes, wiping pulp off his screen. *It's a long story.*), and his initial message had escalated into never-ending conversation. Divorced from the blinding force of his generic handsomeness, Liam was still every bit as charming, funny, and interesting. He sent her songs and memes, jokes and photos of restaurants he wanted to try. In turn, she mostly sent him reminders to study, because her flirting skills had always been poor. Somehow, he seemed to find that endearing, and their banter rolled onward.

If Hudson Graves knew she'd been communicating with his roommate, it didn't show as he leaned against the wall, waiting for her. His gaze was on his phone, ignoring the eyes that roved over him as people passed. None of the students approached, however. Ellory and Hudson were, after all, meeting at the campus founders' museum, a location Ellory hadn't even known existed before

Hudson had texted her and would never have gone to otherwise. She could barely believe they'd squandered a building on a museum devoted to long-dead white men, but if there was one thing rich people knew how to do, it was waste money.

"Hey, Morgan," Hudson said, pocketing his phone. "Ready to go digging?"

"As ready as I'll ever be," she confirmed. "Do you actually think we'll find anything in here?"

"Oh, absolutely not. But I'm bored and we're both free, so why not?"

Ellory snickered, following him inside. A weary student was behind a desk in the small lobby, playing a handheld game. He didn't even look up as Ellory and Hudson passed, and she got the feeling that they could have walked back out with half the museum's items in their arms and he wouldn't have blinked. The museum itself was smaller than Ellory had expected from the size of the building; it was one long hallway, with portraits, plaques, and the occasional preserved item against the back wall. There was another door—a fire exit that led outside—but no obvious way of getting to the rest of the floor.

"Hardly encouraging," Hudson observed.

"Suck it up, Encyclopedia Brown. You did say there would be digging involved, so dig." Ellory reached out to clap him on the arm, then thought better of it. "You take left, I'll take right, and we'll meet in the middle."

His eyes burned into her back as she walked away, but she ignored it. Just like she was ignoring the fact that she had no idea how to interact with him in this provisional space between what they'd been before and what they were now. Were they partners? Colleagues? Enemy soldiers in a temporary ceasefire? She'd seen parts of him that she couldn't forget, yet she didn't know him any better than she had in August. Not really. They weren't *friends* by any definition of the word, but it was still Hudson here with her instead of Tai or Cody. It was Hudson who had been the first to take her seriously. It was Hudson who had offered to help her—no dismissal, no psychoanalysis, minimal snark.

Once, she had been able to rely only on his contempt. Now his faith in her was the one thing keeping her sane as she faced the possibility that ghosts were real, she could see them, and they might be a sign of *magic* leaking into the natural world.

It was uncanny, and not because of the spirits. Her world had tilted so quickly that she was dizzy with it. At least she had a mission to focus on, something easier to investigate than the mystery of Hudson Graves.

Information was as bare as the hallway walls. The founders of the school—Howard McElking, J. Brett Troy, and Richard Lester Odell—had three large gold-framed portraits with the existential quantifier between them. Their interest in the occult and former membership in the New England Society for Psychic Research wasn't mentioned, not even in a single line. They were noted to be an architect, a philanthropist, and a mathematician respectively— which at least confirmed Hudson's interpretation of the symbol— but that was all.

The most peculiar thing about them were the birds; each man gazed severely from the oil painting that captured their pale cheeks and silver sideburns, each with a bird perched on the shoulder of their suits. McElking had a crow, its black talons piercing the fabric of his brown jacket. Troy had a doctor bird—or hummingbird, as she remembered Americans called them—a tiny thing with ruby neck feathers and a straw-like beak. Odell had an owl with black button eyes gazing from a snow-white face and brown body.

They also sat by arched windows displaying different time periods. McElking and his crow sat during a bright, sunny day. Troy and his hummingbird frowned from beside a clear night, the clipped-nail curve of the moon lining the windowsill in silver. Odell and his owl were seated at night as well, but there was no moon visible; instead, their sky was a gorgeous patchwork of off-white stars.

Ellory frowned, taking a picture on her phone. It was probably nothing, but she was here to follow her instincts, and every nerve was alight with suspicion.

The aseptic cream walls, intermittent bronze and gold frames, pristine glass display cases, and ambient museum lighting lent her entire walk a dreamlike quality that was hard to shake free of. All she saw around her were white faces, which wasn't exactly unusual, but something about their serious expressions as they bore down on her from their massive portraits made goose bumps climb her arms. She didn't know if it was her own insecurities or their stone-faced demeanors that screamed, *You don't belong here! Get out.* But she heard it as easily as she could hear her own breathing.

Inhale.

Get.

Exhale.

Out.

Ellory paused in front of a plaque explaining the existential-quantifier symbol and fought the urge to hug herself. She recognized this terror. It was the same way she'd felt at Professor Colt's house, seconds before she had seen the tattoo. That sense of being Icarus soaring too close to the sun, heat cleaving the beeswax from her feathered wings to drop her to her doom. But, instead of being intimidated, Ellory dug her nails into the palms of her hands and breathed past the stone in her stomach. At this point, she was more afraid of *not* knowing. Whatever her mind was trying to protect her from couldn't be worse than this limbo between her reality and the possibility that *magic* underpinned it.

"Morgan."

Hudson was beckoning from halfway down his side of the hall. He'd shed his jacket, and the way he said her name put Ellory on instant alert. He stood before a glass case that held a framed certificate of accreditation, browning with age. His skeptical eyes were not on the faded letters and curling edges of the paper but on the wall behind the display.

"There's a door," he said, before she could question him. "Look there."

The wall was the same sterile white as the rest of the hallway, but as she peered through the glass, she noticed an unevenness that had been invisible to her before. There was a ridge in the flat surface that shouldn't have been there, so far from the nearest corner. The glass magnified it until she could see nothing else. Frowning, she moved from left to right; the door disappeared unless she was looking directly at it, the seam fading into the wall without the display case before it.

"How did you even notice this?" she asked, stepping back. Even that shift in position made it impossible to see the door she now knew was hidden there.

"I'm thorough. And the fact you asked me that makes me think I should check your half of the museum, too," said Hudson. "Hold this."

Ellory took his jacket, and he gripped the glass case, rocking it experimentally. At any other museum, it might have been bolted to the floor to prevent thefts or accidents, but the funds devoted to Warren University apparently hadn't been spent on this collection. Hudson was able to shove the case across the floor until he made a space wide enough for them to fit through. The place it had once occupied was a perfect square of cleanliness in the middle of a dusty floor. Standing in that square made the outline of the door stand out more, though it had no visible hinges or even a knob. Her pulse was setting off fireworks beneath her skin. Her erratic heartbeat made her fingers curl into her denim pants, letting the feel of the fabric ground her in this moment.

What kind of museum stashed an invisible door behind a large glass case?

How many people had gone through it?

And how many of *those* people had emerged alive?

As if thinking the same, Hudson slid in front of her like a broad-shouldered shield. "I don't see any sign of an external alarm," he said, rubbing a muscle in his side. "But I suppose we'll have to take our chances."

Under his hands, the door swung inward with a creak. A cloud of dust escaped into the hall, chased by the stench of stale air and mildew. Hudson coughed twice before bringing an arm up to cover his nose, and Ellory copied the motion as she followed him into the dim room that was roughly half the size of a lecture hall. It took her eyes precious seconds to adjust, seconds during which she heard Hudson's footsteps echo deeper inside, but when she could finally see again, her lips parted in surprise.

They had stepped into an abandoned shrine to the supernatural. There was a grimy glass case containing an old newspaper article about the opening of the School for the Unseen Arts. There were dingy marble statues of the three birds from the founder portraits: a crow whose forehead bore a sun with a line bisecting it; a hummingbird with spread wings, its stomach engraved with a triangle resting atop a cross; and an owl in flight, carrying a circle that had a cross coming out of the underside and a half circle resting on the top. The first symbol looked familiar to her, but she couldn't figure out where she'd seen it before.

Scratched plaques on the statues read, INCANTATION, EVOCATION, and DIVINATION. Written on the back wall, above the art, were two more words: MEMORY and CREATION.

Ellory passed displays on alchemy and vodou, on Santeria and wonder-working, on extrasensory perception and obeah. She passed dust-coated books about magic and mysticism, as well as a framed photograph of the New England Society for Psychic Research, 1953, with younger versions of Howard McElking, J. Brett Troy, and Richard Lester Odell standing front and center. By the time she made it back around to the door, her brain was racing with the implications of this discovery. Warren University *did* have occult origins—and, for whatever reason, they wanted to bury those origins.

Bury but not destroy.

Memory. Creation.

What did that *mean*?

"We should go," said Hudson. "The museum closes for lunch soon."

"How do you know that?" Ellory asked absently, still staring at the marble statues. Invocation, evocation, divination—were those the unseen arts? Had someone been using one or all of them to mess with her memories? Or, worse, to create new ones? Was her tattoo some sort of declaration that remembering gave her power? "Have you been here before or something?"

She didn't see Hudson roll his eyes, but she could *hear* it in his tone. "I read the hours on the sign out front. And something about breaking into a hidden room that *obviously* wasn't meant to be found made me want to keep an eye on the time. I guess I'm strange like that."

"You go ahead and make sure the coast is clear. I'll catch up in a second."

"Morgan—"

"I just need a *second*."

Maybe he heard her porcelain words for the fragile things they were, because he didn't argue further. As soon as he left the room, panic crashed over Ellory in tidal wave tremors. She collapsed to her knees, burying her face in her hands to wait it out. She had held herself together well, too well, because she cracked apart in seismic pieces now. Her body was a prison of short breaths and a roiling stomach, of sudden chills and heavy sweat. She wanted to lie on the floor, but it was filthy and unwelcoming. Her mind screamed at her to breathe. Her nerves simply screamed and screamed and screamed…

Until now, part of her hadn't truly believed her episodes were a sign that magic was real. It was easy to put forth a theory when it felt unlikely, easy to dig into the past when it had been laid to rest. If magic was real, if magic was the reason for her lapses of memory, then it was not only extant but actively being used against her. And until she knew who, how, or why, she was in danger.

Ellory's throat closed. She gripped her curls tightly and counted her breaths. *Inhale, exhale, inhale, exhale.*

It took five rattling minutes before she felt steady enough to get to her feet. Seven before she was able to stuff the last of her macabre theories into a box at the back of her mind. Ten before she felt normal enough to go and find Hudson.

"Want to grab dinner?" he asked. If he cared how long she had taken or about the patches of dirt smeared against the knees of her pants, it wasn't enough to take his mind off food.

"Sure," said Ellory. "You're paying, since I was right."

"Wow."

"You can pick the place."

"Your generosity knows no bounds…"

It wasn't until they were sitting across from each other in a diner that Ellory realized how odd this was. Or, rather, how odd this *wasn't*.

Hudson had chosen a diner called Little House, which was every bit as cozy as its name implied. If not for the window booths and wrought iron marble-top tables scattered around, she would have thought that she was in someone's dining room. The floors were dark wood, and the walls were deep blue, with what looked like family photos for decoration. Brown lanterns dangled in a line from the center of the ceiling, and a bloodred curtain hid the back—where Ellory assumed there was a kitchen and bathrooms—from the front. The waiters were wearing all black with deep blue aprons that matched the decor. She half expected someone's grandmother to breeze in and set a fresh pie on the center of their table.

Ellory hadn't even known this place existed, and yet, when Hudson had pulled into the parking lot, she had been struck by a sense of familiarity. She steered them toward this booth tucked away in one of the back corners, with a view of the street instead of the cars. She'd absently ordered without even looking at the menu. And it wasn't until now that the strangeness of it finally hit her.

After all, she was having a strange *year*.

"I feel it here, too," she said. "I don't recognize this place, but I feel like I do."

Hudson set down his own menu, which he'd asked to keep in case he wanted dessert. Apparently, Little House had phenomenal desserts. "Are you sure you haven't been here before?"

"I'd remember being here in the last three months. Everything *looks* new to me, but I know things I shouldn't know. Like what's on the menu."

"I thought you'd looked it up in the car." Hudson looked down, like he expected to see her phone somewhere on the table. Ellory showed him both hands, her phone safely tucked away. He frowned. "I'll admit that's bizarre."

"More bizarre than the museum?"

"The museum was not in itself bizarre," he said. "The fact that they hid an entire wing in it was."

"I was thinking the same." It would be one thing if the room had been demolished. To be taken seriously as an Ivy League institution, Warren would *want* to hide its occult origins. But they had created a tomb, a forgotten memory waiting to be found by those who knew where to look. "Are we going back after lunch?"

"That would raise some suspicion, even from the most apathetic student worker. No one ever goes in there, let alone twice in one day." Hudson rubbed his face, and Ellory was suddenly reminded that, every time she saw him, he looked more and more exhausted. "I think it's best if we take what we saw and do some independent research."

"I don't know if there are any other books on Warren's supernatural history. Even the one I read was pretty bare," Ellory admitted. "Maybe there's something in the library? It's haunted, after all, so maybe—" She sat up straighter as an idea struck her. "Do you think we should try talking to the Graves Ghost?"

Hudson's mouth twitched. "Of course you want to talk to the Graves Ghost."

Ellory had been thinking of ancient texts and digitized newspaper articles, but the Graves Ghost was possibly as old as the library itself. If she could communicate with it the way she had with Miss Claudette years ago, maybe it would tell her something as impossible as its existence. Maybe it would point her in the direction of books that could help. It spent more time in the Graves than any librarian did, after all.

"I think that maybe we should start with living people," Hudson deadpanned. "For example, maybe my logic professor can tell us more about the symbols we saw. I can ask her over fall break."

"Fine," Ellory said magnanimously. "I'll need that week to get the materials for a séance anyway."

He rolled his eyes, probably sensing that she had never been to a séance and was going to have to google what materials she would need. While American children feared the boogeyman, Ellory had grown up with stories of duppies. The spirits could be malevolent or benevolent, and the former type had been used by her parents as a cautionary tale, especially after she'd come home claiming to see one. She'd memorized all the tricks to keep them away—the herbs, the chants, the number of the local obeah man. She'd never seen herself growing up to summon a duppy of any kind, but desperate times…

At least the Graves Ghost didn't seem wicked.

For now.

Then the rest of Hudson's words sank in. "Wait. You're not going home for fall break?"

"I don't usually go home for fall break," said Hudson as the waitress returned with their food. A bacon cheeseburger for Hudson, with a mountain of golden fries, and Southern-style shrimp and grits for Ellory, with a side of honeyed corn bread that smelled fresh from the oven. Ellory was momentarily distracted by her first taste of the creamy, perfectly flavored grits coating soft pink shrimp, but she still managed to make an inquisitive sound. "I like the quiet," Hudson continued. "Or as quiet as it gets with Boone underfoot."

"Did you two always live close to each other or something?" she asked, thinking again of their easy camaraderie.

"Boone? I met him in freshman year. Liam's the one I grew up with. We're both from Darien."

Ellory blinked. "You...don't seem particularly close."

"Yes, well," Hudson said, contemplating his burger, "that's why you shouldn't date someone you live with." He took a large bite, chewed aggressively, and swallowed. "And no, I don't want to talk about it."

"I wasn't going to ask," Ellory said, stifling her curiosity about what Hudson thought of Liam flirting with her every time they saw each other. "Where's Darien? I've never been."

Hudson launched into a story about his childhood in the coastal Connecticut town, the large houses and the endless blue of Long Island Sound. Ellory was again struck by how normal it felt to be sitting here with him, eating some of the best food she'd ever tasted while watching Hudson Graves smile, *really* smile, a smile that made his cheeks dimple and his eyes crinkle. Beneath the table, their feet touched, his Doc Martens lightly pressed against her years-old Nikes, and the booth felt like a hug. Intimate. Safe.

It was peculiar. It was familiar.

It was...lovely.

AN ARCANE INHERITANCE

She told him about her aunt and growing up in Astoria, the place to which she would return for fall break to remember the world that existed outside the concentrated glitz and sinister glamour of the Ivy League: their rented apartment, their stacks of bills, her multiple jobs, her nosy neighbors. Instead of feeling self-conscious or judged, she blossomed under Hudson's clear interest in her small, silly stories. By the time the waitress brought the check, it was dark outside, and Ellory had several texts from Tai asking where she was and if she and Graves had gone on a date. The idea of such a thing didn't rankle as much as it should have, and it was that more than anything else that finally made discomfort twist in Ellory's gut.

"All right, so fall break," she said as Hudson swirled a signature onto the receipt. "You'll talk to the logic professor about the symbols. I recognize one of them, but I don't remember from where, so maybe that will spark something. Meanwhile, I'll gather what we need to safely summon the Graves Ghost. Anything else?"

"Just don't be surprised if nothing comes of all this, Morgan," he replied, tucking his credit card back into his wallet and his wallet back into the inner pocket of his jacket. His jaw worked like he was choosing his words carefully. "Unsolved disappearances are one thing. The supernatural is quite another. These are the kinds of questions that end only in disappointment or danger."

"If that day at Bancroft turns out to be a folie à deux, I promise to let you *I told you so* me right to my death."

Hudson's eyes were shadowed with a dark intensity that gave her pause. "Well. Let's hope it doesn't come to that."

INTERLUDE

Dean Edwin Thomas Godwin had been among the first to suggest the idea of different classes of magic. Though he never claimed a source for this flash of brilliance, it was rumored he had been inspired by Scholomance, the legendary underground school for black magic in Romania, and the Hermetic Order of the Golden Dawn, the Freemason-founded secret society for occult study and practice in Great Britain.

Magic, he wrote, was at the heart of too many disparate cultures to be nonexistent. And there were too many forms—or classes—to presume that one was superior to another. For those who believed, there was simply ability: what kinds one could and could not do.

Enter the Godwin Scholars.

They tried alchemy and scrying. They learned tarot cards and astrology. They created charms and studied ley lines. Mediumship and mysticism, rune casting and wonder-working. Even Santeria and Kabbalah, Shinto and Māyā, vodou and obeah—religious traditions from around the world that they considered far beneath them

AN ARCANE INHERITANCE

were appropriated for their occult properties and discarded for their refusal to give up their cultural secrets.

There *was* magic a breath away, an undeniable element of the world like death and taxes. The scholars knew it, but they could not unlock it.

In a world of appearances and deceptions, desperation lifts a mirror and forces people to face who they are when no one's watching. For most, this answer is shameful. And for those who have never before known what it is to want, this answer is downright chilling.

Maybe if the Godwin Scholars had chosen failure, there would be no story to uncover.

Instead, their access to magic became an arcane inheritance of lives taken and bodies buried.

13

"I HATE EXAMS," TAI COMPLAINED. "I just want to be hot and rich."

"You're already hot and rich," said Ellory, typing a nonsense conclusion into her international-politics essay. Exam season swung like the Sword of Damocles above them, and fall break was, apparently, no excuse to miss a due date. She had two papers to write and a test to study for; since returning to campus, she had spent so much time in the Graves that she'd started to dream about it. She couldn't be sure she wasn't dreaming now, in fact, except her stress felt very real. "It won't help you pass."

On the other side of the table, Cody snorted. "Don't tell her that. You'll upend her entire worldview."

There was a book open in front of Cody, but they were on their phone, playing Candy Crush. Tai leaned against their shoulder, her eyes glued miserably to her own textbook. Even without counting fall break, it had been a while since Ellory had spent time with her friends. When she'd suggested this study date, Tai had pointedly asked, *You won't be busy with Graves?* This mystery glued Ellory and Hudson together, but she hadn't realized how isolated she'd been until that snide wake-up call.

Now, tonight, she refused to even mention him.

Tai and Cody joked back and forth about old mobile games while Ellory read over her essay a couple of times before submitting it. Her neck and shoulders ached. Pressure built behind her eyes, warning of an impending stress headache. When the words of her second paper began to swim in front of her, Ellory closed her laptop and rubbed her temples.

"You know," said Tai, frowning, "Lor, you don't seem much more relaxed now than you were before fall break. What's been going on with you lately?"

"Are you and Hudson finally dating?" Cody asked. "I've got a bet going with a few of the soccer bros."

"No," Ellory said, avoiding any reference to Liam so that Cody learned a lesson about gambling and friendship. "And fall break was fine. It was good. I'm fine."

All things considered, she *was* fine. Fall break had passed in the blink of an eye, but Aunt Carol had remained in perfect health and Ellory had actually gotten a call from her parents. Their pride over how hard she was working on her political science degree had made guilt ferment in her chest, but not enough guilt to stop her from purchasing the séance materials she'd researched. Otherwise, it was quiet. She learned to make two new meals for Carol's post-stroke dietary plan. She bought the latest *Ironheart* comic. She considered texting her old friends to hang out and went to the Air and Space Museum alone instead.

She'd refused to think about magic and memory at all.

Perhaps *fine* was a stretch, but there was little to be done about how quiet her phone had been that week. High school had been a blur of work and academic achievement, sleepless nights and long days with the goal of qualifying for the kinds of schools that she couldn't afford to attend. Her friends had taken her constant refusals as a sign she didn't want to be invited anywhere at all—and as those invitations had dried up, as those names had fallen farther down her list of open text threads, as the seasons had changed without a single meaningful word exchanged, she'd let them all go.

Now she knew that Polly hated the feeling of wearing wet socks, that Zane was allergic to cats, and that Shug cried at the end of any Disney movie about families. Intimate details about strangers that were two years out of date. Useless residue from the friendships that had evaporated while she'd been buried in her books.

Every second Ellory spent in this country was devoted to building a future that seemed further out of reach the closer she supposedly got. She had to work hard here in order to get there. Then she had to work even harder there to get *over there*. And if she wanted to get up *there*, well, she'd have to work *ten times* harder than that, because she was Black and a woman and an immigrant, and very few people with those intersections ever made it *up there*.

Ellory hadn't figured out if Warren was yet another stop on a still-expanding road of academia—masters, doctorates, postdocs—or if this was finally where all her hard work and sacrifice would pay off. If these were the years she would finally get to live, to thrive. All she knew was that she was tired of treading water until the next wave came.

She rubbed her temples harder. "I need a longer break, I think. Five days wasn't enough."

"You're really not going to tell us what you and Graves have been up to, huh?" Tai asked, leaning forward so that Ellory could see her even with her head dipped toward the table. "Or why you guys are suddenly spending all this time together if you're not dating?"

"I *did* tell you," Ellory grumbled, "and you told me I was cracking under pressure and took me out for lunch."

Tai blinked. "I was trying to help you. If you were upset, you could've said something."

"I'm not upset."

"Can we please not do this passive-aggressive bullshit? This isn't middle school."

"I know you're not accusing *me* of passive-aggressive bullshit—"

"I obviously missed something," said Cody, looking between them. "What's going on?"

With a sigh, Ellory repeated the same story she'd told Tai, about her disappearing tattoo and the day at Bancroft Field, an endless sense of déjà vu and the not-quite-memories that slipped out of reach. This time, she added the note in her own hand, what she and Hudson had learned about the symbol, and the hidden room in the founders' museum, carefully skirting any mention of Hudson at all. Cody's eyes were dinner-plate wide by the time she finished. Even Tai looked apologetic.

"So, what's your next step?" Tai asked. "Or, rather, *our* next step?"

"*Our?*"

"If you're being cursed or whatever, you're not going to deal with that alone. I have sixteen Nigerian aunties on speed dial who could help you."

Cody lifted a shoulder in a shrug. "I think I have a third cousin everyone says is a bruja. I'm not sure it's *true*, but I'm willing to reach out and confirm."

Ellory blinked slowly into the silence that followed, but it seemed that Cody and Tai were serious. She glanced at her phone, face down on the table, and then back at her friends and their earnest desire to help. She'd planned to do this with Hudson, as part of their partnership, but...

She leaned forward and lowered her voice. "Meet me back here at around one a.m.? We're going to summon the Graves Ghost."

"Oh, is that all?" said Tai, before muttering something in Hausa.

Cody placed a hand on her shoulder. "The Graves Ghost isn't even dangerous. It just presses all the buttons in the elevators and pulls books off the shelves sometimes. It'll be fine."

Ellory nodded, hoping Cody was right, hoping it *would* be fine. If not, it wasn't as though her school year could get any worse.

◆

An Ivy League university library was surprisingly easy to break into, even without employing CIA-level tactics. The door was unlocked, which struck Ellory as strange until she remembered she was here for a séance. Like going to a cemetery at night or saying *Bloody Mary* into a mirror, this activity was already on the list of things a person should do only if they were tired of being alive. The Graves Ghost had probably unlocked the door in anticipation of a new friend to skip through the stacks with. Ellory imagined the ghost as one of those sisters from *The Shining*, standing beneath the skylight and waiting for her to take his hand.

She shivered as she took the elevator underground. The *ding* of the closing doors sounded like a cry for help.

Ellory emerged into the fourth floor, her sneakers whispering across the carpet. Tai and Cody had beat her here; they sat side by side at one of the tables, watching a video with the volume low.

Ellory had chosen this floor on a whim, because it was exactly halfway from the surface and halfway from the basement, a liminal space for a liminal act. There was a wrongness to the way the shadows stirred when she expected them to be static, filling the hollows of the empty stacks. The circular skylight that lit the center of the room was like the open mouth of a howling wolf.

She set her bag on the table, the items clattering inside. "What are you watching?"

"Witchcraft explainers, which are an actual thing," said Tai. "And I'm starting to regret every choice that led me here."

"It's not too late to leave," Ellory told her, even though her stomach tightened at the thought. "Both of you. I can do this alone."

"It's like you've never seen a single horror movie." Tai rolled her eyes. "If you're going to summon a ghost, you don't do it *alone*. You also don't do it if you've got some melanin to your skin, but we'll ignore that."

Cody shut off the video. "So, what's the plan?"

Ellory's pulse quivered at her throat. This was the part that made her wish she had invited Hudson instead of her friends. She was sure they could handle themselves, but she didn't worry about Hudson the way she worried about Tai and Cody. Hudson knew what he was getting into. His skepticism was like armor against the supernatural, without being offensive enough to provoke a duppy. At the very least, he would check her work whether she asked him to or not, driven by the same compulsive need to be *better than* that inevitably pushed them to outdo each other.

"Lor?" Tai blinked at her from across the table, her night-dark eyes made darker by the hazy lighting. "What are we doing?"

Ellory infused her voice with the confidence she needed to feel. "I cross-referenced the most common details of the Graves

Ghost legend with news articles about dead young adults from the last century, and I think I found a match." She placed the printed pages between them. "Malcolm Mayhew. He was a junior crushed between two fallen shelves during finals week in 1983. They found him at dawn, dead from blunt force trauma and internal bleeding. The earliest mention of the Graves Ghost that I could find is from 1987, so the timeline fits."

There was a loaded silence.

"You know, I spent fall break at my family's lake house," Tai murmured. "Some people do that."

"Some people don't have a family lake house."

"I wish that were your problem."

Ellory elected to ignore this, rolling up the sleeves of her forest-green hoodie instead. From her bag she pulled a used video game, a pack of Twizzlers, and a bottle of Cîroc Snap Frost Vodka— offerings to Malcolm Mayhew, based on her research of things he'd liked while alive. This was followed by a vial of graveyard dirt to form a circle to contain his spirit. Finally, there was a candle to be placed in the center of this makeshift altar, to light the Graves Ghost's way to the realm of the living.

All she needed now was magic.

The hair on the back of Ellory's neck prickled with warning. She ran a hand over the still-smooth, still-bare skin, and let her next breath out slowly in a futile effort to slow the *thaDUM thaDUM* of her telltale heart. Ignoring the two sets of eyes on her, she constructed an altar as best she could. Her circle was lopsided. The candle was off-center. Every horror movie she had ever watched about summoning ghosts flipped through her mind like the world's worst silent film, monochrome reminders that she was going to die.

"All right," she said, too loud, too earnest. "We have to stand at the points of the circle."

"A circle doesn't have points," Tai whispered.

"Shut up," Cody whispered back.

Ellory stood with her back to the door as Cody and Tai took their positions. Together, the three of them formed an invisible right triangle outside the graveyard dirt. At her instruction, they closed their eyes, and Ellory took one last deep breath before joining them. Darkness pressed upon darkness, blocking out everything but their breathing and the occasional crackle of the candle.

Sometimes the answers for the living rested with the dead. Part of her had always known that. Now she was ready to stop running.

With her eyes closed, Ellory stared into the abyss and waited for something to stare back.

A low buzzing overtook the silence—not bees, like she'd thought before, but the trill of a hummingbird's wings. Her skin warmed despite the cold that made her hands tremble. Images flashed across her lids, like flipping through a deck of playing cards: memories from her childhood, from high school, from the last few months. They began to slow from a blur of color and feeling, and the closer she came to focusing on one, the more fear tightened her chest, warning her about what she was about to see...

Then something hit the floor.

Ellory's eyes shot open, her body unmoving in that absolute silence between two heartbeats. Across the circle, Tai's hands twitched over an upturned chair, like she might still be able to catch it if she tried hard enough. Cody had covered their mouth with a hand, which lowered when they realized the only danger in the library was Tai's ill-timed clumsiness. Ellory stared at her friends, and they stared back, and the candlelight made shadows dance

across hollows of their faces but did little to summon anyone or anything from the void.

Her shoulders slumped. "Maybe I did something wrong."

"I don't know that there's a *right* way to talk to spirits," Tai said, bending to fix the chair. Its sharp wooden legs dug into the carpet, leaving divots when she pushed it back toward the table behind her. "Do you want to try again?"

From the corner of her eye, Ellory saw Cody smother a yawn. Seconds ticked by. Ellory dragged a hand over her clammy face. "No. The longer we stay, the more we risk getting caught."

She made quick work of cleaning up the altar, shoving everything into her bag with frustrated force. A pinch of graveyard dirt spilled over her torn blue jeans, but she dispersed it over the carpet until it almost looked like dust. Cody relieved her of the vodka, shoving it down the side of their shorts for later. Ellory checked one more time that there were no noticeable signs of their presence, and then she checked a second time to be safe.

Tai threw an arm around Ellory's shoulders, steering her toward the elevator. "I never have a dull moment with you, Lor."

Ellory managed a smile. "The whole reason I came to Warren was to entertain you."

The elevator dinged open. Cody entered first, and Tai stepped in after them. Her arm passed through Ellory as if she were a ghost. Ellory blinked several times, but the image before her didn't change. The elevator framed the forms of three people: Cody, Tai, and Ellory's body gazing pensively at the ground between them.

She stared at herself, at her pineapple-shaped updo, her toothpaste-white high-tops, her dark brown knee peering through the frayed edges of the holes in her jeans. That was her, but if *that* was her, then what was *she*? And how had she gotten that way?

She remembered the warmth of her skin, and the terror that had gripped her. The flashes in the dark and the sense that if she focused hard enough, then she could see beyond this world on purpose this time. Even so, she stumbled backward as a frightening truth dawned on her.

Her séance had worked.

But she hadn't *summoned* a ghost.

Somehow, she had become one.

14

Someone cursed. For an instant, Ellory thought it was her, but her voice was not that deep or that far away.

The table to the far right of where they'd been sitting was no longer empty, and the carpet beneath her feet was no longer present. Shiny mahogany wood formed the floor, its lines distorted by a thin layer of mist that coated everything like freshly fallen snow. It reminded her of summers spent at the public pool, diving deep to watch the sunlight warp as it pierced the chlorinated water.

But the figure at the table noticed nothing wrong. He ran his thick fingers through neat brown locs, which fell over the wrinkled collar of his starch-white oxford shirt. Dripping from the top rail of the chair was a black hoodie with the Japanese characters for *Lupin the Third* embroidered across the back. His sleeve was rolled up to reveal a detailed tattoo on his inner forearm of a crow with small black eyes and short black legs. Its feathers pointed, knifelike, toward a flat, square tail near the bend of his elbow. Above its head was the far-too-familiar symbol from the museum: a sun with a line through the center.

And she knew, without knowing how, that this was Malcolm Mayhew. The Graves Ghost, resurrected—or perhaps not yet entombed.

Vision blurring, Ellory crept closer, taking note of the undercut that his locs had hidden from the back. His eyebrows were faded. His mustache curled above his upper lip in a paintbrush swipe. His face was a light brown that darkened closer to his neck, and his round nose bore a silver septum piercing. Below his oxford shirt, he wore plaid patchwork pants in red and black. He scratched his cheek with ring-laden fingers. His large black eyes were walnut shaped.

She smiled when she noticed he had a half-eaten bag of Twizzlers by his textbook. At least her research had been sound.

Wait. She still had lips?

Ellory looked down at herself and tried not to scream. She was a translucent shadow, a figure made of the endless void between worlds, limned in skull-white stardust. She had known—she had *seen*—that she'd been severed from her own body, but it was one thing to watch herself walk away and another to see what little remained. Frost gathered in her chest, an invisible chill that seemed to root deeper the longer she and her body were separated. She staggered, catching the edge of the table to keep herself upright. A pen went flying as she fell through it.

Malcolm Mayhew cursed again. He grappled for his pen, and still he didn't look at her. "I swear this bitch is haunted."

Picking herself up, Ellory stifled a hysterical laugh. If only he knew.

"All right," said Malcolm, "I think I know what I did wrong. But let me check one more thing before I try again."

His chair scraped across the wood. It echoed through the empty library. Moonlight snuck through the skylight, casting a ghostly glow in the shape of a spotlight, but Malcolm sat too far away to bask in it. She could see everything perfectly in the dark, but could *he*?

He rubbed his eyes as he ambled toward the nearby stacks. A watch was on his wrist; it was nearing three in the morning. His pants had suspenders clipped to the back and front pockets. Silver chains swung like pendulums from his belt loops. The shelves consumed him, until not even his shadow remained.

Ellory realized she was about to watch him die.

"WAIT!"

He didn't hear her, couldn't hear her. Maybe it was because she wasn't really here, the memory unaffected by her spectral presence, but no matter how loudly she screamed, her own voice echoed back to her, sounding more mocking each time: *"WAITWAITWAITWAIT."*

Ellory sprinted after Malcolm Mayhew, reasoning that if a table couldn't hold her, then the shelves couldn't crush her. He'd found a ladder and hefted himself up to the second rung, scanning the higher titles. Dust flaked from their aged spines. He coughed into his elbow twice before he hopped to the floor for a fit of sneezing. This time, when he climbed the ladder, he found the right book and freed it from the shelf in a grimy cloud of neglect. He wiped the cover on his pants and turned the yellowing pages with care, lips soundlessly forming the words of whatever he was reading.

All the while, the mist rose from the floor, climbing up Ellory's legs, her hips, her shoulders. The room fell away until all she could see was the silver fog that gathered outside a perfect circle carved for Malcolm Mayhew alone. Behind him, the shelf creaked and groaned like a grandmother standing.

Suddenly, she couldn't move any closer. Her feet were rooted to the ground.

Her stomach clenched. It was time.

Despite the dedicated efforts of those who posted graphic videos to social media of the police's extrajudicial killings, the endless public shootings, the ever-worsening genocides, and the tragic natural disasters, Ellory had never seen someone die before. Her last two trips to Jamaica had been for funerals, but those ceremonies were for the desolate aftermath of death, when tears in stone churches were dried with evening parties outdoors to celebrate the life that had been lived. She had never walked this closely with death, locked in the same room as someone taking their last breaths. It was unsettling in a way she couldn't describe. Her fingers twitched at her sides, aching to intervene. Aching from the knowledge that it was useless to try.

The shelf tipped, books tumbling like raindrops from the top row. Malcolm turned in time to let out a cry drowned out by the falling tomes. For an instant, their eyes locked, and Ellory's heart dropped to her ankles. Of course he could see her now, in this pause between living and not living. She forced an apologetic smile. Malcolm's eyes were wide as plates, sclera ghost white around his dark brown irises.

Before he'd taken even two steps to safety, the other shelf collapsed atop him.

Ellory felt cold for an entirely different reason. Wood creaked and cracked, forming a jagged grave that buried the now-silent Malcolm Mayhew. Books continued to strike the ground, sounding like a boxer hitting a punching bag. One fell open before her, its pages shuffled by the breeze of the fallen shelves.

Then she realized the wind wasn't coming from the fallen shelves. It raked across her shadow skin, and her shadow body prickled with unease as the mist cleared enough for her to see

another figure beyond the wreckage. She couldn't make out the details of their face and clothes, but their hands were tucked into their pockets, and she could tell, somehow, that they were staring at where Malcolm had once stood.

"Sorry, man," the figure said, lifting one hand from their pocket. Their fist clenched, and the wind stopped as abruptly as it had started. When they turned into the mist, she caught a flash of a crow tattoo almost identical to the one on Malcolm's skin—except the bird's eyes glowed an eerie silver. "You're more use to us dead than alive."

Ellory's heart raced. The cold was still there, but fear had crept back in, squeezing like a vise until she couldn't breathe. Because even now, she wasn't alone.

Another figure made of shadows and stardust stood beside her, and she knew without seeing that it was Malcolm Mayhew. She looked at him—at the lack of him—and she could feel his eyes boring into her, as if to say, *Do you see? Do you understand?*

But she didn't understand. Not at all.

Because it seemed almost like that person had used magic. *Real* magic.

Because, if so, then Malcolm Mayhew's death had been a murder.

And if he'd been murdered, then why? And by whom?

Malcolm gripped her shoulder as tightly as an eagle would a mouse. He had no fingers, yet she felt them digging into her until her bone threatened to snap. His touch was so icy that it *burned*, but she refused to scream. She refused. His jaw, or the shadows where his jaw would be, elongated until his head looked like a gaping hole, and from that hole exploded a dozen birds, a hundred birds, a thousand birds, all of them shrieking until there was no room for the sound of her own thoughts—

And she lurched up in bed with a scream.

"JESUS CHRIST, ELLORY," Stasie screamed back from her bed. Her Bambi-brown hair was a mass of silk scrunchies tied together with a bathrobe's belt. She had cream smeared on her face and murder in her eyes. "SHUT THE *FUCK* UP AND GO TO SLEEP."

Ellory struggled out of bed, ignoring the muttered curses of her roommate. In the time it took her to find a pair of shoes, Stasie had buried her head beneath her pillow with her back to Ellory. A muffled "Where are you *going*? It's four a.m.—" followed her out the door, but Ellory didn't stop until she was down the hallway.

Before she could bang on Tai's door, her voice filtered through it.

"—a stupid dream."

"One we both had?" Cody shot back from within, their voice faint, as if they were on the other side of the room. "What in the hell?"

"We just came back from a séance. Of course we'd dream about ghosts. That doesn't *mean* anything."

Ellory stepped forward until her ear was pressed against the wood. Was it possible that Cody and Tai had seen the same things she had? Even the fact that they were awake right now was promising. She didn't have to hold the claustrophobic burden of this memory—this *vision*?—by herself.

"Look, I know it's been a strange year for us," said Tai. Her voice was farther away now, perhaps as she joined Cody on the bed. Ellory could almost picture them there: tangled brown limbs and fond dark eyes; Cody's fingers buried in Tai's hair; Tai's arms locked around their waist; two hearts beating in concert. "But *life* is weird. That doesn't make it magic."

"There are more things in heaven and earth, Horatio, than are dreamt of in your philosophy."

"Quote Shakespeare to me again," Tai purred.

Cody made a sound halfway between a laugh and a moan, and Ellory jolted back from the door with burning cheeks and a complicated emotion swirling in her chest. It wasn't the sharp edge of jealousy that briefly knifed through her when she witnessed her friends' harmonious relationship, but a feeling darker and more cutting. The conversation had told her nothing, and her suspicions were already running away from her. Because it almost sounded like not only had the three of them had the same dream but the three of them had also been experiencing strange phenomena since the school year had begun.

And Cody and Tai were hiding that from Ellory.

She was assuming things. She had to be. The séance had her seeing conspiracies where there were none. Tai—her best friend, her first college friend—wouldn't let her drown in her flights of fancy alone without telling her she'd seen the same things. And even if Tai would, Cody had been willing to hear Ellory out, to believe her. They would have said something. They would have confided in her, with or without Tai.

Besides, there were many things that could be described as strange and magical.

Ellory repeated that to herself as she shuffled back up the hallway, but she felt suddenly, utterly alone.

15

Hudson Graves glowered at her with the fires of Phlegethon in his dark brown eyes. Ellory would have considered being afraid if she hadn't, quite literally, just seen a ghost. Instead of her usual iced coffee, she clutched a large honey-lavender tea with both hands, steam drifting upward in stringy clouds—not unlike the mist from last night. She had waited until the sun had tanned the horizon into a burnt-orange line before texting Hudson to meet her in the same study room as last time. Though she'd expected him to ignore her or to make her wait, he had showed up shortly after Ellory, drowsily clutching his cinnamon roast.

At the time, she'd thought he looked soft, his damp flaxen curls finger combed and his combo of a blackberry knit sweater and blue jeans basic enough to forget he came from money. Then she'd told him what she'd gotten up to last night, and now he looked like what he'd always been: a well-dressed piece of shit.

"Your recklessness in pursuit of this so-called mystery is going to get you killed before you get the answers you're searching for," he said peevishly. "I thought we were in this together."

"I couldn't reach you," Ellory lied over the rim of her to-go cup. "And I didn't get murdered, but Malcolm Mayhew did."

"What you did was incredibly dangerous, Morgan," Hudson continued, starting to pace. "You could've spent too long outside your body and gotten trapped in that void. You could've been hurt by the Graves Ghost. You could've—"

"*But I didn't.* So can we please move on?"

Hudson stopped on the other side of the room with his eyes narrowed. Ellory felt like an old scarf, all frayed ends and loose threads. Every time she blinked, she saw Malcolm's distended jaw, the silver-eyed crow tattoo, the choking mist. Her head was empty except for the sound of his final cry, playing on a loop like the ringing of tinnitus. Hudson could yell at her all he wanted, but she had barely slept in almost two days, and she'd wasted all her energy on sharing her findings.

Magic was real, and it was dangerous. Magic was real, and it had been used to kill at least one person on this campus. Magic was real, and someone was using it to drive her mad.

By comparison, Hudson Graves was nothing.

He seemed to realize that, because he deflated with a sigh and hoisted himself up on the table beside her. A long drink of his coffee followed. Ellory watched his throat bob before turning her blank gaze on the glass doors. This early, anyone who had to go to the Graves usually stopped on the upper floors, as close to the surface and the sunshine as possible. Aside from them, the only other person on the floor was a woman at a desk near the elevator, and she'd fallen asleep on a leather-bound copy of *The Vicomte de Bragelonne*.

"Are you all right?" Hudson asked, setting his coffee cup between them. He smelled like bergamot and shea butter, sharp citrus and smoky earth, like the cinnamon of his drink and the dew of the early morning. "Your hands are shaking."

Ellory observed this fact with such detachment that it was almost like it was happening to someone else. She placed her tea between them, too, and slid her hands beneath her thighs, where they couldn't betray her fear. Today, she had opted to wear black overalls over a pink-and-white-striped crop top; one strap was unbuckled, swinging across her back with every movement like the pendulum of a grandfather clock. Her curls were tugged into a pineapple puff, decorated by a pink floral scarf. It was the kind of outfit she would wear around Astoria, bounding down the stairs of her apartment building to go to the deli, where she could buy Carol aspirin, ginger ale, and a scratch ticket while trying to lure Baker, the cat, out from the shelves.

At Warren, there was an unspoken uniform of neutral colors, collared shirts and blazers, slacks and cardigans. But, right now, Ellory did not want to assimilate. She needed this comforting slice of home in this Stygian place marked by death.

"It was a lot. This entire year has been a lot, but this…" She thought of Tai and Cody again, and her throat closed up. "And you'd rather yell at me than listen to me."

"I can listen to you and not want you to fall apart on me at the same time. What if you cry? What am I supposed to do if you cry?" Hudson made a face. "I left the house so quickly, I forgot to grab my handkerchief."

Ellory rolled her eyes. "You do *not* have a handkerchief."

"I do not. And if I did, I wouldn't waste it on other people's tears."

"Luckily for you, I'd rather eat a live roach than cry in front of you."

"*Thank you*," said Hudson, so effusively that Ellory had to laugh. It was more air than sound, a little amused and a lot exasperated, but it loosened something in her chest that made it easier to breathe. From the corner of her eye, she thought Hudson looked almost proud of himself, but when she turned to face him, the expression was gone, replaced by his usual boredom. "On my end, the conversation with the logic professor went nowhere. She identified the hidden symbols as alchemical in nature, but, to be honest, I think I actually know less than I did before I called on her."

"Are you sure you didn't get stupider without me here to keep you on your toes?"

"A light breeze could knock you over right now, Morgan. You're hardly in a state to be the whetstone to my mind's keen knife."

"Calling your mind a keen knife is vastly overstating its capabilities, but all right."

"I recorded our conversation," Hudson said in a clipped tone, pulling his phone from his pocket. His thumbs flew across the screen, every tap as sharp as his voice. "I'll send it to you, and you can hear for yourself that it wasn't worth the trip."

Ellory stifled a yawn, though she had every intention of listening to the recording later. If Hudson Graves were as smart as he thought he was, he'd have graduated early. Hell, if he were as smart as he thought he was, he wouldn't have believed her in the first place.

"Why are you doing this?" she asked. "It can't be for your thesis. You don't even like me. Unless I'm the subject of your thesis, I don't see how—wait, I'm *not* the subject of your thesis, am I?"

Hudson's eyebrow arched. "I would need your written consent for that, I think."

"You're rich. You don't really *need* anything but less money."

Hudson's other eyebrow joined the first. "You're not the subject of my thesis, Morgan."

"Then why...?"

His eyebrows lowered, his gaze clouding over in thought. A single bead of water slid from his drying hair down the back of his neck, staining his sweater a deeper purple. His white-blond curls shrank close to his skull, as fluffy as a sea of dandelions. As his jaw worked like he was practicing and discarding several answers to her questions, Ellory found herself desperately interested in what he had to say. Neither of them had any reason to be here, to be together, and yet here they were all the same.

And she had room in her life for only one mystery right now.

"If you must know, I've always wanted to be a part of something extraordinary," he murmured without looking at her. "I've always wanted to discover worlds within wardrobes and magic behind mirrors. I know it's childish and impractical and *silly*, but part of me never stopped believing in the impossible. And everything we've researched...it's impossible." He smoothed down the invisible wrinkles across the front of his sweater, then adjusted his collar. Anything, she realized, to distract from his childhood dream laid bare. "Thesis or not, I want to see this through, Morgan. With you."

"That," she managed, "is a lot of faith to put in someone you don't even like."

"I beg you to see a therapist about this obsession you have with how I feel about you."

Ellory's mouth dropped open and then snapped shut without a word. Damn him, he was right. There was no reason for her to want him to like her, no reason for her to constantly toss his inexplicable hatred for her toward him like a bomb, hoping he would finally defuse it. Ellory had always craved validation—she was, after all, a former honors student—but only from authority figures and crushes: Teachers. Parents. Liam. The hot Korean woman in her Spanish class with the lesbian flag pinned to her messenger bag.

Hudson Graves didn't fall into either category, so why did she keep doing this to herself?

She straightened her shoulders and reached for her to-go cup. "I just think it's weird to declare your undying loyalty to someone whose arguments you once called *neonatal in complexity*."

"First of all, you had called me *human coccydynia* not even thirty seconds prior to that. Second of all, I'm committed to the cause, not to you."

Ellory coughed as lukewarm coffee hit her tongue instead of the lavender tea she'd been expecting. Hudson Graves didn't believe in sugar, and the bitter aftertaste of his roast coated her tongue like oil. He gingerly took his cup from her, making a face that said, *I will be throwing this in the trash at my earliest convenience*. His sneer struck her with the realization that her lips had been where his lips had been. Now they both tasted of cinnamon.

That felt unbearably intimate for this not-quite-cordial interaction.

"In any event," Hudson said, still looking put out about his coffee, "Liam used to date a Mayhew. Sophomore year, I think. I don't remember her name."

"Shocking."

He ignored her. "I doubt their bedside conversations dove into exploring the branches of her family tree, but he might know more about the Mayhews in general. If there's one thing rich families know better than anything else, it's keeping up appearances. Malcolm Mayhew's murderer could have had the money and the resources to ensure his death was reported an accident."

"Oh, great. I've always wanted to disappear."

The words turned to ash in her mouth, sending a shudder down her spine. There it was again, that déjà vu, as if they'd had this exact conversation before. As if she'd said these exact words, and it had been more dire than simply tempting fate. Her breathing rattled like a stone in a tin can. The white walls turned black, then white, then black again—or was it her eyes playing tricks on her? Even if sirens weren't blaring from every nerve ending, her body was exhausted. Too exhausted for this level of stress.

"Let me know what you find out," said Hudson, jumping down from the table. "And try not to do any more séances without me, Morgan. If you keep playing with fire, sooner or later you're going to get burned."

The glass door slid shut with the finality of a prison cell.

16

ELLORY WALKED BACK TO MONETA Hall alone, unenthused by the approach of her morning shift at the Powers That Bean. This early, the campus was vacant, as etiolated as a neglected houseplant—or maybe her world was muted by the lack of sleep. She tossed the dregs of her tea in a nearby trash can and buried her hands in the deep pockets of her overalls. During fall break, it had been a relief that life kept moving on despite her mind bisecting it into a *before magic* and *after magic*. Now it grated on her, how normal the university could look. Slowly, the student body would wake and head to class, ignorant of the fact that Warren's emerald lawns and cobblestone pathways were topographic artifice, pristine lies to blind them to the poisonous powers at work underneath.

Of course, that was hardly new information.

Ellory had done everything right—or thought she had. She prioritized her grades and her extracurriculars above all else. She wrote exemplary essays and filled out convoluted forms. She worked to have enough money for SAT classes and application fees. She tried her luck with every single scholarship and grant she qualified for, no matter how small. It would all add up, after all. On paper, she was the perfect applicant. But she got rejection after rejection—not from the schools but from the financial aid she would have needed to attend.

"You're a Black immigrant," Aunt Carol had said from her hospital bed, weak from her latest stroke and still trying to make Ellory feel better. "There's no number of right things you can do to get the same results in this country. You did your best, Lor. Don't hate yourself for losing a rigged game."

Warren University was no different than any other college in that respect: The wealthy bought their way in. The poor begged their way in. Both groups were praised for their admission as if their journeys had been equal. And so did the foul forces underneath remain unseen and unchallenged.

Now they even had magic hidden from the world at large. It was as disturbing as it was infuriating. With every advantage at their fingertips, did they have to hoard magic, too?

Footsteps clomped down the path behind her.

Ellory looked over her shoulder, half expecting to see Hudson fresh from some early-morning detour that had kept him from going home until his first class. But there was no one there. The sound was gone, but *all* sounds were gone. Dawn birdsong and susurrant wind had been replaced by a stillness so comprehensive that her own heartbeat was muffled. Ellory placed two fingers to her chest, feeling the vibrations of an escalating *thadum thaDUM THADUM*. Her skin prickled with warning.

And then the footsteps returned, louder and closer than before.

Ellory ran. She ran before she even knew she was running, blinking to find herself three feet farther down the path. Four. Five.

The footsteps followed—*clomp, clomp, clomp*—as her own feet moved soundlessly over gray stone. On the horizon, the sun bled vermilion and coral, tinting the clouds, trees, and buildings in red orange and pale pink. Ellory imagined her pursuer catching up with her, imagined her own blood painting the quad, the only sign she had ever existed, and her throat closed in terror.

Clomp, clomp, clomp.

Her lungs burned.

Clomp, clomp, clomp.

She ran faster.

Clompclompclomp.

Moneta Hall appeared in the distance as her energy flagged. Unwillingly, she thought of Hudson Graves sprinting across the soccer field, barely winded. She was sweating like a gravedigger in a zombie apocalypse, unable to sustain this momentum for much longer. If she could reach the door… But her student ID was somewhere in her bag, and the footsteps were closer and louder, louder and closer, and she was alone, so no one would hear her if she—

Ellory jolted backward as strong hands grabbed her dangling overall strap. The tear of fabric cracked the silence, and other sounds immediately rushed in: Her wheezing breaths. Her cry of pain as her spine hit the pavement. Her bag rattling across the ground, hurling her books into the grass.

A shadow hovered over her, features obscured by the sunlight they blocked. The same hands that had torn her clothes now wrapped around her throat, silencing her scream. She clawed at their wrists, but the grip didn't loosen. Black dots gathered at the edges of her vision as she contorted her body, trying to dislodge this person from their perch. Their knees shifted until they pinned her

AN ARCANE INHERITANCE

hips to the ground. Their thumbs dug into her windpipe. Ellory's lungs howled for air. Her limbs sighed their defeat, getting weaker and weaker.

"We will warn you only once, Ellory Morgan," said an androgynous voice. As Ellory gazed upward, she realized it was not that the person's features were obscured—it was that they had no features at all, their face a silkworm-white mask with deep divots where their eyes, nostrils, and mouth should be. "The more you pry, the more likely you are to get hurt."

Ellory's hands hit the ground. Her eyelids fluttered. *Air. I need air. I...need...escape...*

In that static darkness, a memory—

"When was the last time you saw sunlight?"

The sudden brightness that slammed through the open curtains blinded her. Her room was dim, and she was hunched over a notebook with every joint throbbing. It could have been hours; it could have been days. All she had to show for it was a half-full notebook and the sneaking suspicion that she was being watched by forces more powerful than she could even imagine. Three alchemical symbols were labeled atop the latest page: a triangle resting atop a cross (sulfur), a circle with a cross coming out of the underside and a half circle resting on top (mercury), and a sun with a line bisecting it (salt).

"I'm so close," she murmured. The Old Masters had fused too many different mythologies together for their curriculum, but slowly and surely, she was decoding the method to their madness. Her throat was dry. She gratefully accepted the water bottle that was handed to her, draining half of it before she attempted to speak again. "All the pieces are here. I need to put them together before the Old Masters put me in the ground."

"Ellory..."

She lifted her gaze from the lined paper to his lined face. They were the same age, but there were bags beneath his eyes. His frown was so deep, it wrinkled the skin around his mouth. His complexion was wan, as though he were the one who'd spent the last few hours—days?—buried in research. But the thing that drew her attention most was the darkness of his eyes, not purely because of their soil-brown color but because of the shadows that lingered within them. She had seen him angry and aloof. She had seen him happy and hopeful. She had seen him sorrowful and sincere. She had no reference in her mental catalog of his moods to match this one. Her stomach dropped.

"Hudson." She searched his gaze. "What aren't you telling me?"

"I—"

He turned to the window, let the golden sun hide his expression. She got to her feet, hungrier for answers than food, and reached for him. Her hand disappeared into the radiance of early afternoon, but before she could touch his skin—

Light erupted between her and her attacker. Their bony knees, their viselike hands, it all disappeared. Ellory sucked in precious oxygen as she rolled onto her side. Her fingers traced the bruises forming on her neck, the raised skin burning hot to the touch. When she searched for the person without a face, however, they were gone.

In their place, the path had been scorched. Gray stones were blackened. Several of them were cracked, revealing flattened dirt and ash beneath.

Ellory swallowed past the pain in her throat. Her heart pounded. No matter where she looked, she could see no sign that there had ever been another person out here with her. And yet she could still

AN ARCANE INHERITANCE

hear that nondescript voice hissing down at her as she slowly lost consciousness. She could still see Hudson Graves, his face carrying a secret that his lips refused to tell. She could still feel hands around her neck and soft notebook paper beneath her ink-stained fingers, a confusing swirl of sensations that made it impossible to relax.

It took her a long time to force herself back onto her feet. Moneta Hall watched dispassionately as she approached, her petrified gaze jumping from shadow to shadow. She flinched at a thud like it was a gunshot, only to realize someone had flung open the door to the dormitory to let the first stream of students out onto the grounds. The sun was crowning the trees now, a sunflower yellow that was entirely too cheerful for the darkness she had witnessed.

What was that?

I'm losing my mind.

No, said that stubborn side of her she couldn't quite ignore. *I'm regaining it.*

That had been a memory, not madness. Something that her tattoo begged her to remember. Something lost that was now found. She couldn't keep rationalizing this when she had seen—chased, even—the unexplainable. Her fingers returned to her throat, where the hot skin had already begun to swell into raised bruises. It was all real. This was all real.

But the farther she got from the scene, the more the details of her recovered memory slipped through her fingers like beach sand. She scrambled for her phone to record it all in her Notes app, but she'd forgotten to collect her bag. She paused outside Moneta, torn between returning for it alone and running upstairs even if it meant someone would steal her things. There was a yawning chasm where her memory had been, and all she could recall now was blinding light and—and what?

Magic.

I don't want to forget.

Ellory raced back the way she'd come, finding her bag and her discarded personal items strewn across the grass. The burnt stones were gone. Birdsong intertwined with the chatter and laughter of students and professors on their way to class. Wind caressed her skin like it was any other autumn day.

By the time she finished typing into her phone, the memory was as dim as the room she could now barely describe. She could *read* the sentences she'd written, but she couldn't visualize them, and the more that she tried, the more nauseous she felt. Dread and déjà vu clung to her the longer she stood in this spot, staring at the place on the path where she'd been attacked. Where she'd pulled sunlight from her own mind and wielded it like a shield against—she looked down at her phone screen—the Old Masters.

We will warn you only once.

Her head hurt. She rubbed her arms absently.

The more you pry, the more likely you are to get hurt.

Clutching her bag to her chest, Ellory ran back to Moneta Hall with that threat ringing in her ears.

INTERLUDE

"THEY'RE ALCHEMICAL SYMBOLS—SPECIFICALLY FOR mercury, salt, and sulfur if I'm not mistaken. The Swiss physician Paracelsus also dabbled in alchemy, and he identified these three chemicals as the tria prima, or the three primes of which all materials are composed. We've learned better, of course, but until the eighteenth century, many alchemists believed these could be combined to create entirely new elements."

"Why, though? Did these mean something or do something specific?"

"In theory, mercury was a fluid element. It represented air, mind, volatility. Salt, a solid, was base matter, representing the body, the earth, and water—permanence. And then sulfur, that was spirit, fire, combustibility. Alchemists believe that by adding different levels of combustible sulfur to a solvent of mercury, they could create anything, leaving a residue of salt behind."

"Huh."

"You look more confused than you were when you walked in, Mister Graves."

"I sort of am. I guess I don't see the logic…no pun intended."

"Beliefs aren't always logical, but they do tend to follow patterns. Humanity has applied the rule of threes to their world since the beginning of time, from the valknut to the pyramids of Giza, following the earth's natural patterns. You might find it illogical to ascribe symbolism to elements, numbers, and shapes, but it's no more outlandish than the field of science, which disproves its own long-standing theories every few years."

"What about you, Professor?"

"What about me?"

"Do you think these alchemical symbols could be magic?"

"…"

"Professor?"

"I think…magic is another form of belief. Perhaps the strongest form there is. If enough people give something power, then, yes, I would say it could be considered magical. Sorry, what class did you say this was for again?"

—Transcribed by Ellory Morgan from a recording by Hudson Graves

17

LIAM BLACKWOOD PERPETUALLY LOOKED AS though he had stepped off a runway, and today was no different. His rich brown hair curled brightly over his forehead, his ivory skin lazily kissed by sun. He'd attracted a small crowd of admirers, and he spoke to them softly, flashing a smile that almost warmed the crisp autumn day. His hands were in his pockets as he leaned against the side of an indigo-colored car.

"Is that a fucking Rolls-Royce?" Tai asked, her eyes wide. Ellory, who had no idea what a Rolls-Royce looked like, shrugged. "It's the latest Rolls-Royce!"

"Wow," Ellory deadpanned.

"If you saw the price tag of that car, you'd be scared to even look at it, let alone put your ass on those seats."

Ellory wasn't thinking about cars or price tags. She was thinking *only* about Liam, with the kind of fierce determination that Tai wouldn't understand. After all, Ellory hadn't told Tai about her early-morning altercation. She didn't tell anyone but Hudson, and Hudson didn't even bother to answer her text message. After days of staring over her shoulder and calling the increasingly annoyed campus police to drive her home from her closing shifts, Ellory grew tired of being afraid. She immersed herself in arcane histories and occult mysteries for far too long, treating it with the same importance that she treated her schoolwork. For once, she wanted to try being a normal woman on a normal date with a normal man, one who actually enjoyed her company. So, when Liam had invited her to go apple picking with Boone Priestley, Ellory had jumped at the chance.

The fact that it would get her off this haunted campus was a bonus.

Liam spotted Ellory over the head of the woman he was talking to, and he waved. His fans turned to look at her, confused and then surprised and then annoyed, but Liam didn't seem to notice as he slipped past them. Ellory wasn't used to this—being wanted and being envied for that want—and she didn't know what to do with it. Her body felt like a series of disconnected limbs rather than a functioning unit as Liam closed the distance between them, smile bright. Her hands found her pockets, then straightened her hat, then tucked a stray curl behind her ear. She was stuck between trying to seem nonchalant and feeling painfully awkward.

Beside her, Tai leaned against the doorpost. "Blackwood," she said with a nod. "Nice car."

"Thanks," Liam replied without taking his eyes off Ellory. "It was a birthday present." He stepped closer, his voice becoming feather soft, as if they were the only two people in the world. "Hey, you look amazing."

They were going apple picking, so Ellory had dressed for apple picking: a loose-knit thermal top, a gold cotton parachute vest, black leggings, and waterproof lace-up boots. Her beanie was gold, her peacoat was olive green, and her dangling earrings were a gold line of stars that almost touched her shoulders. She didn't think the outfit was anything special, except that the deep V-neck of her top showed more cleavage than usual. His eyes hadn't dropped below her face, though, so maybe it wasn't *enough* cleavage.

"Thank you," she said with a shy smile. "So do you."

Ellory barely remembered to say goodbye to Tai as she floated to the car, Liam's hand on her back. Yes, some normalcy to her school year was long overdue.

Tucker Farm was located forty-five minutes away from campus, passing through at least three towns along the way. The scenery alternated between quaint colonial houses hidden by long stretches of greenery, shopping centers with banks that looked more like manors, and so many trees stretching over the guardrails to reach the road that they swallowed the sound of passing cars. Liam admitted to being a fan of R & B, and after a brief moment of discomfort ("You didn't ask me out because of some jungle fever bullshit, did you?" "Some *what?*"), he gave Ellory control of the aux cord so she could test him with the intros of some of her favorites. He'd just guessed Ashanti's "Foolish" off nothing but six notes when they pulled into the farm's half-empty parking lot.

Waking sunlight gilded the few cars they passed. Liam backed into a space near the entrance, then helped Ellory out of the passenger seat. A duo waited by the front gate, but Ellory's gaze was first drawn by a single muscle car that stuck out among the sedans and SUVs. Her smile inverted. Only Liam's hand in hers kept her from stopping in her tracks.

"Isn't that—"

"Hey, guys," said Liam, as the pair turned to reveal Boone *and* Hudson. "I hope you weren't waiting long."

"'Sup, Morgan," said Boone, who wore a black hoodie beneath a black sherpa-lined trucker jacket. His ebony hair spilled from beneath the hood, bouncing when he nodded in greeting. "Thanks for letting me crash your date."

Hudson's lips thinned as he stared at their joined hands, but he didn't comment.

"I thought you had plans today," Liam said to him.

At this, Hudson finally looked up. Not to meet their gazes, because that would have been the polite thing to do, and he certainly wouldn't be caught dead being polite in Ellory's presence. Instead, he looked off into the parking lot, his black peacoat adorned by a light-gray wool scarf.

"He canceled," Hudson said tightly. "I hope it's okay if I come."

Ellory, who minded a great deal, let Liam assure Hudson that they were happy to have him. She had been excited to get to know these people with the saintlike patience to not only know but also *live* with someone like Hudson Graves. But Hudson himself being here, this man who acknowledged and discarded her at a whim despite all they'd been through… Her body was hot with embarrassment.

Liam's arm circled her shoulders. She flinched as he tugged her against him, and the concern in his fawn-brown eyes made her feel like an ass for it. "Everything all right?"

Ellory briefly entertained the idea of being honest with him, making them watch as Hudson climbed back in his stupid Plymouth Barracuda and drove home alone, but smiled instead. Her arm slid around Liam's waist. "Everything's perfect."

They ambled behind Boone and Hudson into the fields bisected by a dirt path that was still slick with yesterday's rain. The undeniable smell of manure was tempered by the scent of fresh grass pearled with dew, butter-yellow dandelions, and baby-pink peach blossoms. A ginger cat stretched out in front of the barn, tail curling back and forth as it watched their approach. Inside, there was a shop that offered jams and cider, apples and pears, wreaths and pies. Fridges in the back carried milk, cheeses, cream, and alcohol. The entire space smelled like hot chocolate, freshly mixed and up for sale in stainless steel beverage dispensers.

"Professor?"

Ellory turned at Liam's surprised greeting to find Preston Colt standing there with a basket full of Brie, Parmesan, and cheddar cheeses. He was wearing a powder-blue cable-knit sweater and beige slacks, and he looked larger divorced from his salon suits, Clark Kent glasses thrown off to reveal Superman underneath. His smile was still warm, the crinkles by his eyes deepening despite his confusion.

"Mister Blackwood, Miss Morgan, what brings you to Tucker Farm?" They were still pressed against each other like magnets. Colt's smile widened. "Ah, perhaps that's a stupid question."

"What are *you* doing here?" Boone asked, though not unkindly. He fiddled with the ring on his middle finger, turning it over and over.

Colt lifted his basket. "I may be biased, but this is some of the best cheese in the state. I'll accept nothing less on my sandwiches, Mister Priestley."

Behind them all, Hudson remained silent. His desire to speak to a professor outside of class must have been limited to salon nights only. Colt didn't even bother to look his way, as though used to this treatment, and that infuriated Ellory, because it was one thing to ignore *her*, but it was an entirely different thing to ignore the man who held her future in his hands. Ellory wanted to shake Hudson, afraid his rudeness would reflect poorly on her, barring her from any more gatherings. Instead, she remained a tense line at Liam's side, hoping her polite smile would keep Colt from noticing Hudson at all.

"Well, don't let me keep you," said Colt, winding his way past them. "The weather's supposed to be quite good today."

Ellory dropped her arm from Liam's waist and watched Colt leave, feeling like she should say something, anything, to capture his attention. What if she'd been too quiet? What if he thought her frivolous for going on a date when she could have been studying? What if he mistook her insecurity for Hudson's insolence?

But he was gone before she could cobble a sentence together, disappearing into the too-bright morning with his brimming basket of cheese.

"He's such a weird old fuck," Boone commented. "But he's got the right idea. We should clear out before the rest of that crowd comes lining up for fresh produce."

"He's not *weird*," Ellory finally managed. "He's brilliant."

"Do you want to stop by the hospital on our way back? You might need emergency surgery to remove your lips from his ass."

"Boone," Liam sighed. "You promised you'd behave."

"This *is* me behaving."

"Well, behave over by the refreshments, would you? Ellory, I'll be right back."

Before she could make a single sound of protest, Liam went to get baskets, and Boone wandered toward the drinks. She and Hudson were left hovering by the entrance like awkward children whose parents were late to pick them up from kindergarten.

He still wasn't looking at her, so she studied him from the corner of her eye, trying to figure out what he and Liam could possibly find to talk about. Despite growing up together in Darien,

Liam and Hudson had turned into two different people—and not just because they occupied such viscerally opposite ends of her occipital lobe. Liam was all summer, warm as sunshine, a golden boy in every sense of the word, while Hudson was deep winter, human permafrost, who smothered all signs of life beneath an icy exterior. There were some similarities—they were, after all, both popular brown-eyed athletes—but even in that they differed. Liam welcomed people close to the bonfire of his personality, while Hudson's mysterious-loner routine made them desperate to impress him. Liam was an active captain of the lacrosse team, while Hudson played soccer like he couldn't avoid it. Liam's eyes were the brown of a toasted marshmallow, while Hudson's were the brown of graveyard dirt.

"I forgot that you'd be here," said Hudson, piercing the uncomfortable silence. "I can head home if—"

"And leave it to me to explain to your roommates that you left because of me? Absolutely not. You'll pick some damn apples, and you'll like it."

Hudson's lips curved upward. "Will I?"

"No, you don't get to do that right now," Ellory said, her tone barely shy of waspish. "You didn't answer my texts. I was attacked, and you couldn't even be bothered to ask if I was all right."

"You were *what*?"

"We're not *friends*, Graves," she hissed. He had turned to face her, and their height difference rankled when her fury crackled between them like an electric storm. She wanted it to strike him down until he was beneath her, where he belonged. "If I'm texting you *at all*, you should assume it's actually important."

Hudson ran a hand over his face. "Boone took my phone. When he gets mad at one of us, he hides our phones, and—this is irrelevant. I assure you my dislike of you isn't murderous in nature." His hand dropped back to his side. The regret in his eyes made her anger wither. "I didn't get your texts, Morgan. I swear I didn't. What do you mean you were *attacked*?"

Ellory frowned suspiciously. "Do you know about the Old Masters?"

"Ready to go?" Boone said, shoving a basket between them. Ellory caught it before it hit the ground, her heart composing a blast beat in her chest. In that moment of uninterrupted eye contact, she had seen something flash in Hudson's dark eyes. Something that looked like fear. "If we focus," Boone continued, "we can be done before nightfall."

Hudson's silent intensity snuffed out like a candle flame. He took a basket from Liam and headed outside without another word, Boone trailing behind him.

Liam passed Ellory a disposable cup of hot chocolate, heavy with whipped cream and rainbow marshmallows. "I hope you like sweets, because that's all Boone got."

"Yeah, this is great," Ellory said, staring after the two men. "Thanks."

The cup warmed her hands, but her skin prickled with nerves. What did Hudson Graves know that she didn't?

◆

The Tucker Farm orchard was a sprawling maze of apple trees and browning grass. Narrow trunks and feathered branches spilled clouds of leaves into the air, apples of all colors weighing them down. They ranged from four feet to eight feet, crowded together to block Ellory's view of even the nearest rows. Once Boone and

Hudson disappeared down another path, she and Liam swiftly lost sight of them. The orchard even swallowed their footsteps, until it was so quiet Ellory felt like they were sharing space with ghosts.

She had spent far too much of the walk trying to figure out a way to get Hudson alone, to demand everything he knew about the Old Masters, but she hadn't been able to think of a thing. They weren't friends. He wasn't even supposed to *be* here. While she was mollified that he hadn't been ignoring her intentionally, she was still on a date, and how would it look to abandon Liam Blackwood to drag Hudson Graves deeper into the trees for a whispered conversation?

Ellory shot one more glance in the direction Boone and Hudson had gone before forcing herself to let this go. For now.

She and Liam picked apples in a companionable silence, pausing only to do the occasional taste test. After the third time Liam managed to find the one sour apple in the bunch, she started calling him a jinx. He lobbed a half-eaten apple at her, which she dodged easily, and chased her laughing form through the trees. Apples spilled from their baskets, but neither of them stopped to notice. There were apples everywhere, after all.

Ellory let Liam press her against the trunk of an apple tree, still giggling. Fine golden hair dusted his arms as he trapped her between them, his palms against the bark. His hair flopped over his damp forehead, loose from its artful style. He looked like a Botticelli painting.

His gaze dropped to her mouth, pupils expanding with palpable desire. Ellory nodded her assent, her hands gliding over his strong shoulders.

Liam kissed her, a soft brush that deepened into curious exploration. He tasted like coffee and mint. Sunlight fell through the trees, warming her face and making her lids glow a fiery red. He leaned closer—his chest against her chest, his hips against her hips—and she slid her arms around his neck to hold him there as one kiss bled into another and another. She'd forgotten how much she liked kissing as a destination, rather than a rushed journey to the bedroom. She could feel him hard against her, but there was no urgency to any of it. This was nice. He was nice.

Everything was so…nice.

They were swathed in sunshine and birdsong, so it took Ellory a moment to notice the dissonant chord in the sonata. Her eyes opened, briefly studying the messy curl of Liam's eyelashes before moving beyond the curve of his golden cheek. A crow sat on the branch of a nearby apple tree, watching them with beady black voids. *Eyes* seemed like the wrong word for those fathomless holes, trapped in shadow despite the brightness of the day. Its knifelike beak pointed to the right, and its wings were pulled close to its skeletal body. The crow did not blink, and neither did Ellory. Unease rippled through her chest until she yanked back from Liam's abruptly claustrophobic kisses.

"What?" he asked, breathless and distracted.

Ellory, whose breathing was even, swallowed past the lump in her throat. "Nothing. Nothing, I—we should keep moving." She didn't have to feign her shiver. "It's kind of cold."

Liam's gloved finger traced the line of her jaw before he pulled away completely. "More of that later."

"Definitely," she promised.

Her basket was in the grass, apples trickling out in a waterfall of red and gold. More crows had gathered there, prodding at the fruit in a way that seemed more menacing than curious. One lifted its wings and squawked when she reached for the basket handle, and no fewer than six birds dropped from the trees to surround it. A murder of crows stared her down, daring her to try her luck.

"Hey," said Liam, his back to her, his own basket safely retrieved, "I wanted to thank you for letting Hudson crash. I know the two of you are kind of weird about each other, but I would've felt shitty about him being home alone after his brother blew him off again."

Ellory straightened, the birds forgotten. "Hudson's *what*?"

"His brother. He never told you about Cairo?"

Ellory lifted her eyebrows.

"Right, stupid question." Liam laughed. "Cairo is Hudson's older brother. Six years older. They used to be close when we were growing up, but then..." He made a vague gesture that meant nothing to Ellory. "Anyway, these days Cairo's pretty unreliable, but anytime he shoots an email, Hudson shows up."

Ellory did not want to feel bad for that walking hangover, but her delicate heart squeezed anyway. She knew the sting of missed calls and broken promises, the justifications and excuses that preserved the illusion that someone who couldn't even manage to be present still loved you in their own way. Her parents had sent her away because they wanted more for her. Intellectually, she knew that. Emotionally, she had been taking care of herself and Aunt Carol since she'd first set foot in America, and sometimes that didn't feel like love at all.

She couldn't pinpoint exactly when her independence had become the result of an innate knowledge that the only one that she could rely on was herself, but she knew she had felt like an adult long before the law recognized her as one. Disappointment was baked into her existence.

It was uncomfortable to have something like that in common with Hudson Graves.

"Oh," Liam said, followed by muffled laughter. "You're not getting those back."

He had noticed the crows. They'd multiplied since she'd last looked, covering her basket like flies swarming a rabbit carcass. Apple shards dotted the ground, torn apart by sharp beaks and sharper talons. Every crunch sounded like the breaking of a bone. Ellory's unease returned with a vengeance, her mind on a crow tattoo and a midnight murder.

She grabbed Liam's sleeve as he tried to walk past her. "It's fine. Let them have it."

"You sure?" Liam looked completely unbothered by the birds, but Ellory's pulse was jagged and uneven. It was nearing winter. Shouldn't most of them have flown to warmer locales?

One crow snapped up a chunk of apple and stared at her unblinkingly. Its twitching head seemed to say, *You're next.*

Ellory's fingers tightened around Liam's sleeve. "Let's keep moving."

"All right," Liam said easily, prying her hand from his sleeve so he could hold it. "I don't mind sharing."

They sank deeper into the trees, but no matter how far they walked, Ellory couldn't shake the feeling of a thousand beady eyes hunting her through the orchard.

18

THEY WALKED THE ENTIRE LENGTH of the orchard, until their basket was overflowing and Liam was wearing smudges of her lip gloss. Now Liam tapped out a message to someone on his phone, the sun overheard creating a halo of light in his dark honey hair, and Ellory lingered a pace behind him so she could observe him. She was unsure *what* she was looking for, except that she wasn't finding it in his relaxed gait and soft smiles. In a school year of sinister occurrences, Liam Blackwood was like a Disney prince, a happy ending waiting for her acceptance. But his perfection only made her feel more fragmentary.

Still, as far as dates went, this hadn't been the worst. It almost was a shame to ruin it.

"You know," Ellory said, drawing Liam's attention away from his phone, "when I met you, I really didn't think I was your type."

His smile widened. "And what do you know about my type?"

"Hudson told me the two of you used to date."

"How did *that* come up in an argument?" Liam tossed her a curious look, but all she did was shrug. "Well, he told you the truth.

He and I dated for about half of freshman year." He slid his phone back into the pocket of his jacket. "But isn't it a little early to be talking about exes?"

"I'm not on a set schedule." Ellory picked up her pace so they walked side by side again. She kept her tone light as she continued: "He also mentioned a woman—something Mayhew, I think?"

"Farrah."

She let the silence unspool, thick and awkward, inviting clarification. But Liam apparently felt no need to continue. Leaves crunched beneath their boots. His smile was gone. Ellory could tell that if she pressed him for any information about Malcolm Mayhew, he would close faster than a clam's shell. Just the family name had created such a marked shift in his demeanor that it was like looking at a stranger.

Ellory adjusted the apples in her basket, arranging them so that the stems were pointing upward. "Did you somehow have a worse breakup with Farrah Mayhew than with someone like *Hudson Graves*?"

Liam snorted, almost as if he couldn't help it. "Hudson isn't as bad as you think he is. He's…intense, yeah, but he's loyal. Giving. Funny. A great kisser." He paused. "Not better than me."

"I'd sooner kiss a skunk right in the anal glands," she said pleasantly, "but go on."

"Our families got along really well, so it was easy with him until it wasn't. Farrah's family…they were different. They were…" Liam's mouth twisted into a peculiar kind of frown. It wasn't pure sadness or anger, but there was an interred pain there. Before Ellory could follow this lead, he shoved his basket toward her. "I need to use the bathroom. Do you want to wait for me or—"

"I think I can find my way back to the giant barn," Ellory said, her fingers closing around the basket handle. The weight of the fruit strained her muscles, but it was mild enough for her to ignore for now. It was the strain in Liam's expression—the not-quite-smile etched onto his face—that drew most of her attention. "I'll meet you up there?"

He saluted her with two fingers and then disappeared in the direction of the outhouse. Ellory typed FARRAH MAYHEW into her Notes app as she picked her way through the underbrush. Something about the Mayhew family had unnerved Liam, even to this day, and his evasiveness wouldn't keep her from finding out what. At least his reaction confirmed that there was something to find out.

She frowned at her screen. Her portable notes read like a grocery list of supernatural mysteries, some of which she could no longer remember the context of. It should have reassured her, that her memory problems weren't the result of brain degradation, but she was no closer to figuring out who *was* causing it. She needed to do more research, but first she needed to get out of this orchard.

Apples rolled from the basket, each hitting the ground with a soft *whump*. Ellory followed a grass path outlined by soil and apple trees that tangled together like hedges to block her view. The morning birdsong had faded into the occasional caw or rush of wings, but even that was muted, as if the orchard existed in its own world.

Liam hadn't gone far, and neither had she. Somehow, Ellory still felt unbearably alone.

She walked faster, ignoring the way the uneven shafts of sunlight ruptured the leaves. Shadows formed and dissolved in her peripheral vision. Her breaths distilled into frost clouds before her. Every heartbeat sputtered like an engine backfiring. Even at their leisurely pace, the walk through the orchard hadn't taken more than an hour. Now the path was endless, the trees identical.

Ellory stopped, hand tightening on the basket handle. "Liam, maybe—"

Behind her was nothing and no one.

She could see no sign of the tracks Liam should have made through the underbrush. She couldn't even see the end of the orchard or the leaf-tangled gate that had invited them to turn back. Her heart beat faster as she realized that she was somehow trapped in this open area. The clustered trees were the bars of her prison.

Not again. Not this again.

The unfamiliar yet symmetrical surroundings reminded her of getting lost on campus, of the sudden déjà vu that had saved her from wandering alone in the dark. The rain and the shadows had kept her company then, but this was worse—this violent sunlight, the world still in vivid color as it distorted around her. This way, she could see it happening and feel her own helplessness. It wasn't a matter of finding her way; it was a matter of not losing her mind.

Remember.

She broke into a run. Dirt and grass, trunks and leaves. Wind iced her face, dried her throat. She bent over, gasping for air, no closer to the barn than when she'd started. Everything looked the same, except the sky. The sun had been high above, a white-gold eye assessing her lack of progress. Now it had gone red orange, painting the tops of the trees the color of cinnabar. Once periwinkle, the cloudless sky had darkened to pale lapis as the sun prepared to set.

She'd been out here for hours.

How had she been out here for hours?

"Liam!"

Liam! Liam! Liam!

The orchard echoed her voice back to her mockingly. Ellory scrambled for her phone, checking pocket after pocket. The basket slapped the ground as she checked every pocket again, this time with both hands, turning them inside out. Coins. Lint. Keys. Headphones. No phone. No phone. *No phone.*

Despite the chill, Ellory scrambled out of her coat and shook it. Lip gloss and a silica packet fell free, but there was still no sign of her phone. She'd used it, a second or an hour ago, and now it was gone.

Her hands shook as she replaced each item in each pocket and gathered as many apples as she was willing to carry, giving herself time to think. The orchard closed at 5:00 p.m. The others wouldn't leave without her. She had a coat to keep her warm and apples to keep her fed and hydrated. She could survive the night if it came to that.

But it wouldn't come to that. She wouldn't let it come to that.

She walked, and the sun set. She walked, and the moon rose. She walked, and the stars twinkled like they knew something she didn't. Ellory finally collapsed in the grass, frustration building to a screaming pitch. Someone did not want her to leave the orchard, and all she was doing was wasting energy. She rolled onto her back, eyes clenched shut against fearful tears. The reality of her predicament had finally caught up to her, making her shiver in the dark.

The word she'd been avoiding as she walked finally unfurled in her mind: *magic.* She had been a fool to think she could have one day free of magic if she left the campus. Now that she knew what to look for, it stalked her everywhere. Her world was not normal. She was not normal. Whatever force was working against her—the School for the Unseen Arts, the Lost Eight, the Old Masters—wouldn't allow her to eke out even one wonderful day from the mess her life had become.

Now the attempt would cost her.

Inexplicably, Ellory wished that Hudson were here. She wouldn't have to explain the impossible to him. She couldn't bear to believe that he would have a plan, but he might piss her off enough to come up with one herself. The whetstone to her mind's keen knife.

Her eyes popped open as the long-faded bruises on her throat began to throb. Ellory thought of that featureless face and nondescript voice that had warned her away from her investigation. The details were still hazy without her Word document in front of her, but they hadn't killed her, even though they must have wanted to. Why hadn't they killed her? She strained to remember, but her impressions of that day were evanescent. Even the attack itself seemed like something she had only imagined until confirmation bias made it true.

Overhead, a star twinkled in a quick flash of light. Ellory pushed herself into a sitting position, brows creasing. Light...something about light... What she wouldn't give for some *light*...

She looked down and gasped. Her palms were illuminated, golden beneath her skin and shadowed where her veins crisscrossed her muscles. That day at Bancroft, a brightness had consumed her vision before she'd stopped that soccer ball from slamming into her face—before *she* had stopped it, with magic. Now her hands were drawing on some well of power that pushed back the dark. Her weakness had converted into a sudden strength, and she was not going to ignore this gift.

Ellory scrambled to her feet, afraid that the light would be extinguished if she looked again. Not only was it still there, but a sphere of it also rose from the center of her palm to hover like a firefly. Mouth trembling, Ellory called another and another and another until she was surrounded by these tiny rays, until the light in her hands had transformed into an undulating wave of glowing bubbles.

I need to get out of here, she thought.

And the lights obeyed.

They surged into the trees, creating a shimmering path for Ellory to follow. The layout of the orchard had changed into a maze. Instead of neat rows of trees separating paths for visitors to walk along, she was tearing through a forest of identical trunks and emaciated branches. She realized she had left her apples behind and hoped, with a spike of fear, that these lights were leading her to safety instead of death. The trees that should have borne fruit were empty, and she could *feel* eyes watching her from the underbrush.

And then: "Morgan!"

That distant call.

"Morgan!"

Ahead, an aggressive rustling, heavy footfalls.

"Morgan!"

She started running. Her foot caught a root, and her arms windmilled to keep her body from toppling over. The swarming trees shifted around her, widening until a path formed. She could see Hudson Graves, his flashlight pointed in her direction, his voice shouting her name. Her summoned phosphorescence traced him for a moment before disappearing as though they had never existed. Ellory locked eyes with Hudson, hers wide and his wider. Her feet swallowed the distance between them in seconds.

"*Ellory*," said Hudson. His hands gripped her shaking shoulders, his flashlight now rolling in the grass at their feet. "Where the hell have you been?"

"I—"

"Are you hurt?"

He pulled off his peacoat and wrapped her in it. His eyes were midnight black as they searched her face. His hands were everywhere, gloved fingers brushing protectively over her body, looking for wounds internal and external. Every touch ignited a bonfire of sensation, a comforting and familiar warmth.

You just want to get your hands all over me.

That's not the only thing I want.

Ellory's breath caught, their voices ringing in her ears. Echoes of a conversation they'd never had. Only Hudson kept her grounded in the present. His coat smelled like shea butter and bergamot, a scent that was becoming increasingly familiar. His hands were now on her collarbones, where he'd fastened the first button over her frigid skin. He stared at her, stared *through* her, and the absurdity and terror of the last few hours hit her all at once.

She could have died in there, wherever *there* was, and she had no idea if they would have found her. She felt dizzy, detached, like her body was a puppet and she was absently tugging the strings for movement. She could have died. That disorienting magic could have killed her if she hadn't found her own.

Someone wanted her *dead*.

Cold seeped through her. She gripped Hudson's wrists, blinking back tears. "It was—I saw—someone attacked me *again*—"

"Okay, okay," Hudson murmured. "Tell me about it while I walk you back. Your boyfriend is worried."

"He's not my boyfriend," said Ellory, automatically.

Hudson's arm wrapped around her shoulders, tugging her close to his heat. She shivered her way through the story as he led them back to the orchard. With Hudson at her side, it was an orchard again. Apples dangled from branches. Nighttime sounds—crickets and frogs, owls and cats—filled the pauses between her words. Grass whispered beneath their feet, no longer dry and dead.

They crossed the tree line to a clear path that led back to the fence, where Liam and Boone were waiting with their own flashlights. Boone had his free hand on Liam's arm, as if he'd been holding Liam back for as long as he could, and Ellory swallowed. She didn't consider Liam her boyfriend, but that didn't mean she wanted to worry him. Especially not over something she couldn't explain.

Hudson squeezed her shoulder, voice low enough for only Ellory to hear. "I'll look into the Old Masters as soon as I can. Everything is going to be okay, Morgan. I swear it."

She didn't believe him, couldn't believe him after the last few days, but there was no time for further conversation. Liam was already in front of her, his expression twisted with guilt.

"I should never have left you alone. I'm so sorry, Ellory."

"No, I—no." Ellory put some distance between herself and Hudson, curling her fingers into the inside of his coat as if that would stop them from shaking. "I should have waited. Anyway, I'm fine. I'm just mad I lost my phone."

Liam looked like he wanted to ask several more questions, but all he said was "Let's get you home."

Ellory let him take her to the parking lot with a hand on the small of her back. Boone fell into step behind them, silent as a wraith. She didn't hear Hudson, but she could feel his gaze searing into the back of her head. She burrowed deeper into his peacoat, hoping its smell would stave off the panic that still hovered at the edge of her awareness.

She glanced back at the orchard. An owl perched on the topmost rail of the fence. Its unblinking eyes gleamed like ghost candles. Behind it, the orchard slumbered, pretending that it had never tried to swallow her whole. The owl's head turned, spectral slow, its neck folds and jutting feathers making it look twice its size. Its talons gripped the fence so tightly that she could almost hear the wood crack, and its eyes, those bulbous fucking eyes, tracked her every move.

Ellory watched the owl and the owl watched her, and though she was too far away to hear anything at all, its cry echoed in her head like a corpse bell.

PART II

THE SINISTER ELITE

They scare the singing birds of earth away
As, greed-impelled, they circle threateningly,
Watching the toilers with malignant eye,
From their exclusive haven—birds of prey.

"Birds of Prey," Claude McKay

INTERLUDE

THERE IS MAGIC IN THE bones of this world: in the soil and the waves, in the air and the billions of souls that pollute it. It lives and changes, fades and lingers. On the campus of Warren University, magic gathered like shadows at dusk, painting everything a color that few know how to see. The school's motto was the only hint that most had of the world beneath this world, of the magic that breathes and breathes and breathes…

Exstat. There exists.

In legends and folktales, magic is woven into the fabric of existence. In occult secret societies and classified CIA programs, magic is a ritual, a hypothesis, a field of study that can make or break empires. These days, magic is like a mist, slipping through the fingers of anyone who tries to clutch it too tightly. It is sacrifice. It is accidental. It is in the hands of too many and too few. It is a dwindling resource in a century of dwindling resources, and you never know where it might find you.

But it *will* find you.

And magic—the magic of bones, of shadows, of legend—always leaves a stain.

19

ELLORY SLEPT UNTIL SUNDAY AFTERNOON, interrupted only by work and a call from Aunt Carol that ended with Ellory ordering fresh fruits and vegetables to be delivered to their Astoria apartment. Her body acted on autopilot, fine-tuned from years of *doing*; caretaking was so second nature that she could pour into her aunt's health from an emotional well so empty that cobwebs lined the bottom. Without the luxury of free time to have the breakdown that waited in the wings of her mind, she was stuck with a general malaise that discolored the world around her. Stasie was as disinterested in her as ever; the few times they were both conscious in the dorm, Stasie either had headphones in or was on her way out.

The package alert, then, came as a genuine surprise. It was a break in the monotony.

Tai found her in the mail room, waiting for the student concierge to return with her package. Tai's braids were decorated with a deep red head wrap, which was tied into a bow to allow them to tumble down her back. Ellory, who had simply pulled her hair into a bun, felt underdressed as Tai threw an arm around her.

AN ARCANE INHERITANCE

"You didn't tell me how the date was," said Tai, rocking them from side to side to the tune of a song only she could hear. "Did Blackwood earn a second one?"

It took Ellory a second to remember the date at all. Her mind was full of magic and murder, her thoughts spilled across the page of the Word document upstairs, where she'd recreated the notes she'd taken in the orchard as best she could. She'd had no space for the memory of why she'd been in the orchard in the first place until now. "It was nice."

"Nice? *Ouch*."

"No, I—that's a good thing."

"Not with that expression, it isn't."

Ellory didn't know what her face was doing, and she was too tired to figure it out. Liam was nice. The date had been nice. And none of that mattered right now. She let Tai string together several platitudes about fish in the sea and the world being her oyster and then rank the dating apps by "vibe." The fluorescent lights pulsed like Ellory was hungover, and there was an enormous yawn trapped in her throat that she didn't dare let out until Tai was done talking.

"Here it is," the concierge said, dropping her package on the counter.

Ellory stared blankly at the box. It had a picture of a cell phone emblazoned on the front, which she recognized as a new model that would have been obsolete by the time her own stopped working. If, of course, she hadn't lost it at the farm.

"I..." She blinked at the woman. "I didn't order this."

"I get off in ten minutes," the concierge said in a pleading tone. And then, when Ellory opened her mouth to protest further, she continued: "*Ten minutes*. Take it."

She shoved the box closer to Ellory, revealing a small envelope taped to the far side. Ellory turned the package to pull it off while the student slipped away to help someone else. Her name was written in neat cursive, and the envelope was closed with a wax seal. That alone was enough to raise her suspicions, even before she saw that the seal was stamped with the letters *LB*.

Liam Blackwood.

And that was how she ended up in an Uber to Liam's off-campus housing, the box balanced in her lap like it was full of snakes. It was impossible to forget Liam was in a different social class considering how he dressed, but there was a difference between making out in an apple orchard and accepting gifts it would take ages to repay him for. Their relationship hovered in that undefined stage between *just for fun* and *exclusive*, and she refused to introduce this kind of power imbalance so soon.

Or ever, if she had her way.

Her pulse skipped involuntarily when she saw the Barracuda parked out front with the hood flipped up. She and Hudson hadn't had class together yet, so she had no idea what version of him would greet her today. The man who had believed her wild tales of magic and ghosts, who had held her like she was a rare first edition when he'd found her in the orchard? Or the elitist bully who scowled at the sight of her, who made the *and* in *Ellory and Hudson* feel like a chasm full of barbed wire, too wide and perilous to cross?

But it wasn't Hudson with his hands buried in the guts of the car. It was Boone, his dark hair pulled up into a tiny ponytail and his sleeves rolled up to his elbows. He wore a pair of black overalls over a blue sweater, and there was a smudge of oil beneath his left eye. She opened her mouth to greet him and choked back the words.

With his forearms bare, Ellory could clearly see the tattoo of a sun with a line through the center that decorated Boone's inner wrist. It was the same symbol she'd seen in the hidden museum, the one that had looked so familiar to her. The alchemical symbol for salt, the element of permanence. She watched the tattoo wink in and out of view as Boone fiddled with the inner workings of the car, stark against his almond skin when he dragged the back of his hand across his weeping forehead.

Boone took one look at her and snorted. "We told him not to buy you a new phone."

Her mouth hung open. She closed it.

"I have no idea if he's even here." Boone gestured to his wireless earbuds. "I've been swamped. But the door's open if you want to check."

Ellory remained rooted to the spot, torn between asking about the tattoo and pretending she hadn't seen it. Would Boone pin her to the ground with his hands around her neck, threatening her away from the conspiracy he was clearly a part of? Despite the fact that they were outside, Ellory was aware of how *alone* they were. These storybook homes and cream-shuttered windows hid helpers or bystanders, and she wouldn't know which one the neighbors would choose to be until it was too late.

"Morgan?" Bonne raised his eyebrows. "You need something else?"

Ellory swallowed and shook her head.

Inside, the house was the kind of quiet that signaled no one was home. The lights were on, but there was no music or conversation. The television was cold, the kitchen abandoned. Eucalyptus branches were sunning in a blown-glass vase on the windowsill, making the air smell of forest and mint. Hudson was in his bedroom, wearing a pair of headphones as he pored over a textbook in bed. Fruit snacks spilled from a bag by his elbow. When Ellory studied, she looked like a gremlin, her hoodie drawn over her frizzy coils, well-deep bags beneath her eyes, pimple patches decorating her jaw. Hudson's cozy sprawl could have come directly from a pinup.

She stepped inside, locking the door behind her.

"Morgan," he said, expression inscrutable, "we have got to stop meeting like this."

"Boone has one of the alchemical symbols tattooed on his wrist." Ellory pressed her back against the wood, her ears alert for any movement in the hallway. Her paranoid mind was comforted by the lack of sound. He hadn't followed her inside. Thankfully. "Whatever's going on here, I think he's a part of it."

Hudson sat up, his left foot tucked under his right thigh. He drummed his fingers against his bent knee, and Ellory remembered too late that he and Boone weren't simply close but also acted like family, all soft glances and inside jokes. In a war of words, Hudson had no reason to believe in her instead of Boone. And the longer the silence went on, the more Ellory wished she'd kept her suspicions to herself.

"Boone does have a tattoo of a crow on his chest, now that you mention it."

The bird wings she'd seen the tips of around his shirt the first time they'd met. Ellory opened her mouth and then closed it, staring at Hudson instead. Of all the things he could have said, she had not been expecting that.

"He's also the editor in chief of the school paper," Hudson continued, unaware of her shock, "which, by its very nature, means he definitely knows more than he should. If there's a conspiracy on campus, he'll be the first one there."

She didn't blink.

"Morgan?" Hudson said. "Did you hear me? Boone might—"

"Yeah, no, I—yeah." Ellory shook her head, biting back a smile. "Do you think he's dangerous? If he's involved with them, maybe he's spying on me. Maybe I shouldn't come by here anymore."

"I don't think he's *dangerous*, per se. He's not—well, he's not subtle enough for that. If he wanted to attack you, he would do it without playing games. But I think it's worth keeping an eye on him in case he *does* know something." Hudson made a thoughtful sound. "Hey, what if you join the paper?"

For the second time, shock silenced Ellory's mind. "Me?"

"It'd be suspicious if *I* showed a sudden interest after four years, but he doesn't really know you. Besides, the *Warren Communiqué* is legendary, so it wouldn't even be weird for you to want to write for them."

Her ears rang. She almost asked him to repeat himself, because it seemed like he was handing her everything she had ever wanted in the form of a concrete reason to make time for the newspaper. All her reasons for avoiding it caught fire, and a fresh determination grew from their ashes. When it was no longer about her selfish wants, it was easy, too easy, to say yes.

"That's a great idea," she said too quickly. "I could keep an eye on him there."

Hudson nodded. "And I can keep an eye on him at home. It wouldn't be safe for me to confront him, considering he has access to where I sleep, but I'll watch him more closely and text you any updates."

"Unless he hides your phone."

"Indeed."

Despite how the sight of the tattoo had rattled her, Ellory's lips twitched in amusement at Hudson's return to formality. Her relief at being so easily believed calmed her enough to look around. His room felt different in the light of day, without the thumping of bass beneath the floorboards and a packed house of drunken partiers. Hudson was in sweatpants again, this time paired with a band T-shirt so worn that she couldn't identify the band. He'd made some effort to organize his books, because the piles were smaller and the bookshelves sported labels: MEMOIRS. ROMANCE. ESSAYS. SCI-FI. FANTASY.

"The real reason I came was to return this," said Ellory, holding up the box. "While I appreciate the thought—"

"He left for lacrosse practice a half hour ago. And you need a phone."

"I've already ordered a phone," said Ellory, who had not. Hudson lifted his eyebrows as if he knew, so she amended, "I'm going to order a phone. This one is too much on at least three different levels."

"That's Liam," Hudson murmured, taking the box and wedging it onto his side table. "Too much on at least three different levels."

The statement wasn't fond, but it also didn't sound like a condemnation. Ellory considered asking if that was why they'd broken up—if Liam had been too charming, too earnest, too generous for a porcupine like Hudson Graves to take—but then decided that she didn't care. Her eyes swept the room from ceiling to floor, catching on a shelf near the window labeled OCCULT. The books there looked new, their spines hardly even bent.

"So far, everything I've learned about the Old Masters...well..." Hudson began. He stopped to wrinkle his nose, and his next words sounded like they were being yanked out of him. "It seems that I was wrong."

Ellory's gaze snapped back to his. "Did you say you were *wrong*?"

"I thought we were poking at the past, trying to solve a mystery that's been cold for decades. But someone in the present wants those secrets to stay buried—"

"You said you were wrong."

"—and has the magic to silence you—"

"Can you say it again? I want to—wait, fuck, I don't have a phone to record you on."

"You are such a child," said Hudson. The corner of his lips twitched like he wanted to smile, but he managed to suppress it in time. Ellory hated the flutter of pride that took root in her chest. They were a few years out of their teens, and yet Hudson often acted like middle-aged businessman rather than a twenty-one-year-old college student. Even humoring her juvenile teasing made his eyes sparkle. "*Yes*, I was wrong. But if that's true, you're in danger and *you don't have a phone*. I don't feel good about letting you leave without one."

Ellory glanced at the box. He had a point, and yet… "I told you that I'm going to order one. I'll be able to buy a new one myself after my next paycheck. That's a week from now."

"Then use this one until then. I promise you that Liam can still get it refunded."

"Fine."

"*Fine?*" Hudson was frowning. "You're more rattled than you're letting on. I don't think you've ever agreed with me that fast."

"Of course I'm rattled. I really thought I was going to die in there. If it hadn't been for those lights—" Ellory swallowed the words before they could choke her. "Anyway, I'm fine."

Hudson was silent for so long that she was sure he would call her on the lie, and she had no idea what she would do if he did. Her experience in the orchard was always waiting to unbalance her again, stealing any semblance of peace—though she was more relaxed than she'd been in a long time for being able to voice her fears to someone who understood. Thankfully, Hudson didn't push.

Instead, he said, "Where do you think the lights came from?"

Ellory paused. "I…hadn't thought about it."

"I have a theory, but I'm not sure you'll believe it." When she gestured for him to continue, he cleared his throat. "I think you might have conjured them yourself. You felt scared and unsafe, and you summoned a way out."

He was right. She didn't believe it.

Men like Hudson—born with a silver spoon up their assholes—didn't understand women like her. He had admitted to her, all those days ago, that he had never stopped believing in the impossible. Meanwhile, Ellory's life had been one slow realization that she was not special. She was no secret royal who would be whisked away to a palace in the hills. She was no great beauty poised to be scouted in a shopping mall. She would never win the lottery or become the unexpected beneficiary of a reclusive millionaire's inheritance. Men like Hudson were born into greatness, destined for greatness, would have greatness thrust upon them whether they appreciated it or not.

Women like Ellory disappeared—well-behaved and forgotten by history.

Her skepticism must have showed on her face, because Hudson pushed forward with the stubbornness of a man who loved a debate. "You stopped a soccer ball in midair. You successfully hosted a séance. You blasted an attacker off your struggling body. Even before all that, by your own admission, you've been seeing ghosts your entire life. Why draw the line at conjuring lights? If magic exists—and we surmise that it does to explain any of this—then you clearly possess the aptitude."

Ellory discarded three different arguments before accepting that she had no words for the tempest of emotion his words had created. Strung together, those events seemed less like a series of coincidences and more like...like magic. But if she had magic, why was it only showing itself now? Where had it been when her parents had slowly stopped calling? When her aunt had been in the hospital? When she'd watched her classmates move on to college while she remained behind, trapped by medical debt too large to bear the additional weight of student loans?

She would rather have been struck by a soccer ball and lost in an orchard than live with the claustrophobic panic of the last three years, watching life pass her by while she remained in the same place.

Ellory could no longer deny that she had done things that defied rationality. But every time she wanted to believe in them, in herself, reality crashed back in to remind her that even in a magical world, she was so far behind. That magic was something that happened *to* her, not something that worked *for* her. That she was powerless, not privileged.

"At the very least," Hudson said when she didn't speak, "let's not rule it out."

"Did you find anything interesting in those?" Ellory nodded toward the OCCULT shelf, tabling this discussion for another day. "They look new."

"Well, we have an exam tomorrow, so I haven't had the chance to read them."

"Can I borrow a couple, then? I can help with—" Ellory's stomach dropped as she twisted around to face him. "We have a *what*?"

"An exam. In con. law. It's in the syllabus." Hudson smirked. They might have gotten closer while working together, but it was clear that he was back in his element. A king on a throne of academic excellence. "It's not worth *that* much of your grade. You'll probably only drop down to a B, and I have every confidence in your annoying determination to raise that back to something respectable."

"Are you forming words? I don't speak your particular brand of asshole." Ellory grabbed the phone box and stuck it under her arm. "I need to go home."

Hudson waited until she had almost made it to the door to say, in a tone that felt overly casual, "You know, you can study here until Liam gets back. He's been worried about you, too."

"You want me to wait for Liam?" she asked, puzzled. Her hand was inches from the doorknob, but she'd gone to all the trouble of taking an Uber here, and the only thing waiting back at her dorm was her roommate's judgment and Tai's concern. Besides, she could at least trust that Hudson's notes were as detailed as hers. "Is this your way of saying you approve?"

"Is this your way of saying you want my approval?"

"Of the two of us, I'm not the one who wastes time craving impossible things."

Hudson rolled his eyes. "Let's take this party to the kitchen. I want something more substantial than fruit snacks."

20

E LLORY HAD ONLY A FEW hours before she needed to be at Powers That Bean. Usually, she would spend those hours taking a long shower, doing last-minute homework, or—if she was ahead in her assignments—streaming a new show so that she had half a chance at making conversation with her classmates. A lack of free time meant her knowledge of pop culture was a couple of months behind at best, and the people she hoped to endear herself to were usually talking about the latest episode of things she'd never even heard of, let alone found time to start.

Today, however, she spent those hours at Bancroft.

It had been two days since Hudson had planted the idea in her mind, and her attempts to suppress it had only made it more insistent. Magic. No, *her* magic. Could there truly be such a thing? Bancroft still bore the scars from her last visit, a circle of cracked dirt and dead grass. Winter's premature chill had driven everyone to the gymnasium, where the indoor track would provide them with whatever exercise the weight room and rock-climbing wall didn't. There was no one to see her squat and press her gloved hands to the soil.

She expected a jolt like lightning up her arm, a heat like touching a pot with her bare hands, perhaps even a shimmer in the air that faded when she looked directly at it. But nothing happened. The ground was cold. Ants scuttled out of her way, disappearing into the grass. Blackened dirt clumped beneath her nails, but that was all. That was normal. If not for the fact that she had somehow caused this...

Even as she thought it, Ellory's mind wanted to again reject the idea of *her* magic. There had been a time when Ellory had believed. She checked the back of closets for a hidden road to Narnia, she left windows open for Peter Pan to take her to Neverland, and she stared unblinkingly at her bedroom lamp in an attempt to develop Matilda's telekinesis. Magic was something that hummed in the veins of the world, and if she could only find a way tap into it, she would feel it in her own blood, this endless possibility and limitless power. Even America had seemed like a magical place when she'd first flown over it, all rippling greenery and smooth gray lakes, mist-topped mountains and red-brown fields, bigger than several Jamaicas put together. A land of dreams—where she was the dream of her ancestors, every breath another word in her evolving story.

But her parents, and Aunt Carol, expected her to grow out of it. Belief in things that only she could see was childish, and speaking to the dead was a cause for concern. She stifled any magical potential to pursue a concrete future, proving her worth with grades and certificates, ribbons and trophies.

Warren had brought that potential roaring back. The university was steeped in the occult, calling to that deadened part of her that the world had forced her to forget.

Still, it was easier to accept the existence of magic than to accept that *she* could wield it.

AN ARCANE INHERITANCE

Ellory reminded herself to channel the confidence of a mediocre white man and got back to her feet. Another quick glance confirmed she was alone. She frowned at the circle, fingers twitching restlessly at her sides. Maybe magic was a matter of intention. That day, she hadn't wanted the ball to hit her in the face. That morning, she'd wanted desperately to be able to breathe. In the orchard, she had wanted to find her way. Life had taught her many times that wanting and having were two different things, and they rarely intersected for people like her. But maybe magic was different. Maybe it was that invisible line between have and have-not.

She thought of grass, thick and green, crawling over the dirt in an eruption of slender blades. She thought of rich soil brimming with its own kind of life, worms and beetles, fungi and bacteria. She thought of stones and caps, of sticks and discarded wrappers, the debris of the day-to-day stretching across the quad. Unbidden, the words from the hidden museum floated across her mind: *memory* and *creation*. She remembered what Bancroft had once looked like, held that image in her head, and imagined herself nudging her present to match that past.

Doom clawed across her skin. Her neck burned with fresh soreness. Her hair quivered in a sudden gust of wind almost strong enough to carry her off her feet.

Ellory clenched her eyes shut, breathing through the nausea and unease.

And then it was over. She opened her eyes.

The circle was gone, replaced by a carpet of grass that cupped her sneakers. It was the wrong color for November, a vibrant viridian that was more common in spring. The quad around it had faded as autumn trudged on, speckled with red and gold leaves blown from the surrounding trees, and it made the formerly burnt circle look unnatural. But as Ellory stepped back to admire her handiwork, she at first felt nothing but a rush of excited pride.

Magic. She had done *magic*.

A hysterical laugh escaped her. No matter how many times she rubbed her eyes or turned away only to look back again, the grass remained there as if it had never been gone.

Her head began to ache, a tightness similar to the stress of studying too long—but worse. The image of Bancroft, lush and bright beneath the summer sun, faded. It felt as though her mind were wiping itself clean like a blackboard, erasing old information without making space for anything new. Ellory looked down, and no matter how hard she tried, she couldn't remember anything but the blackened pit that Bancroft had once been. This vibrant new lawn she had conjured was brand-new to her, even though she had reconstructed it from memory.

Pain flared in Ellory's neck, from an ache to a sting. Her knees wanted to buckle, but she managed to remain upright. *Remember.* Magic ate at her memories, she realized. To alter reality, she lost her grip on it, recollection by recollection. Ellory swayed on her feet, dizzy from the implications. From the soreness. From the weight of not knowing what she'd already lost.

Caw. Caw.

Crows streaked across the sky, ink black against the silver overcast. Below, a pack of passing students watched her from the other side of the field, whispering among themselves. Ellory would have smiled, but her muscles felt like they were under someone else's control, and the pain still lit her body like a circuit board.

By the time it became semibearable, the students surrounded her in a half circle of reluctant concern. Two of them hung back, radiating an air of *don't make this my problem*, but the remaining three were in the middle of offering to walk her to the health center.

"No, no," said Ellory, proud of her voice for sounding normal when she felt anything but. "I'm fine. Dizzy for a second."

"See?" said one of the men in the back. "We're going to be late if we don't hurry up."

"It's a movie, Brayden," said the woman in the center, rolling her eyes. "We can start it from the beginning." She toyed with her phone, searching Ellory's face. "Are you sure you're okay? I don't want to hear later that you collapsed after I left."

"I won't collapse. Promise."

Brayden made an impatient sound. His companion hissed at him to shut up. It took Ellory five more minutes of calm assurances and stifled flinches to get the group to move on, and by then the pain had lessened even further to an ache that she could live with. Once she could no longer see the students, she pulled out her phone, already knowing what she was going to see in the blurry, badly centered photographs.

RemƎmber.

Her tattoo was back.

◆

"You're terrible at this," said Hudson, his voice flatter than the Great Plains.

Once again, Ellory had been hoping to find him working late in Graves Library. Instead, she'd searched every floor but the basement and turned up nothing but a handful of study groups and one student in a suit taking a video call in a private room. She lingered outside the building now, her phone pressed to her ear, her free hand tracing her still-sore tattoo. Magic had brought it forth, which made it likely that her magic—*her* magic!—was the thing Ellory was trying not to forget. That only opened more questions, but it was a strong enough theory for her to reach out to Hudson before her closing shift at Powers That Bean.

And he was, as always, unimpressed.

"I thought I'd be happy when you got your phone back. Now I'm wondering why I called," she muttered. "I did magic, Graves. *Real* magic!"

"Or you gave yourself brain damage."

Ellory rolled her eyes. "I'm perfectly healthy. I can't imagine how disappointed you must be."

Hudson sighed as though *she* were being tiresome. It was amazing, how belligerent people could twist any situation to blame their own bad attitude on those who had to deal with it. "I'm happy to be your partner in this supernatural investigation, but I can't be the only one of us who cares whether you live or die. What good are answers to a corpse?"

The darkened path before her faded into the background as her mind stretched miles away to imagine Hudson Graves as he probably was: Dressed cozily. Sprawled out on his bed. Brow so furrowed that its grooves were considering buying permanent real estate on his forehead. Book open in front of him as he took a study break to answer her call. She could see it perfectly, as if she'd witnessed him like that a thousand times before, and the sudden shiver of familiarity made her tattoo throb anew.

"I didn't actually think it would work," she said, rubbing at it again. "Now I don't really know what to do with myself."

"What do you *want* to do?"

Ellory considered and discarded several answers to that question.

She wanted justice for Malcolm Mayhew, whose name history had already forgotten. She wanted to know what she'd lost, what had compelled her to tattoo herself in a fruitless attempt to remember. She wanted to use magic for some sort of good, even if she had no idea where to start.

"I want to show you," she decided. "I have work soon, but maybe tomorrow?"

"I don't know if that's a good idea." She heard the rustle of papers, the light notes of some R & B song in the background. "I've devoted more than enough of my time to this endeavor lately. God forbid my grades begin to slip."

Ellory blinked. "You *asked* to do this with me."

"And now I'm asking that you leave me out of this. You're more than capable of handling things, especially considering how much you love to run off on your own."

Her mouth worked, but no words sprung forth. The night's darkness stalked close as she thought of that man who had led her to safety with his arm around her shoulders, his body shielding her from a labyrinthine forest. The man who had softly promised to learn all he could about the Old Masters, all because they might have threatened her. The man who had listened to her accuse his childhood friend of subterfuge and come up with a plan for her to further investigate.

Realization sliced through her like a hot knife through butter. "You're afraid."

Hudson fell silent. Red-orange circles illuminated the night. A trio of students hovered near the side of the Graves, passing lit cigarettes back and forth despite the crisp air. Others traveled in packs around the quad, the occasional burst of laughter crackling through the air. Behind her, the library was still, but she could feel the miasma of stress that seemed to permeate the building. Every sweating student was a sacrifice to its academic altar.

"I suppose questioning everything is a good trait in a lawyer," Hudson finally said, and he sounded almost bored. "What conspiracy have you centered me in now?"

Ellory put some distance between herself and the Graves, narrowing her focus to the man whose family had paid for it. "You found something in your research that scared you, didn't you? That's why you want to distance yourself."

"Wanting to focus on school while attending a school is a symptom of terror? Fascinating."

Her cheeks heated. "Who are you protecting, Graves? Is it Boone? Or is it the Old Masters themselves?"

"Oh, please." Hudson made a frustrated sound. "Every odd thing that's happened since the start of the school year has somehow involved you, yet you claim *I'm* keeping things from *you*? You don't even involve me until after the fact."

Ellory's fingers tightened around the phone. He was right, and she knew he was right, but he was also being incredibly infantilizing. Her instincts were shrieking that something was wrong, and she was more inclined to trust them than to trust him. Even after this school year had made her question everything she thought she knew about herself and her world, she could still recognize a diversion.

"I *know* you're lying to me. I don't know about what, but I'm going to figure it out. I'm going to figure all of it out."

"It seems you have everything well in hand, then," Hudson deadpanned. "Good luck with that."

Click.

Ellory stared down at the blank screen of her phone for a full thirty seconds before it sank in that Hudson had hung up on her.

Affronted, she called him back and left a voicemail that would surely get her arrested but felt good in the moment, all four-letter words and passionate speculation about his place in whatever version of hell existed. She was breathing hard by the time she wedged her phone back into her pocket, nearly dropping it twice in her haste, and only the fact that Hudson would absolutely call the police on her—and be justified in doing so—if she turned up at his house kept her rooted in place.

Well, that and the fact that her shift began in twenty minutes, and she needed money more than she needed to throttle him.

"Admittedly," said a familiar voice from behind her, "this explains so much and nothing at all."

Ellory turned with her heart in her throat. Tai stood in the tombstone of light that stretched from the door of the library, her arms folded. A canvas bag stuffed with books rested against her hip. Her eyebrows were almost one with her hair. Whatever she saw in Ellory's expression made her smile.

"Yes, I heard everything. It seems we have some catching up to do, but I know you've got work," Tai continued. She marched forward, looped her arm around Ellory's, and tugged her in the direction of the bus stop. "Let's talk over coffee."

21

THIS CLOSE TO MIDNIGHT, POWERS That Bean was a wasteland. A table at the back housed four customers, all of them on their laptops with bags beneath their eyes and coffee cups the size of trophies half-empty beside their keyboards. Ellory had consumed a large coffee of her own before pinning on her name tag, tying her apron with a double knot, and stuffing her hair into a jaunty cap with a praying coffee bean on the front. Her leaden feet had to be forced into heading to the counter to relieve the other barista, because Tai was waiting with questions Ellory didn't know how to answer.

But all Tai said was "Can I get a small Earl Grey tea with three sugars?"

Ellory went through the motions, keeping one eye on the back table in case they flagged her down for more coffee. Tai drank her tea while flicking through her phone, giving Ellory time to wipe down the counter and check the espresso machine. Her shoulders eventually lowered, the knot of anxiety in her chest easing. Part of her knew Tai was doing this on purpose, letting

Ellory have this space to speak in her own time; even so, she was grateful.

"I heard you and Cody one night," Ellory said, which wasn't where she had meant to start at all. Tai's brow furrowed, so she charged on. "You were talking about magic—or they were. You had each other to confide in, and it felt like I was outside of that. Like I needed to have my own secret keeper."

"Who did you pick?" Tai asked. "Please tell me it wasn't Blackwood."

"Graves."

"Oh, of *course*."

Ellory frowned. "Why did you say it like that?"

"You're obsessed with each other," said Tai, matter-of-fact. "Of course you'd ask him. Of course he'd say yes."

Ellory retreated to collect an order from her only table. Whether the coffee shop swelled with crowds or dwindled to a single table, she treated her work-study with the reverence it deserved. Textbooks and clothes and school supplies weren't covered by her scholarship—nor were her tickets home to see Aunt Carol during breaks. Powers That Bean was her kingdom and her captor, where she kept order and pleased patrons with ruthless efficiency at the cost of studying time and social engagements. At least on slow nights, she could have a textbook open under the counter to stay on top of her classes. The times she worked late, watching raucous students stumble from party to party on the other side of the glass—well. It would all be worth it when she graduated.

Tai was waiting with her chin propped up on her hand, her Earl Grey tea drained. The scent of bergamot lingered in the air, making Ellory think reluctantly of Hudson. Tai's phone was face down on the table, her full attention like a blunt weapon. "This isn't about Cody or me. Are you ready to tell me what else has been going on?"

And Ellory finally was. Her entire school year, recontextualized through the framework of true magic, from the séance and the murder she had witnessed to the field and the nature she had healed. The longer she spoke, the more relieved she felt. Every moment had seemed so surreal that keeping it to herself, preserving it only in her notes, had helped her feel in control. But Tai listened without judgment, so much so that Ellory couldn't believe she had taken so long to confide in her best friend.

"Wow," Tai said when she was finished. "Magic, huh?"

"I know." Ellory deflated atop the counter, her arms dangling dramatically over the front. "I couldn't believe it either."

"It's been an unusual school year. Even before the séance, I've felt like…something is off." Tai stared to the side, where nothing but empty tables and scattered chairs waited for acknowledgment. "I tried calling my aunties, but they couldn't explain this inexplicable familiarity. The way the universe seems to bend to me sometimes. The way I feel too small and too large for this world." Her expression melted into something sheepish. "I sound confused. I didn't want you to think—"

"No, I—I've been feeling the same way." Ellory had straightened at some point during Tai's confession. Now her hands closed over Tai's wrist, a comforting gesture to ground them both. "Graves has been trying to help me figure it all out, but part of me was still fighting this…until today."

"What was it like?" Tai's eyes were wide, her voice breathless. "Doing magic?"

Several words crowded the back of Ellory's throat, each of them inadequate. It felt like loss—draining and all-consuming—and also like strength—as rightness in a world that had always been wrong. It felt like sickness; it felt like panacea. It felt limiting and limitless. Instinctively, her hand found the back of her neck again, rubbing against the tattoo she couldn't see.

"It was like stepping into a memory," she finally said, clearing the counter of Tai's empty cup and abandoned tea bag. "It's not a good memory, but it's not a bad one. It just…is. You wonder how you could have ever forgotten that life could be like this—and you dread what it means for you, for the world, that life can be like this. Words don't do it justice."

"I want to see."

Ellory glanced at the back table, where one of the students had fallen asleep on their keyboard. Their laptop screen was illuminated with an incomprehensible PDF scan, incomprehensible not because of the distance but because the text was illegible, letters bleeding into one another from age. Ellory would have passed out rather than deal with that, too.

"Maybe during my break," she allowed.

On the night shift, her break consisted of being allowed to sit down behind the counter; with no one to relieve her, she couldn't abandon her post. Tai called Cody, who showed up in a long hoodie and leggings, their hair beneath a navy baseball cap. While Tai and Ellory went out back, Cody hung around the counter, ready to summon Ellory if anyone needed anything—or, worse, if her boss did a surprise drop-in.

Outside, the moon was almost full, lined by a slip of darkness no larger than a hangnail. Dumpsters were wedged against the back of the coffee shop, and gray garbage bags peeked out. The grass was dull even without the wash of moonlight, wheat-yellow patches broken by soil and stone. Tai leaned against the building, wrapping her winter coat tighter around her as the cold tore through the night, sinking into places it didn't belong. Ellory flexed her hands at her sides, trying to find that string of power that had wound within her at Bancroft.

But there was nothing.

It wasn't even as though there were a notable absence of something. That would have roused her suspicions, given her a mystery she could sink her teeth into. Instead, her heart beat, and her breath flowed in and out of her lungs, but there was a lack of that *something more* that had overtaken her on the field. She felt no more powerful than a leaf swept along by the wind, and it scared her, this impotence, how easily it rendered her weak.

Ellory clenched her eyes shut, rifling through a lifetime of memories. She opened her mind in offering, inviting the magic in to take and to create. A field of grass. A ball of light. A pack of birds. Something. *Anything.*

Her eyes jumped open.

No goose bumps flared along her arms. No pain singed her nerve endings. If there was sentient power in the universe, it was ignoring her. Her mind was intact, and she should have been happy about it, but this left her empty in a different kind of way.

This came with the sour taste of failure.

Tai shifted, her puffer jacket crinkling in reminder of her presence. Ellory's cheeks heated as she stared at the ground until her eyes watered. It was like Bancroft had been a dream, and she had awakened into the real world where magic was the stuff of Disney movies and fairy tales, reserved for girls with golden locks and evil stepmothers. The fire in her face spread to her stomach, a kind of shameful resignation that said, *You should have known better.*

"Your break is over," said Tai. Her gentle voice was like a slap. Ellory didn't turn. "Tell Cody I'll be in soon."

Tai took a breath, as though to say something, and then decided against it. Ellory waited until her footsteps faded to drag the back of her hand across her eyelids, wiping away the gathered tears. She glared at the grass as though it had personally betrayed her, but the only response she got was the rattle of the dumpster lid in the wind.

22

Ellory made her way to the building that housed the *Warren Communiqué* office that Friday. Her phone was silent in her bag, undisturbed by messages or calls. She had made no effort to reach out to Hudson, and he had made even less effort to reach out to her. If he thought his silence would derail her investigation, she was excited to prove him wrong. If he had abandoned her to protect Boone, she wanted to know why. And if she had other reasons for her nerves as she approached the front doors, that was something she could keep to herself.

She had walked by this place many times on her way to one class or another, but she'd never allowed herself the luxury of slowing down to admire it in earnest. It was done in a Gothic style, with a single pointed arch that bore a stained glass rose window. The black door in the gray-washed stone was decorated on either side by columns with two lions carved into them. Inside, marbled hallways led to an elevator that declared the *Communiqué* was on the top floor. The staircase was directly to the right, with a sign on the door that said ROOF ACCESS.

Ellory tugged her cropped hoodie down over her bare stomach as the elevator took her to the penthouse. She buttoned and then unbuttoned her coat. Her hands couldn't decide whether they wanted to stay in her pockets or not. The many times she had imagined coming here, it had been under such different circumstances. Now she couldn't even stand in an elevator without hearing the disappointed voice of her aunt Carol, chiding her for wasting her time on a money sieve like journalism. Even if she had a good reason.

Even if she wanted this.

Ding.

Ellory had expected the floor to be quiet, but people filled the area, sitting behind desks, laughing by the stained glass window, pushing a whiteboard from one glass-walled office to another. A printer was running, loud and steady. The air smelled of coffee and excitement. Eyes latched onto her as soon as she stepped out of the elevator, but when she tried to find the prying gazes, there didn't seem to be a single person looking up from their computer.

To her left was a container full of the latest issue of the *Warren Communiqué*, a front-page story bragging about the victory of the soccer team at an away game. Ellory realized she was searching the crowd in the picture for Hudson and dragged her eyes away.

"Well, well, well," said Boone, appearing from behind a column. In defiance of the weather, he wore a short-sleeved black shirt with a deep V-neck that revealed a hint of the crow tattoo across his chest, and tan cargo pants. Somewhere on his ink-covered arms was the alchemical symbol she was looking for, hiding in plain sight. There was a marker behind his ear and a cap embroidered with TWC over his messy hair. "They told me we had a novice, but I didn't expect it to be Miss Ellory Morgan."

"Hi, Boone," she said, ignoring the sudden kick of her pulse. "I didn't know you were on the newspaper."

"I run the newspaper," he corrected. "I was made editor in chief this year. Walk with me."

With his back to her, it became even more obvious how guileless he was in her presence, as if they were old friends. It was the performance of a lifetime if he was truly involved with the Old Masters.

Boone took her to one of the glass offices, which had a round table, several empty chairs, and a whiteboard that was half-full of what was labeled STORY PITCHES. Without the label, Ellory never could have guessed, because all she saw was DUCKS, FOLLOW-UP, THAT ONE FUCKING DELI, and a picture of what looked like the Babadook.

He slid the door closed and threw himself down in one of the chairs. His booted feet found the table, lifting the front legs of his chair off the ground. "What can I do for you, Morgan?"

"I know it's late into the semester, but I was wondering if you guys are looking for new reporters?" Ellory settled into a chair of her own, but she couldn't seem to get comfortable. She crossed her feet at the ankles, right over left, then left over right. A wayward pen had been left on the table. She straightened it. "I have an idea for an article I'd like to write, if so."

Boone looked more curious than convinced. "Why the sudden interest in the paper? You don't need to befriend all of us to date Blackwood, you know."

"This isn't about Liam," she snapped. Then she swallowed. "I mean—"

"Don't you dare fucking apologize. I like you more with your claws out." There was a twinkle in his eyes that would have put the stars to shame. "I meant that you haven't expressed an interest in the paper before now. Hell, even when it comes to people who are majors, I always ask them the same questions: Why are you really here? What do you want out of being a reporter?"

"The truth." Ellory was surprised by how easily the answer came. How right it felt. How it didn't feel like she was only talking about this tangled mystery. "I know that newspapers control the conversation and that all of them have their own agenda to push. But I'm here because I want to find the truth. I want to write stories that illuminate some dark corner of our knowledge of the world. I want that truth to be powerful."

Her hands trembled on the table. That sense of déjà vu was back, like she had given this speech before, like she'd sat in this room before. She looked around, trying to place the glass walls and the curious faces pretending not to watch them from the other side of it. The muted bubble of the coffee machine making another round for the already-frazzled reporters. The gorgeous prism of colors the glass window stretched across the floor. The tapping of keys as people put the finishing touches on stories that could change the world—or at least the campus.

It felt familiar and unfamiliar.

It felt like magic.

Maybe Hudson's logic professor had been right. Maybe believing in something *was* its own kind of magic.

Her eyes returned to Boone, who was watching her in silence. She straightened her shoulders. "I'm going to pitch you my story now."

"The floor is yours," said Boone, a smile buried in the corner of his mouth.

Ellory had devoted her weekend to cobbling this idea together, inspired by her endless recordings on the strange happenings on campus. She'd practiced her casual, passionate tone, shaping the piece into something that was publishable, sensational, and a perfect excuse to be found in places she shouldn't have been. Now she told Boone the highlights of her research into Warren University history and the legacy families who had built it. A feature on each of those families would not only expand their understanding of the school, she said, but it might also result in extra funding for the newspaper. After all, who didn't love good press?

"Which is not to say that it would be a fluff piece," she concluded. "I plan to ask tough questions, then verify with interviews and independent research. But I looked at old articles here and in local papers, and it's been a while since these names were spotlighted. I think no matter how the story turns out, they'll be flattered."

Boone's chair hit the floor, and his feet joined it a moment later. He walked over to the whiteboard, freeing the marker from behind his ear to write, FAMOUS FUCKERS. She caught a flash of his tattoo and swallowed, silenced by an inexplicable hope that she was wrong, that Boone had nothing to do with the Old Masters at all.

"Welcome to the *Communiqué*, Morgan," he said with a grin she had no idea how to interpret. "Let me start you on the merch closet."

◆

Even though Ellory was balancing a hat, two hoodies, a T-shirt, and a PopSocket on top of her bag, she was buoyant with joy. It wasn't a real assignment, and she wasn't really on the paper, but her invigorated body hadn't gotten the memo. The usual clamor of Moneta Hall couldn't hold her attention. Instead, she ruminated on ways to approach the article.

Her favorite part of a story was all the legwork that came before writing it. Research and sources. Leads and fact-checking. She might have pitched Boone an excuse to do what she was already doing, prying her fingers into the history that Warren wanted to keep hidden, but she still wanted to impress. Besides, she now had full access to a digitized archive of *Communiqué* issues, a budding list of families she wanted to interrogate about Malcolm Mayhew, and an excuse to spend more time with Boone until she could use him to get to the Old Masters.

Everything was connected. She had to figure out how—even if that meant working alone.

The elevator *ding*ed open, and she shuffled out onto her floor. An unusual tension seeped into her muscles, but she chalked it up to her expanding to-do list and the endless tasks that would fill her afternoon. It wasn't until she rearranged everything she was carrying to find her room key that she realized she was being watched.

A hooded figure stood in front of her dorm room, too short to be Stasie and too suspicious to be Tai.

Ellory's gasp drew their attention. Time slowed, but her heart rioted in her chest. She took in the scene as a series of piecemeal images: White plastic. Sharp edges. Bottomless blank eyes. Every thought fled her head except one: *They're back.* Because the person hovering in front of her closed door wore a white mask with divots in an empty face to indicate where their eyes, nostrils, and mouth should be. Their hood was drawn, hiding any hair, and their clothes were so nondescript that she couldn't have described them even though she was looking right at them.

This was the person who had attacked her on the quad.

It had to be. She hadn't heeded their warning, and now she had caught them lurking. Ready to ambush her. Ready to enforce another one of the Old Masters' arbitrary, clandestine rules.

Her throat lit with phantom pain as she swallowed, though the bruising had long since faded. There was time to run. Right before the elevator was a door to the staircase. She could probably sprint back to the lobby in time to alert the security guard. If this person caught up to her, if they *pushed* her, then at least she would go down trying to escape. At least she would die doing something more substantial than writhing on the ground, begging for air, as alone as Malcolm Mayhew had been on that terrible night.

No.

Ellory was so fucking sick of running. If they wanted to turn the Lost Eight into the Lost Nine, then she would not make it easy for them. The Old Masters could have her life, her magic, only by taking it from her. She was tired of being the prey. She wanted to be the hunter.

Sometimes, justice looked like vengeance.

Sometimes, violence called for violence.

Sometimes, rage was power.

Another beat passed during which she and the enforcer faced each other. Then Ellory dropped everything she'd been carrying and lunged at their neck.

"*Bitch*," they bit out in that androgynous voice as they stumbled into the wall. "You should have listened when—"

"*You* listen," she snarled back. "I'm not afraid of you. Of *any* of you."

Ellory threw a punch. She had never punched someone before, but she knew enough to keep her thumb on the outside of her fist. She wanted to crack that stupid mask in half and see who was underneath. They knew who she was, what she was doing, what she *could* do. She had the name of only one member—Boone—and even that was a guess. Would the Old Masters be as threatening with their identities laid bare?

Her knuckles throbbed, sending agony shooting up her arm. She'd punched the wall, not that infuriating mask. The enforcer had twisted out of her grasp and was sprinting for the stairs while she clutched her aching hand, checking to make sure she hadn't broken anything.

Enraged yet elated, Ellory raced after them.

Inside the stairwell was silent except for her furious profanities and the pounding of two sets of feet. She hoped her screaming would draw attention from other residents, that the stairs would flood with curious students who would help her catch the intruder. The doors remained closed, the floors beyond still, as if she had once again been cut off from the wider world.

The enforcer leaped over the railings like a comic book villain, keeping at least one flight of stairs between them. Ellory's lungs burned, and sweat glued her clothes to her body. Her legs, which had gotten more exercise in the last few months than they had in her entire life, were on fire. But she didn't falter. Her focus had narrowed to a single mission: capture and interrogate.

Fifth floor.

Fourth floor.

Third.

Below, the lobby door swung open with a *thud* that echoed up the stairwell. The enforcer stopped short, halfway between the second and first floors, trapped between Ellory and—

"Morgan," said Hudson Graves, and she had never been so happy to see him in her life. "I could hear you cursing from the *front door*. What's going on in here?"

The enforcer decided their chances were better with Ellory and whirled around to disorient her with the full force of their uncanny lack of expression. Ellory expected her momentum to hurl her directly down into a punch, but instead she was blasted off her feet by an unnatural gust of wind. She landed in a pained heap on the stairs, her arms and legs as limp as a discarded puppet's. The back of her head ached. The world swam. She could taste blood at the back of her throat.

"Ellory!"

Footsteps approached, each one echoing in her skull like a jackhammer. Everything was too loud and too bright. Her ears were ringing. When had her ears started ringing?

A figure hovered over her—masked and feral with rage. "This ends *now*."

It took her a moment to remember who this was, where she was, and why her sore body had gone cold with fear. They raised their leg, and Ellory realized too late that she was about to be stomped to death in a residence hall's stairwell with no one but Hudson Graves to watch. Tears stung her eyes. She begged her limbs to move, but the fall had rattled her skull. Her neurons could fire all they wanted. Nothing was listening.

Her final thought, absurdly, was the hope that Aunt Carol followed her dietary plan without Ellory around to nag her. At least one of them deserved to live a long life.

But death didn't come for her. Instead, Hudson did.

Fire erupted in the stairwell, the indigo and violet of the hottest part of a blaze. Their shadows flickered against the wall. Flames twisted around the handrail, bolting like a snake in the grass. One minute, the enforcer's foot was speeding toward her skull. The next minute, fire gripped their limbs, their waist, their chest, like burning chains holding them in place. Smoke fizzled from their clothes, followed by the sour scent of burning flesh. The enforcer screamed and screamed as the chains expanded until the stranger was completely covered in light.

And then they exploded, leaving behind a scorch mark the exact size and shape of their body. As if they had been burned out of existence.

But *how*?

Head throbbing, Ellory traced the fire back to its source. Hudson stood with his hand on the rail, flames twisting downward from his bicep. As she watched, they retreated from the wall, back to Hudson's outstretched arm, and then collapsed without so much as a curl of smoke to prove they'd once been there. Hudson was breathing hard, his own eyes so wide, she could see the whites of them from where she was sprawled. His shock didn't just mirror her own, but somehow exceeded it.

"*Ellory*," he repeated, shaking himself. He closed the distance between them and pulled her limp body into his arms. "You're okay. Everything's okay."

It was unclear whether he was talking to her or himself. Either way, she blinked.

"Do I have a concussion," asked Ellory, "or did you use magic?"

Hudson looked down at her. "You definitely have a concussion."

"But you used magic?"

"I—" He stared at the wall. His hand adjusted its grip on her legs, holding her more securely against him as he descended the stairs. It wasn't until now that Ellory realized that whatever fire he'd conjured hadn't touched her at all. If she hadn't been looking, she wouldn't even have known it was there. So much for thermodynamics. "I need to take you to the health center."

"Since when can you do magic?"

"Morgan—"

"*Don't* lie to me," she said. He paused at the lobby door, probably because of how much bitterness she had packed into those four words. "Is this what you've been hiding? Why would you lie to me about this when you *know*—"

Her head throbbed. She saw one Hudson and then two Hudsons and then one again. She clenched her eyes shut, desperate to keep her lunch down.

"The health center," Hudson repeated. "Then we can deal with— whatever that was."

Ellory nodded wearily and let him carry her into the light.

23

THE NURSE PUT HUDSON IN charge of monitoring Ellory for the next twenty-four hours, assuming that they were together and ignoring their fervid protests to the contrary. Ellory was given Tylenol and a lecture from Hudson before he took her to the student center, where she received a six-pack of ginger ale, an ice pack, a bottle of water, and a second lecture. She let Hudson preach about the dangers of leaving her phone behind, because they were in public and she was more concerned with checking every nook and cranny for more masked figures. But as soon as they were back in the car, she glared at him.

"You can do magic," she accused, "and you didn't tell me."

Hudson paused with his hand on the keys. Instead of starting the engine, he dragged that hand over his face. "I didn't know."

Violet-gray clouds had overtaken the once-blue sky. Gentle rain began to fall, plinking against the roof like an intermittent drumroll. They were still in the parking lot of the student center, but the streets had emptied in light of the weather. There was no one to witness Ellory and Hudson in his Barracuda, arguing about the esoteric turn their lives had taken, and there was some comfort in that. Ellory opened her water, downed her pills, and stared through the wet windshield.

For a while, the raindrops provided the only sound.

"I didn't want to watch you die," Hudson murmured. "But I was too far away to do anything about it…until I wasn't."

"Yeah, I understand that," said Ellory, remembering Malcolm Mayhew and the murder she couldn't prevent. Her frozen limbs had forced her to bear witness to something that haunted her to this day, and she wouldn't wish that on anyone. "What I don't understand is *how*. How could you not have known? How could you listen to everything I told you, everything I experienced, and not…?" *Confide in me, too.* Ellory's throat was tight with an emotion worse than anger. She was hurt. Hurt that he hadn't trusted her the way she'd been forced to trust him.

No, she hadn't been forced. She'd wanted to. Maybe she'd even needed to.

"I've always believed in the unbelievable," said Hudson, "but it feels different when it's *me*. Surely you can understand that, too."

Ellory knew he was referring to how hard she had fought against the idea that she might have magic, even after she'd accepted that magic did exist. But it still wasn't enough to mollify her. He could have shared his suspicions. He could have admitted he had questions at all. He could have done anything but show up to help her again and again while keeping such a large part of himself hidden from her.

If he could cover this up, what else was he hiding?

He knew her, but had he ever allowed her to know him?

Hudson started the car. She stared out the window as they pulled onto Falstaff Road, driving south back to Moneta Hall. Soon, he would foist her off onto Stasie—or, more likely, Tai—and go back to ignoring her, leaving her frustrated under the guise of letting her rest. He was reliably unreliable, while she had been attacked for the second time this month by people who wanted to silence her at any cost. Ellory's eyes traced the angles of his face in the mirror the graying sky had turned her window into. Rain carved his reflection in half, making him look like both monster and man.

"What were you doing at Moneta?" she finally asked. "I thought you were busy 'studying.'"

"Boone told me you'd left the *Communiqué* office, but you weren't answering your phone. I…worried."

"Tell Boone to mind his own business."

"I mean, I'm the one who asked how you were doing, but I'll relay the message. Why weren't you answering my calls?"

Ellory remembered again that her phone was still—hopefully—in a heap on the sixth floor with the rest of her things. She had put it on Silent before going to the newspaper office. "Why would I? You said you were done."

"Morgan," he sighed.

"*Don't*. Don't talk to me like I'm the problem."

"No, I—you're right. I'm sorry. I did say that. And I shouldn't have. That's why I was asking about you. I come with a peace offering."

Hudson tipped his head toward the back seat, where each turn caused a stack of books to slide from one side of the vinyl seating to the other. A battered tote bag was on the floor; it had clearly made a valiant effort to contain the books before sinking out of sight, defeated. It was joined by a pair of black soccer cleats, tied together by the laces, and Hudson's Montblanc sling, each pocket zipped tight.

"I pulled these from my shelf because they mention secret societies and esoteric traditions. Maybe you'll get more out of them than I did."

His tone was different. She was used to his arrogance, his peevishness, his introspection. This was a clipped discomfort, like he was hesitating over every word while trying to seem like he wasn't. The acetaminophen had eased her physical pain, but mentally she still felt out of sync with the hazy world. Except him, her enigmatic sometimes ally.

"I can't trust you if you don't trust me," Ellory said, closing her eyes. She was exhausted all the way down to her bones, but she doubted she would sleep tonight. At least not until she had a theory about why that enforcer had chosen her room to wait in, and if they'd actually gotten inside, and what they had touched or taken if they had. "You encouraged me to believe in my magic. You gave me a way to investigate Boone. You've been there for me twice in the wake of these attacks. But you hid your magic from me. You didn't notice that you live with someone who has the ideograms of the Old Masters *written on his skin*. And I feel more unsafe right now, in this car, than I did bleeding in that stairwell." Her eyes opened, meeting his gaze through the windowpane. "Out there, I know who the enemy is. In here, I don't even know *you*."

"Morgan—"

The car came to a stop in front of Moneta. Ellory unbuckled her seat belt, eager to put some distance between them. With or without a concussion, she couldn't think in Hudson's presence. Every time she tried to hold on to her anger at him, he inevitably wore her down. But her anger was a gift and a shield. It had protected her from the person in the mask, and it would protect her from a man who knew only how to lie.

He caught her hand before she could get out of the car.

Ellory stopped, but she told herself it was because the rain had gotten heavier and she didn't have an umbrella. With the door open, the evening wind bit through the car, making her shiver. She reluctantly turned to face him head-on, meeting eyes the dark brown of Southern sweet tea. His thumb touched her pulse point, and an infuriating warmth suffused her body at the way he was always so gentle with her.

"Should I walk you up?" he asked. "In case that—person is still hanging around?"

"You didn't kill them?"

"What? *No*. Do I look like I kill people?"

Ellory stared at him. Hudson scoffed.

"I'm pretty sure I kind of…banished them. If I'd *killed* them, there would have been a burnt body. And no matter what you think, I've never killed anyone before. I wouldn't be *okay* afterward."

Ellory's foot was getting wet where it rested on the pavement. She settled back into her seat, but she didn't close the door. Hudson deserved for his precious car's precious internal detailing to get water damage. He deserved worse than that, but she was too tired for punitive justice. All the while, he didn't let go of her hand, and she didn't make him. It was the only thing keeping her steady.

"Whatever you think of me right now, I'm on your side, Morgan. I *want* you to remember what you've lost. I want the Old Masters to be stopped. I want…"

I want you. And I'm tired of pretending I don't.

Yeah? Then do something about it.

Ellory gasped back to the present. She yanked herself from Hudson's grip and escaped into the rain.

"I need to think," she said, slamming the door. On his expression, open in a way it hadn't been before, eyes tinged with an inexplicable grief. On the words she'd heard as clear as day, their voices having a conversation they'd never had. On this emotionally draining day, which was tearing her soul to pieces faster than any magic.

His lips silently formed her name. Ellory turned and fled into Moneta Hall without looking back.

◆

That night, Ellory crashed into a slumber so deep that Rip Van Winkle would have been jealous. She'd told Stasie that someone had attempted to break into their dorm, and she'd listened to her roommate tear security a new one before ordering a camera for the door. She'd told Tai about her trip to the health center, and Tai and Cody had spent the rest of the night checking on Ellory's head, leaving notes with time stamps so she would know they'd come to visit. When she woke up to an empty room the next day, her headache and nausea had ceased, and she felt less wrung out. Her stress hadn't fully faded, but she was learning to live on high alert.

By late afternoon, she judged herself healed enough to read, devouring the occult books she'd gotten from Hudson. The tote bag was waiting outside her door, off to the left so no one would trip over it. She'd found it on her way back from the bathroom, and her stomach had flipped at this small consideration. Research was easier than thinking about *him* and all the tangled emotions his lies had embedded in her.

Two of the books were useless—if fascinating—histories of haunted artifacts and men made myth. Nicolas Flamel and Ostanes. The Bronze Lady and the screaming skull. They were great for contextualizing how the natural became the supernatural, even just

AN ARCANE INHERITANCE

in tall tales told by the superstitious, but there was nothing specific to her situation.

The third book covered secret societies, and it was halfway through that one that Ellory finally found something worth adding to her notes.

> *The Old Masters have maintained their anonymity to such an extent that it is impossible to confirm their existence. Though largely based on hearsay, their clandestine activities are said to have roots in the Central Intelligence Agency (CIA). Or, perhaps, their ongoing activities were simply legitimized by the CIA.*

Hudson had been right. This section was a mere page and a half compared to other chapters, so it wasn't exactly enough to qualify as a break in the case. But something about it filled her with a heavy sense of significance, and she lingered over each word.

> *From the beginning, they have walked hand in hand with the occult. Starting with the New England Society of Psychic Research and then peppering the declassified Stargate Project with their members, the Old Masters are rumored to have wanted power unlimited to the natural world. In writings alleged to have been rescued from the burnt journals of rumored member Arthur O'Connor I, there are notes on occult magic and psychic phenomena from around the world, including alchemy, Māyā, ESP, and more. But when questioned, O'Connor, a former*

dean of Warren University, claimed ignorance of any such journals or organization.

Buzzwords leaped out at her as she read the paragraph again. *New England Society of Psychic Research*—the same group the founders of Warren University had allegedly belonged to. *Arthur O'Connor*—the same surname as her surly roommate. If he was a former dean, then she might be able to find a book in the founders' museum gift shop, or at least there might be a mention of him on one of the displays.

The section concluded with the acknowledgment that the Old Masters were not as legendary as Skull and Bones nor as powerful as the Illuminati, but rumors of their recherché activities had never entirely faded. Ellory read the page three more times to make sure she wasn't missing anything and then rubbed at the back of her neck. Goose bumps made her skin feel rough, and she knew that sickening dread would soon follow.

She took a shaky breath and refused to give in. She'd found a new lead, and she had the resources to investigate, people who would help, even if they didn't know everything they were helping with. And yet her heart continued to pound like she was about to be attacked again. She massaged the space between her breasts, begging her body to calm down.

Stasie came clattering through the door a half hour later, her arms laden with shopping bags. She dropped them on her bed and wiggled her knit cap off her penny-brown hair, which had recently been cut into a short wavy bob. Christmas was only a couple of months away, but Ellory doubted a single one of those purchases was for anyone other than Stasie herself.

Her suspicions were strengthened a moment later when Stasie

tugged a powder-blue wool sweater out of one bag and held it up to her chest. It was crocheted to look like a heap of snowflakes had joined hands to make a shirt. Pearl drops decorated the round collar. "What do you think?"

"It's got holes in it," Ellory pointed out. "It can't be very warm."

"It's meant to be *stylish*," Stasie said, rolling her eyes. "Luxury sweaters are wasted on the poor."

"A sweater can be stylish *and* practical—"

"Are you going to be in here all day?"

As always, Ellory had already failed the Stasie O'Connor test required to earn basic human respect. Stasie unpacked her clothes with the put-upon attitude of a wine mom who had found her prosecco bottle empty when she needed it most. If Ellory stayed, the rest of her night would be filled with eye rolls and passive-aggressive grunts from Stasie's side of the room.

"I could finish this up in the library," Ellory said, saving and closing her document, "*if* you answer a question for me."

Stasie paused in the middle of folding an oversize scarf. "You couldn't afford it even if I told you."

"It's about your family, not your clothes." Ellory took a moment to grab her temper with both hands and force it to a standstill. "Do you know an Arthur O'Connor?"

"My dad or my grandfather?"

"Um, your grandfather."

"We call him *Artie*. Well, *I* call him *Pop-Pop*, but…" Stasie frowned. "Why?"

"I'm working on an article for the paper, and, as he's a former dean of the university, I thought he might be able to help me. Do you have his number?"

"I'm not giving you Pop-Pop's phone number. He'd have my head."

Ellory resisted the urge to record the conversation, if only because she would have to notify Stasie that she was doing so and Stasie would definitely stop talking if she did. "So, you two aren't close?"

"If I asked for your mom's personal phone number, would you give it to me?"

Ellory swiftly changed tactics. "Your family's prestigious. I want to make sure I'm talking to all the right people."

There was a brief silence, during which Ellory could tell that Stasie was turning those words over for any sign of ridicule. She kept her expression open and her smile as genuine as possible, waiting Stasie out. This was a girl who had introduced herself as a member of the house of O'Conor, who had the O'Conor crest as one of her wall decorations, who took her family very seriously. Too seriously, if you asked Ellory, but that had never been her problem before now.

It seemed like ages before Stasie's face softened. "I mean, I guess I could get you in touch with my parents while I see if Pop-Pop even wants to talk to you."

Her eyes were bright with pleasure, as if the key to the intricate lock of her personality had been flattery all along. Ellory supposed she should have figured that out sooner.

"That would be amazing," she simpered. "You're the best, Stasie."

"I know." Stasie went back to folding her clothes. Then she glared in Ellory's direction. "Now get out."

INTERLUDE

From the moment a child is born, they begin to forget.
Life is a series of memories formed and lost, experiences repressed and replaced. Parents catalog first words and first steps, bronzing childhoods to keep in stasis. Friends remember jokes that last longer than the friendships. Trauma enters the bloodstream and pumps beneath the skin, creating muscle memory from a moment the conscious mind has long forgotten.

Even when reduced to ash, the embers of memory still burn bright. A scent can unfurl a forgotten dream. A slant of sunlight can spark a repeated conversation. The sound of laughter can draw out a riddle without a punch line.

Perhaps that is all déjà vu is in the end: a spark of memory, adding color to the portrait of the world. A kind of natural magic that begs the practitioner to think, to feel, to be—again and again and again. We exist in a world that demands too much of some and too little of others, but in this we are all made equal. We live to forget. We forget to live. We capture special moments in our palms and cling to them until they slip through our fingers, a daily sensation so normalized that we don't even notice the loss.

But without those ephemeral experiences that make up the fabric of a soul, who do we become?

24

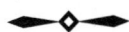

OMICRON CHI LAMBDA PARTIED LIKE they had invented it. Liam helped Ellory out of the passenger seat, and her sneakers immediately flattened an abandoned water bottle that shot brown droplets of liquor into the gutter. She had worn a mesh corset top, black with pale pink floral embroidery, and a pair of high-waisted black jeans. Her shoulders and belly button were freezing, but Tai had assured her that the inside of the frat house would be like a furnace.

As was often the case with these things, Tai was right.

Music loud enough to make the walls tremble. Writhing bodies slick with sweat. Alcohol bottles on windowsills and side tables. It would have reminded Ellory of the night that she and Liam had met, but this was less of a party and more of a rager. Just squeezing through the crowds without ending up wearing someone's mixed drink was an exercise in patience. Only Liam's hand on the small of her back, the tips of his fingers barely dipping into her pocket, kept her from getting lost in the crowded, cavernous room.

A week had passed since she had unofficially joined the paper.

She hadn't heard from Stasie, and she hadn't reached out to Hudson, but she *had* heard from Liam, and his texts had pulled her from her frustrated spirals. She had continued to scour books and search the internet for further signs of the Old Masters, she continued to watch her surroundings for looming enforcers and glitches in the Matrix, but it was nice to have Liam remind her that there was more to her life than school and murders.

She wished only that it were enough to settle her conflicted heart.

This was their second date, and Ellory still felt like she was playing a role—and she couldn't decide if she wanted to commit to it or not. She hardly qualified as a prize to be shown off, but there had to be a reason he took her out only in group settings. It felt performative rather than intimate, and yet she always had a good time.

Maybe her mind was trying to ruin this for her. It wouldn't be the first time.

They pinballed from group to group until Liam introduced her to the entire lacrosse team, all carbon copies of his build and charisma. "This is my…Ellory," he said, and it was only a little awkward. Ellory knew the polite thing to do would be to correct him with a decisive label, but she also didn't want to define the relationship because it was *the polite thing to do*. Instead, she told a man who identified himself as Beau that she liked his shirt.

"Oh, thanks," he said, beaming down at the photo of a slumbering toddler on the front. "That's my kid. Do you want see a better picture?"

Six pictures in, Liam slipped away to find them some drinks. Eleven pictures in, Ellory's curiosity won out.

"Do I pass muster?" she asked, winding a curl around one of her fingers. It sprang free, framing her face. "I know Liam's dated the likes of Graveses and Mayhews, so I'm a little worried."

Beau's eyes flicked to her and then at something over her shoulder. He cleared his throat. "That was a while ago. Blackwood talks about you *all* the time."

Joy bloomed in her chest. Still, she turned, catching sight of a woman standing near the wall with a Corona bottle in one hand and her phone in the other.

Her skin was unseasonably golden, blessed with the color of an increasingly invisible sun, and long lashes surrounded eyes the pale gray of mountain mist. Reddish-brown hair framed her face in a tight curl pattern, decorated by a silver headband that matched her sparkling long-sleeved top. Her earrings dangled toward her shoulders, shaped like guillotines.

Their eyes met, and Ellory's cheeks grew hot.

"Is that her?" she asked without daring to be the first to look away. "His ex?"

"I don't want to be involved," said Beau. "But yes. Can I interest you in more pictures?"

Ellory wandered toward the woman—the Mayhew—before he had even finished speaking. With everything going on, she had completely forgotten to track her down, and now the party was secondary, another step on the inevitable path to truth.

To her credit, the Mayhew woman didn't pretend she hadn't been staring. Those gray eyes watched unblinkingly as Ellory cut through the crowd, her eyebrows lowering as the space between them shrank. She put her phone away and took a sip of her Corona, leaving a perfect smudge of pomegranate lipstick.

"Hey," said Ellory.

The woman smiled. "Hey."

She introduced herself as Farrah Mayhew. Her handshake was firm but not combative. Her nails were painted lily pad green. She was strikingly pretty in a way that made Ellory glad she had missed the entirety of her relationship with Liam. Independently, Farrah and Liam drew helpless longing gazes. Together, they must have been devastating. A bisexual's nightmare. Ellory would never have gotten any studying done.

"So, you and Liam, huh?" said Farrah. "Ugh, sorry." She ducked her head, her cheeks alight with a rose-petal blush. "Asking about it probably makes me seem like an asshole, but I can't help myself."

"I'm willing to abandon decorum if you are," Ellory said. "Though my question is going to be a lot more morbid."

Farrah took another sip of her Corona. "I'm intrigued." But clearly, whatever Farrah had expected her to bring up, Malcolm Mayhew wasn't it. She blinked twice, birdlike, eyebrows knitting together. "My uncle? How do you know about that?"

"I stumbled on the wrong article at the right time, I guess. Do you know much about him?"

Farrah's mouth opened and closed. She looked down at her bottle, thumb circling the lip. "Not really. He was my father's younger brother. He died here on campus." Her wry smile returned. "I'm a legacy student. That's not the legacy I would've chosen, but at least you're only the second person to ask me about it this week."

"Second?"

But even as Ellory's lips formed the question, she knew down to her marrow what—who—had gotten to Farrah first:

"Hudson Graves."

◆

The next two hours of the party passed in a blur. Ellory stayed close to Liam's side, laughing at jokes she couldn't remember and cheering at stunts that needed the intervention of the campus police. Every so often, she would feel eyes on her, but the sensation would fade as soon as she turned around. Farrah had left the party. Beau was playing a drinking game. Liam crowded Ellory against a kitchen counter and kissed her with a mouth that tasted of vodka shooters and weed. Even though she'd been drinking nothing but soda, she felt drunk on his attention.

Ellory retouched her hair and makeup in an upstairs bedroom, her skin slick with sweat. There was a vanity mirror here, plus a desk that was laden with abandoned beer cans, makeup-remover wipes, and a snapped nail file from those who had used the room before her. Under the lights, her dark skin glowed and the bags beneath her eyes looked deeper, like gathered shadows at the bottom of lit basement stairs. She should have gotten Farrah Mayhew's number before she'd left, or at least asked her more questions. Maybe she could get her info from Liam on their way home, but that might invite unwanted questions.

She blotted her lipstick with a tissue, frowning into the mirror. Or maybe she could demand answers from Hudson, since he'd already done her work for her.

It always came down to Hudson Graves in the end.

Ellory nodded a greeting as she passed another woman stumbling in with a mascara wand held aloft. But she had taken only two steps when a sudden flurry of cool air through the hallway drew her into another room. This open bedroom was dark and sparsely decorated, but sheer curtains ruffled in the same breeze that offered her scant relief from the heat of the party. She should have gone back downstairs—where she'd left Liam in the kitchen playing bartender, even though the only mixed drink in his repertoire was a rum and coke—but she felt like a cartoon animal following a scent trail to a freshly baked pie on a windowsill. There was nowhere to go but forward. There was nothing to see but what lay at the end of that trail.

Hudson Graves glanced back at her from a balcony railing.

"Of course," they said as one.

With his back against the handrail, his face was cast in shadow and impossible to read. The sky was the silver blue of a swordfish, stars like spilled glitter across the dark. This hidden balcony was barely large enough for three men of Hudson's size, but it was perfect for the two of them; she placed her hands on the railing with almost enough room between them to open an umbrella. Out here, the music was muted, and the night was cold. Hudson smelled of lager and shea, with the underlying musk of long-dried sweat. The glass door occasionally rattled, but a pleased sigh fell from Ellory's lips as the chill wrapped around her sweaty body.

Somewhere, she heard the sharp cry of an owl.

"There are owls on campus?" she asked almost without meaning to. Trees crept like burglars toward the fraternity, trapped beyond the white-gold circle of the porch lights, but everyone else was inside. Her shoulders tightened. "Is this frat part of—"

"I've been to parties here before, and I've never seen anything strange," said Hudson, before she could work herself into a panic. "I think there have always been owls by Warren. Owls and crows. Hummingbirds and robins."

Releasing a slow, meditative breath, Ellory chanced a look at him. Beneath his peacoat, he wore a mint-green collared shirt beneath a black sweatshirt with the Capricorn constellation in gold on the front. Under it were the words AMBITIOUS, RELIABLE, and HONEST. He'd paired it with herringbone slacks in a shade of paper-bag brown. He looked like he'd been on his way to a poetry reading and instead stumbled into this frat party. She half expected him to have brought a book.

When her gaze returned to Hudson's face, she caught him studying her outfit with mild amusement. She curved her body toward him, her hip against the railing, and raised her eyebrows challengingly. "Enjoying the party?"

"I needed a break," he said. He lifted a Keystone Light to his lips, throat bobbing as he emptied the can. Then he pitched it through the narrow crack in the glass door, where it clattered somewhere out of view. "Enjoying your date?"

She turned back to the empty yard. "I needed a break, too."

Hudson made an understanding noise, which took away some of her shame at the admission. She'd spent the whole night feeling like she wasn't having *enough* fun, going through the motions of a part she was the understudy for. If she'd asked, Liam would have been happy to leave with her, and maybe that was why she hadn't asked. He was making the effort to draw her into his world, while she hadn't even let him set foot in her dorm. Sometimes, the curve of his smile made her stomach swoop like she was at the apex of a roller coaster. Sometimes, it felt like she was just passing the time until they both got bored.

But Hudson didn't need to know that.

"I met Farrah Mayhew downstairs," Ellory said. "She said you'd talked to her about her uncle Malcolm."

"Are we just going to ignore how we left things, then?"

Ellory had never thought of Hudson Graves as awkward, but a muscle in his jaw ticked as they fell into silence. It was like he was unsure what to say to her when they weren't at each other's throats. There was something impossibly endearing about it. She couldn't tell how much he'd had to drink, but it had clearly taken a hammer to those walls he lived behind. He was an exposed hermit crab, and she felt, suddenly, that she could either watch him die or build a new protective shell around the softness he was showing her.

His hands were in the pockets of his coat, his face turned away, but she could feel him watching her in his peripheral vision. Waiting for what she would do next.

Most of the time, she existed in a state of rage, some of it directed at him. After she'd gotten over her hurt, she'd felt a certain relief at having a concrete excuse to push him away. No part of her school year had been normal, but he made her volatile, until not even she knew what her next move would be. It was exhilarating, but it was also exhausting.

She was tired of feeling angry. At him, anyway.

"I shouldn't have said some of those things," Ellory admitted. "But I meant others. I need to be able to trust you, Graves. I'm already questioning everything. I don't want to question this."

A light flashed in the gloom. Hudson pulled his phone from his pocket, the screen facing her. She caught the name—CAIRO—before he squinted down at it, frowned, and let it ring out. "I know Liam told you. About my brother."

"He told me that you *have* a brother," Ellory corrected.

"Cairo's older by six years. I'm the only member of the family he still speaks to, and even then, barely." He returned his phone to his pocket. The curtains swayed back and forth, shifting the chiaroscuro of his face. That muscle ticked again, like he was uncertain how much he wanted to tell her but certain he wanted to be heard. Ellory held her breath, held perfectly still. Then: "I don't blame him. If I could get away from us, I'd do it in a heartbeat."

"Yeah?" Ellory said, instead of *I'm sorry*. "Are they all as bad as you?"

Hudson chuckled at that, though it was a low and bitter sound. "Worse."

He sank to the floor, his back still against the railing, his legs sprawled before him. Ellory almost joined him, but she assumed it was the cover of darkness and the illusion of privacy that had him baring his soul. She didn't want to take those security blankets away.

"The first time I did magic, I was nine, I think…" he said without looking at her. "My father is a cruel man. His standards aren't simply exacting; they're impossible. Cairo and I are his living legacies, so he's harder on us than anyone else. And when my mother stood up for us, they would have fights. Vicious, brutal fights that lasted for days. Weeks. One week, I just…lost it."

Ellory could see the picture his words painted, of a little boy in a little suit—for she couldn't imagine Hudson Graves in anything else—pressed against the wall behind his mother as his parents tore into each other with a violence at odds with their opulent surroundings. The swirling guilt and rage and fear consolidating into a desire for the fighting to stop. Cataclysmic magic that reverberated through his body, shattering the windows and drawing his wary brother from the bedroom down the hall. Standing there with glass shards at his feet and his heart beating out his chest and blood leaving narrow rivulets between his nose and lips.

And then darkness.

Her vision felt familiar, felt *right*. Like a kinship she had always felt between them had revealed its thick roots, and now something powerful could grow.

"When I woke up, they said I had imagined it. I could barely remember anything, so it was easy to believe all these years. Coincidences could be explained away. This strange awareness I have, this pull toward the inexplicable, that was just my personality. But when you came to me, when I started helping you, I didn't just want answers for you. I wanted answers for myself. I just had to go home to get them."

Ellory glanced down at him. "You went home?"

"Well, if I had magic, then I must have always had it, right? If I couldn't trust my memories, I wanted to go through the family records. So I confronted my parents and—and it's true. My father, my brother, and I can all do magic. And they've known since I was *nine*." Another bleak laugh shattered his composure. "The worst part of it is that I suspected that something changed that year. There was a shift in the way my father looked at us, treated us. Everything got worse." Hudson's hand tore through his platinum curls. "Sometimes, I wish he hated us. It would have been easier than squeezing droplets of affection from a riverbed gone dry."

The remnants of his story faded into the night, leaving the air thick with vulnerability. Familiarity shivered through Ellory's body again, as if she'd heard this before. She had never met Hudson's father, and yet she could almost picture a stern white man with his son's dark eyes, demanding and detached. The ensuing silence threatened to choke all the life from this moment, silence in which Hudson could put himself back together and regret everything he'd shared.

Ellory's shoulders curled in on each other as she opened a wound of her own. "I get that. I—to be cruel, my parents would have to be present. Since they sent me here, I've spoken to them a handful of times, and every time they say they love me. I *know* they love me. I just wish—"

"That it mattered."

"That it mattered," she confirmed in a whisper. "But I don't even feel it."

"I get that." The echo of her words from his lips made another shiver run through her. His head tipped back, *thunk*ing against the balustrade. "I shouldn't have told you any of that. I must be drunker than I thought."

"You shouldn't have hidden the magic thing from me in the first place. I would have understood. I would have believed you. As for the rest…I won't tell anyone about your family. We all have things we don't say out loud." Carefully, Ellory sank down beside him. Their thighs brushed. "Is everything all right? No offense, but you don't strike me as the kind of guy to drink to excess. Too uptight."

Hudson snorted. "I'm not uptight."

"You're wearing a button-down to a frat party."

"I like this button-down."

"Graves."

"I'm *tired*, Morgan," he gritted out, gaze on the remote sky. "Of all of it. The pageantry and the exams and the fucking *rot* of this place. Magic is real, and yet, every day, we march a little closer to death, wasting hours and hours performing for people who will never give a shit about us. Who will lie to and use and discard us. I'm tired of it." She couldn't be sure in the dark, but his eyes seemed brighter than usual. "If my family had magic at their fingertips all this time, then *anyone* could, and we wouldn't even *remember*. But with Cairo gone, I'm the one thing keeping my family together. I'm our only chance. Even with my faith in them shattered, I can't live down the disappointment in my father's eyes. I won't. Fuck this, but fuck him most of all."

Hudson's breath caught. Ellory had closed her hand around his, and even with the full force of his attention on that, she couldn't bring herself to let go. He'd gone as still as a startled rabbit, like he'd forgotten they were real people with real limbs. His eyes found hers, so wide that their whites were like moons in a penumbral eclipse. She looked back steadily, searchingly.

"Would it be so bad," she murmured, "if we *actually* tried being on the same side for a while?"

"No," he whispered back, "I guess it wouldn't."

His fingers slid between hers. Their palms kissed. Ellory studied the shadows gathered at the other end of the balcony, because if she thought too much about what she was doing, what they were doing, she would have to put a stop to it.

"I'm tired, too," she said. "Going here feels like everyone was born with boats, while I'm only just learning to swim. The great lie of higher education is that getting a degree—hell, getting as many degrees as you can—is the only way to be successful. My aunt's bought into it. My parents have bought into it. And here I am, killing myself for a piece of paper in the hopes of getting a job I don't even want." It burned to admit it, but he was burning with her. Their truths would keep them warm. "I don't even want to be rich. I want to be happy. That's what success means to me. But I just don't know any other way to get there."

"I imagine it's a lot easier without some arrogant rich guy mocking you in your classes," said Hudson, thumb tracing her skin in a comforting glide.

Ellory was surprised into laughing. "God, you were such a *dick*. Are you going to finally tell me why you hate me so much?"

"I don't hate you, Morgan. I just had no reason to like you."

"And now?"

"You're fine." A smile tugged at his lips. "I'm only slightly indifferent."

"Careful. I might swoon."

It felt good, to share a laugh with him, like they were inching toward something that had been inevitable from the start. His gaze fell to her mouth, tracked the path of her tongue as it wet her lower lip. Her lashes dipped to half-mast, the rest of her senses roaring to awareness. His scent, shea butter and bergamot. His touch, smooth, warm skin wrapped protectively around her hand. His eyes, an endless sacred darkness focused wholly on her. She could hear his every shaky breath, feel how much he wanted her in the quiet between each one, and the night around them tightened in anticipation.

She could imagine perfectly, what it would be like to kiss him, the softness of his lips contrasting with the scratch of his stubble. He'd hold her just shy of too tight, fingers leaving bruising marks across her dark skin that she would fit her own fingers to for days afterward, heat pooling between her thighs every time she remembered this moment. They would devour each other if they could, her body hungering for him in a way she'd never felt for anyone before. She would even let him take her right here, on a semipublic balcony, her jeans dangling from one ankle as she rode him against the railing with only the stars to witness. His teeth set in her shoulder. Her hands shoved beneath his shirts. Their primal cries of pleasure.

It felt like salvation.

It felt like a memory.

"I miss you all the damn time," Hudson whispered. His words sounded like they encompassed so much more than their recent time apart. Her chest ached with every tender breath. "I miss you so much, it ruins me."

"What if you don't remember? What if you never do?"

"You'll remind me." She turned into the darkness, her hands cupping a face she knew as well as her own. Stubble scratched her fingertips as she tipped his jaw up until their gazes locked. "Hey, you trust me, don't you? Try trusting yourself."

He snorted. "Myself? I was a monster before I met you."

"Finally, you admit it." She waited until she saw a reluctant smile on that sharp mouth. Then her expression sobered, because she needed him; this wouldn't work without him, without both of them together, even when they weren't. *"But you're not that guy anymore. I trust you. We can end this."*

"Okay," he sighed. He turned his head, pressing a kiss to the inside of her wrist. *"I... Okay."*

Inside, glass broke, and someone swore just loud enough for Ellory to hear. The music paused briefly, then roared back in, disinterested in whatever chaos it was burying. Whatever that—vision, memory?—was, the details fled on the wind like a kaleidoscope of startled butterflies.

Ellory slid her hand free. It felt cold. "I should get back to Liam."

"Have fun," Hudson said evenly.

Something about his voice made Ellory want to snatch the words back, to linger in this little world, but the moment was over. It was enough to end on a truce, their weapons lowered so they could both live to fight another day. Besides, *if* anything happened between them, it would not be on the balcony at a party she had come to on a date with another man. Her hunger could not be sated at the funeral of her morals.

Shame heated her cheeks as she mumbled a goodbye. When she dared to take one last look, Hudson was sitting in the same spot, half hidden by the curtains, his hand curled in the space she'd occupied, his eyes on the stars.

25

LIAM DROVE HER BACK TO Moneta in a silence broken only by the radio. Ellory had returned to the party but not to Liam, vacillating between emotions she wanted to sort before she hurt anyone but herself. Away from the lure of Hudson's siren eyes, she was faced with the cold reality that her imagined tryst with Hudson had filled her with more passion than a single kiss from Liam. She yearned to be upstairs with him but hid in the living room until Liam found her instead.

Even under the haze of inebriation, Liam recognized the shift in her mood. After the first time she pulled away from his searching hands, he didn't reach for her again. He'd sobered up with some food and water before asking if she was ready to leave, and he didn't seem to mind that Ellory couldn't look at him.

Louis Armstrong and Ella Fitzgerald crooned "Can't We Be Friends." She wondered if he'd chosen this song on purpose.

They eased to a stop in front of Moneta Hall. The jubilation of a frat party extended even here, where students milled out front, their laughter ringing through the air. Windows glowed on every floor, rooms alight with activity. Louis and Ella had moved on to singing about a lovely day for two people together despite the storm. Ellory stared into the rearview mirror, took in her flushed face and guilty eyes, and told herself to stop being a coward.

"Liam—"

"I know," he said without looking up from the steering wheel. "You want to break up. Or I guess stop doing whatever we're doing, since there's nothing to break."

Ellory's shoulders slumped. "Yeah."

Liam turned down the radio, until the jazz legends' voices were reduced to a low hum. His hands gripped the wheel until his knuckles blanched, his shoulder muscles tight beneath his shirt. It was rare not to see a smile on his face, and the lack of one now made Ellory's stomach swirl with guilt.

"I can tell when someone isn't into me," he continued, visibly relaxing inch by reluctant inch. "You were hard to read sometimes, but I could sense that you were losing interest. I guess I just hoped you might change your mind, since you hadn't ended things yet."

"I hoped I would change my mind, too."

He pressed his forehead against the back of his hands so she could no longer see his expression, only the bounce of his dirty-blond hair as it fell over his forehead. Part of her was glad, because she no longer had any right to his raw emotions. The rest of her was just exhausted.

After this, she was not having any more hard conversations in people's cars. It was claustrophobic, to be trapped in a vehicle with the consequences of her actions.

Liam's throat bobbed. "It's Hudson, isn't it? You have feelings for him."

Ellory didn't deny it. She couldn't. The guilt was thick enough to choke her.

"He's a great guy," said Liam, quietly. "He tries to act like he's not, but he's got a big heart. I think the two of you would be good together, in case you're worried." He lifted his head, and his expression had smoothed into something so falsely amiable that Ellory couldn't look at him anymore. She stared out at the quad until she heard him clear his throat. "I don't want you to think I'm taking this well because I didn't like you. I really fucking like you, Ellory."

"I know," she said miserably.

"I'm glad you ended it before...before it got messier. I deserve to be with someone who likes me best, you know? And so do you. Even if it's not me. I just..."

Ellory longed to touch her forehead to the cool glass, in the hopes that the chill would chase away the burning in her tear ducts. She longed to escape this car, in the hopes that racing to her dorm would put all this awkwardness behind them. She longed for the feelings she'd hoped would grow for him, because it would be easier to feel the same way, and she could do with a little ease in this school year.

Instead, she whispered, "You just what?"

"I just," Liam continued apologetically, "wish that someone would choose me back. At least once."

Her heart felt like it had ruptured. *I want it to be you*, she didn't say. Hudson Graves was rude and superior. He ran lava hot and tundra cold. His mind and tongue were weapons, and he often made her feel so incensed that she wanted to throttle him. And none of it, not one substantial personality flaw, mattered when she was with him. All she wanted was to be the focus of his severe attention. All she wanted was to be close to the fire that burned deep within those cold brown eyes. All she wanted was to be shielded by his protective fury, inspired by his sharp intelligence, held by his surprisingly gentle hands.

On paper, Liam Blackwood was perfect. In practice, Hudson Graves was perfect for her.

Ellory stared down at her lap. "What happened between you and Farrah Mayhew? I met her at the party, and it seemed like... I don't know. She speaks highly of you."

"She broke up with me," Liam said. There was an unspoken story behind those words, but Ellory didn't pry. She didn't have a right, after all. "We still see each other sometimes, but it's—I don't go where I'm not welcome."

"I hate to be so cliché, but I really do hope we can be friends." Ellory picked at a loose thread on her jeans. "I like you, Liam. I like spending time with you. I'm sorry I didn't realize what kind of feelings I had sooner, but I don't want to lose you entirely. If you're ever up for it. It's okay if you aren't."

A pale hand covered hers. She glanced up to find Liam watching her, his fawn-brown eyes gentle. There was pain there, but there was affection, too. The warmth of his touch was not the thunderous crackle of a lightning bolt but the comforting heat from a fireplace in the deepest winter.

"We'll be all right, Ellory," he whispered. "I'll need some time, but...yeah, I think I'd be up for that. Someone has to call you out on your incorrect Sherlock Holmes opinions."

She smiled, only slightly hesitant, and he managed to smile back. When his expression began to tremble, she knew she had overstayed her welcome. Liam withdrew his hand, and Ellory climbed out of the car. The wind numbed her ears, her stomach. Liam waved, and Ellory waved back, and with that, he was gone.

Her first college relationship was over with less fanfare than a daily weather report.

Liam's car disappeared around the corner.

It's Hudson, isn't it? You have feelings for him.

Ellory buried her face in her hands, fighting the urge to cry as if she were the one who had gotten her heart broken.

26

Ellory had expected Hudson's liquid courage to cause morning regrets, but she woke up to a text from him complaining about the brightness of the sun and warning her to take ibuprofen before attempting to do a single thing.

> **graves:** that voice telling you to get out of bed without it is the devil talking

Unlike some people, she texted back, I have an early shift today so I didn't get drunk.

Her reciprocation forged a tentative new connection between them, in which it became common for her phone to flash with his name. Not as often as Liam's golden texts had come, but often enough that Ellory began to look forward to them. There was a freedom to Hudson over text that was absent when she saw him in person. He was a fountain of darkly funny one-liners that made Ellory giggle in between the helpful links and random questions he sent over the course of the next week.

It made her feelings both harder and easier to ignore.

"I go on runs here," Hudson said dubiously when he met her on Riverside Campus. Since she had no way of knowing what would happen, she'd told him to dress in his favorite clothes, clothes he considered so innate to his personal style that they were practically a part of him. He had translated that to mean the same peacoat, that obnoxious yellow sweater, and a pair of frayed jeans she'd never seen before. Somehow, he looked incredible. "The paths are straightforward. How did you possibly get lost?"

"Magic," Ellory deadpanned. "Which is why we're here."

The orchard was too far. The Graves was too haunted. And the quad—Ellory had altered her path to her classes to avoid that stretch of grass for weeks. Riverside Campus, prismatic and desolate in the November cold, was perfect for her third attempt to cast magic intentionally. The trees, those that still had leaves to brag about, had gone scarlet and butterscotch, lime and amber. Sunlight rippled through the canopy, painting the foliage with buttery light. The babble of the Connecticut River was as peaceful as a lullaby. After a stormy few days, this clear morning was rife with magical potential.

It had been only natural to demand Hudson work with her. If she was bargaining parts of herself for power, she wanted someone who would criticize what she'd given away. Someone who would remember what she'd lost and perhaps complain until she found a way to regain it.

hudson will hǝlp

Her note to herself had been right, that day. Instinctively, she was drawn to him instead of Tai and Cody, and that had to mean something. There was a difference between a crush—the butterflies and obsession, the confirmation bias of every interaction—and her thorny feelings for Hudson. The high highs and low lows could not explain how badly she wanted to know and be known by him, to be liked, to be *wanted*. This craving was like no crush she had ever felt.

Hudson made a face at the mud lingering from the rain. "Your logic is sound, but your taste continues to be questionable, Morgan. I know a better place than this."

Baffled by her own taste, Ellory rolled her eyes. "I hope it's a better place to hide a body, because I plan to leave yours there."

"It's always nice to have goals," Hudson said archly. "Follow me."

He led her down a quiet running trail, occasionally peppered by a dog walker or a sweatband-wearing athlete, and through a thicket of trees reduced to nothing but knotted branches. He moved with the confidence of someone who had been to this area many times before, the same confidence that had flooded her that rainy night she'd been lost in these woods. She stifled a ridiculous urge to ask him if they'd come here together before. Hiking with her once nemesis wasn't something she'd just forget.

"Here we are," Hudson said. "Better, right?"

They were in a clearing, the yellow grass feathered with multicolored leaves. The Connecticut River was louder here, like they were near a small waterfall, and there was a pond near the right side that had a single duck cutting across its rippling surface. Its black wings were tucked tight to its brown body, its green-and-black head turned away. The sky was framed by golden-red trees, thin clouds ambling across a cerulean blanket.

Ellory didn't realize how much stress she'd been carrying until her shoulders dipped, free from the weight of it all. "All right. I'll let you have this one."

She spread the blanket she had brought a few feet from the lake, then sat cross-legged atop it. As good as the sun felt on her skin, it wasn't enough to settle her stomach or her mind. Hudson gingerly sat down next to her, gaze expectant, and trying to seem competent was taking more energy out of Ellory than any spell had.

"I want to try divination," she said, tugging her almost-full notebook out of her bag. After twice leaving her phone behind, she had made it her new go-to for portable notes. "After the party, I realized I've done two of the three. I can restore Bancroft Field, and I can summon the Graves Ghost, but I haven't tried reading the future or anything."

"Divination isn't just about the future. You tried to summon the Graves Ghost, but instead you divined what really happened the night he died." Hudson took her notebook, flipping through the pages until he found her badly drawn replica of the summoning circle and her hastily scrawled description of all that had happened afterward. "He didn't appear to you until he was already dead...again. So I'm not sure that counts as evocation."

Ellory frowned at her own notes, feeling like she was missing something. Malcolm Mayhew wasn't the first ghost to appear to her without answering her questions. Death had followed her all her life—from Miss Claudette to the Lost Eight—and she felt, instinctively, that she had a unique talent for drawing the deceased to her. If there were only three forms of magic, then what she had done and seen defied categorization. Her frown deepened. Even in this, she didn't belong.

"Let's try it anyway," she decided, retrieving the book and spreading it out in front of her. "I'm not changing my plans based on your guesses."

"I'll go first. I want—can I go first?"

Even before he glanced hesitantly her way, his tone made her answer easy: "Of course."

Hudson closed his eyes and took a breath. "Who's hunting Morgan? Tell us where to look, where to start."

Ellory was glad he couldn't see her so she could manage her surprise that this was the first of his questions. She would have thought he would want confirmation that Boone was innocent of what they suspected or more information about what else his family was hiding from him. Hudson using his magic to protect her—again—made her stomach flutter.

Wind whistled through the clearing, lifting her braids off her shoulders. The clouds moved no quicker, but leaves shot across the ground in swirls of color. A frog leaped into the water, its protruding eyes the only visible sign that it was there. Ellory could no longer see the duck at all, even though she didn't think she'd seen it fly off.

Hudson's lids flickered like he was having a bad dream. His lips parted, but no sound came out. His hands had curled where they rested on the blanket, his fingers like claws against some imaginary attacker.

"Hey," said Ellory, "are you all right?"

She touched his shoulder and gasped.

Night fell. Lightning flashed across the violet sky, surrounded by spidery branches torn free of leaves. The woods were pitch-black in between lightning strikes, and there—in the flare of illumination—figures stood as still as the trees around them. Everywhere Ellory looked were unfamiliar faces, their eyes gleaming in the unnatural light. Every time she caught one, their heads decayed like corpses. Skin bloated and then sagged. Nostrils leaked purge fluid that, even from here, smelled like death. Maggots crawled from blackening eye sockets. She could barely pick out any defining features before they were gone.

The few remaining faces were ones she didn't recognize.

Except one.

Except Preston Colt.

The professor stood between two trees that leaned against each other like lovers, his hands in the pockets of his tweed suit. She recognized his salt-and-pepper beard, his jaunty pocket square, but she didn't recognize the expression on his face. With every flash of lightning, his skin turned translucent, revealing a hollow-eyed skull with bared teeth on the left side of his face. His right side remained opaque, wearing a half smile that felt drawn with cruelty.

Ellory eased onto her knees. "Professor?"

Someone screamed so loudly, her word was drowned out. More people had appeared in the clearing, these ones visible even without the glow of the lightning. Four men and four women—none older than their midtwenties, all of them noticeably people of color—circled a blanket, holding hands.

Eight strangers.

Eight young adults.

The Lost Eight.

The sound had come from one of the men, perhaps Manuel Sharp, whose throat widened in a river of red that soaked into his denim jacket and gray turtleneck. To his right, a woman who might have been Olivia Holloway screamed as her skin burned, from brown to pink to white to black and flaking. Then the next person and the next person and the next person, dying in some horrific way before her, shrieking at the top of their lungs as they did, until all she could hear, all she could see, were these people who could have been her classmates suffering in ways she could never have imagined.

A single phrase cut through the cacophony, like a lightning strike of its own: *"Wake up. Wake up! WAKE UP!"*

"Stop it," Ellory whispered. Then, louder, clapping her hands over her ears: *"STOP IT!"*

The vision faded with a final echoing scream. Sunlight momentarily blinded her, and the rush of the Connecticut River returned in place of the lightning. Ellory rubbed her eyes, damp with tears, but, when she could see again, Riverside Campus had returned to normal. Even the frog and duck were back, casually moving around each other in the pond.

Her breath tore from her chest, and her head throbbed, and she knew what was about to happen if she wasn't quick enough.

"Did you see—"

Ellory ignored Hudson to dive for the notebook, scratching a quick summary of everything as gaps began to appear in her memory. Hudson realized what she was doing and freed a pen from his bag, taking the next page, writing down what he had seen. Between the two of them, they painted a complete picture of a nighttime meeting, of decaying corpses, of unknown figures who couldn't—shouldn't—have been there.

She stopped writing only when her headache eased, dropping her pencil from shaking fingers. She'd expected for the entire vision to be gone, but she could still remember what she had written. The decaying corpses and the screaming victims. Professor Colt and a salon of minorities dying before him. Her stomach twisted with revulsion and fear. If that memory hadn't been taken, which one *had*?

Hudson stared blankly at his own handwriting. "I don't remember any of this."

"Don't worry," Ellory said, swallowing the urge to vomit into the grass. "I have it. I just don't know what I *don't* have." It was unsettling, but she didn't want to linger on it. Not now. Not when she'd done magic, intentionally, for the *third time*. She couldn't miss what she didn't remember, but she could move forward. She had to move forward, before that vision drove her mad. "I saw Professor Colt. If those were the Old Masters, then—"

"Fuck." Hudson pressed the meat of his palms against his eyelids. "Is anyone we know not suspicious as hell?"

"He *was* at the orchard. How well do you know him?"

"As well as any student. My parents would probably know more." He dropped his hands, squinting down at the notebook again. "This really happened? I don't remember—"

"Welcome to my life since August," said Ellory, climbing to her feet. Her legs nearly collapsed beneath her but, thankfully, decided to hold her weight at the last minute. "You talk to your family. I'm going to do more research into the Lost Eight. I think they have something to tell me."

27

THE DAY OF PROFESSOR COLT'S next salon, she didn't hear from Hudson at all. After the fifth unanswered text, she realized she was running out of time to get ready and frowned her way to the shower, hoping—in vain—that something would be waiting for her when she got back. The idea of going alone disoriented her almost as much as the flash of Colt among the trees, a warning she wasn't entirely sure she could afford to believe. After all, a recommendation from the sexagenarian professor could set her up for life.

Still, she packed her pepper spray and her Taser just in case; they were more reliable than magic. Then she tried Hudson one more time before calling an Uber. His robotic voicemail informed her that his inbox was full.

Professor Colt's face lit up when he saw her at the door. He'd chosen a tweed suit with an orange pocket square that made it look as if he were wearing the foliage around them. His eyes were the blue gray of the winter sky, and his beard had been shaved down to stubble that outlined his square jaw in silver and blond.

It was so much like her vision that she almost fled, except she could hear the other members of the salon behind him, people who wouldn't spit on her if she were on fire, and she was struck with a sudden unfairness that they were inside and she was not.

She needed this. Needed Colt. If he was hunting her, she would have to make herself harder to hunt.

"I was beginning to think you wouldn't be joining us," Colt said. "Mister Graves hasn't arrived."

"He might not be coming at all. Can I—"

"Of course, my dear. It's a pleasure to have you, with or without Mr. Graves. Come in, come in."

Ellory could tell that he meant it, but she couldn't tell *why* he meant it. Her fingers itched to ring Hudson one more time, but he already had an abundance of messages and a missed call. Not even Aunt Carol would try that many times; she would already be halfway to Hartford after three messages at most. Boone must have taken his phone again.

Hopefully.

Ellory willed herself to think about nothing but the salon; it felt like a spotlight was on her, an unaccompanied interloper in a space that had been carved out for people older, richer, more talented. The rest of Colt's guests were gathered near the fireplace, which was currently lit. The orange and yellow flames cast the room in warm tones that made it feel all the more inviting.

"Where's Graves?" asked Duncan Something-or-Other. "Did he finally get tossed out?"

"And replaced by her?" Kendall Rhodes frowned. "I doubt it."

"Maybe she killed him," said Sofia Aston. "There was this weird tension between them last month."

Ellory bit the inside of her cheek to keep from reminding them all that she was standing right here. They knew that. They were enjoying it, in fact. Ellory had met people like this in high school, who fed on negative attention. Ignoring them never solved the problem, but it felt good to turn her back on them to stare out the window instead.

Colt joined her, smiling. His mustard suit made him look like a golden emperor, but she saw no trace of the malevolence that had been so evident in the clearing. "The gardener overseeds her every autumn," he said, jutting his chin toward the yard. "There's not much to be done about the trees short of replanting them, but I do so hate dead things."

"You could replace them with evergreens," said Ellory, wondering if the school groundskeepers would claim overseeding to explain the abrupt change in Bancroft Field. "Junipers and spruces, maybe."

"Too festive, for me. But I'll bear that in mind."

If he found it absurd to be standing here, talking to her about tree species while his regular salon attendees whispered poison behind them, it didn't show in the lines of his face. Should she ask him about the Old Masters directly, or would that only get her killed? Was this salon part of the recruitment effort, or would his guests be shocked if he killed her before them and buried her underneath his dead trees? Ellory tried to slide her trembling hands into her pockets before remembering that, unlike her coat, this dress didn't have any. She twisted her fingers in the folds of the skirt instead.

"So Hudson didn't tell you he couldn't make it?" she asked, finally turning away from the view.

"He rarely does," said Colt, unbothered. "These salons are difficult for him. The rest of the group envies him in many ways. They think he's my favorite."

"Well, is he?"

Colt's smile widened. "It would hardly be appropriate for me to play favorites, Miss Morgan. I've done this too many years for that. But I do see a lot of myself in him, more so than I do in Kendall, Duncan, Sofia, Quentin, Miles, Percy, or Gaia."

It took Ellory a moment to realize that Gaia was the girl she'd thought was named Greer. "How so?"

"I choose my cohort based on talent, potential, and, I'll admit, connections. Talent is something many people are born with. They may cultivate it, but they may also take it for granted. Connections, as I'm sure I don't need to tell you, grease the wheels of this world. Knowing the right people at the right time offers the kind of protection that not even money can buy. But potential...it can be hard to find students who aim to reach their full potential. Mister Graves is one of two, in the entire time I've been hosting these." Colt rubbed at his bare chin, shaved so closely that she could hardly see the silver of his stubble. "He's never been content to coast on his talent. He reads ahead. He asks questions. He has a hunger in him that appeals to me as an educator. He will do great things, and I want to be a part of his journey." A wry laugh escaped him. "Perhaps I *am* playing favorites."

"No, I think you're right," Ellory said carefully. "I've always... seen that in him."

"I see that in you as well," said Colt. "Mister Graves can be very withdrawn, so I was surprised when he brought a guest at all. But in the short time I've known you, I see your similarities. Have you considered—"

"Professor," said Gaia-Not-Greer, appearing between them with a look of strained politeness. Her blond hair was pulled up into a messy bun, which made her look like she should have been teaching classes herself. "Can you come and settle something between Sofia and me?" Her blue eyes cut in Ellory's direction. "You don't mind if I borrow Colt, do you, Morgan?"

"Not at all—"

But Gaia was already dragging the professor away, leaving Ellory alone by the windows. The whispering on the other side of the room grew louder, interrupted by performative laughter that sent a clear message. The setting sun looked like the glowing eye of a monster, waiting for her to fail.

Ellory took a deep breath and braced herself for a nightmarish evening without Hudson as her shield.

◆

Dinner had a Southeast Asian influence: pancit miki bihon, which blended egg noodles and rice-stick noodles, shredded cabbage and stripped carrots, shredded chicken and chicharrones; skirt steak skewers with caramelized marinade and a side of nước chấm; tofu pad thai, the rice noodles flavored with sweet-and-sour sauce; Cambodian chicken and rice soup garnished with a lime wedge and garlic cloves.

Ellory forwent the wine in favor of water, letting the conversation wash over her instead of contributing. She didn't want to be drunk around these people normally, but she especially didn't want to be drunk around people who might want her dead. Her phone was in her lap, the screen remaining dark as the night wore on. At one point, Miles tried to press her for information about Hudson's whereabouts, his eyes narrowing when she told him she didn't have any.

"Then why did you come?" he asked. "Not that you're not welcome. It's just a little strange, don't you think?"

Ellory lifted her eyebrows. "You seem to have a lot of thoughts you want to share."

"The rest of us busted our asses to get chosen by Professor Colt for this year's salon," said Miles, leaning forward so that she could smell the rosé on his breath. He wore a silver tie that stroked her arm as he invaded her space. "And you just, what, slept your way in? It's not fair."

It wasn't fair that Miles's grandfather had possessed a billion dollars in start-up money to loan to his father. It wasn't fair that Miles's father could still oppose things like the Godwin Scholarship for elevating disadvantaged students into spaces like this. It wasn't fair that Miles could look at her and assume she could have gotten here only on her back—and that he would look down on that when he didn't seem to have anything that wasn't handed to him thanks to an accident of birth. At least if she had slept her way into the salon, she would have *worked* for it. Miles dripped with the egotism of a man who had never struggled and never would.

"Leave her alone," said an unfamiliar voice on her other side. Percy, the quiet one, didn't lift his gaze from his plate, but his mouth was twisted into a scowl. "That's so fucking sexist, man."

Miles snorted. "I'm just saying what the rest of you are thinking."

"I'm thinking you're an asshole, actually," Sofia, sitting on Miles's left, chimed in. "And that you're probably projecting. Which of your professors are you sleeping with to have the grades to be here?"

Miles's suntanned cheeks grew dark with an angry flush. He drained his wineglass, glancing quickly at Colt to make sure he was still buried in conversation with Kendall. When he spoke, it was acidic. "And why are you here, Aston? Didn't your family go bankrupt in the last hospitality crash?"

Sofia rolled her eyes. "I can't believe I ever dated you."

While Sofia and Miles argued over who was to blame for their breakup, Ellory loosened her grip around her fork. Her nails hadn't broken the skin of her palm...this time. She wanted to be angry at Hudson for leaving her to suffer these people alone, but she had chosen to come, despite everything. She was choosing to stay, in the hopes that all this would be worth it, and she was choosing to bite her tongue so as not to come across as the belligerent one. But Miles's accusation did more than make her feel small. It made her feel like the basest sum of her sexual parts, worth nothing in his eyes but what was between her legs. Her mind, her personality, her appearance—those things could not possibly have charmed Hudson. No, they had to have fucked.

It made her ashamed of every time she'd ever been aroused in Hudson Graves's presence, and who was Miles to have that kind of control over her thoughts?

Carefully, she set her fork down on the table before she stabbed him in the thigh with it. She had been so focused on the dangers of magic that she had forgotten the everyday danger of a man who thought his money made him worthy of having stupid opinions.

Dinner wrapped up soon after. Ellory helped Colt's cook clear the plates, mostly so she didn't have to risk walking out with the rest of the group. Her thoughts were a tangled wasp's nest, buzzing with her anger, and she was afraid of what she might say to them. By comparison, Colt—who had yet to do anything to her that she could prove—seemed like the lesser evil.

"I was hoping I could catch you alone," he said, stepping back into the dining room. The table was clear between them. He rested his hands on the back of his chair. "I have an unusual proposal for you, if it's of interest."

"Okay..." Ellory's hand hovering near her bag and the pepper spray concealed within.

"The spring semester will be here before you know it. I've looked into your transcript. Your grades are impressive, even more so given you successfully juggle your coursework with your work-study. If it wouldn't be too much for your schedule, I'd like to take you on as a student assistant for my research next term."

Ellory blinked, all thoughts of sinister secret societies and overt misogyny forgotten. "Me? But—I'm just a freshman."

"You're hardworking and reliable. You manage strong personalities with an unexpected grace. And, according to your professors, you already show a strong grasp of political theory. You're one of the most engaged students in your classes." Colt glanced toward the hallway. "I know you had some sort of disagreement with the others at dinner, but I hope you won't let what one or two students think of you stop you from considering my offer. It's unorthodox, but I do feel you're the right person for the job."

"I—I'd love to." The agreement could not come out of her mouth fast enough. It wasn't exactly a recommendation, but it was an opportunity. She would have the same access to him that she did to Boone on the *Communiqué*, a path to information she couldn't get otherwise. If he was innocent, it would look good on her résumé. If he wasn't, as she increasingly suspected, she could keep an eye on him, even *stop* him, from the heart of his own research lab. "What sort of work is it?"

"I'll send you all the details so you can make an informed decision. But I typically spend my fall term teaching and my spring term doing field research with around four or five student assistants. However many my grant will allow. You'll be the first."

Ellory swallowed past the lump in her throat, unsure if the

sudden onset of tears was because of the stress of the night, the emotional whiplash of getting everything she'd ever wanted, or the obvious trap he was trying to close around her. "Not to talk you out of this...but are you sure? We've only just met, Professor."

"I trust my instincts about people." He checked his watch. "Anyway, let me call you a car. It's late, and you'd best get back to your dormitory."

Ellory's hands shook as he called a car service, but, thankfully, Colt didn't seem to notice. It would be a lot, adding something like this to her already-packed schedule. She would have less time for dates and parties, and even less time to study for her actual classes. But if she could do this—the work *and* the investigation, learning *and* spying—then her future would finally look bright.

"Hey, Colt," she murmured, once the car was three minutes away and she could slip back into her coat. "You said earlier that Hudson was one of two students you've seen potential in. Who was the other?"

"Oh, that was so long ago." A shadow passed over his face, like he was remembering something unpleasant. "It was a boy by the name of Malcolm Mayhew. Sadly, he died young."

Ellory froze with her arm only halfway through the sleeve. "Malcolm Mayhew was a part of your salon?"

"Yes. Did you know him?"

"No. I just met his niece, I think." She yanked her coat all the way on, her heart pounding. Somehow, she hadn't expected him to drop this lead into her lap, and now she wasn't sure if he suspected her or if his confusion was genuine. *Idiot. Idiot!* "Would it be strange if I asked you for a list of all your attendees? I'm...working on something, a research project of my own, and I think it might help."

"I suppose that would be fine," Colt said, his eyebrows drawing together. "It's hardly private information."

Ellory thanked him and hurried outside to meet her car before he could ask follow-up questions. Or worse.

INTERLUDE

OWL—Divination/Mercury

- Wisdom
- Protection
- Omen
- Powers of prophecy

HUMMINGBIRD/DOCTOR BIRD—Evocation/Sulfur

- Messenger
- Love
- Luck
- Reincarnated souls

CROW/RAVEN—Incantation/Salt

- Trickster
- Harbinger
- Creation
- Huginn ("mind") and Muninn ("will/memory")

—Excerpt from Ellory Morgan's notebook

28

Despite her reluctant excitement, Ellory managed to prioritize the salon list over the student-assistant details. The offer still didn't feel real, and part of her worried that she would open the email to find Colt had simply written an apology for his impulsiveness, that it had been a cruel test she had failed by accepting. Besides, she couldn't deny the hum of excitement that she felt as she downloaded the salon list, the feeling of making progress, of having a random suspicion confirmed. With a notebook open on the bed beside her hand, she combed through the names for any she recognized.

She had to read the list twice to make sure she wasn't hallucinating.

Arthur "Chip" O'Connor II and Malcolm Mayhew had been in the same cohort from 1982 to 1983. Or, rather, from 1982 to when Malcolm Mayhew was murdered.

It felt significant, though she couldn't put her finger on why. The Mayhews were the kind of family known to the Graveses and the Blackwoods, so there was no reason why they wouldn't have also associated with the O'Connors. But there had to be something she could get out of Stasie's grandfather that would give her somewhere to start looking for the other person who had been in the library with Malcolm that night. If it had been Stasie's father, that would be more than enough reason for a cover-up.

Maybe this wasn't her mystery to solve, but she was too invested to turn back now. It was all connected somehow. She was sure of it. She just had to figure out what the murder had to do with the magic, what the birds had to do with the Old Masters, what the salons had to do with the School for the Unseen Arts. All the research she'd done, all the unrelated pieces she'd gathered, blurred together in her mind without making a sensible picture.

Once again, she wished she could reach Hudson. But he still hadn't answered her messages.

"*Magic*," Aunt Carol said flatly, when Ellory took advantage of the empty dorm room to call. "What do you mean by *magic*?"

She had no idea where Stasie was, but her roommate had yet to give her a number to reach her grandfather with. In the interim, Ellory continued to work—or pretended to work—on the newspaper article where Stasie could see: She had taken out library books on the history of the school, she had printed out photos of former deans on which she scrawled legible notes, and she had even gone as far as to act like she was talking to one on the phone. Stasie hadn't responded to any such silent pressure.

Left to her own devices, Ellory had gone down a rabbit hole about the Lost Eight and ancestral magic that ended with this phone call. But faced with her aunt's disinterest, she couldn't imagine trying to explain the absurdity of her life to someone who hadn't witnessed it. Carol would change fifty years of opinions on mental health just to have Ellory committed to a psych ward.

She slathered leave-in conditioner into the section of hair she was detangling, trying to keep her tone light. "We're doing a segment on legal protections for folk healers and cultural home remedies. It made me curious if we ever had anyone in the family like that."

"Your mother had an affair with an obeah man once."

"Wait, really?"

"*No*. But that's how ridiculous you sound."

Ellory stifled a sigh that would only get her in trouble. She hadn't expected Aunt Carol to suddenly confess that she was part of a hidden magical dynasty that had passed their abilities down to Ellory, but she hadn't expected to be outright mocked either.

Not that Ellory could blame her. A month ago, she would have found the idea laughable, too.

"There was no affair," Carol relented. "Your father *did* visit an obeah man when you were young, though. I told him not to mess with things he didn't understand, but you spent most of your childhood talking about duppies and doctor birds. Your parents thought you'd be cursed or something. He didn't give me the details, and I didn't ask. But whatever advice he got from the obeah settled his spirit."

Obeah, though many practitioners didn't call it that due to the scorn she could hear in her aunt's voice, still thrived across Jamaica. Through spellcasting and communing with spirits, obeah followers could heal or harm, see the future for advice, or search the present for lost objects. She'd been told two things about them her whole life. The first was that they were born with their abilities. The second was that they were the last resort of the desperate.

She'd never had cause to think about them before, let alone form an opinion. Now she wondered if her father had sensed her magical potential and gone to the obeah about it. She would call him and ask if she'd thought there was a chance he would actually answer.

"I talked about duppies?" Ellory asked as she typed that dutifully into her notes. "What duppies?"

"It started after Miss Claudette died in a shop fire, and then suddenly you could name dead people all over town who came just to talk to you." Ellory had no idea who Miss Claudette was, but she added the name to her notes as well. "Doctor birds are also known as god birds. The Arawak believed they carried the souls of the dead or that they were reincarnated souls themselves. They're supposed to be quick as a devil, but you could catch one of them in your hands. It wouldn't fly off until you let it go." Carol kissed her teeth. "I see why Desmond got scared. But it was all silly superstition."

"This is really helpful, Auntie," Ellory heard herself say, turning the page of her notebook until she reached the three bird symbols. The hummingbird—the doctor bird—stared up at her from above EVOCATION. "Thank you. Have you been taking your medicine?"

Carol kissed her teeth again. "I'm not a child, Lor."

"Is that a yes?"

"Mi wi tek dem now," grumbled Carol. "Jeezam peas."

◆

On Ellory's next visit to the *Communiqué* offices, Boone introduced her to the editors, identified the various conference rooms, and told her which snacks in the break room he'd already claimed. If she'd expected him to ask for a progress report on her story, she was soon disappointed. Boone, it seemed, cared little for micromanaging. She'd said she was working on the piece, he told her, and unless she came to him for help, he would assume that was what she was doing.

"The woman who ran the paper before me was always up in my business," he added as he showed her the printers, each of which apparently had names. "I nearly quit so many times, and journalism is my major. If I do that to any of you, you have my permission for a mutiny."

"I'll stick a pitchfork in the merch closet," said Ellory. "Just in case."

Boone smirked. "Well, there's certainly room in there now, with how much shit you took home."

She nodded at the sweatshirt he was wearing, sourced from the same closet. "You're the one who's a walking advertisement right now. I'm already starting to miss your tattoos."

"You like the ink, Morgan?" Boone glanced down at his arms. "You didn't strike me as a tattoo person."

"I'm not, really. It's just weird to see you without them." Beside them, a printer spit out an article draft. "I guess I have favorites of the ones I've seen?"

"Yeah?" Boone rolled up his sleeves until his forearms were bare. "They all tell a story, if you're that interested. Hit me."

He told her about the anchor on his extensor carpi ulnaris and how it was a reminder that, even when he thought he'd hit rock bottom, there was still further to go. He told her about the constellation on his biceps, which represented Orion's Belt ("or, as we call it in Mexico, Los Tres Reyes Magos"). By the time she worked her way around to the sun with the line bisecting it, he'd made her laugh so many times that she almost regretted asking.

"Oh, that?" he said, glancing down at his inner wrist as though the tattoo meant nothing at all. "That's the alchemical symbol for salt. According to Paracelsus, it's one of the tria prima—three primes—of alchemy. It represents earth and the material body, the fixed principle of existence, the purification of matter. And salt itself is said to protect from evil spirits and bad luck."

"I thought I'd seen that symbol somewhere." Ellory made a thoughtful sound before her eyes met his. "Does it have anything to do with divination?"

"Like alomancy? That's when you toss salt in the air and read the patterns it falls in."

He didn't pause, didn't blink, didn't flinch. Ellory stared him down, connecting his tattoo to the very label the hidden museum had given it, and Boone seemed for all the world like they were just exchanging fun facts. Should she push him in such a public place? Or should she retreat, glad that he didn't seem to suspect her of anything for now?

Just when she was about to back off, an inscrutable smile crossed his face.

"This is starting to feel like an interrogation," Boone said. "Do you want to grab a conference room?"

Ellory paused. "I'm good out here, I think."

"Oh, come on, Morgan." His eyes sharpened. "You're not afraid of me, are you?"

It wasn't about fear, she wanted to point out, but that would give him the upper hand. Instead, Ellory squared her shoulders and followed him to one without glass walls, tucked into the corner of the space between the windows and a kitchen.

Boone snagged a bag of pretzels on the way, whistling a reggaeton song she didn't recognize. The door itself was made of glass, which made her relax only slightly. She was less afraid of Boone than she had been of Colt, but that didn't mean she wasn't afraid at *all*. He was taller than her and likely stronger than her. He knew the newspaper office better than her, both the layout and the staff. If he wanted to make her disappear for asking the wrong questions, he could manage it easily on his home turf.

Boone dropped down at the head of the table, in full view of anyone who walked by, and popped a pretzel in his mouth. Ellory tried not to feel like a rabbit taking a meeting in a wolf's den.

"If you want to ask me about magic," he said once he'd swallowed, "then just ask me, Morgan."

Ellory missed her chair. She caught herself on the back, bending her finger the wrong way, and fumbled onto her feet. Amusement flashed in those dark eyes that watched her from across the table. She charted the distance between herself and the door, wondering if she could make it to the hallway before he cast some spell.

"I'm not going to hurt you, Morgan," Boone continued. "We're just going to talk."

"I believe you." Her voice didn't shake, which was the only good thing about this confrontation. "You've been *so* trustworthy up until now."

His smile widened. "I told you that I like you better with your claws out. Sit."

Ellory sat, if only because she had no other choice. There were pens and pencils on the table, but he'd sat far enough away that she couldn't stab him with one. She'd never stabbed anyone before anyway. She could try and cast a spell if needed, but she still hadn't figured out what the last one had cost her, and she was wary of doing more magic until she did. He had her dead to rights, and they both knew it.

She clasped her hands together so they wouldn't betray her fear. "Are you a member of the Old Masters?"

"Not by choice, but yeah." His smile was a bitter thing. "I'm a loner, not a joiner, but they don't really ask, you know?"

"No, I don't know. I don't know anything. I don't know why you would—" She swallowed. "Is this why I haven't been able to reach Hudson? I thought you just took his phone, but did he finally ask you outright and you made him disappear like—"

"I would *never* hurt Hudson," Boone snapped. She had never seen him angry, and his fury filled the room like poison gas. Gone was the mocking troll who seemed to make light of everything, and in his place was a warrior ready to defend his liege lord. "He's not just my best friend. He's my brother. I would never, *ever* hurt him."

"Did he know you have magic?"

"No."

Ellory frowned dubiously. "Do you know *he* has magic?"

"Yes. And if you know what's good for you, you'll help me keep that to ourselves. The Old Masters don't react well to power they don't control."

Piece by piece, Boone seemed to pull himself back into the insouciant man she remembered. Hudson was a sore spot; she would file that away for later. It was surreal to be sitting here, having this conversation, with the kind of openness she usually shared only with Hudson or Tai and Cody. Though she'd seen the tattoos, she hadn't really believed Boone could be an enemy until now. He seemed like the kind of guy who wouldn't believe magic existed even if he knew about it, just to be contrary.

A loner, not a joiner.

Maybe that was why he was giving her answers.

"You talk about them like they're normal," Ellory said carefully. "Like this is normal. They're *killing people*, Boone."

He tilted his head, puzzled. "Are they?"

"Y-yes," she sputtered, but suddenly she wasn't sure. She'd assumed the Lost Eight and the Old Masters and the School for the Unseen Arts and Malcolm Mayhew had all been connected, but what if they weren't? "One of them threatened me away from looking into their group. Twice!"

"The Old Masters," Boone said on a sigh, "are a bunch of stuffy old white fucks too stuck in their ways. They recruit off this campus and others around New England, but it's usually from old money and founding families. I mean, you don't co-opt a term like *old masters* without being full of yourself, and money makes their research go 'round."

"Research into the occult? Like the School for the Unseen Arts?"

"What's that?"

Ellory frowned again, filing that line of questioning away for later. "Well, what do you mean by *research*? Do they not have magic of their own?"

"Not much, as far as I can tell. They find gifted people and bleed them dry." Sympathy crept into Boone's eyes. "You're a Godwin Scholar, right? That's one of their main recruitment tools. They use their money and power to make sure your other options dry up, and then they use their scholarship exam to test your aptitude for magic. You attend Warren for free, and the Old Masters snatch you up like they're doing you a favor. They've been doing it for decades."

Ellory's lips parted, but no words came out. It felt as though she'd been punched in the stomach. She thought of the schools she'd gotten into and the financial aid she'd seemed incapable of getting. She thought of how many nights she'd spent feeling like a failure, incapable of living up to her own potential. She thought of how the offer for the Godwin Scholarship had appeared like the sun breaking through the clouds, giving her a second chance.

The idea that all of it—every long cry, every sleepless night, every abandoned dream—had been the machination of some shadowy society made her want to overturn this table and scream.

"They…" she finally managed, "they didn't recruit me, though. They threatened me to stay away, remember?"

"Yeah, that's what I find weird about this whole thing…" Boone tapped his fingers against the desk. "It's possible they didn't want you to find them before they found you, but even that doesn't explain it."

"Have they threatened Hudson?"

"Not on my watch." His eyes narrowed in warning, but this time she could tell his anger wasn't directed at her. "If they *were* going to recruit him, it would have happened already. I don't know why they skipped him over, but it can't be anything good. I've been keeping him off their radar since freshman year. Hell, you're the only other person I've talked to about magic. Like, actual magic." He snorted. "You know why I got this tattoo? Because I've been hoping to find more of us. But no one's ever asked me about it—even Hudson. Not until you."

"I'd never even done magic before I came here. I…I thought it was the school."

"It might be. I heard this is where it all began, and my magic's more powerful here." Boone leaned back in his seat, arms behind his head. "I've suspected you might be like me for a while. See, I'm good at creating liminal spaces. A place within a place, where everything slows down and I can just breathe. I felt one forming in the orchard when Liam came back without you. It took me *hours* to comb through the void and find you, but by the time I did, you had these lights leading you back to us. That wasn't me, Morgan. That was all you."

"Why the fuck didn't you *say* anything, then?" Ellory asked. Her voice shook with lethal anger, but she managed not to yell at him if only because she didn't want their conversation to leak through the glass door. Her knuckles had blanched from how tightly her hands were fisted together, keeping her from strangling him. "I thought I was going out of my mind, and you knew about magic and the Old Masters, and you didn't say shit to me. *Why?*"

"Because these are dangerous fucking people," Boone retorted. "Do you think this is a game? I haven't seen anyone die or be killed since *I* was recruited, but that doesn't mean you're wrong about that. The Old Masters make up the highest echelon of society, the kind of people with the kind of power you couldn't even dream of. They could wake up one morning and decide to start a war or bomb a city out of existence with a single phone call. And that was *before* they had access to magic. I won't let them get to Hudson, but I barely fucking know you. Consider this your warning to back the hell off."

Through his angry words, Ellory could sense a thread of fear. Fear not for what they would do to her, but for what they would do to him for having this conversation. It only made Ellory angrier, because that fear was exactly what allowed people like the Old Masters to maintain their power. Someone had to stand up to them. That someone clearly wouldn't be Boone.

"If they're so dangerous, then why are you telling me all this?" she finally asked. "Especially in a public office."

"We're not in a public office." Boone tipped his chin toward the glass door behind her. Ellory glanced over her shoulder and was hit by another wave of shock. She and Boone were still standing by the printers, his fingers pointing at tattoo after tattoo, her head bobbing along with whatever he was telling her. It was like the night she had summoned the Graves Ghost, except her stomach swooped with sickness at being able to stare at her own body for this long, acting independently of her soul.

Magic. He'd done magic right in front of her, and she hadn't even noticed.

"See?" Boone said, drawing her attention back to him. "I'm good at liminal spaces. And I found out what you've been doing with Hudson. We're having this conversation because I'm hoping if I give you the answers you want, then you'll give me something I want."

"What do you want?"

"Leave him out of all this. *Please*," Boone said, crushing his pretzel bag into a crinkling ball. "I can't lose him to these people. No matter what you think of the Old Masters, I'm not your enemy, Morgan. But for Hudson, I will be." He got to his feet, tossing the bag into the nearest trash bin like he hadn't just threatened her. "Now let's get back out there. This spell holds for only as long as it takes our conversation to end, and I don't want to disappear in front of a room full of professional gossips."

You don't get to tell me what to do, Ellory bit back, breathing until this tidal wave of frustration passed. Boone was entitled, but did she expect any different from someone who would join the Old Masters? At least he was willing to talk. For now.

"Okay," she lied. "Let's go."

29

E LLORY AWOKE TO VOICES.
It was early, too early, for Stasie to have guests in their dorm room. Ellory's satin bonnet had shifted in the night, freeing her curls to the air, and her oversize Batman T-shirt had shifted with it, revealing her shoulder and collarbone. The blankets were tangled around her bare legs, and her boy shorts were riding up her butt. It was in this state that she contemplated finally killing her roommate. She would end up in jail, but it might be worth it. Every time she thought Stasie had reached the apex of how annoying she could be, she invented a new level.

Grunting, Ellory opened her eyes, only to find that one of the voices belonged to Hudson Graves.

Hudson stood in front of the closed door, his hands in his pockets as he eyed the dormitory like it might give him a contagious disease. There were bags beneath his eyes and a frown on his mouth, but he was here, he was *here*, and Ellory sprang into a sitting position at the sight of him.

Then she remembered that she wasn't wearing a bra and crossed her arms over her chest.

"What are you doing here?" It came out more waspish than she had intended, but her state of undress made her hyperaware of herself. And him. And him seeing her breasts like this for the first time, sagging drowsily toward her stomach. "You haven't been answering my calls."

"I've been asking myself what I'm doing here for five minutes now," said Hudson, wrinkling his nose. "I don't remember these dorms being so small..."

"I wanted a single," Stasie said, sitting cross-legged on her bed. She was fully dressed, her tablet in her lap. "But my parents didn't want me to be antisocial."

Ellory frowned at her tone until she realized what was bothering her: Stasie sounded *nice*. Flirtatious, even. She watched her roommate watch Hudson through her light-brown lashes, and Ellory's frown deepened. That explained why Stasie had let him inside the dorm while Ellory had been sleeping, yes, but it made Ellory even angrier about the violation. Stasie was wearing full makeup, her hair in perfect waves that cascaded toward her shoulders. Ellory looked like a troll doll, her nipples poking at her shirt in the cold room. Knowing Stasie, she'd done this on purpose.

Ellory wiped at the corner of her mouth, relieved to find she hadn't drooled. Small miracles.

"Can you wait in the hallway while I get dressed?" she asked, pulling her blanket up to her chin. Hudson stopped scanning the room and scanned her instead, as if realizing for the first time that she wasn't ready for the day. His lips parted like he wanted to say something, but he just nodded sharply. Ellory didn't relax until there was a closed door between the two of them. She glared at Stasie. "New rule: no boys over while I'm asleep."

Stasie discarded her tablet and stared at Ellory with more interest than she'd ever had before. "How do you know Hudson Graves? He asked for you specifically. I thought you were dating Liam Blackwood." She paused. "Speaking of, how did you manage *that*? I cannot believe you have more of a dating life than I do when all you do is study and pass out."

Ellory ignored her to throw on her laundry-day bra and whatever shirt-and-jeans combination that wasn't visibly stained. When she opened the door, Hudson was leaning against the wall opposite the dorm, looking, if possible, more exhausted than he had inside. She so rarely saw him appear anything less than perfect, but he'd left a trail of cracks in the facade for her to find: His coat was improperly buttoned, his curls drooped from beneath his beanie, and his skin had the kind of pallor one usually associated with a fever. The urge to put him to bed was so strong that she closed the door tightly behind her before she could act on it.

"Let's walk and talk," she said. "You look like you need coffee."

Hudson followed her without argument, stifling a yawn. "I saw your messages and came right over. I went home like we talked about, but then there was a family emergency."

"Was the emergency that you lost your phone?"

"No," he admitted. "But I forgot to check it with everything going on."

"What was it, then?"

"My brother. He showed up at the house."

Ellory discarded her first three questions and settled on her fourth: "Is that why he was calling you?"

"No, he was calling me because he wanted money. It's unusual for him to go back to Darien. It was…" Several seconds passed in silence before Hudson settled on something: "Exhausting. My parents hadn't seen him in long enough that all three of them had forgotten how much they hate one another, and I had to mediate at least six disagreements."

Ellory saved the rest of her questions for when she'd gotten some coffee in him. When they reached Powers That Bean, Wynne, who often worked the morning shifts because most of her classes were in the afternoon, gestured for Ellory to get behind the counter and make her own. The morning rush had resulted in a line that wrapped around the room, and it was either that, or they would be waiting at least an hour for their drinks.

She and Hudson ended up on one of the benches that ornamented the campus, this one overlooking the quad. Hudson had already downed half his roast by the time they found the bench; the other half followed as soon as he sat down. Ellory, drinking her coffee at a more measured pace, tried to rein in her concern and failed.

"Did you not get any sleep?" she asked.

Hudson tossed his empty cup into a nearby garbage bin. "I told you I came as soon as I got your messages. That was about two hours ago." His dark eyes were now alert enough for her to read the apology in them. "Did you still get to go to the salon? Was it horrific?"

"Worse than that," Ellory groaned. "Those people—"

"I *know*."

The entire story of their time apart spilled out of her, starting with the salon and ending with her conversation with Boone. Hudson didn't question her offer from Colt or her anger at Boone for the lies he'd told them both. He just listened until she ran out of words and had to replenish her energy by finishing her coffee. Her attempt to throw it into the trash can missed by at least two feet.

"This whole time..." Hudson said, when she returned from picking it up and placing it in herself. "Part of me didn't truly believe Boone could be an Old Master until now. Especially not after I discovered my magic. I thought anything strange that happened around our house was me, not...."

He sounded as baffled and betrayed as Ellory had been. Still, her mind couldn't settle. "You really had *no* idea? How is that even possible? He said you're as close as brothers."

"Boone's always been a facetious person. He's sarcastic even when he's telling the truth. If I hadn't witnessed everything we've seen this school year with my own eyes, I probably wouldn't have believed him even if he'd done magic right in front of me. And he *hasn't*." Hudson wasn't looking at her, but there was a tick in his bearded jaw. "Everyone is so concerned with protecting me when all I want is the goddamn truth."

"Yeah," Ellory murmured. "I know how that feels. I just have no idea what to believe anymore."

"Believe *me*. We agreed to be on the same side from now on, didn't we?"

Ellory's cheeks warmed as she remembered that night on the balcony, his hand in hers and her mind on the ways their bodies could move together. He was right, though. He had been nothing but open with her since, he had driven through the night to get back to her side, and she was letting her anger at Boone and fear of Colt poison their budding partnership.

Along the quad, students rushed to get out of the cold, carrying books or bearing heavy backpacks. Someone sped by on a skateboard, wearing a massive pair of headphones. Hudson watched them with the thousand-yard stare of a man fighting a war on too many fronts. Ellory decided then and there not to add another battle.

She placed a hand on his arm, a touch light enough to be brushed away. Hudson released a shaky breath. "Anyway...everything I learned at home lines up with what Boone told you. Another former dean—Dean Godwin—took a major interest in all manner of magic, which he eventually distilled into three kinds: evocation, incantation, and divination—summoning, spellcasting, and scrying. Each with their own alchemical symbol, a kind of code for like-minded people to translate. But Boone was also right that magic is dangerous. That's why my parents didn't want me to remember that I could do it. It's been twisted into this dark version of itself somehow."

"Maybe that's why the School for the Unseen Arts closed so quickly. Maybe they couldn't figure out how to do magic without some sort of sacrifice." Ellory thought of the soccer ball she had stopped, of the dead patch of grass she'd left behind and the memory she had surrendered in order to fix it. She thought of how magic had drained her of more than she could even remember, how power—real or imagined—always had a cost. "Do you think the Lost Eight and Malcolm Mayhew have something to do with all that? He had that crow tattoo, so maybe he was studying magic."

"And, what, he became a sacrifice?"

"Maybe. Or maybe he knew too much. Maybe they all knew too much…" The back of her neck began to ache again. Ellory rubbed it, refusing to let the pain derail her. "Boone said the Old Masters are a secret society—and we know they tried to warn me from getting too close to their secrets. What if those who don't get in are dealt with, and those who do get in are sacrificed?"

"That's a terrible way to run an organization."

"I have a theory, but I need to do more research into the Lost Eight. I need more than their names at least. I can probably do that at the *Communiqué*." More of Boone's words rang in her ears, clawing at the back of her mind. *The Old Masters are a bunch of stuffy old white fucks too stuck in their ways.* Meanwhile, she and

Boone, Tai and Cody, and Malcolm Mayhew and the Lost Eight—they were all people of color. There was a pattern to follow, a deadly past that threatened her anarchic present. "But if we're right…"

"Morgan, all we have right now are a lot of maybes with little evidence. Are you all right?" Hudson turned to her, his eyes narrowing on her hand. "What's wrong with your neck?"

"I think my tattoo is coming back. Like it came back when I did magic for the first time."

Ellory's hand covered the space she knew the message would be, scrawled in her handwriting with that backward *E*. He reached for her, pausing inches away until she nodded, and then pulled her hand away from her neck. His fingers brushed her skin, leaving goose bumps in their wake as they lifted her curls. He leaned closer, and Ellory could feel his sharp intake of breath.

"You told me about this," he said, "but even still I didn't…"

"It comes and goes," she whispered, remaining motionless. She was afraid to breathe, in case that would jolt him into movement. His fingers were tracing the letters in a soothing stroke, and his soft exhales were warm on her exposed skin. He smelled like coffee and, beneath that, his usual woodsy citrus. She wanted to inhale him. "Every time I learn something, I feel this pain or this dread… It feels like a curse. It feels like someone cursed me."

Just like her parents had feared. Maybe the obeah magic had never cured her at all.

Ellory lifted her head. They were so close that she could count every line in the bags under his eyes. She could see the hazy edges of his irises, like he had been drawn by someone with shaking hands. She could see the bumps across his otherwise-smooth skin. She collected reasons to break his gaze, but in the end, none of them mattered. He was looking at her, and she was looking at him, and his hand was on her neck, and her hand was on his arm, and that was what mattered. She had hated him and trusted him, competed against him and reached for him, and he was here. That mattered.

"We'll figure this out," he said, so soft, so tender. "You and I. Together."

"Thank you."

She licked her suddenly dry lips. His pupils expanded. Once again, the air between them caught fire. Her breathing thinned. His cut out entirely.

Hudson dropped her hand as if he'd been burned. He cleared his throat and stood. "Thank you for the coffee. Sorry again for being MIA."

Ellory felt like she'd run a marathon only to find no one waiting at the end. Embarrassment crashed through her. She got to her feet, unable to look at him. "It's fine. I just hope you're all right. If you need to talk—"

"I know where to find you now," he said. "I'll text you later?"

"Sure, of course."

"Okay."

"Great."

Awkwardness pressed down on them like a weight. Ellory wanted to run. She wanted to scream. She wanted to rewind to the moment she'd felt closer to him than ever before and stay there. She wanted not to want that.

And then warmth enveloped her. No, not warmth, but Hudson, pulling her against him in an unexpected hug. Her cheek touched the fabric of his coat. His chin pressed against her forehead, scratchy from his beard and yet somehow perfect. She closed her eyes, her arms looping cautiously around his waist, expecting him to shove her away at any moment. Instead, he pulled her closer, and it broke something inside her. Tears gathered at the corners of her eyes, and she had no idea why.

She hugged him tighter.

"Together," he said again, a solemn promise that she had no choice but to believe. "We'll figure this out."

PART III

A MAGIC MOST FOUL

They beat us to surrender weak with fright,
And tugging and tearing without let or pause,
They flap their hideous wings in grim delight,
And stuff our gory hearts into their maws.

"Birds of Prey," Claude McKay

INTERLUDE

A DETECTIVE IS A SEEKER of justice. A journalist is a seeker of truth. After three students vanished, journalists swarmed the campus of Warren University to do what the detectives could not. Willem Pendel was one such journalist, a Pulitzer Prize–winning reporter whose investigative pieces had appeared in the *New York Times*, the *New Republic*, and the *New Yorker*. He had noticed a pattern of unexplained disappearances, and it was his intention to write a nonfiction book about whatever he found out.

According to Pendel, the administration was remarkably helpful. He was allowed to examine dormitories and classrooms. He was allowed to research in libraries and retrace steps across the quad. He was allowed to study student records and interview living family members. It was the evidence that gave him trouble. It was nonexistent, as if Letitia Rose, Manuel Sharp, and Angel Mclaughlin had never walked these unhallowed halls. Pendel had written takedowns of well-protected government figures that had left more of a paper trail than three students from two different decades.

Instead, he wrote about the peculiarities of Warren. The rooks and hummingbirds and owls that gathered on campus in eerie packs, living peacefully together while watching the students with eyes that held an almost-human wisdom. Their unorthodox start and the rumors of paranormal activity that they had never quite shaken. The Old Masters, a secret society that no one could truly prove existed, and the Godwin Scholars, a not-so-secret society that contributed reams of esoteric research to the world.

That book would never reach publication. Willem Pendel was found dead of a heart attack in his office at the age of thirty-three, face down on his own notes. His final page of writings included sketches of birds, each one more detailed than the last, staring up at the ceiling with a peculiar sort of malice that gave his widow chills.

30

WINTER BREAK TURNED THE CAMPUS into a ghost town—and Ellory loved it. Her shifts at Powers That Bean were quiet, her customers largely international students who didn't have the money or the desire to hop on an expensive flight home for the holidays.

Snow had yet to fall, but the weather was preparing for it: every day was subzero, and the grass crunched beneath her boots when she crossed the frozen quad. Decorations appeared in the fir trees and building windows, cutouts of Santa and Stars of David, snowflakes and dreidels. A lake in town had frozen over, and she occasionally saw students heading toward the bus station with ice skates hanging by their laces off their arms.

The holiday season, for Ellory, was a gift and a nightmare. Retail shifts were hellish, packed with the kind of customers who made her wish it were legal to hunt other humans for sport. When she'd worked at Midtown Comics, she had been yelled at more times than she cared to remember for not having the exact issue of the exact comic series someone wanted at seven o'clock at night on

Christmas Eve. But there was also a hopefulness in the air that was unmatched by the rest of the seasons, a sense of camaraderie and togetherness that she had always loved. It was like the world forgot to be cruel, because the sight of snow and the ringing of sleigh bells forced a collective calm.

Ellory would have felt calmer if Aunt Carol hadn't taken her decision to spend an extra week at school so hard. "Don't tell me that you're starting to like it up there," Carol had huffed over the phone. "This is your home. *I'm* your home."

"And you always will be," Ellory assured her. "But Liam invited me to his family's Christmas party, and it would just be easier to get there from here. I'll be back in Astoria right after."

"*Liam*," Carol repeated. "I thought you broke up with him."

"I did." Ellory winced at the reminder of letting that slip. "But we're friends. We're fine."

It was Ellory who wasn't fine. She had been able to think of little else but Hudson Graves and the way his breath had caught as he stared at her mouth on a cold bench just off the side of the quad. She had moved on so quickly that it was as if she had never liked Liam at all, and still he'd broken the stalemate between them with this invitation. He was a far kinder man than she had ever deserved, and her heart did not care at all.

"I guess I'll see you after your fancy party, then," Aunt Carol said, somehow making it sound like Ellory was getting kidnapped rather than choosing to spend extra time at school. "Don't get arrested."

Ellory had rolled her eyes and said her goodbyes.

The day of the Christmas party dawned without fanfare. Ellory took her time in the shower, getting dressed, and packing, luxuriating in having the room to herself. She took the bus to the Metro

North, even knowing that Hudson probably would have driven her if she'd asked. It was over an hour from Hartford to Darien, so, of course, she hadn't asked.

Where Hartford was bisected by a river but otherwise landlocked and forested, Darien was a small coastal town that looked like it belonged on a postcard. The Long Island Sound was a gorgeous ribbon of blue, lined with gray beaches, piers with white boats, and pink and brown boulders. She passed redbrick buildings, a school that looked more like a barn, and several long driveways leading to houses that were probably too expensive for her to look at.

The Blackwood house was one such manor. Her taxi carried her to a colonial-style stone-and-shingle home located on two wide acres of land at the end of a private lane that stretched for what felt like a mile. It was two stories tall, with three arched roofs and a chimney. Stone steps led up to a front door wedged between two beige columns. To the right was a wrought iron fence that led around to the back of the property, and after that was what looked like an attached garage.

Ellory already felt underdressed.

Liam opened the front door before she'd even ascended the stairs, beaming down at her. Christmas music poured into the yard, a Bing Crosby classic with muffled words. A smile tugged at Ellory's lips at the sight of this bright and beautiful man, so unabashed in his enthusiasm for life. What was wrong with her that she couldn't have mustered up equal affection for him? What was wrong with her that he hadn't been everything she could ever want?

He hugged her so tightly that he lifted her off her feet, and Ellory felt nothing, absolutely nothing, except the faint desire for someone else to be holding her instead. She swallowed down a wave of shame. "Hey, Liam."

"All good, Ellory? Come meet everyone," Liam said as he set her down. "I can put your bags and coat in my room for safekeeping, buddy."

He was trying. Ellory owed it to him to try, too.

Everyone turned out to be his parents, two polite white people who shared their son's smile and golden tan. His father asked her about her classes and laughed at her jokes. His mother straightened his hair when he returned from putting away her bags and encouraged them to head upstairs to enjoy the party. Ellory hadn't even noticed that every guest on the main floor was much older than them until they went upstairs and she began to see people under thirty. She wondered if Hudson's parents had been among the main-floor attendees. She wondered if she would recognize them if they were.

The speaker on the second floor was playing more modern Christmas covers. Someone she recognized from the lacrosse team grabbed Liam to "deal with an issue in the master bedroom," leaving her to make her own way through the crowd. Tai was supposed to come with Cody as her date, but she hadn't texted since that morning. Gaia-not-Greer Hammond and Kendall Rhodes were in one of the empty bedrooms, laughing over their wineglasses. David Chang Vargas was beating someone at cards in another empty room. Two men were kissing fervently in what Ellory hadn't known was a closet until it was too late.

Without a drink, she thought the party had too much noise and too many strangers for her to enjoy herself. She found a den brimming with coolers and grabbed a light beer to nurse while she explored the rest of the floor. It took her five minutes to realize she was looking for an empty room or a quiet balcony—or, rather, for someone who tended to escape to those places—and groaned internally.

She was such a mess.

Ellory wandered back downstairs, dodging the small crowds talking about vacations she would never take and assets she would never attain, until she reached the kitchen, where she had met the Blackwoods. A sliding glass door let her out onto a covered patio that overlooked an empty pool. A black iron table surrounded by matching chairs with tan cushions beckoned her. Evergreen trees blocked the view beyond the pool, and the night hid her from the lit-up windows. With the music and chatter muffled, Ellory took her first real breath of the day.

She was *such* a mess.

taiwo: omw. are you there yet?

Ellory replied in the affirmative and tipped her head back. The arched ceiling blocked the sky from view, but she could imagine that the stars cared little about her. It was oddly reassuring, how minuscule they all were in the grand scheme of the universe. How irrelevant.

She reached for her bottle and missed. It hit the floor instead, shattered glass and fizzing beer spreading before she could stop it. Ellory cursed, and then, because it felt good, she cursed again. She had nothing to clean the stones with, but she could at least pick up the glass before someone got hurt. She reached for a large jagged piece...

...and straightened, her body buzzing with anger and intoxication. She wished it were just the drinks—three, four, maybe five— that she'd had tonight, but she knew it was also him, his presence and the way it overshadowed everything until she could think about nothing and no one else. She held the glass shard like a weapon, and his eyes flashed.

"Are you going to hurt me, Morgan?" he said in a low voice, stepping forward. He bared the elegant line of his throat to her, all smooth brown skin. "Let me make it easy for you."

She flicked the glass shard into the dark bushes. "I don't need to hurt you to get you to shut up." Now she was the one to step forward. She covered his Adam's apple with one hand, her fingers poised to squeeze. "You think I don't see how you look at me?"

He didn't lower his head. His words were growled to the stars: "How do I look at you?"

Instead of pressing down, her hand slithered across his skin until it settled on the back of his neck. She forced him to stare down at her, burning gaze to burning gaze. His full lips were sneering; his dark eyes held a challenge. Ellory pushed his head down farther, until he was looking down her scoop neck.

"Like you want to fuck me," she said. "Like you already have, and you're aching for another round."

He could have broken her grip so easily, could have put some distance between them, but he didn't. Inside, a party raged, all drunken students and screeching music to dull the monotony of life, but, out here, Ellory had never felt more awake.

"As if I'm the only one aching." He reached back, captured her wrist. Tugged her forward until she was pressed against him, the swell of his interest teasing her with dark promises that made heat pool between her legs. "As if I'm the only one who wants this."

"—Morgan?"

Ellory gasped back into the present. Hudson knelt before her, gazing down at her hand, ignorant to the ghostly touches that had left her breathless. She followed his line of sight to see blood dripping from her palm; the pain caught up with her a moment later.

She'd clenched her fist around the shard of glass she'd picked up while lost in her—what? Reverie? Memory?

It had been so vivid, so *carnal*. She could still hear herself moan as he entered her from behind, still feel his hungry kisses against the back of her neck. It was the first time she'd heard them, seen them, without Hudson already in front of her, and it was that more than anything that made her wonder if these flashes of memory could be real.

Could they really have...?

"Come inside so I can take a look," said Hudson, extracting the glass shard from her hand and making a face at the mess she'd left behind. "Someone will deal with that later."

Did we know each other before? Ellory wanted to ask. *Sometimes, I—I see these things, or I hear these things, and they feel like things I've forgotten. And it's always about you. It's always you. Please. Please, it's driving me mad.*

Ellory didn't realize she was swaying into him until Hudson's breath hitched. She ached to feel his mouth on hers, his hands on her, even here on the back patio of Liam's Christmas party. Between her vision and Hudson's worshipful stare, she felt utterly licentious.

She moved closer. His eyes reflected the distant stars as they flicked down to her lips and up again. Otherwise, he held perfectly still, and she couldn't tell if it was from shock or expectation. She tilted her head, and his eyelids lowered, and now he was the one moving toward her. Their lips were a hair's breadth apart, and she felt hot all over, and he hadn't even touched her yet.

It was irrational.

It was inevitable.

And Hudson pulled back, his expression shuttering. "Come inside, Morgan. You're hurting yourself."

He might as well have slapped her, because even that would have hurt less. Ellory swallowed all the things she wanted to say, settling for a simple nod instead. Without the warmth of her arousal, she felt hollow and cold. Her bloody hand still stung, but it was secondary to her bruised ego.

There was nothing she could say to explain or excuse herself—and he didn't offer anything either. In the howling silence, all she could do was follow Hudson as he tugged her into the house, leaving the shards of her dignity behind.

31

Classes restarted, indifferent to the depressive spiral Ellory had fallen into. The New Year was meant for resolutions and manifestations, but she had spent it in bed, the blankets wrapped around her as tightly as a burrito, watching the ball drop without emotion. Several times, Aunt Carol tried to lure her out of her room, but Ellory left only to shower or use the bathroom. If Carol hadn't brought her meals to her, she might not have eaten.

Her first semester at Warren University felt like a test she'd failed, and she had dreaded returning to campus only to stumble over another forgotten memory or unsolved mystery. She had broken the heart of a man who liked her too much, her heart bore cracks from a man who liked her too little, and she was no closer to figuring out who was trying to kill her. Every aspect of her life was overwhelming, and there was no reprieve in sight.

Her coursework remained as difficult as ever, which at least gave her something else to do with her brain besides focus on everything she'd done wrong. Hudson brought her new books on the occult to flip through and didn't ask questions when she was quick to leave. Sometimes, she thought his eyes lingered on her, but most of the time, it seemed like wishful thinking.

She read the books on the floor of Tai's dorm, mainly because Tai kept doing wellness checks to their room that were starting to annoy Stasie. Take-out containers surrounded them. Tai was shoveling chicken and broccoli into her mouth while studying a textbook with oily fingers, the kind of carelessness she could get away with since she didn't need to resell them for money at the end of the year. Ellory, who had already finished her chicken wings and french fries, handled Hudson's books more delicately, until she found something of interest.

"It says that Warren University is supposedly built over the lodges of the Old Masters," she said, finger tracing the paragraph as she read. "'The founders of the school bought acreage large enough for the Old Masters to meet in secret, and from those grounds rose a school more legendary than any aspiring secret society.' That's got to be about the School for the Unseen Arts."

"Or it's nonsense," Tai said without looking up.

"If their lodges used to be here, maybe they've left something behind that I can dig up." Ellory wrote it in her notebook anyway, even as she acknowledged that Tai was right. As with most of the things she'd learned in her research, this amounted to nothing but more questions. "It's at least nice to read a book that acknowledges that they existed."

Tai made a dubious sound, but Ellory ignored her. Since that night at Powers That Bean, Tai had reported a distinct lack of magical occurrences in her life, and she seemed much happier for it. She wanted normalcy, and who was Ellory to take that from her? Her best friend was still willing to let Ellory bounce ideas off her and ramble on about the occult. If that was all she could get, she would take it.

"Why did they need more than one lodge?" Tai asked, collecting the empty containers to dispose of in the hallway's trash chute. "How many Old Masters were there?"

"If I had to guess, I'd say they had at least three." She could almost see them, log cabins of the kind Abraham Lincoln had lived in, each one labeled with wooden signs that bore painted images of birds: a crow, a hummingbird, an owl. "But as Hudson so thoughtfully pointed out, all I have are guesses."

Ellory set that book to the side and moved on to the next: *Haunted Hallowed Halls: A Collection of Campus Ghost Stories*. She settled into the first chapter, while Tai left to take out the trash, and then read the next and then the next. By the time she looked up again, Tai was lying on her bed, on the phone with her sister. Ellory's lower back ached, her elbows numb from propping up her head for what felt like hours.

Tai paused long enough to say, "Nerd. I've never seen someone read themselves into a coma like that before. Kehinde says hi, by the way."

Ellory stretched. Her bladder was spitting threats of a UTI in her future. "Tell her I said hi back."

She returned from the bathroom to find that Tai had taken her phone hostage.

"Nope," she said when Ellory made a swipe for it, using the two inches she had in height to her advantage. "We're going out for dinner. You've either been sulking or studying, and it's too much now. Go put on something that isn't sweatpants."

Ellory looked down at her loose gray pants and semisheer top. If not for work and class, she likely wouldn't have gone outside, and her favorite part of every day was shedding her middling attempts at fashion for something she could lie around the dorm in. Tai, Cody, and Hudson made up most of her contact with the outside world; even her class engagement had dropped in favor of robotically taking notes while her mind was a thousand miles away.

This investigation hadn't just consumed her life; it had consumed her. And she'd let it, because it was easier than fixing all the things she had broken.

Tai was right. Ellory knew it. And yet... "Can we have a raincheck on—"

"*No.*" Tai nudged her toward the door with a hip and an expression that promised trouble if Ellory tried to argue with her again. "If you're not back in ten minutes, I'm going to kick down your door."

If Hudson was bothered by Ellory summoning him to her side after classes without warning, he didn't show it. Snow dusted the ground, so light that it had already melted in high-traffic areas, and flakes hung on the shoulders of his peacoat as he approached.

His hair, newly dyed, had a fresh golden tint to the silver, but it wasn't enough to stop him from looking a bit like Jack Frost, personifying the season in the form of a mischievous sprite. His high cheekbones and broad nose, his thick eyebrows and smirking mouth, all of it contrasted with his tartan scarf and mahogany leather gloves to make him look like a fey professor—too otherworldly for this campus and yet an inextricable part of it. When he stopped in front of her, the sunniest thing about this cold gray day, her heart skipped a beat.

AN ARCANE INHERITANCE

She avoided his eyes. "Thanks for coming. I didn't want to do this alone."

"Thanks for calling," he replied. "Walking into danger without anyone to watch your back seems to be a habit of yours."

"And yet I'm alive and unharmed, so, if anything, you're extraneous."

"Or you're particularly lucky. Luck runs out."

"Does your arrogance ever run out? I've been wondering that since I met you."

From her periphery, she saw his mouth tick up into a smile too quick for him to stifle. Ellory hid a smile of her own, comforted by old patterns. The changing landscape between them had not taken this away, at least, and it was easier to communicate in swapped witticisms than to wade into anything deeper.

Bailey Library loomed over them, its attached clock tower chiming three bells. As the oldest library on campus, it looked more like a basilica, built in a Romanesque style with sloping roofs and narrow windows. The interior was cathedral, lit by the sun streaming through the clerestory windows, with vaulted ceilings and gorgeous frescos of scenes from classic storybooks. Alice chasing a white rabbit toward Wonderland. Odysseus tying himself to the mast with wax in his ears to avoid the sirens' song. Gatsby staring across the bay toward the green light that represented his yearning for Daisy.

Ellory often thought Bailey was too suffocating to study in; it was more of an altar to the literary gods, and she wasn't pious enough to ignore that none of the frescos featured scenes from books by Black authors. Walking past dozens of white characters, suspended in their famous tales, only reinforced her fear that she didn't belong at the university. At least in Graves, she could pretend that she did.

Hudson paused by the elevator that would take them up to the reading room. "Maybe we should try the rare-books room first? That's in the basement."

Ellory's chest felt tight. "Why?"

"If I had something to hide, I would keep it in a place with few visitors."

The strangled sensation only worsened. He pressed the DOWN button, and she had to clench her fists at her sides to keep from slapping his hand away. She didn't want to go down there, and she had no idea why she didn't want to go down there, except it reminded her of her first week on campus and her exploration of the Graves, that feeling of being buried underground. Trapped.

There were stairs, she told herself. If anything happened, she had an escape route. She had Hudson.

But the anxiety persisted until every breath became a struggle.

The elevator descended into the bowels of the library.

Once the doors opened, Ellory trailed after Hudson, concentrating on placing one foot in front of the other. The rare-books room was at the end of a long, dimly lit hallway, interspersed with flickering lights. There was a humidifier to keep the books at the optimal temperature, but even the sound of it running wasn't enough to hide the skittering of vermin in the corners. Their footsteps were loud on the stone floor, warning anyone present that they were getting closer. Not that there was anyone down here.

She hoped there was no one down here.

"What should we be looking for, exactly?" Ellory whispered as the light bulb flashed another warning. "I don't think any ghosts are going to jump out and introduce themselves."

"Hidden passages. Discarded journals." Hudson unlocked the heavy doors, his expression cast in shadow as the light flickered off again. "Ghosts are appreciated, but not required."

Ellory had never been inside the rare-books room of any library. Shelves wrapped around all four walls, making space only for the door that had let them inside. A glass cage took up half the room, filled with even more books, whose yellowed pages looked like a single touch would dissolve them. There were desks with books stacked on top of them and podiums with books open on them. Dark lamps hung over them as the humidifier droned on.

She rubbed the goose bumps that had risen on her arms, unsure if they were being caused by the temperature or from the nerves that churned in her gut. But the sooner they found something, the sooner they could leave.

Haunted Hallowed Halls featured an entire chapter on Graves Library, but there wasn't anything about Bailey. Ellory had suggested meeting at the bigger library instead, but Hudson had made the sound point that anything buried on campus was likely to be in the oldest buildings rather than the newest. While he tugged at the spines of the books on the shelves, probably hoping for some cartoonish wall panel to slide open, Ellory wandered over to the nearest desk. Every book had an embossed title, and every spine was unbroken. She would have thought they were brand-new if not for how faded the text was. A small brush was abandoned by the side of one stack, the dust of newly cleaned tomes clinging to the bristles.

The hairs on the back of Ellory's neck stood up.

She peered over her shoulder, but nothing was there. Hudson moved silently around the room, and the humidifier roared its presence, but neither explained the way her instincts had shot to life, every nerve ending crying, *Danger, danger, danger...*

She turned her attention to the drawers. In the first one, she found more brushes and a larger feather duster. There was a notebook with numbers scratched on every page, and a key card that looked at least a decade old. The next drawer revealed pens, an empty planner, and an opened pack of batteries.

Her skin prickled with the feeling of being watched. She stopped with her hand on the handle of the third and final drawer, straining to listen. Beyond the humidifier, beyond Hudson's fruitless search, she could have sworn she heard a whisper.

Danger, danger, danger…

Ellory opened the drawer with shaking hands. It was empty.

Her heart was racing. She rubbed her chest as she knocked the drawer closed with her hip. "Hey, maybe we should—"

That was as far as she got before all hell broke loose.

32

IT STARTED WITH A RUMBLING. Ellory cut her sentence short to stare wide-eyed at the shelves, which vibrated like they were at the epicenter of an earthquake. The books quailed with them, rustling against one another like leaves in the wind. Hudson backed away from the ones he'd been examining until he was standing between her and the trembling walls, arm extended to keep her from trying to get past him.

A red book slid free of the shelf and shot toward them.

"Get down!" Hudson called.

Ellory hit the floor, the impact reverberating up her arms. The book slammed into the desk, right where she had just been standing. Hudson, crouched next to her, was still staring at the shelves in open horror. A blue book shook loose and hovered in the air before flying in their direction. Then a green book, a gold book, a leather-bound brown book—faster and faster, each pausing to search for them every time. Dust clung to Ellory's skin as she rolled out of the way, throwing her arms over her head in time to avoid getting concussed by a first edition of *The Mysterious Affair at Styles*.

"The desk," she shouted. More and more books joined the cacophony, swirling into a tornado of paper in the middle of the room. "Get under the desk!"

Hudson threw out a hand, and a podium screeched across the room to shield them. Whatever memory he had sacrificed to cast that spell saved them just in time. Hardcovers hit the walls, one another, the glass case, and the latter began to crack under the assault. Book after book struck the podium so hard that the wood splintered, and still they kept *coming*. Ellory flinched and huddled closer to Hudson; his breathing was calm where hers was labored, and she tried to match his level of peace before she hyperventilated.

Magic is dangerous... It's been twisted into this dark version of itself somehow.

It wasn't that Ellory hadn't believed Hudson when he'd told her that. She just hadn't thought magic itself would try to kill her.

The shelves emptied until the final book clattered to the ground inches away from Ellory's leg. Tension leaked from Hudson's body, but Ellory was on high alert. The shelves were shaking, even with nothing on them, and fear had been her friend and protector so far. When Hudson shifted to move the podium, she grabbed his sleeve.

His eyebrows lifted curiously, but before he could speak, the shelf opposite them tilted forward.

It collapsed to the ground hard enough to make her jump, taking a desk and three podiums with it. Wood panels cracked down the center. Books spilled from beneath with torn pages and bent covers. Ellory saw silver bolts in the wall, silver bolts that should have kept these shelves standing through another World War.

Then a second shelf crashed down.

"We have to get out of here," Hudson whispered. "Someone will come and investigate. Worse, one of the shelves is behind the glass case, and if it shatters—"

Ellory imagined trying to pick her way through sharp wood and sharper glass—if, of course, those shards didn't end up embedded in her body. Her hand throbbed with the phantom pain from Liam's Christmas party. "Lead the way."

He took her hand and kicked away the podium.

Together, they ran for the doors, sliding down the back of a broken shelf as the third worked itself loose of its bolts. The books surged from the ground and followed them anew, forcing them into a zigzag pattern to avoid being struck. Ellory's grip tightened around Hudson's as her free hand knocked a book off course before it could smash into the back of her head. They hit the door at a run, fumbling with the handle and tumbling into the hall.

The third shelf came down, and the glass case exploded with it.

It sounded like it was hailing indoors. Crystal pieces flew everywhere, coating the floor, pitter-pattering against the window in the door, slapping the walls as though they were trying to escape. The books the case had been protecting were covered in a thin layer of glass, and the humidifier rumbled in displeasure as pieces sank into the holes on its sides.

A shadowed figure stood in the center of the destruction, hands raised as though to protect themself from a strike. Their mouth opened wide, white teeth stark against their obsidian body, and they screamed until Ellory's ears began to ring. That scream echoed through her head, filled her chest, made her legs shake. Only her hand in Hudson's kept her on her feet.

"What?" he asked. "What is it?"

Ellory opened her mouth to explain, only to see that the figure—the ghost—was gone.

"Are you all right?" Hudson turned her to face him. "Are you hurt?"

"I—"

"What the hell happened down here?" A Bailey librarian emerged from the elevator, her heels clacking across the floor, her eyes alight with fury. "What did you do?"

"We didn't do anything," Hudson said quickly. To Ellory's disappointment, he let go of her hand. "Didn't you feel the earthquake? It destroyed the room with us in it. We nearly died."

"What earthquake? We're in *Connecticut*." The librarian shooed them away from the door and then gasped. "What on—how could—oh my god."

"Unless you're suggesting we can unbolt shelves from the wall and shatter a glass case with just our hands," Hudson continued, unruffled, "then I think you should take us at our word. And instead of suing for reckless endangerment, I'll see to it that my family restores this room to its former glory."

"I—" Her hand covered her mouth. She couldn't drag her eyes away from the window. "That would…that would be great. Are the two of you okay?"

Ellory knew the smile she gave as an answer was the wrong side of manic, but it was all that she could manage given the circumstances. She let Hudson and the librarian discuss the tentative details of the restoration on the way back upstairs so she could wring her hands in silence. Hudson had been right. Bailey Library *was* a place of magic, but that magic had become dark and dangerous. If she had come alone…

Hudson gave the librarian an actual business card and then walked out at a leisurely pace that grew urgent as soon as they had turned the corner at the end of the block. He slid in front of her before she could go any farther, his forehead creasing.

"Seriously, are you all right, Morgan? It's not like you to be so quiet."

The joke fell flat. Ellory shivered, her mind replaying the attack. She wrung her hands again and paused. There was a smear of crimson near the base of her palm. "What...?"

A quick check made it clear that the blood was not hers. But that meant—

Hudson rolled up his sleeve to show her his bleeding arm. There was a deep crevasse that could have been done only by a particularly sharp glass shard and a crimson scratch like he'd caught himself on one of the broken shelves. She blinked, and the red almost looked like another sleeve, there was so much blood. She blinked again, and it was bad, but it wasn't *that* bad, but he'd still gotten injured to protect her, and she didn't know how to feel about that.

"*You're* hurt," she said numbly. "Why didn't you tell me you were hurt?"

"It hardly matters—"

"It matters to *me*." Ellory reached for him before realizing that touching him would only hurt him further. "My dorm is closer. Let's go."

◆

As if the universe knew that she needed a victory, Ellory's dormitory was empty when they arrived. Clothes were strewn across Stasie's bed, which meant she would be gone for hours, as she usually only put that much effort into her outfit when she had people to show up. Maybe Ellory had gotten really lucky and Stasie was on a date, one that would keep her from making eyes at Hudson and giving him whatever he asked for.

Not that Ellory was any better.

"Sit there," she said, pointing him toward her bed. "I'm going to wet this cloth and come back."

When she returned from the bathroom, Hudson was sitting on the edge of her bed. He'd shed his coat and his sweater, leaving him in just a slate-gray button-down. One sleeve was rolled up to his bicep, the cuffs dotted with rust-colored stains. He stared at his folded hands instead of any of her things, though she wouldn't have been surprised if he'd already gone through her books. Hadn't she done the same thing to him at that party back in September?

She couldn't believe it had been four months since her perspective on Hudson Graves had first changed. She couldn't believe it had been four months and she still didn't know where they stood.

"I'm going to clean the blood, and then I'm going to put on some antiseptic, and then I'll bandage you up, okay?" she said, pulling her desk chair over so she didn't have to join him on the bed or kneel in front of him. Both things were far too intimate after the last few weeks. She needed to keep her hands steady and her thoughts focused. "This shouldn't take long."

"Shockingly, I know how first aid works," Hudson murmured, though he presented his hand without further complaint. "I could have done this myself."

"Just because you can do it yourself doesn't mean you should have to. You're hurt because of me."

"I'm hurt because of a poltergeist in the rare-books room. I don't see where you fit into that."

Ellory bit the inside of her cheek to keep from arguing with him. Letting him bait her into snapping at him would only make her feel worse. She wiped at the blood as gently as she could, her eyes flicking up every now and then to make sure she wasn't hurting him. He watched her intently but didn't flinch. He didn't even seem to blink.

She swallowed and moved on to the antiseptic.

"I think," Hudson said, his voice barely above a whisper, "something we did in there triggered a protective spell. Spells fall under the realm of incantation, which might mean Bailey Library once housed that school."

"We're not going back there," said Ellory. "Even if I wanted to, they're going to cordon it off until they can fix the rare-books room." She smiled up at him. "Nice job using money to get us out of trouble, by the way."

"What else is it for?" Hudson returned her smile with a hint of mischief. "Money will make the greatest skeptic to ever exist swear there was an earthquake even when there's no such thing in the news. She'll spread our story for us, and we'll be in the clear."

"You disgust me." Ellory smoothed the bandage over the last cut and sat back, admiring her handiwork. "Maybe I should have gone into medicine. I have at least six nurses in the family, you know."

"I couldn't see you as a nurse. Your bedside manner is poor."

"Excuse me?"

"You're incredibly bossy."

"That's a good skill for a nurse. And you're patched up now, aren't you?"

Hudson laughed. "I think nurses are kinder about it."

"I'll rip this bandage off and send you to a nurse right now."

He caught her wrist before she could pretend to make good on her threat. Ellory had leaned closer in the process, and now she froze, waiting to see what he would do next. His free hand hovered by her face, not quite touching her cheek but close enough that she could feel the warmth of potential. That intense, unblinking gaze had returned, but there was something soft about it, as if he not only saw something in her but liked it more than he knew how to express. It should have scared her, this closeness and her reaction to it, but it felt right. Normal.

She wanted to pull away, to reject him like he had rejected her at the party. But she was suspended by how being close to him made her feel a belonging that she struggled to capture anywhere else. The déjà vu that had led her down this path roared back to life.

There's something to the concept of people who feel like you knew them in another life, Aunt Carol had said. *Maybe you did. Our brains can only store so many memories, and we're already losing the earliest ones from this life before we're even halfway through it. Who's to say this is the only life we've ever had?*

If that was what all these echoes of memories had been telling her, that this was not the first life she had ever lived, then she was sure Hudson had been a part of the prior one. It was the only thing that made sense.

"Did we know each other," she mused, "before I lost my memories?"

Hudson's eyes had been tracing the curve of her cheek in an invisible caress. Now they snapped back to meet hers. "What do you mean?"

"Sometimes, it feels like we've had conversations before, gone to places together before. Like I know you better than I should. Like—" She pressed her lips together before she could tell him about her daydream. "Like we should know each other better than we do. Is it just me?" A pleading note had woven its way into her voice, and she cleared her throat to be rid of it. "I can't be the only one feeling like this. Am I?"

Hudson's hand dropped to the bed. He was pulling away from

her again, and she didn't know how to stop it. "I...I should go to the health center. Not that I don't trust your work, but...just in case."

"Hudson—"

"Morgan," he said, standing. "I can't, okay? Whatever it is you want from me, I can't give it to you. Not—*I can't.*"

Ellory deflated. If this was a preview of what it would be like to tell him how she felt, then she would die with her crush unspoken. She enjoyed their push and pull, but not when it came to her emotions. She was too old for games and for men who still played them. If he wanted to be partners in this investigation and nothing more, then that was what he would get from her.

"I guess I'll see you later, then," she said, her voice hoarfrost cold.

Hudson mumbled something that might have been a goodbye or might have been an apology. Either way, Ellory ignored it.

33

Ellory had read the *Warren Communiqué* at least three times by now and was already on her fourth by the time the bus dropped her off at Riverside Campus. She had turned in her article on Warren's famous families weeks ago, and she'd done a round of edits with Boone that had been so brutal she had been sure he'd found out that she was still working with Hudson and this was his revenge. Now here it was, on the fifth page of the *Communiqué*, below the fold, but bearing her byline: THE TANGLED ROOTS OF WARREN'S FAMILY TREE by Ellory Morgan.

Her first byline since high school, in one of the most famous student periodicals in the country. If she hadn't been in public, Ellory might have cried.

Disappointment tugged at her that she couldn't share this accomplishment with Aunt Carol, but she pushed it away. Tai and Cody had been so thrilled for her that they'd insisted on celebratory dessert after she got back from, as Cody put it, *Sherlocking around campus, looking for ghosts*, and that would just have to be enough. She didn't want anything or anyone to steal the smile on her face today. Which was also why she hadn't called Hudson to tag along. They hadn't spoken since she'd bandaged his wound, and she intended to keep it that way for as long as possible.

He lived inside her head in a way she didn't live inside his. He'd made that clear more than once. Space would be good for them both.

The morning was cold and misty. Fog rose off the Connecticut River and hung around Riverside Campus. Trees appeared every few feet, hidden in the haze, and dewdrops painted every flower and grass stem. Ellory's hair went from frizzy to disastrous after only a few minutes, making her wish she'd brought a hat. The first time she'd been to Riverside Campus, it had been raining and she had been disoriented. At sunrise, even the mist was painted a dusty pink, and the tree-lined path that twisted farther into the woods and the pond beyond looked like the Yellow Brick Road. Danger waited around every bend, but now she knew how to recognize it. To fight back. To survive.

Ellory was certainly hoping to find magic again, but if it found her first, she was ready.

She walked until she reached the clearing. The surface of the pond was still, grass growing as close to the bank as it could get before mud took over. Bur reeds and flowering rushes decorated the edges with pops of color: pinks and oranges, yellows and greens. After their successful—if terrifying—divination session, this was as good a place as any to summon Letitia Rose.

Like the rest of the Lost Eight, Letitia had left few facts about her life. She'd been a scholarship student. She went by the nickname *Tabby*. She'd come from a large family. That was all Ellory had learned, aside from the tiny black-and-white class photo she had found in an old paper, where Letitia's dark brown face had been

wedged between two beaming white classmates, her smile more measured.

Almost like she knew what was going to happen to her and couldn't pretend to care about anything else.

Ellory used the printed photo as the center of her circle, adding a series of things she had guessed that a woman in the 1960s might enjoy: a lava lamp, a pair of bell-bottoms, a copy of *The Sound of Music*. A flutter drew her attention to the path, where a charm of hummingbirds had gathered to flit from drooping flower to drooping flower. She couldn't remember if they had been there before, but it was reassuring to see them now. It meant the souls of the dead were already listening.

She stood back from her circle, making sure it was closed and identical to the one she'd made in the library. Her phone had no service, but she had told Tai where she was going. If anything went wrong, *someone* would find her before the day was through. Despite not returning her feelings, Hudson had cut himself to pieces to help her, while she'd shied away from casting even the smallest of magic. It was her turn to sacrifice. It was her time to end this.

Ellory glanced at the hummingbirds one last time. Then she closed her eyes and let the darkness take her.

It was surprisingly easy to put herself in Tabby's shoes in the hopes of connecting with her from across the veil. Her story felt familiar: a Black woman vaulted into an elite space and left to fend for herself among predators who didn't care whether she lived or died. If she thrived, she would be a credit to her race. If she failed, she shouldn't have been brought in to begin with. She wondered if Tabby had been born in America or if she had immigrated here, if the Civil Rights Movement had been something she longed to be an active participant in or if she just wanted to exist in peace, if her family ever pressured her to get the right kind of job and make the right kind of friends no matter her personal desires.

Ellory sank deeper and deeper into the darkness, opening herself to whatever might reach back. The stink of rot made her open her eyes.

Fish cluttered the muddy bank. A bluegill, a largemouth bass, a fathead minnow, and several more floated to the top of the pond, wafting toward her like shuffling zombies. They smelled rancid, like they'd not only died but had been dead for years. Their swollen eyes seemed to accuse her. Their scaled bodies had putrefied, leaving wet holes in their skin through which their narrow bones were visible. Their open mouths leaked pond water and pus onto the ground.

Ellory covered her nose, fighting the urge to gag as more and more of them washed ashore. She loved seafood, but she wasn't sure she could ever again eat a fish without thinking of a smell so rancid that it burned the back of her throat. The fish kept coming, more of them than the pond could possibly have held, until a frog dropped atop the small pyramid. Its pale mouth fell open, and a ball of light floated into the air between them with a small cascade of brown-blue water.

The ghost light hovered there for a moment before plunging into the mist.

Ellory hurried after it.

She kept her phone in her hand, hoping to get a signal, but it remained dead as she followed the light through the woods. The farther she went, the less confident she became that she could find her way back to the university buildings. Every tree looked the same, and the mist was even thicker here, hiding the path she had taken.

Conjured lights had led her to safety when she'd gotten lost in the orchard, but that didn't mean each one was trying to help her. She imagined wandering around the woods until it got dark, her legs aching and her body shivering, as the ghost light made sure she didn't stumble over anyone who could take her to safety. She imagined sitting down against a tree's rough bark and falling asleep, only to freeze to death there as the morning mist turned to evening snow. She imagined Tai finding her like that and having to tell Aunt Carol that Ellory had killed herself trying to save herself, and people like her, from the machinations of the Old Masters—a mystery no one had asked her to solve, a theory no one had asked her to validate.

She tugged her coat more tightly around herself and promised she would try to find her way back after five more minutes.

Seconds later, the endless treescape ended in a large clearing. A dilapidated building, all wooden beams and a shingled roof, perched like a pigeon on a phone line. It looked like a one-room schoolhouse from colonial times, but the bell tower was taller than any she'd seen in pictures before, so tall she was reminded of the story of Rapunzel. The door was both caved in and boarded up, decorated by a dusty keyhole arch. A sign had swung down from over the door, one corner pressed into the stone steps that led up to the entrance. Most of the text was missing, but Ellory could make out a single letter:

Ǝ.

She had never heard anyone mention a building like this on Riverside Campus. It hadn't been on her map either. Ellory was sure this clearing hadn't existed before she'd drawn her summoning circle, and the fact that the light continued to hover at her shoulder lent credence to the theory. Tabby's spirit may not have shown up, but perhaps she had sent the ghost light to show Ellory the truth.

Overgrown grass tangled around her boots as she fought her way toward the building. Arched windows with dirty, broken glass hung on either side of the door. A thick spider had made an elegant web in one of the remaining sections, and its legs twitched at Ellory's approach. She gave it a wide berth as she circled the schoolhouse, looking for a way in. At the back, she found a door with a hummingbird knocker that had rusted with time. It creaked open easily, sending a cloud of dust into the air.

Ellory coughed into the bend of her elbow. "Hello? Is anyone here?"

The first floor was one long room. She saw misshapen rows of desks with attached chairs, each one of them broken; a domed ceiling, and a ladder that led to an overhang; an abandoned blackboard, cracked into three pieces; and several filthy textbooks with holes in the equally filthy pages.

Rectangular objects leaned against the walls, covered by tarps. Ellory tugged one free to reveal a portrait, newer than anything in the room. It was painted in the same style as the ones of the Warren founders in the museum, but this one was labeled DEAN ARTHUR O'CONNOR I. Stasie's grandfather frowned at Ellory from the center of the oil painting. A crow was perched on the windowsill behind him, which, like the painting of Howard McElking, had sunlight streaming through the glass.

Ellory freed another portrait. This one read DEAN PRESTON COLT and featured a younger version of the professor she'd come to know so well, a snow owl cupped between his hands. He was in front of a stained glass window that she recognized from the *Warren Communiqué* office, and, like in Richard Lester Odell's portrait, a moonless starry sky in different shades was on the other side of the glass.

The third and final portrait was of Dean Nathaniel Graves, a stern-looking white man with curly black hair and narrow black eyes. A hummingbird hovered by his shoulder, and he gazed out a window into a midnight sky empty except for a crescent moon.

My father is a cruel man, Hudson had said. Ellory was looking at a painting of Hudson's father, a man deeply entrenched in magic, who had, nonetheless, gaslighted his own son into believing it didn't exist.

Disgust made her hands shake. She wanted to carve his portrait up, but she took pictures of all of them instead. Arthur O'Connor was the only one of the three who had ever been dean of Warren University as well, and there was no reason for these portraits to be commissioned, let alone here, if Colt and Graves had been deans at other schools. They had run one of the three magical disciplines of the School for the Unseen Arts: evocation, incantation, and divination.

Colt was part of this, just like her vision had warned. And he was, at least, close enough to answer her questions—whether he wanted to or not. If she could figure out how to tie this back to the paper, to weaponize the silence between his answers, she might get him to reveal more than he'd intended. It had worked for interviews with tight-lipped sources during high school. The trick was never revealing how much you already knew.

A scream cracked the silence of the schoolhouse.

Ellory jumped, whirling around, but she could see no one in the dim room. The scream ricocheted off the walls, building upon itself, until it sounded like a chorus of panic. She turned and turned, but no matter where she looked, there was nothing. Just that endless clamor, a ghostly wail of ancient pain.

Clapping her hands over her ears, she stumbled toward the door. A rectangle of light beckoned her to freedom until a shadow filled the space. Ellory skidded to a halt, her ears still covered, squinting at the figure limned by the sun. She could feel eyes on her, but the person was silent, and if they heard the screaming, they were unaffected. She got the sudden urge to put some distance between her and this stranger, and she gave in with three large steps back. The figure didn't move.

"H-hello?" she said, her voice swallowed by the screams that still deafened her. "Who are you?"

The shadow charged toward her. This time, Ellory was the one to scream.

She threw herself to the side, narrowly avoiding being tackled by a person she still couldn't see. She could no longer blame the sun for casting them in shadow. Their form was nondescript, as if her eyes hadn't adjusted to the darkness. Their face was blank, not in expression but in features: They had no nose, no eyes, no mouth, just sunken crevices where those things would be. Their skin was corpse gray, and as she watched, their muscles swelled and their legs elongated until they were six feet, seven feet, eight feet tall. Their nails were needle sharp as they reached for her.

But this was not the person who had attacked her on the quad or at Moneta.

This was no masked enforcer. This twisted creature was an assassin.

Ellory rolled back onto her feet and ran.

The floor shook as the monster chased her down. The scream that had weakened her abruptly cut out, leaving Ellory with nothing but her quick breaths and desperate steps to keep her company. Her pursuer was as silent as a cemetery: no breathing, no growling, no threats. Her heart leaped to her throat as every rumbling step brought it closer and closer and closer...

The door had never been so far away.

Talons pierced the back of her jacket, scratched her spine.

Ellory threw herself into the sunlight, her face wet with tears. A clawed hand stretched out, only to dissolve upon contact with the outside air. One minute, the monster was stretching the foundations of the door, desperate to drag her back into its lair, and the next minute, it was gone in a flutter of black spots that clouded her vision. Still, she kept running, cutting through the tall grass and past the tree line. Then and only then did she slow enough to glance back again.

The monster was gone, but so was the clearing, the building. In their place was a thicket, and the winding path that led deeper into campus. Her heaving breaths combined with the sound of rushing water, a sign that she was close to the riverbank.

If not for the sting of the scratches and the chill wind that had already found the hole in her only winter coat, Ellory might have thought she had imagined it all.

She fell into the grass beside the path, pressing her hands against her closed eyes. "Holy shit."

"Are you okay?!"

Her blurred vision resolved itself into an upside-down Hudson Graves. There were twigs and dirt in her hair, and she was pretty sure she was bleeding, but this was just as unbelievable as the danger she had escaped. Ellory was so confused that she allowed him to pull her to her feet. He dusted off her sleeves and then reached for her hair before seeming to realize what he was doing. He cleared his throat, stuffed his hands in his pockets.

"I followed you," he said gruffly. "I saw you heading into the woods *alone*, and I thought maybe—you might need—I don't know."

Ellory noticed, belatedly, that he was dressed in the kind of clothes people typically went running in: stretch leggings and comfortable sneakers, a long-sleeved breathable shirt and headphones wrapped around his neck. Sweat beaded at his temples, and his coat was nowhere to be seen.

"I don't need you," she heard herself say. "But I'm glad you're here."

Slowly, invitingly, she tipped her head forward. Hudson studied her for a moment and then stepped closer to pick the debris out of her hair. Ellory wanted to fold herself against him, to close her eyes and know that she was safe, but she held herself still before she embarrassed herself again. His touch was gentle and focused. She let that soothe her frazzled nerves instead.

"What happened?" he murmured.

"I think I found one of the buildings for the School for the Unseen Arts," Ellory said. "I did a summoning spell, and it led me to a clearing with a schoolhouse in it. I think it might have been the oldest one, going back to Letitia Rose's time." She told him everything she had found inside but excluded the portrait of his father. She would tell him, eventually, but not now, not like this. She thought of how small he'd sounded on the balcony, recounting how many lies his family had told him, and she didn't want to cut him with another one when he was already so worried. "I think something terrible happened there. That scream...it was like the death echo of Malcolm Mayhew's murder. It was *awful*. If this is where Tabby died, then she was in incredible pain the whole time."

Hudson cupped her cheeks, his thumbs caressing her damp face. Her breath caught. She hadn't realized that she was still crying, and now she was paralyzed by the look in his eyes, the protectiveness of his touch, the safety she'd found in his company.

"I'm so glad you're okay," he whispered. "So, so glad."

"I'm getting mixed signals here," she whispered back.

Hudson laughed, more breath than sound, more relieved than amused. "I care about you, Morgan. Isn't that obvious by now?"

Ellory was frustrated with him, and perhaps she always would be, but she couldn't deny he was right. It *was* obvious. He had worried about her, and he was here. Every time she called him, he was there. Even when she didn't call him, he was there. She had spent her entire life living for other people, embodying her parents' hopes, keeping track of her aunt's medicines, making her own meals even when she worked late. She didn't need Hudson Graves, or anyone else, to take care of her.

But damn did it feel good that someone wanted to.

"We need to talk to Colt," she said, shuddering at everything she had just seen. "Maybe he's the key to tying all this together. And, even if he isn't, I want to know whatever he knows."

34

Ellory's scheme to get Professor Colt alone worked with only a minor snag. He didn't have office hours as a rule, leaving that to his TAs, so she pretended to have additional questions about his spring research project. He agreed to let her come to his house, and Hudson agreed to go with her for backup. She didn't mention how quickly he agreed or that he'd have to skip a class in order to be there. He didn't mention the smile she couldn't bury for the rest of the day or how confidently she laid out the questions she'd ask, knowing she'd have him behind her.

That was how she ended up in a car on her way to Colt's house, hoping she was doing the right thing. She wasn't particularly afraid of the professor, not now that she had some level of control over her power, but she *was* afraid of magic's dangerous possibilities. She had been weakened and chased, attacked and cursed, and she worried that this was only the start of it all. Magic was powerful enough to rewrite her memories and alter her reality. It was powerful enough to kill for.

The car dropped her off at the end of the drive, but there was no sign of Hudson. She checked her phone—five minutes away, he'd texted ten minutes ago—and approached the house. No Hudson there either. She checked her phone again, and then she peered at the front door, where a scarecrow decoration winked from atop the familiar skull knocker. Had he gone inside without her, or was he late? Should she ring the doorbell? Should she walk back down the drive to wait for him?

Something felt off.

Ellory shared her location with Tai and Cody, then scrolled through her contacts until she found Hudson's number. But before she could call him, the door swung open.

"I thought I saw someone wandering around out here," said Colt with a welcoming smile. "Please, come in."

Someone, not *someone else*. Ellory hovered on the steps, knowing that she should wait for Hudson. But what was she supposed to say? *Give me a minute, Professor. I need to wait for a surprise guest?* It was now or never.

Keeping one hand on the Taser Tai insisted she carry with her these days, Ellory stepped inside. She had caught Colt in the middle of grading papers. Stacks of them topped the coffee table in the study, along with a lukewarm mug of tea and a plate empty of all but a single smear of jam. As Colt left to put the kettle back on, Ellory sat in one of the armchairs. The papers had enough red swipes on them to make her nervous about taking his class in a couple of years. A low flame filled the fireplace, making the room cozy. It was impossible not to relax when faced with the combination of Colt's soothing presence and his aesthetically pleasing home that seemed to croon that comfort was a luxury he intended to afford.

Of course, that was exactly how he wanted her to feel. His

unique power was putting people at ease while feeding from them like a leech. Ellory forced herself to remember that.

Colt returned with two mugs and a tray of honey, sugar, and tea bags. She grabbed one, and he took the other, choosing an Earl Grey tea bag to mix into his water. Ellory copied his motion with oolong tea and slowly stirred honey into the drink to disguise the fact that she didn't actually plan to take a sip. At home, she and Carol had a honey container shaped like a bear. Colt kept his in a silver-plated dish engraved with pomegranates.

"The myth of Persephone is one of my favorite classics," he admitted when he caught her staring at it. "A woman of multitudes, the goddess of spring and the ruler of the underworld, so loved that her earthen mother cursed the world with six months of winter, so loved that her deadly husband was, by most sources, the only one who never strayed. Light and dark personified."

"I didn't know you liked myths," Ellory said, holding her mug with both hands in case she needed to throw a hot beverage and run. "Do you know any about birds?"

"Birds," Colt repeated, amused. "There are thousands, even millions, about birds. Did you want to hear about any in particular?"

"Owls. It's for another *Communiqué* article."

"Owls." Colt drank from his own mug, shifting into a more comfortable position on the couch. "It depends on the culture. Owls can be prophetic creatures or ruinous ones. They can symbolize wisdom or calamity. In the words of Lady Macbeth, 'It was the owl that shriek'd, the fatal bellman, which gives the stern'st good-night.'"

"So they're associated with divination," Ellory murmured, watching Colt closely. It felt like they were dancing on a knife-edge, and any wrong word would ensure she'd never leave this house again. "Like those free psychic readings you can get all over the place?"

The line of questioning didn't seem to disturb him. "I can't say I have any interest in the esoteric, Miss Morgan. Astrological charts and tarot cards and the like just seem like a way to rob us of our own free will. Maybe it's my old age, but I want the future to remain a surprise. I want to wake up every day not knowing what to expect."

Ellory remained silent, watching steam curl from her mug.

"Not," Colt continued, "that there's anything wrong with the esoteric. There are many reasons people need to believe in a higher power. Especially in times of strife."

"Yeah, I could see that. The school hasn't been without strife either, I've heard."

Colt sighed. "What school is? Since you asked me about Malcolm Mayhew, I suppose you've been looking into the disappearances. Awful, awful things."

Ellory glanced at the window, half expecting to see Hudson crossing the lawn, late but whole, pissed that she'd dived into trouble without him again. But this turn in the conversation made a lump form in her throat, the bad feeling she'd had outside following her here. Hudson should be here. Hudson *would* be here. With or without a phone, he'd find his way here.

Her grip tightened around the mug to keep her hands from trembling. "There hasn't been a disappearance since, right?"

"Not to my knowledge." Colt finished his tea and set the empty mug on the tray. "Unless, of course, you count Mister Graves."

Ellory froze. "What?"

"That was a joke, Miss Morgan. Perhaps in bad taste, given the subject matter... My apologies," said Colt. "I meant only that he missed my last salon without a word."

Ellory set down her mug, unconvinced. Her heart pounded against her rib cage. *Hudson should be here.* "Have you heard from him today?"

"I haven't. Why?"

She wanted to overturn the tray and demand answers, but there wasn't a hint of recognition in Colt's eyes. Either he was a remarkable liar, or he genuinely had no idea what she was hinting at—and, most likely, he thought he was indulging her in some random tangent. She didn't dare get into her more specific questions without Hudson—*should be here, should be here, should be here*—and yet she felt like she'd hit another dead end by coming.

Maybe the same curse that had taken her memory had also taken Colt's. If the School for the Unseen Arts was willing to kill students to protect its privacy, they might have cast spells of forgetting on the former deans as well. People too important to kill, but with too much information to be allowed to roam the streets.

No matter what, she was wasting her time here. She had a Taser, hot tea, and her screaming instincts, which wasn't enough to keep her safe without Hudson and his magic. Colt was older, more experienced, and that made him too dangerous to follow through on her plan right now. Eventually, she might be able to get him somewhere public. Until then, she got to her feet. "I just remembered that I'm late for something. Thank you so much for your time, Professor. I'll email you my questions about the research when I have a free moment."

Colt blinked. "Well, all right. Is something wrong, Miss Morgan? If you're in some sort of trouble…"

His kindness only terrified her more.

"I don't want to take any more time from your grading." She was already halfway to the door, her thoughts tumbling over one another. "See you at the salon."

But even when she made it outside, she could still feel his eyes burning into her back.

◆

Ellory's call to Hudson went to voicemail, so she sent him a text to call her later. She spent the rest of the day until her shift at work theorizing in circles and waiting for Stasie to come back so she could demand, once again, that she turn over her grandfather's phone number. As usual, her roommate let her down, and Ellory went to serve coffee to the exhausted masses with no more answers than she'd started her day with.

She was so close, that was the worst thing. The puzzle was almost complete, but the parts that were missing were just large enough to keep her from seeing the whole picture. She'd written everything down in her notebook, hoping that writing notes would help shake a realization loose, but all it had done was make her wrist ache. She needed to talk to more people. She needed to do more research. She needed at least one more séance, with another member of the Lost Eight.

She needed Hudson to *tell her he was okay*, but her text went unanswered.

Ellory got back to her dorm at eleven at night, smelling like coffee beans and caramel sauce. Stasie was already asleep, a sleep mask protecting her eyes from the light. Instead of shaking her awake, Ellory sat in the hallway to call Hudson one more time, hoping he hadn't been summoned home again.

"The number you have dialed is out of service..."

She frowned and ended the call. Tried again.

"The number you have dialed is out of service..."

Again.

"The number you have dialed is out of service..."

She checked her call log, but it read GRAVES (3) like normal. She tried Boone once, twice, three times, but the same bizarre message greeted her each time. Boone was one thing, but *Hudson's* number being out of service made no sense. Even when he'd last been home, her messages had gone through and she'd reached his voicemail just this afternoon, full though his inbox had been. To be out of service now...

The strangeness of it made Ellory too anxious to sleep. She rose with the sun to take a taxi to Hudson's, but immediate action didn't soothe her the way it usually did. The closer she got to his off-campus housing, the harder it was to breathe. Her body was in the midst of dealing with some horrible truth that her mind had yet to catch up with. That clawing dread would choke her before she ever got to see that Hudson was all right.

Hudson had to be all right. He *had* to be.

The car had barely stopped before Ellory was surging out and jogging up to the door. Hudson's Barracuda wasn't in the driveway, which didn't help her shaky nerves. Ellory managed to ring the doorbell only once, but she paced restlessly on the porch until she heard footsteps approaching.

Liam opened the door dressed in a matching slate-gray pajama set. His feet were bare, and his hair was smushed on one side of his head, as if he'd been sleeping on it. He blinked at her in confusion. "What are you doing here, Ellory?"

"I'm looking for Hudson. Do you know where he's gone?"

Liam's eyebrows drew together. "Who?"

Ellory wasn't in the mood for jokes. She stepped forward until Liam backed away to let her inside. "I can just wait in his room," she said, leaning down to unlace her sneakers. "I don't want to interrupt whatever you were doing before I got here."

"In whose room?" Liam asked.

"This isn't funny."

"I'm not kidding. And, not to be rude, but do you know what time it is?"

"Hudson will be—"

"Okay, seriously"—Liam grabbed her shoulder, keeping her from moving deeper into the house—"who's Hudson? I'm the only person here."

Ellory's stomach dropped. She turned slowly, studying Liam's face. He was serious. She forced herself to sound calm. "Hudson Graves? He's—you don't know someone named *Hudson Graves*?"

"I don't," Liam confirmed.

"What about Boone Priestley?"

Liam smiled drowsily. "Are these hot goths?"

Ellory stared at him until he yawned.

"If you're staying, I'll put the coffee on," he said, rubbing his left eye. "In fact, you should stay. You sound—I'm worried about you."

Ellory allowed him to deposit her on the couch. As soon as he was out of view, she left the house in a daze. Hudson's phone number was out of service. Liam—his ex, his roommate—had never heard of him or Boone. Part of her hoped that if she waited there long enough, Boone would reopen the door, laugh at her for believing in his and Liam's practical joke, and tell her that Hudson had gone to the gym or into town or somewhere, *anywhere*.

The door remained closed. Everything was still.

She walked down the road until she could no longer be seen from the windows. She sent a text to Tai, to Cody, to Stasie, even to the one person she knew from con. law: have you seen hudson today? Each one replied the same way: who?

Each one struck her like a blow.

The journey from the house back to campus flattened to nothing. One minute, Ellory was summoning a taxi. The next minute, she was in Graves Library—which was missing the plaque she sneered at every day—searching ancestry sites and local newspapers, searching *Forbes* and class records. Hudson Graves, twenty-one, senior at Warren University, didn't exist, as far as the internet was concerned. His parents had one child—Cairo Graves—who had never attended Warren—or, indeed, any college at all.

The next time she checked her phone, his number was gone.

Ellory blinked, and she was in her dorm room, searching her shelves for the books Hudson had lent her and finding nothing. She sank onto her bed, wishing that she'd taken a picture of him or a picture of the two of them together, something she could hold on to as proof of this tear in reality.

Her surroundings blurred. Tears fell, first one and two and then a steady stream of sobs that tore her throat raw. All the times she'd felt alone before now couldn't possibly compare to this hollowness. It was like losing a limb that she kept trying to walk on, like breaking a heart that she'd thought was already too broken to work. Ellory wiped angrily at her wet cheeks, but her body continued to shake because nothing made sense, nothing made any fucking *sense* anymore.

Ellory screamed into her pillow until her voice went hoarse and she could finally think.

Boone had warned her that he would protect Hudson at all costs. Had he done this? Had he dropped them both into some liminal space where she couldn't reach them, leaving her the sole victim of the Old Masters' ire?

She rejected the theory as soon as it formed. She'd seen Boone's magic, and it left copies behind to fill the void left by their absence. Hudson and Boone hadn't just disappeared; they had been erased from existence, from memory.

RemƎmber.

Someone—Colt, perhaps—was messing with her. She'd gotten too close to the Old Masters and the School for the Unseen Arts, and Hudson had suffered for it. They wanted her isolated and afraid. They wanted her weak and doubtful. She was outside their control, and that made her a problem.

All her life, Ellory had tried her best to be accommodating. She was Black and she was a woman, and that intersection made her determined to be polite, decorous, unproblematic. Never sassy or angry. Never too sexual or too prudish. Never a clown and never a nerd. She welded herself into the mold society left open for her, and she tried not to ask for anything more.

What had it gotten her? A safety net of a person that only she remembered. A thousand questions with answers that would make her sound like she should be committed. A nightmare she couldn't wake up from that had taken the one thing she hadn't realized she had to give.

No more.

She could not, would not accommodate this. She could not, would not accept it.

She was tired of making herself small so that other people could feel larger than life. She was tired of lies and secrets, of being controlled by hidden figures in the dark. She was tired of feeling scared and powerless, especially at the hands of people scared of *her* power.

AN ARCANE INHERITANCE

If they wanted a problem, then she would become a problem—and she would make them regret that they had pushed her to this point.

INTERLUDE

For magic to live, something must die. Luckily, death comes in as many forms as magic. The world requires balance, and magic collects its debt in sacrifice. To rewrite the rules of reality is to give away something one can never get back. The cost of the sacrifice must equal the power of the spell, or the magic will take and take until it's satisfied. Until there's nothing left.

Some say that's why the Godwin Scholars rebranded themselves. Magic was no longer something to be worked for, studied, or exalted. Magic was their master, and they were its slaves—a role reversal that sat poorly in the parts of their minds that knew, in theory, that owning people was wrong but felt, in practice, that only owning *white* people was intolerable. In the 1980s, magic became evil and dark, a putrid shackle that linked its wielder to Lucifer himself.

This turn did not inspire the Satanic Panic that launched with the 1980 publication of *Michelle Remembers* by Michelle Smith and Dr. Lawrence Pazder. But, as with most societal upheavals, the right sort of people found a way to use it to their advantage. By that point, three of the Lost Eight had gone missing, enough to raise eyebrows but not enough for true alarm. Three students in thirty years was hardly newsworthy, except maybe at a Hartford bar just before last call when the stragglers began to speak of spirits that existed outside their glasses.

For the length of a decade, Warren University was no more than what it appeared to be: an Ivy League institution, accessible to only the highest echelon of society and the handful of scholarship students they peppered across the campus to corral in time for brochure photos. Magic was a direct line to hell, and no learned man would *ever* mess with demonic forces.

Unless, of course, they were not the ones who had to sacrifice.

35

"ARE YOU MOVING OUT?" STASIE asked as Ellory raided the room for more things to stuff into her backpack.

She had a Taser, a water bottle, granola bars, Greek yogurt, a flashlight, a change of clothes and shoes, and a portable battery for her phone, but she still felt like she had packed too light. There was no instruction guide on how to confront a secret society of possible magicians about messing with her life, her head, and her heart. She was making it up as she went along.

"Maybe," she said, as she shoved a hoodie, a notepad, and a pen into the bag. "I don't know when I'll be back, so you might get your wish for a single after all."

"Should I be worried?" Stasie lowered her voice as if there were anyone but them around to hear her. "Is this a cry for help?"

"If I were going to cry for help, it wouldn't be in front of you. No offense."

"None taken."

Ellory added batteries for the flashlight, the pepper spray and rape whistle they'd been given during welcome week, and her wallet.

Then she zipped up her bag and hoped it would be enough. She'd gotten by on nothing but her own determination so far, a drive to solve this mystery that not even she could explain sometimes. But this wasn't just dangerous. It was potentially lethal. A truly smart woman would have unpacked her bag, gone to bed, and waited for whatever spell had been cast to erase Hudson Graves from her mind.

But Hudson had gone through hell just to help her. She had to do the same for him.

"Hey," Stasie said before Ellory could go through the door. She took what might be her last look at her roommate and was struck by just how *young* she was. Her face was bare of makeup, and her hair was down; she wore a pair of baby-pink silk pajamas, and her eyes were Bambi bright. Stasie O'Connor was only eighteen years old, fresh out of high school, and determined to find her place at college, and she looked it. "You weren't, like, the *worst* roommate in the world."

Ellory smiled sadly. Maybe in another world, another life, they could have been friends. Stasie was spoiled and vain, inconsiderate and churlish, but she would have the rest of her life to grow out of that. Maybe they could have learned from each other, helped each other, listened to each other.

But this was the hand this life had dealt them, where Ellory felt a rush of affection for her roommate only when it seemed likely she would never see her again.

"You kind of were," she said, smile widening at the offended wrinkle of Stasie's nose. "But I like you, too."

Then she hurried out of Moneta Hall before anyone—especially Tai—could stop her.

◆

The ground floor of Colt's house was already lit like he was in the middle of a party. The next salon wasn't for a few more weeks, but the shadows passing behind the windows made it clear that he wasn't alone. Ellory had been hoping to break in, to get the drop on him, to confront him with what she knew. She considered returning to the dorm, regardless of how much Stasie would make fun of her, and trying again tomorrow. But by tomorrow it might be too late. By tomorrow, she might have forgotten Hudson and Boone, too.

She would try to sneak in the back, hide in a closet until the party was over, and—and what? Threaten her meal ticket with a butter knife? Who did she think she was?

Before she could make a decision either way, the front door swung open. Colt stood bathed in golden light like Zeus on Mount Olympus, a small smile on his face. She didn't know if it was the shadows cast or if it was because she knew the truth of him now, but he cut a sinister figure, and his smile was an austere slash across an otherwise-remote face.

"Our guest of honor. I saw you coming." He stepped back, one hand still on the doorknob. "It's time we have a frank conversation, don't you think?"

Ellory approached the house as if drawn by an invisible cord. Colt watched her with the focus of an eagle on the hunt, taking her coat like this was just another night while she walked herself to the study. The glittering room was full of people, none of whom she recognized. Some of them wore white masks like the enforcer had, hiding their identities even among their peers, but the rest were just strangers. Old white fucks, as Boone had described, wearing Rolexes and furs, diamonds and designer shoes. Despite everything, she half expected to see him here, but she didn't. As far as she could tell, she was the only person with any melanin to her skin in the room.

Colt appeared behind her. "We know you've been looking for us, and here we are. In a manner of speaking, anyway."

Ellory gasped as she regained control of her own body and stumbled to put some distance between herself and Colt. This forced her farther into the room, on the outskirts of this anonymous crowd, but even that felt safer than being near someone who could puppet her as if he owned her. "Why? You already had me right where you wanted me, and you let me leave. You took Hudson and Boone. *Why?*"

She didn't dare mention Tai and Cody. If the Old Masters didn't know about them, Ellory wanted to keep it that way.

"Mister Graves and Mister Priestley were tools that we gave you to get you where you needed to be," said Colt. One of the masked guests handed him a wineglass of golden liquid, and he swirled it before taking a sip. "You no longer need them, and neither do we."

Ellory placed her back against a nearby wall, forcing Colt to come to her. She could see the entire crowd from here, and an inlaid flat-screen TV that she could swear hadn't been there the last time she'd been here. It played camera footage of a dark platform lit by orbs of blue light. The aging arches and vaulted ceiling looked almost familiar, but not as familiar as the faces she could see floating in two of the orbs.

"Tai? Cody?" she blurted out. "Where is that? *Where are they?*"

Were Hudson and Boone there, too?

"Since its inception," Colt said with the relish of a man who loved to hear himself talk, "the School for the Unseen Arts has been a bastion for the Old Masters, their friends, and their families. Magic is a tool to influence the world, as powerful as any other. It sits alongside money and connections, meant for the hands of those who know what to do with it. It's organized and controlled.

A precious resource that we wield for only the most necessary of circumstances. But, every so often, people arrive who have an aptitude for what we call *wild magic* but would more accurately be described as *ancestral magic*."

Ellory swallowed. "Me."

"You. Tabby Rose, Manuel Sharp, Angel Mclaughlin, Olivia Holloway, Tasha Butler, Eugene Kang, Kristopher Douglas, and Joel Carroll. Taiwo Daniels and Cody Flores."

The rush that usually came with being right never materialized. Instead, all she felt was dread.

"Where are they?" she whispered through a suddenly dry throat. "What have you done with them? What are you going to do with me?"

"You haven't guessed?" Colt took another sip of his wine, a frown deepening the creases by his mouth. "They're asleep, Miss Morgan. In the decades it took to get the spell right, sacrifices were an unfortunate necessity to power our magic. But now things are so much more civilized. Now we siphon it, and we use the power to change the world. In the meantime, they sleep. *You* sleep. And the magic gives you a beautiful shared dream, a fictitious realm crafted by all of you in tandem, as long as you don't. Fight. Back."

The dread, Ellory realized, and the times she had felt like she couldn't breathe when the déjà vu was strongest. She'd been testing the boundaries of her world and her memory, and the siphoning spell had punished her for it. When she'd investigated the library and the schoolhouse, she'd outright been attacked—and that explained the familiarity. She squinted at the television again, her heart racing. The schoolhouse. This was the layout of the schoolhouse. The monster had driven her from searching further, from searching above, but she recognized those walls and floors.

There was no time. There was no *time*. She dragged her eyes from the TV to take note of all three exits—the one to the hallway, the one to the kitchen, and the windows that overlooked the yard. She couldn't get to any of them. Not yet. Especially not when, as Colt had just displayed, their magic was far more powerful than hers, and she wouldn't even see it coming.

"I thought we were having a frank discussion, Professor," she said as she formulated a plan. "Start making sense. How can I be asleep if I'm standing right here?"

The room went silent. As one, every head in the room turned to them, blank masks and blank expressions. The eyes she could see were ravenous, like she had something they wanted too badly for her to survive its theft. Ellory's body coiled tight, her hands fisting at her sides. The crowd inched closer step by step, moving in unison like a toy army, and Colt stood at their head with the casual air of a man used to getting his way.

"I think you're very bright, full of potential," he said. "I like you very much. I pushed for your induction rather than contribution to this hecatomb, but we live in a democracy and all that." Behind him, the Old Masters crept closer and closer, blocking the windows, the fireplace. "I promise this won't hurt."

"I don't," Ellory said, charging forward.

Colt was too surprised to plant his feet. They went down together in a splash of white wine, and Ellory recovered first. She scrambled up and headed for the kitchen, which, she remembered from helping the cook clean up, opened out into the yard. Once she escaped, she could think, she could process, but not here in the heart of these well-dressed vultures who wanted to suck magic out of her dying body. She expected the crowd to try and grab her, to stop her, but they stood like androids that had powered down, their heads bowed to look at a cursing Colt.

Honestly, at this point in the school year, advanced robots wouldn't even surprise her.

The kitchen door was locked. Ellory fumbled with it, keeping an ear out for movement from the study. *Click.* She turned the knob, hurled the door open, and nearly collided with someone.

White mask.

Nondescript clothes.

The enforcer.

Ellory reached for her bag too slowly. The enforcer dropped to the ground, sweeping her legs out from under her. Ellory hit the paneling with a pained cry, her hips burning from the impact. Standing over her, haloed by the fluorescent lighting, the enforcer looked like a duppy, the malevolent kind, ready to make off with her soul.

Their gloved hands reached up to remove the mask, and Gaia Hammond smirked down at her.

"Got you," Gaia crowed.

A rage like nothing Ellory had ever felt coursed through her. "You *fucking* bitch—"

She gripped the front of Gaia's clothes and rolled, slamming her down. She landed on top of the cursing woman and reached for something, anything, to shut her up with. Her searching fingers found the mask. Instead of beating Gaia with it, Ellory cracked it in half right by the woman's head. Gaia flinched, and it felt good, so good, to make her the terrified one for once. Every conversation they'd ever had played on a loop in Ellory's mind, combined with every time she had cowered from Gaia's masked face and every time she'd swallowed her retorts to Gaia's victim complex. This was who was terrorizing her? Some blond-haired white woman who was more afraid of being called a racist than she was of actual racism?

"*I'll kill you*," Ellory snarled, drawing her fist back.

"PROFESSOR," Gaia screamed. Tears peppered her reddening face, and she looked pathetic and small without her mask to hide behind. "SHE'S HURTING ME."

Ellory would have been stunned by the audacity if Gaia hadn't reminded her of how much danger she was in. Ellory drew her up by the collar and slammed the woman's head against the floor, taking a sick satisfaction in her pained cry. It wasn't enough to knock her out, but it did disorient her enough that Ellory felt safe climbing to her feet.

The doorway was filled with Old Masters.

Somewhere, Colt's rickety voice commanded, "Stop her."

Ellory grabbed her bag and fled into the night.

36

ELLORY HAD EXPECTED IT TO be difficult, if not outright impossible, to find the hidden clearing again, but it was as if Riverside Campus were eager to suck her back into its concealed areas. Fear made her surroundings smudge together. Every sound was an Old Master seconds away from capturing her. Her vision blurred, and her chest burned, and she was sure she must have looked unhinged to anyone who saw her, but the campus was empty and dark. She could see only the path ahead, which led her all the way to the lake without injury.

Tai and Cody needed her. Hudson and Boone, if they were sleeping there as well. She wouldn't let them down.

She was in the middle of drawing a summoning circle—frantic edges, bare of offerings—when the ghost light appeared to lead her way. It vibrated, as if it, too, were in a hurry, as if it knew that she wasn't safe lingering here. The rotting pile of fish had been cleared since she'd last been there, but the flowering rushes drooped like they were considering an early grave, too.

She had her Taser in one hand and her phone in the other. It did little to stave off the anxiety of knowing that she was being hunted like a duck during the fall season. Everything Colt had revealed tumbled around her throbbing head, the proprietary way he'd said, *This won't hurt*, as if that would be her only problem with what the Old Masters were doing. With what they had done. It made her sick, even more sick than not knowing what she would have done if they had inducted her. Would she have given up on her investigation, ignored all red flags like Boone, just for a taste of that same power? Would she have forgotten the Lost Eight if she'd been given the magic to keep Carol healthy for the rest of her life?

She *didn't know*, and she hated herself for that.

Every time she blinked, she saw Hudson's face: his half smiles when he didn't want to admit he found her funny, the aloofness he wore like a shield against being taken advantage of by a populace who saw his last name first, all the soft affection he poured into his friendship with Boone. He had been the first person to believe her, the person who had helped her most, and at some point, he had become a support system she couldn't bear to lose.

They had taken him from her as easily as they'd tried to take her power. And that, she knew, she could never let stand.

Let the rest of the world forget him. That was their mistake to make.

She would remember and remember and remember.

The ghost light zipped through the trees, and Ellory hurtled after it. She slapped branches and leaves out of her path. She skidded over rocks and twigs. Her foot caught in an exposed root that sent her tumbling onto the leaf-coated ground, scraping her palms and sending another zing of pain from her hip down to her ankle. Light hovered over her, waiting for her to get her bearings, but the cold earth had slapped some sense into her. Riverside Campus was alive with rustling and shouts, the Old Masters bearing down on her, and she was running out of energy. Even if she made it to the hidden tower, what then? Another creature could be waiting. Or, worse, they could surround her and starve her out.

How could David take on Goliath? Even with a Taser, not a slingshot, Ellory felt outmatched.

Yet Letitia Rose had sent her a guide, a way to escape the fate that she hadn't. Ellory owed it to Tai and Cody, to Hudson and Boone, to the Lost Eight and to herself, to keep going.

She pushed herself up and hobbled onward.

The shingled roof of the schoolhouse crested the trees, like a lighthouse directing her through rocky waters. Ellory was so busy staring at it that she almost didn't notice the person who stepped into her path. She slipped to a stop, inches away from colliding into the broad chest of Liam Blackwood.

"No." The word fell from her lips in a breathless plea. "Not you. Please not you, too."

"It doesn't have to be like this." Liam looked like he had the first day she'd met him: white-and-black-striped polo and loose blue jeans, clean-shaven jaw and swooping chestnut hair. He was so handsome that it pained her, though not as much as his presence. "They'll stop chasing you if you stop running. Don't you want to stop running?"

Ellory shoved past him, but he caught her by both wrists. She was on a mission, but he was lacrosse captain. Her struggles for freedom were laughable in the face of the easy strength he was using against her. She could use magic, but she felt too raw, too volatile right now. She might kill him. She didn't want him *dead*.

"I don't understand." Her eyes stung, but she refused to cry any more tears over this man. "If you're one of the Old Masters, why did you even ask me out?"

"I'm not one of the Old Masters." Liam looked *sad*, like he knew whatever he said next would be no better. "I'm a part of your dream, Ellory."

"Sorry...*what*?"

She stopped fighting, stopped moving, stopped *everything*. Colt had said something similar, but the desire to escape and rescue her sleeping friends had pushed the bizarre revelation about herself to the back of her mind. Now, trapped and forced to face it, she could feel her surroundings blur as though the backdrop to this conversation were unnecessary. As though she and Liam were the only two people in this world.

"You're dreaming. You've been locked in a dream for three years now, and you're only now awake enough to recognize the truth. This is how the Old Masters siphon magic. They've crafted a spell that lets you slumber while your magic feeds theirs. The magic allows you to live a full life in the world the dreamers have created, occasionally moderated by an Old Master. In your case, your moderator was Preston Colt. Your part of the dream was me." He looked down as though seeing himself for the first time, his black plimsolls lined with dirt from his trek through the hazy forest. "It's an amazing likeness, but the real Liam Blackwood doesn't know who you are. I'm just a story you were telling yourself, encouraged by the spell to distract you from the truth you'd forgotten."

"Hudson," she whispered. "I'm in love with Hudson."

"You were," Liam admitted. "In your waking world. Until the Old Masters found out. And found you two."

Ellory's mouth opened, but she couldn't speak. Tears streamed steadily over her cheeks. She didn't remember being in love with Hudson, but she'd *felt* it, hadn't she? Every time they'd been together in this fictitious version of reality, she had been focused on him above all else, like he was the only real thing she knew. Those half conversations had been lost memories, returning to her whenever they bonded anew, giving her the strength she needed to break free of the spell's control. And he'd disappeared because she'd overplayed her hand.

He was in danger, and it was all her fault.

He had loved her, and her love had destroyed him.

"Wait." Ellory shook her head before the guilt could debilitate her, her thoughts snagging on something Liam had said. "You—you're the one who forced me to admit that I had feelings for Hudson. You basically pushed me into his arms. Why would you do that if you were just a distraction?"

Liam finally released her. He slid his hands into his pockets and shrugged.

"It wouldn't make any sense for the spell to do that," she continued as the ghost light sailed around them, illuminating them in a circle of sunflower yellow. Reminding her that she was free, that she had to move, that every second she wasted was another second her loved ones were in danger. "If you were just a distraction, you would never have let me go. You would have fought for me. You would have done anything to keep me away from Hudson, from the truth about the Old Masters." She stepped forward until she was close enough to place her hand over his chest. His heart beat beneath her fingers, strong and true. "Maybe this world isn't real. Maybe you aren't either. But what we felt was real, Liam. You love me. I saw it. I still see it."

Those chocolate-brown eyes melted under her scrutiny. Real or not, this was a man who was still not over her. His heartbeat raced beneath her touch. He leaned closer to her, as if aching for a kiss, and then turned his face away to look at the forest behind them. "I do. Love you, I mean. I want you to stay here with me. Everyone else has forgotten about Hudson, and I'm sure you can, too. We can have a real shot if you just…stay." He reached up to cover her hand with his. But this time, he wasn't trapping her. This time, he was pleading. "Please, Ellory. Don't fight them. Stay."

"I can't," she murmured, her free hand reaching up to turn his face back to her. She wanted him to see how serious she was. She wanted to see the love that she was giving away. "I'll die. And even if I don't—even if it's not for a while—they're never going to stop until someone stops them, Liam. People have died, and people will die, unless I stop them."

"That doesn't have to be your problem."

It was every doubt she'd ever had, every time she'd felt scared and alone, every turned back and ignored epiphany in her quest to eke out some normalcy from her school year. Liam was right. She could take his hand and stop running. She could give in to the Old Masters, let them take her memories of Hudson and Boone, let them take her magic along with it, and build a life here in this constructed space. If she really was creating a dreamworld, then she and the others could make it kinder and softer than the one she'd left behind. She could succeed here in ways she never could out there, instead of making herself miserable fighting something stronger than herself.

She could. But Ellory knew she wouldn't. And if Liam really was a part of her, then he knew it, too.

"*Someone* needs to make this their problem," she said, her voice quiet but firm. "If I'm going to die, I want to die experiencing all the pleasure and pain the world has to offer me. I want to die doing, being, and feeling something *real*. Something better."

Liam's throat bobbed as he swallowed. He leaned into her touch with a heart-shattering smile that was painful to look at. "Okay."

"Okay?"

"This is exactly what I like about you, Ellory. You actually give a shit, you know? So many people have forgotten how." Reluctantly, he extracted himself from her grip and stepped past her to face the looming trees. "I'm not part of their spell, Ellory—I'm part of *you*. I am *your* creation. And I'll hold them back as long as I can. You go. End this."

Ellory fought back a sob. "Will you be okay?"

"I don't exist, remember?" He glanced at her over his shoulder, and this smile was more like the ones she remembered, golden and bright and devastating. "Just do me a favor? Give the Liam out there—the real Liam—the chance to get to know you when you wake. As friends. He deserves that chance."

"I will." She wiped her damp eyes. "I love you. Even if it's not like that, I want you to know—"

"I know," Liam said warmly. "Goodbye, Ellory."

"Goodbye, Liam."

The ghost light shot onward. With one last look back, Ellory followed.

37

THE SCHOOLHOUSE WAS EVEN MORE worn down this time, like it was crumbling around the tower that marked the Old Masters' true base. The grass was even thicker, more treacherous to run through. Ellory waded through waist-length strands that clung to her like chains, forcing her to yank her wrists and ankles free of their grasp. Her light hovered by the hummingbird door, indifferent to her slow progress. Wishing she'd brought a knife, Ellory ripped the plants from the ground, tore their vines from her arms, and flicked burrs from her clothes without caring about the scrapes they left behind.

Her tears had dried. Her resolve had calcified. Whatever was inside that building, she was ready to meet it.

She shoved the door open and entered with her Taser lifted. No monster lay in wait. Instead, the ghost light illuminated a trail to the far wall, beyond the shattered blackboard on the opposite side of the room. Ellory kept her eyes and ears open as she inched forward, waiting for the shadows to coalesce into something that was hopefully weak against electricity. But all was still and silent except for the spiders that sprinted across the windowsills and the spectral light that watched her without eyes.

As soon as she made it to the wall, the ball disappeared, submerging her in darkness. Ellory stuffed her phone into her pocket and replaced it with her flashlight. It took two tries for it to click on, but she managed to aim it at the spot where the ghost light had been. There was an inverted hook on the wall, pointing in the wrong direction to hold anything up. Ellory reached for the hook, and it slid downward like a light switch with a low *click*.

The wall popped outward.

Because it wasn't a wall, not completely.

It was a hidden door, like the one at the museum.

Before she could touch anything else, something yanked her backward. She hit the filthy floor hard, new aches and pains exploding across her ribs. A clawed foot pressed against her throat, squeezing her windpipe, emptying the air from her chest. It was attached to a corpse-gray leg, thick with muscles and visible veins, and a body that hunched over her to create a shadow larger than any human could. The monster—the assassin—tilted its featureless face down to her, and a seam opened near the bottom of the blankness, widening into a black void of serrated teeth.

Its breath smelled of death.

"No," Ellory whimpered. Those needlelike talons pressed into her throat, bruising her skin, drawing blood. She couldn't swallow. She couldn't breathe. Black spots danced before her eyes. "No."

Her heart slowed. The world grew dark.

She had made it this far and would go no further.

This school would be her grave.

"NO!"

She conjured fire, detonating it outward from her chest like a

bomb. Red and yellow flames struck the monster through the gut, and it flew backward until it hit the opposite wall. Air. Precious air. Ellory wheezed, her neck stinging with every shaky breath. Her hand stretched out, increasing the temperature of her blaze, searing the beast from the inside out as it writhed above the portrait of Arthur O'Connor. The monster was large enough that part of it extended to the ceiling, but she could see its skin flaking over the light and power tearing through it. There was no screaming, no sound at all but her own breathing.

The beast crumbled. Ash rained to the dusty ground.

Ellory took a moment to collect herself, to wipe her tears and heal the pain of her neck. Her nerves shook for longer than she wanted, but she'd come close to death too many times this year to blame herself for it. Swallowing hard, she pushed herself to her feet.

She continued on.

Behind the hidden door, a set of dark stairs led upward. Ellory replaced her flashlight with her Taser, keeping one hand on the wall to guide her while her eyes adjusted. She couldn't hear anything over the sound of her own shrieking heartbeat. The scent of mildew and disuse was thick, but a single line of light lay ahead—another false wall, another door, another room she could explore. She realized that she was trembling from something worse than the cold, but even still she couldn't stop.

They're coming for you, said a nasty voice in her head. *Liam can't stop them. They'll come for you. They'll kill you. You'll die here with no one to mourn you.*

She kept going until the spiral steps turned into a concrete floor. The door swung outward silently, revealing a hallway lit with fluorescent bulbs. There were three closed doors on either side, as well as one opposite her that opened onto another set of stairs.

Each door was labeled, and Ellory read the markers as she passed: DEAN, CLASSROOM 1, CLASSROOM 2, LABORATORY 1, STORAGE, and LABORATORY 2. She tried each knob, but they were locked. The brass of them looked newly polished, in contrast to a bottom floor that was doing its best to persuade her that no one had been there in centuries.

"Morgan."

She turned. Boone Priestley had emerged from Classroom One dressed all in black, his tattoos coiling around his bare arms and the sides of his neck. He looked both terrified and resigned, like he'd been hoping not to find her here and didn't want to be the one to do something about it.

"You piece of shit," she accused. "You *did* erase yourself and Hudson from this world."

"It wasn't me, goddamn!" said Boone. And then, quieter: "I get why you think so, though. I mean, I deserve that."

"What's down there?" Ellory jabbed her flashlight at the final door. He was lucky he was too far away for her to beat him with it. "Is it Hudson? Is this where they're keeping him?"

Boone bit his lip and didn't answer.

"They don't care about you!" Ellory snapped, frustrated. "They care only about your magic. Once you're no longer useful to them, they'll make you disappear, just like Letitia Rose, Manuel Sharp, Angel Mclaughlin—"

"Morgan, come on—"

"—Olivia Holloway, Tasha Butler—"

"You don't understand, okay? You weren't born into this shit like we were. Sometimes, you have to take the hits so someone else doesn't!"

"—Eugene Kang, Kristopher Douglas—"

"I told you these people were dangerous, and you still—"

"Joel Carroll, Malcolm Mayhew. Me." She stared him down, her jaw set. "Are you going to let me take the hits so you don't, Boone? Do you think that's what Hudson wants?"

Surprise flickered across his face. "You remember."

"We were together. Before. Weren't we?" When he didn't answer again, she ranted onward, stepping closer and closer to him. "We were together, and the Old Masters found out, and now I'm here and he's not. And I know it's because we fell in love again. I know I did this to him. You tried to warn me, and I didn't listen, and I'm sorry for that. But if you want to protect him, if you actually want to save him, then you'll stop doing their bidding and *help me*. If we end this, no one has to suffer again. Not him, not *anyone*."

A wrinkle appeared between Boone's eyebrows. She could see the conflict on his face, could see how badly he wanted to do the right thing. But he still had no idea what the right thing was, and she had grown tired of waiting for him to figure it out. She couldn't risk him stopping her.

"Morgan," he began before she smashed him over the head with the hefty flashlight.

Boone crumpled to the floor, and Ellory ran for the next set of stairs.

The next floor was more of the same—locked doors that were once classrooms, dust and blackened grout along the walls—and the floor after that. It wasn't until she found the stairs that led to the rooftop that Ellory slowed down. There were no footsteps behind her, and there were no more obstacles ahead of her. It felt like a trap, but it was one she had to walk into.

She thought again of Rapunzel from the Grimms' fairy tale, her hair shorn, her prince blinded, her body banished to the wilderness—all because a sorceress had wanted to keep the princess for her own. There had been a happy ending to that fairy tale, but Rapunzel been blond-haired like Gaia. Ellory wasn't sure that girls who looked like her, with thick-textured black hair, got that golden ending.

Ellory took a deep breath and pushed on.

As soon as she took the first step, she nearly toppled down the stairs when nausea punched her in the stomach. Her legs felt as weak as a newborn's. She leaned against the wall to keep herself standing, swallowing again and again to keep bile from rising. Sweat coated her skin, and her breath came in sharp pants. Deep aches bloomed across her skin. She looked down to see bruises circling her ankles and inching up under her jeans. Purple-brown marks sprouted across her arms.

Her legs gave out. She gripped the railing as she slid downward until she was sitting in the center of the staircase, breathing like she'd run a marathon.

What's happening to me?

The top of the stairs seemed oceans away, but she was seized by the urge to crawl back the way she'd come. Boone might have been unconscious, or he might have been bleeding and pissed, but he wouldn't hurt her. She knew that now. Not as long as hurting her would hurt Hudson.

Ellory almost turned, but the thought of Hudson cleared her head. Another protective spell, she realized, one trying to keep her from wading deeper into the lodge. She climbed to the next step, dizzy.

By the time she made it to the top, black spots danced in her vision. Her lips were dry, but her fingers were too weak to get the water bottle from her backpack. If she didn't keep moving forward, if she paused for even a second, she knew she would pass out.

Feet turned into inches, which turned into centimeters. Her shaking hand found the doorknob and turned.

Her breath caught.

The rooftop was lit by bluish glows that came from several globes filling the otherwise-empty space. A cloud-covered sky bore down on them, flashes of stars barely visible between the battlements. Lightning sparked across the surface of the orbs, obscuring the shadowed figure at each center. But the one directly in front of her was close enough for Ellory to see that it was not her kidnapped friends that floated in the middle of this living magic.

It was her own sleeping body.

38

ELLORY'S LEGS STILL COULDN'T SUPPORT her weight, so she could do nothing but crawl forward in a trance. That was her curly hair in its usual high bun, that was her deep brown skin tinted blue by the magic, those were her full lips, her broad nose, her curves wrapped in her favorite green hoodie and blue jeans. She was fast asleep, though occasionally her eyelids would twitch as though she were about to awaken. Every time that happened, another spark of lightning flashed across the globe she was trapped in, and the twitch dissipated into restful sleep.

From her spot on the floor, she could make out the figures in the nearby globes, just as she'd seen them at Colt's house. Tai slumbered in one, her beautiful face tipped to the side, her lips parted. Cody was in another, curled into the fetal position with their legs pulled up to their chest. Sofia Aston. David Chang Vargas. Ximena Moreno. Imani Khalif. The bright cages continued on beyond what Ellory's strained eyes could see, holding an untold number of her classmates captive in this underground prison.

But not Hudson. Where were they keeping Hudson?

Ellory turned back to her own body, trembling with dread. She had been here before, *seen this before*, and she had been terrified then, too. This fear was too ingrained to be new, and she couldn't think, couldn't *breathe*; her heart was trying to beat its way out of her chest—

She dragged herself closer,
  close enough to reach
    out
      and
        touch.

The room went black.

◆

"Wake up."

Ellory gasped into something like consciousness, but she could tell from her translucent limbs and her crepuscular surroundings that she wasn't awake. Before this year—before magic—she had always thought of her dreams as gossamer threads of imagination that disappeared in the dawn, nothing to worry about or retain. In the short time since she'd accepted that everything she thought she knew was a dream, she was getting better at grounding herself within them, at separating the real from the fake.

This was not real. She was in that hollow void that seemed to follow her wherever she went, that endless blackness where souls waited to send her a message. And, as always, she wasn't alone. The Lost Eight circled her, their solemn faces staring down at her with pity.

"Do you see now?" asked Letitia Rose, stepping forward to help Ellory to her feet. "They take us, and then they take from us, until we have nothing and we are nothing. But you're different. Special."

"I'm not special," Ellory whispered. "They took from me, too. Isn't that why I'm here?"

"You're not special because of the power you were born with," said Eugene Kang, a handsome Korean boy with round cheeks, a wide nose, and thick lips. "You're special because you're *kind*. You chose to care about us. To research our stories and restore our voices."

"You knew that this was bigger than you," Angel Mclaughlin added. She was a bronze-skinned girl with a septum piercing. "You cared that we were lost. You wanted to find us, and you did."

Ellory looked from one face to another, and though she should have been scared by where she was and what she had seen, she felt held. Protected. Even with Letitia breaking the chain, there was strength in the circle of ghosts around her, beside her.

"What do I do?" She looked down at her hands, through which she could see a floor that was little but shadows. "I have to stop them, but how?"

"You already know," said Kristopher Douglas.

"You already have," said Joel Carroll.

Olivia Holloway touched her shoulder. "For now, stall them. When the time comes, you will have our power to aid you."

"But first," said Letitia Rose, "wake up."

And then she slapped Ellory across the face.

◆

Strength returned to her in increments. As soon as she thought her legs could hold her weight, Ellory rolled onto her feet. She was too far from the tower wall to put her back to it, but she wielded the Taser like a sword as she stared down the rooftop. Even if she hadn't felt like she was being watched, she could *see* eyes in the tenebrous distance, dozens of them pointed in her direction. There was no safety in these watchful gazes. There was only the knowledge that she was trapped in this dangerous place, with these dangerous people, and she had no idea what the Lost Eight thought she already knew.

"I know about the School for the Unseen Arts," she said, trying to sound braver than she felt. Comforting herself with the facts she *had* gathered. "I know that you guys have been killing students of color once they're no longer of any use to you. And I know you made everyone forget about Hudson except me. Why did you take him? Stop hiding in the shadows, and *answer me*."

The orbs began to move, creating a circle of illumination before her. Into that circle stepped various pairs, an elder and a younger, a master and an acolyte, each someone she recognized from her investigation. First came two generations of Arthur O'Connors, so similar in appearance that they could have been clones. Stasie's father, Chip, had her brown hair and pixie-like features, though he was taller and broader than she was. Her grandfather—the misleadingly named Pop-Pop—had silver hair, a silver mustache, and blue eyes the icy color of a blizzard. Half of her expected Stasie to be with them, smug and sinister, but her roommate didn't materialize. Perhaps she was too young, or too spoiled, to have merited an invitation to this exclusive club.

Next, Preston Colt, leaning heavily against Gaia Hammond. Then, Boone Priestley, twisting her flashlight in his fingers like it was a baton. Miles Clairborne, grinning with malicious satisfaction at how helpless she looked trying to point the Taser at so many people at once. Nathaniel Graves, Hudson's father, who cut an even more imposing figure in real life than he had in his portraits.

And beside him—

"Hudson," she breathed.

He looked at her like she was a stranger, dressed in an olive sweater over a beige button-down, black slacks, and matching boots. His peacoat was open, his hands in its pockets. He was taller than his father by three inches, but next to Nathaniel, he looked smaller. Diminished.

She should have noticed that he wasn't chained or gripped, wasn't visibly injured or reaching for her, but the testimony of her eyes was swept away beneath a powerful relief. Hudson was here. He was alive. The tower was full of living batteries and human leeches, but Hudson was *here*, and together they would figure this out.

"You know," said Nathaniel Graves, before she could ask what he had let them do to his son. "Every time we find you here, this situation plays out a little differently. After three years, I thought I might be bored, that you would be more trouble than it was worth to contain you, but Hudson was right. Your power is of great value to us."

"*Us?*" Ellory echoed. She lowered the Taser, feeling foolish as she looked at Hudson for the second time. As the fact that he was standing with them, rather than with her, finally sank in. "What do you mean *us*? Hudson, what does he mean *us*? Are you—are you one of *them*?"

His eyes were empty. "Yes."

Ellory was trembling again. If she hadn't been gripping her only weapon, she would have wrapped her arms around herself. "I don't believe you."

AN ARCANE INHERITANCE

He was like a robot rebooted to factory settings. There was no flicker of emotion on his face, no trace of anything they'd shared over the course of the school year. The warmth. The joy. The *trust*. She would have thought she had created him, too, but she would never create a version of him that watched her like she was no more interesting than a fly hovering over a too-full trash can. Maybe months ago, but not now. Not anymore. Not after all they'd become to each other.

"Hudson," she managed, "tell me it's not true."

"I can't." His jaw ticked. "Ellory, I—"

"You performed commendably, Mister Graves," said Colt. He steadied himself, waving Gaia away so he could lord over Ellory without assistance. "Don't you see the beauty of it? The entire world you've been living in was catered to take you down the same paths in different ways. You, Miss Morgan, have the strongest wild magic we've found in a while. In almost four years, you've powered spells so small and so large, it's like we're back in a time when magic was everywhere. Our spell needs you to repeat certain actions, to gain certain knowledge, to return to certain places. It reinforces the boundary of the siphon."

The conversations that had felt familiar. The confrontations that had seemed inevitable. The truth she could never escape, not really, because it was not in her nature to stop searching for it. Ellory hadn't been making leaps and putting puzzle pieces together to form a whole picture. She had been guided by an invisible hand down a path to the same discoveries, threatened just enough to make her dig her feet in and then baited into standing right where they'd always wanted her to be.

For the hundredth time, she felt like crying. She forced the tears back, refusing to show them any weakness. "My aunt—"

"Thinks you've been taking winter and summer classes. Your calls with her have been short, vague. You've been more effusive by email. Soon, she'll be told you've gotten a job far away from here." Artie O'Connor chuckled, his voice like the rasp of a serpent. "Or perhaps we'll tell her you've died. It doesn't matter, in the end."

Boone nudged Hudson's shoulder until he took a step toward her. Ellory raised the Taser again, and Hudson stopped, his face brightening with the arrogance she'd once hated him for. That last, small part of her that doubted he was really a part of this curled up and died at the smirk that crossed his face. Beside his father, he'd been a lifeless puppet, waiting for direction. Standing before her now, he had come alive, and all she saw was a monster.

"You're not going to hurt me, Morgan," he drawled.

"Are you sure about that?" Her thumb flicked the button, feeding current between the two points of the Taser. "Come closer, and let's find out."

"You're not going to hurt me, because we've been through too much together for that. I've seen the way you look at me. I know you've begun to remember." His hand covered her wrist, lowering the Taser until it was back at her side, and she let him because he was her weakness, a vulnerability she could no longer hide. "We were in love, once."

Ellory bit the inside of her cheek, refusing to give him the satisfaction of confirming that she knew. Their gazes locked, and Ellory could see it then, everything she couldn't recall but had subconsciously been searching for. The way his eyes softened when he looked at her. The visions of intimacy that had plagued her all year. The way she was drawn to him like a moth to a forest fire, ready to die just to be close to him.

It hurt worse than his betrayal. Seeing him with the Old Masters had stung because she had finally allowed herself to trust him. The painfully slow restoration of her feelings—a love three lifetimes strong—had made her soul cleave in two.

She hated him. She'd missed him.

"Every time we reset your school year," Hudson whispered, "you always end up here. You always remember."

His thumb traced her wrist in gentle circles. The dissonance between his tender touch and his cutting words was too much to bear. She looked down at their linked hands, and her body relaxed under the familiar gesture. Every time he did this, a shard from their old life together cut through the fog of her mind, forcing her to focus only on what was true. Her eyes widened with realization.

This was no simple affection. This was a spell. One he'd been casting all year.

But a spell for what?

"I need you"—his voice dropped even lower—"to remember."

Wake up.

Ellory's head snapped back with a gasp. Her brain flooded with memories, each slotting into place like they'd always been there. She saw their first meeting in the classroom, a different conversation with the same competitive vibe, the way Hudson followed up on her answer to a question with reasoning that undermined her, the way Ellory followed up on his follow-up by citing an obscure case that proved her point beyond reasonable doubt.

She saw their first kiss at a frat party, half-drunk and wild with desire, a moment that ended with her riding his thigh on the very balcony on which they'd almost kissed in her dreamworld. She saw the awkward aftermath in which they tried to ignore the heat between them only to end up making out in library stacks and empty hallways, hooking up in her dorm room or his.

She saw his tea grow hot in his hands, the first small sign of magic that drew her suspicion, and the investigation that unfurled afterward. The same clues in different places. The same books in different stores. The same realizations in different contexts. She saw herself receive a formal invitation to join the Old Masters, her furtive conversation with Hudson. Ascending the stairs she had just climbed before her world had gone black, Hudson's name the last thing on her lips.

Her eyes burned with a new wave of unshed tears as she lowered her chin to stare at him. "I remember everything," she said, lashing the words like a whip. "You knew the whole time. You lied to me and set me up. You basically *delivered* me to them."

"Despite all his excellent work, Hudson is not yet a full member of our society. He has a pedestrian weakness for you that we've had to stamp out." Nathaniel Graves placed a hand on his son's shoulder and squeezed in a facsimile of parental fondness. Hudson's eyes briefly closed, and Ellory remembered with a pang how much his father's good opinion meant to him. How rare it was. He had lied about forgetting his own magic, but he hadn't lied about that. No matter what happened next, this was *killing* him. "We wanted you sooner, but there were…concerns about how Hudson was handling things that forced us to pull him out."

"I still think we should have let Hammond finish her off," said Chip O'Connor, scowling at her. "Whatever hold she has over the boy is too strong. Let Hammond kill her, and bring Hudson to the lodge for further correction."

"Seconded," Gaia said, lifting two fingers like she was at an auction.

Ellory glared at her. "Fuck you, Greer."

"Who the hell is Greer—"

"It would be a *waste*," Nathaniel Graves shouted over them all. "Her power is too strong. Hudson has come to his senses. He has returned for his graduation. He will put her under himself, and he will not disappoint me like his brother has."

Behind them, Miles Clairborne snorted. She didn't know whether the version of him she'd met had been real or invented, but it was clear there was no version of him that cared for Hudson. Boone began to click the flashlight on and off, making dots dance before her eyes.

Through it all, Hudson didn't let go of her wrist, didn't stop the steady glide of his fingers against her pulse.

"Incantations aren't as you see them in the movies," he said. "You don't say some special words and watch the magic happen. You have to set an intention, surrender a memory, and from that loss, you have to build. This is my creation." He tugged the Taser from her grip. "When I'm finished talking, you'll go back under, and you won't remember any of this."

Light.

Dark.

Light.

Dark.

Light.

Remember.

"It will be August, again. Maybe we'll meet then. Maybe we'll meet later. But no matter what, you'll always...end up...here."

Boone extinguished the flashlight and tucked it into his back pocket, staring at the two of them with an inscrutable expression. Ellory couldn't move. Couldn't speak. She could only watch as Hudson stepped back, her Taser in his hands, and smiled a smile that didn't reach his hollow eyes.

"Goodbye, Ellory."

Light erupted between them. Someone screamed.

And then there was nothing left.

39

*S*HE DRAGGED HERSELF CLOSER, CLOSE enough to reach out and touch—
The room went black.

So this was how it felt, to tear herself in two.

When Boone had done it that day at the newspaper office, she hadn't even noticed them walking away from their bodies to have a conversation of the spirit. When she splintered herself now, her body collapsed and surrounded in one world and slumbering peacefully in another, her spirit floated between them like a swirling air current. She was aware of the conversation—*stall them*—and the need to escape—*wake up*—but it felt like she was soaring through layers of the atmosphere, fighting against the gravity of the spell that had kept her yoked until now.

Even while as insubstantial as a thought, she could feel the weight of that magic against her soul. She could soar as high as she wanted, but, inevitably, it would pull her back down, her memories erased, her timeline reset, her school year beginning anew. Her power was their power.

Again

       And again

              And again

                      Until.

◆

"When was the last time you saw sunlight?"

◆

"You just want to get your hands all over me."

◆

"I want you. And I'm tired of pretending I don't."

◆

Memory by memory, Ellory dragged her spirit toward the light. Every time she tired, she felt a jolt of sizzling energy—the magic of the Lost Eight, carrying her, strengthening her—and she climbed further out of the fog.

◆

AN ARCANE INHERITANCE

"What if you don't remember? What if you never do?"

◆

"Are you going to hurt me, Morgan? Let me make it easy for you."

◆

"We can end this."

◆

And then she paused. She had time for one goodbye.

◆

Tai and Cody sat across from her at Little House, sharing a catfish po'boy and potato wedges. Ellory knew at once that this wasn't real—or rather, that this was another memory she had plunged into—and yet she took the time to enjoy it. Afternoon sun slanted through the blinds, and Tai was wearing one of the corset tops that made her breasts look amazing. Cody, in their soccer uniform, fed Tai a potato wedge, and Ellory instinctively made the same grossed-out face that she'd made then, even though there was nothing disgusting about two people so deeply in love.

Especially not when it might be the last time she ever saw it.

"Are you sure about this?" Tai said after she'd swallowed her potato wedge. "Who's to say Graves is even being honest with you about how much he knows about magic? He didn't tell you about it in the first place, right?"

Cody pried the blinds apart with two fingers, and Ellory realized that it wasn't the sun that cast lines of light and shadow across the table. There was nothing outside the restaurant but a network of roots, each glowing blue. Lightning shot through them, erupting like fireworks outside the window.

A network of borrowed power, calling for her attention. She was so close to freedom, to the light, to ending all this. The spell was nearly complete.

Ellory ignored it for a little while longer, reaching across the table to take her friend's hand in hers. They were still asleep, in the waking world, but she would save them soon. And if she didn't, well, at least she got to see them one more time.

"I'm not sure about anything," she said. "But I have to try. I have to protect us."

"Who's going to protect you?" Cody asked, carefully separating a shrimp from the sandwich. "And don't say Graves. I don't trust him either."

"Then trust *me*, because I do." Ellory took Cody's hand, too, the one that wasn't covered in shrimp grease, and she smiled soothingly at both of them so they wouldn't notice her memorizing their faces. "Hudson will help."

"Okay," Tai said without hesitation. "I trust you, Lor. Of course I do."

"And we're here," said Cody. "If you need us for anything. You might have to work with Graves, but you don't have to do it all alone. Got it?"

Light flashed in the corner of her eye again. Her reckoning waited only for her to reach out and take it.

"Got it." Ellory drew her hands back, fighting tears. "I have to go."

"We're not finished eating," said Tai, eyebrows drawn together in confusion.

Ellory squared her shoulders and headed for the door. "It's time for me to remember."

◆

Ellory awoke in a bed both familiar and unfamiliar. She recognized the soft feel of these thousand-thread-count sheets, but it had been so long—too long—since she had seen the world from this perspective. Books stacked precariously on every flat surface, covering the floor except for a narrow trail cleared between the door and the bed. *Reel to Real* by bell hooks annotated on the side table, an ornate bookmark just pages from the center of the novel. A constellation of glow-in-the-dark stars on the ceiling, the only compromise on the subject of a night-light in the room.

The door opened.

She sat up as Hudson strolled in wearing a pair of frayed black jeans and nothing else. Thin black hair spanned the skin between his pectorals down to his dark brown nipples. A trio of tattoos lined his inner bicep: the alchemical symbols for salt, sulfur, and mercury. His toned chest and soft stomach glistened with water. A small mint-green towel hung from around his neck.

"This," he said with a smirk, "is the liminal space you've created, is it?"

Ellory settled against the bed frame, admiring the view. "You're welcome."

Hudson left the door open as he dripped his way across the room. She leaned into his touch like a flower in the sun, her eyes sliding closed as he pressed their foreheads together. He smelled like bergamot and shea butter, momentarily distracting her with a memory of the first time they had showered together and she had complained, for three days after, about his expensive, though fragrant, Yves Saint Laurent soap.

"We don't have much time," he said, trailing kisses down the line of her nose. "I can keep talking for only so long before they get suspicious."

"And Boone?"

"Holding the spell and clearing your way out. I told you he just needed a push."

"Or a flashlight to the head."

"Whatever works." Hudson grinned. "We have until the flashlight goes out a final time."

Ellory's answering sigh was shaky, both from his proximity and from the reality of what she had to do. There had been no guarantee that this would work. In fact, it *hadn't* worked for three years, three long years in which Hudson was forced to play the role of dutiful son and aspiring initiate while trying desperately to get her to remember the plan *she* had come up with.

With the full context of three years of memories, she could see his desperate fingerprints all over her school year. The *RemƎmber* tattoo, copied from her own notes in her own hand and bespelled to appear whenever she came close to the truth. The *hudson will hǝlp* note buried in her favorite bookstore, right on the shelf where her research would inevitably take her. His easy belief in her theories contrasted with just enough sharp resistance that she took his attitude as a challenge to overcome. He had left a trail of breadcrumbs formed of the memories they'd made together in her freshman year, and she had finally followed it to the right gingerbread house.

Now all that was left was to trap the witch in the oven and escape with her riches.

Her hand cupped the back of his neck. A tear slid down her cheek.

The only problem was that Hudson was one of the witches. He always had been, and he always would be. Unless she trapped him, too.

"It's okay," he said, brushing his thumb across her damp cheek. "I deserve this. After everything, I—"

"Stop it," she snapped. "You're nothing like them."

"I was. If I hadn't met you…"

The Hudson Graves she had met in her first year at Warren had been arrogant and cruel, trapped in a sycophantic prison of his own making. His brother, she would learn, had been meant to carry on the family's lineage in the Old Masters, but that night when Hudson was nine years old had proven that he was far more powerful than Cairo could ever be. Nathaniel Graves turned his attention to Hudson, and Cairo turned to drink, his addled mind addled further by the memory spells that tore any mention of the Old Masters from his brain. Hudson was watched and molded for a future that didn't belong to him. Cairo dropped out of college and disappeared into the heartland.

It was like I'd spent my whole life asleep, Hudson told her once beneath the cover of night, his fingers buried in her hair, *and then you came along with your sharp mind and your wild magic, and I remembered what it was like to live.*

Hudson hid how potent her wild magic was from the Old Masters for as long as he could—but in that she foiled him at every turn. One flash of power unspooled into an investigation that put the School for the Unseen Arts on Ellory's radar…and put her on their radar as well.

Either I bring you to the lodge to be siphoned, Hudson confessed, *or they'll kill you and say it was for the good of the world. You don't know them like I do, Morgan. They're dangerous families with dangerous power, and they don't care what they have to do to maintain it.*

The world runs on dangerous power and the people who abuse it, Ellory replied. *That doesn't mean we should let them win.*

Together, they schemed late into the night. The next morning, he brought her to the clearing in Riverside Campus, and she had been a living battery ever since. Until now. Until the Old Masters had finally trusted Hudson enough to let him enter her dreamworld to strengthen the siphon—and he had weakened it instead.

Every time we reset your school year, you always end up here. You always remember. I need you to remember.

Incantations aren't as you see them in the movies... You have to set an intention, surrender a memory, and from that loss, you have to build.

In the fabricated world, Hudson stalled for time, confronting her with everything the Old Masters needed to hear. In this liminal space formed by Boone's magic, seconds stretched into minutes that gave them time to be together before the spell they were constructing took hold. Another tear slid down Ellory's face, and then another, and then another. It wasn't fair.

It just wasn't fair.

She and Hudson had been born in two different worlds, yet they had both been set aside as lambs for slaughter. She was doomed to scramble and struggle for even half the recognition that others received as a rite of passage. He was doomed to live a life decided for him before he'd been born, isolated in an ivory tower that claimed to work for his benefit.

The Old Masters needed to be stopped. There would be no justice as long as this secret society continued to exist.

But why did the people underfoot always have to be the ones to sacrifice? The ones to lose?

"It's okay," Hudson said again. "I've had the honor of watching you fall in love with me again and again. Now give me the chance to fall in love with you a second time." He cupped her face in his hands with a sad smile. "Loving you is the best thing I have ever done. As easy as taking a breath. You're not a weakness, Ellory. You're my strength. The best part of me, the best person I know. I don't need magic or memories. I just need your word that you won't give up on me."

"I won't," Ellory promised. "I couldn't."

He kissed her, and it tasted like goodbye. Ellory slid down the bed, dragging Hudson on top of her, over her, burying herself in his warmth and scent and skin. His head tilted. Her mouth opened. His teeth grazed her lower lip, and she groaned, wishing they had *time*.

Her magic was finally hers again, and for a moment, with his hands sliding up her shirt and hers undoing his belt, she considered turning her back on the real world. She could build them a new one, one in which they didn't have to struggle, one in which they could walk hand in hand down flowered paths, drink cheap supermarket prosecco on picnic blankets, and argue over modern art on museum days. Everything her imagined Liam had offered her sounded tempting if it was Hudson's hand in hers. She could make them immortal, pass the centuries together with the kind of love they wrote sonnets and songs about, watching the world change, changing the world. They would never hurt again. They could finally rest.

But it wouldn't be real.

And they deserved something real.

"I love you," Hudson said fiercely, his face pressed against the side of her neck as he slid inside her. His hips slammed against hers in a familiar rhythm, and she could feel him deep, *deep* where he belonged. She wrapped a leg around his waist, taking him even deeper, and choked out his name. "I love you, I love you—"

Ellory dragged his head back up to hers, kissing him again and again. "I love you. I won't forget. I'll never forget you again—"

He said her name like an oath, and her orgasm spilled over her.

For a moment, everything went dark.

Then light erupted between them as two worlds collided and tore them apart.

40

SOMEONE WAS SCREAMING.

Ellory was back on the roof of the tower, surrounded by blue light. Instead of a globe caging her body, magic pumped through her blood, lit her arms, her hands, her chest, waiting for her to direct it. Tearing free of her dreamworld, emerging from Boone's liminal path into freedom, she was awake for the first time in almost four years, back in the real world, harnessing her real power.

The screams grew louder. Ellory looked down.

The older Arthur O'Connor was on his knees, his head thrown back as light poured from every orifice: his eyes, his ears, his screaming mouth. His son writhed beside him, clawing at his own face as if he could tear the power out from under his skin. Blue bolts sizzled toward Preston Colt and Nathaniel Graves, forming the links of chains that dragged them to the floor. They, too, thrashed around in impotent fury, but none of them could break free of her magic.

Their magic.

Because she wasn't alone. She never really had been.

One by one, the ghosts of the Lost Eight appeared on either side

of her, their smiles victorious. They had told her that she'd know what to do, and she did. She had needed only to *remember*. This plan was hers to execute. This power was hers to command. These enemies were hers to destroy. They had thought they had her right where they wanted her, but Hudson had warned them of the truth:

This is my creation.

"This is *my* creation," Ellory said, raising her arms.

Magic spider-webbed toward her as Letitia Rose, Manuel Sharp, Angel Mclaughlin, Olivia Holloway, Tasha Butler, Eugene Kang, Kristopher Douglas, and Joel Carroll linked hands with one another and with her, feeding more power into the roots she had woven between them. She had never met them, and she never would, but she cared enough to tell their stories. She had summoned them from a past that had forgotten them. Their spirits rippled with the kind of magic that had been restored to them only in death, and they gave it, all of it, to her.

Ellory slashed the air.

Again and again and again.

With each sharp movement, a globe shattered into sparks that then faded, freeing the disoriented bodies of the students inside. She destroyed all the cages she could see, and then she felt for the cages she couldn't see and destroyed those as well, until she was certain every siphon had been cut off.

Her attention returned to the Old Masters, powerless except for the stolen magic still contained inside their traitorous bodies.

Without shadows for them to hide in, she could target them one by one. Gaia Hammond doubled over, vomiting as Ellory's spell ravaged her, eating away her powers from the inside out. Miles Clairborne was trying to claw a path to the stairs, but he was crying, weak and pale, and she knew he wouldn't make it. Even if he did, his magic would not. She tore it from his body like she was ripping out his still-beating heart, her mouth a grim line.

She did not revel in his pain, but she didn't try to ease it either. This was what he deserved.

This was what they all deserved.

From that loss, you have to build.

Tai approached her, followed by Cody and Sofia, David and Ximena. She opened her mouth to tell them what she was doing, but there was no need. After being freed from their orbs, they had watched for long enough to piece together her retribution, and they were ready.

Their hands glowed as they drew on their magic to build her spell—not a sacrifice but a gift. They shuffled like newborns learning to walk again, some of them using the stone walls to hold themselves up. But like the dead students they likely couldn't see and had almost become, they fed their magic to her so she could do what none of them had been able to do alone.

Because it was not just about the Old Masters. It was about the privileged.

It was about the people like Gaia and Miles, born in ivory towers, who thought that taking was their birthright.

It was too much power in the hands of the hidden few.

Ellory would end it all, here and now.

Beneath them, the floor began to shake. Ellory could *feel* every magic user, each of them a point in her mental web of light, and one by one, she siphoned that magic away. More screams rang out, an unholy symphony of pain, but she wasn't worried. By the time she was done, they wouldn't remember any of this. Their memories would be the price of their own destruction. The Old Masters wouldn't just be buried but obliterated.

Tabby Rose.
Manuel Sharp.
Angel Mclaughlin.
Olivia Holloway.
Tasha Butler.
Eugene Kang.
Kristopher Douglas.
Joel Carroll.
Malcolm Mayhew.

Those were the ones who deserved to be remembered. Not as the Lost Eight or the Graves Ghost, not as sacrifices for a rich white man's definition of a better world, but as people—wild magic or not—who had lived full lives that were taken too soon. The Old Masters had erased their names, but Ellory would make sure no one ever forgot them again. She would say their names until they passed into legend.

If magic faded from the world, maybe that was for the best. It was not the problem, but it had become a problem simply because of how it had been wielded. There would always be those who coveted what they did not have, who believed that the only way they could be powerful was if someone else was powerless. There was nothing to do with such a system but to tear it down.

"Lor," Tai said, grabbing her shoulder. Her voice was strong, but her grip was weak. "The tower is collapsing. We have to get out."

"Go," Ellory said without taking her eyes off the writhing bodies of those who had thought they could control her. Control everyone. "Boone is waiting to get you out."

Then he and Hudson would be next. Their magic would be destroyed, and their memories would be sacrificed. Even though Hudson had agreed, even though he'd said it was for the best,

AN ARCANE INHERITANCE

Ellory already knew she wouldn't be able to face him again without crying. It wasn't fair that they carried the taint of a legacy that needed to be abolished.

But they had been complicit in the Old Masters' crimes, regardless of their reasons. They had allowed people who looked like them to be used so that they could each play at being "one of the good ones" in a system that had never been designed for their benefit.

Hudson was right. This was for the best.

Still, she would save them for last.

Tai still hovered by her shoulder. "But what about y—"

"*Go.*" Ellory wiped at the blood that began to leak from her nose and shook her friend's hand off. "I'll be fine."

It took a few seconds for her to hear the scramble of feet toward the stairs, but she waited until the last of them had faded before she unleashed the full weight of her wrath.

Magic was sacrifice.

And it was finally time for the elite to be the ones to surrender.

Ellory lifted her hands to the ceiling and tore it all down.

41

THE FIRE THAT HAD TORCHED half of Riverside Campus was still the main topic of conversation at Professor Preston Colt's salon. Sofia Aston and Percy Wallis sat side by side on the couch, having a conversation that made Percy's face flush pleasantly. Tai Daniels and Cody Flores were in the kitchen, helping the cook carry tonight's dinner—Samoan inspired—to the table. Professor Colt and Imani Khalif lingered over his wine cabinet, a glass in his hand and a borrowed book of poems in hers. Liam Blackwood and Farrah Mayhew had disappeared, likely to kiss in the mirror-lined hallway that led to the bathroom. Ellory had caught them more than once, and each time, the quiet happiness on Liam's face had made her hurry away smiling.

With each passing day, she slowly relaxed. Colt *was* a phenomenal actor, but he was normal even with no one to perform for. He taught his classes and held these salons. He went to the farm for fresh cheese, and he did TED Talks in his wide collection of tweed suits. He no longer smiled like a man with a secret more substantial than his own intellect. And Ellory would continue to keep an eye on him to make sure that remained true.

In the meantime, there was no reason not to take advantage of the fact that his offer to work with her had very much been real. Maybe during her original freshman fall semester, it had been a means for *him* to watch *her* for signs of magical potential, but his recommendation would still open doors for her once she graduated for real.

He owed her that much.

"Hey."

Ellory tore her eyes from Colt to focus on Liam, who had appeared at her side with two glasses of a dark liquid she assumed was brandy. His sweater was royal purple, and his hair was windswept, and he was smiling, always smiling, even here in the waking world, where they barely knew each other.

"You know the point of these things is to network, right?" He extended one of the glasses. "You can't keep wallflowering. We can all see you."

Ellory took the glass, but she didn't drink from it. "Is it wallflowering if I'm in front of a window?"

Behind her, the sun had finally set, a half-moon taking its place against the navy sky. Colt had never planted those evergreen trees, since that conversation had been erased alongside the dreamworld and the Old Masters, but the bare branches that remained were beautiful in their own way. They were a testament to the resilience of living things, that they could lose it all and still blossom given a little time.

Like them, she just needed a little time.

Liam chuckled around his next sip. "Come sit with us. Farrah wants to ask you about your research project with Colt."

"And you?"

"Me?" He shrugged. "I think you're cool. Come prove me right."

Ellory was no more able to resist him here than she had been in her dreamworld. She let his golden retriever–esque enthusiasm sweep her away, until she was sandwiched between Liam and Farrah in the dining room, deep in conversation about school assignments and bookstores, lacrosse practice and charity functions.

It wasn't that Ellory had avoided Liam since destroying the Old Masters and putting the Lost Eight and the Graves Ghost to rest, but she hadn't gone out of her way to fulfill her promise to a man who didn't exist either. Her memories of what hadn't been were as painful for her as the three years of time she'd lost, trapped in the tower of a lodge that no longer existed, and she already felt out of sync with the world. Tai had Cody. The other Godwin Scholars had one another. Ellory had a love that only she remembered and an aunt she spent half her phone calls lying to.

She'd started keeping a journal, just so the things she'd lost in that world—the memories of Miss Claudette, of the attack on the fictitious quad, of all the things magic had taken away without her even realizing—were preserved. She was strong enough now to pick which memories she wanted to give away to cast her spells, but it calmed her to know that something, somewhere, would remember what she couldn't.

But Ellory couldn't sulk forever, especially not in the wake of Liam's innocent olive branch. She had freed herself—freed them all—so they could live a life that they chose. It was time for her to start living it.

After all, the pain was part of what made it real.

◆

The journalism major at Warren University was a prestigious murder weapon.

Ellory stared in dismay at her blank Word document and the article she hadn't written that was due to her editor in four hours. Boone had moved the deadline three times already, and she dreaded asking him for another extension. He was a nightmare to work under. Her writing had never been better, but her sanity had dwindled to frequent daydreams of slamming his head into one of the printers.

It was only three weeks into the spring semester of her freshman year—the semester she'd missed the first time around—and already stress flavored the stagnant air inside Graves Library. Ellory had witnessed six breakdowns in the hour since she'd claimed this table, and she was doing her best to avoid becoming the seventh. Two freshmen giggled their way through a muted video on their phones, and that was the only levity in the room. Every other station was packed with studying students, red-eyed and pale, carrying flasks filled with either coffee or vodka.

Ellory wouldn't judge either way.

She returned her attention to the cursor that mocked her with every blink. Then a shadow fell over the table, and her article became the last thing on her mind.

Hudson Graves stood before her like he'd stepped from the pages of an airline magazine. His hair was styled into its usual fade, but the black curls that tumbled over his forehead were not, for once, dyed white blond. His natural hair color looked good on him.

Then again, what didn't?

"Can I sit here?" he asked, as though he expected her to stab him through the hand. "All the other tables on this floor are full."

Ellory stared at him for a little too long before she managed a silent nod.

Every day. She had come to the Graves every day in the hopes of catching a glimpse of the man pulling out the chair across from her. Since she had switched her major, they no longer had classes together. Colt's research project had become her new work-study, so she and Hudson didn't run into each other at the coffee shop. And she wasn't bold enough to take a car to the off-campus housing of three graduating seniors who barely knew who she was.

So she'd come to the Graves before and after classes, staying until she ran out of work to do and felt guilty hoarding a table from someone who actually needed it. All she had learned so far was that Hudson must have come to the library only to see her, because without their preexisting relationship, he was *never fucking here.*

Until now.

"Yes, my family donated this library," Hudson drawled without looking up from his textbook. "Please stop staring at me."

"Huh? Oh. No, that's not—no."

He gave her a disbelieving look. "That's not...?"

"All my eloquence went into this article, I'm afraid." She rubbed her eyes and forced herself to focus on something other than how beautiful he was. How much she missed him. How much time they'd already lost. "And the only thing I've even written so far is *Warren University.*"

Hudson's mouth twitched like he wanted to smile. "I thought you seemed familiar. You work with my roommate on the *Warren Communiqué.*"

"I suffer from your roommate on the *Warren Communiqué.*"

The smile broke free. "We do have a bet going on which of you will attempt to kill him first."

"If he keeps going the way he's going, it'll be more of a *Murder on the Orient Express* situation. We'll each grab a letter opener and just lay into him."

She mimed stabbing, gratified when Hudson chuckled. There had been a tension to his shoulders under the weight of her gaze that slowly disappeared as he warmed up to her. He brought up Julius Caesar, comparing her to Brutus. She countered with the Praetorian Guard, as one who wouldn't act alone without benefit to the group. They moved from Roman history to Greek plays to Egyptian gods, their work forgotten on the table.

Ellory felt it then: That push and pull. That give-and-take. That sense of a circuit completing, igniting a spinous connection between them. Sometimes, love was driving through the night to reach the other's side or the gift of a warm coat in a cold orchard. Sometimes, love was heated touches and whispered secrets and fighting through the dark to be each other's light. But sometimes love was an exposed wound, combative and destructive and obsessive in its desire to be expressed.

She and Hudson were not in love, not yet, perhaps not ever. But she had chosen him again and again. He had found her again and again. Their lives were meant to be intertwined. In a volatile world, they were the only thing that made sense.

I've had the honor of watching you fall in love with me again and again. Give me the chance to fall in love with you a second time.

"I have to finish this article," she said reluctantly. An hour had passed, and he was keeping a list of her favorite Hercule Poirot mysteries, but if she missed her deadline, then Boone might stab *her*. "But would it be inappropriate of me to ask for your number?"

His eyes sparkled. "So you can find out what I think of the books?"

"Something like that."

Hudson wrote it down on a new sheet of paper, which he pushed across the table. When Ellory reached for it, their fingers brushed, and she felt a spark that left her breathless. He was still staring at her when she looked up, searching for something she knew he wouldn't find. Not yet.

But as she wrote her number under his, tore the page in half, and passed it back, she thought, *Maybe someday.*

Of all the things reclaiming her magic had given her, perhaps the most important of them all was *time*. Magic had ensured Aunt Carol always had her heart medication, pills duplicated whenever she ran low, so they could both reduce their hours at work. Magic had eased her financial insecurity, credit cards paid off with money they didn't really have, so she had the space to do things she wanted instead of only things that she needed. That was all true power was, in the end: the ability to live a comfortable life.

Without the Old Masters, those who remembered that magic existed had been reduced to the circle of students she had rescued from the tower. They had yet to gather in the same room again, but sometimes Tai, Cody, and Ellory would drive out to the farthest reaches of Hartford and practice what little wild magic they had retained. Sharing their magic for stronger spells. Collapsing in joyful exhaustion to watch the passing clouds. If Sofia, David, Imani, or Ximena still used their powers, Ellory wasn't close enough to them to ask.

But they were free to make that choice. The ghosts that had once haunted the campus were finally at rest. And no one but her editor had tried to kill her lately.

For now, that was enough.

"Maybe I'll see you around, Morgan," Hudson said, packing up his bag and lingering by the table.

"Ellory," she said. "You can call me *Ellory*, if you want."

"All right."

There was a wrinkle between his eyebrows, like he wanted to say something more but couldn't imagine what that something more would be. He visibly let it go and wandered off with a wave that was only slightly awkward coming from him.

Minutes later, her phone buzzed on the table, and the screen flashed with his name.

graves: hello ellory

Her smile widened from the rush of new beginnings. *Someday* had never felt so close.

Just like that, her writer's block cleared, and the opening of her article poured out of her like something from a partially remembered dream: WARREN UNIVERSITY STARTED AS A JOKE...

READING GROUP GUIDE

1. Ellory identifies herself as someone who isn't "needy enough for a single needs-based grant." How does her relationship with money guide her choices in the story despite not coming from poverty?

2. What do you think draws Hudson and Ellory to each other beyond their academic capabilities? What traits do they have in common? In what ways are they foils of each other?

3. How did her relationship with Liam help Ellory clarify her relationship with Hudson? Do you think there was something that she could have done differently by the end of her relationship with Liam?

4. Ellory is a first-generation immigrant who was born in Jamaica and moved to America when she was a kid. How does this fish-out-of-water perspective shape her views about hard work and success?

5. It takes Ellory a while to truly begin questioning her reality and commit to the mystery unfolding on campus. Would you have waited until the same point? Which event would have spurred you to investigate sooner (or later)?

6. Warren University is a fictional university, but it acts as an amalgamation of several higher education institutes. Which parts of academic and social life there felt the most relatable to you?

7. Hudson and Boone's childhood bond is painted as both a good thing and a toxic thing at various parts of the story. How do the two boys help each other? How do the two boys hurt each other?

8. Tai and Cody's romance provides a stable contrast to Ellory's tumultuous love life throughout the book while at times isolating her when she needs someone in her corner. How do Tai and Cody each prove that they are always there for Ellory? In what ways could she be a better friend to them?

9. The Lost Eight are both a secret and a legend on the Warren campus. How can we raise awareness for those invisible people whose names are too often forgotten by history?

10. Both Ellory and Hudson have issues with their families despite being varying degrees of close with them. How do their families shape the people they became? How do our families shape the people we become because of or in spite of them?

11. bell hooks is a beloved writer to Ellory and Hudson—and many real people across the world. What is your favorite bell hooks quote or work and why?

12. At the end of the story, Ellory and Hudson's relationship has drastically changed. Where do you think their connection will go from here?

A CONVERSATION WITH THE AUTHOR

***An Arcane Inheritance* is your adult debut. Why did you want to tell this story for an adult audience?**

   I've always planned to be a hybrid author who writes for both the young adult and adult age categories, but *An Arcane Inheritance* came to me fully formed as an adult book. I knew I wanted to talk about someone who started college "late" as a means of grappling with how behind I felt on African-American history my entire life, and thus Ellory would be in her early twenties. I also knew that this would be less of a coming-of-age story and more of a grappling-with-a-past-much-larger-than-you story. For that, I needed a level of maturity that some of my more impulsive teen characters lack, but not so much maturity that they wouldn't be a little reckless. *An Arcane Inheritance* best fits in that new-adult college-set age, but it's definitely more for adults who have already struggled with much of what Ellory is struggling with than it is for children with college ahead of them.

Like you, Ellory is a first-generation Jamaican immigrant. What else do the two of you have in common?

That's really about it! Like me, Ellory wanted to major in journalism, but unlike me, she's instead majoring in political science out of a sense of obligation toward the sacrifices made on her behalf. I wrote her as being from Jamaica, because that was easiest and that's what I know, but she was her own character from the start. I can't say I'd do even half of the things she does in the book!

How did you go about crafting Hudson Graves as your male lead?

I love the academic rivals-to-lovers trope in general and especially in dark academia, so I really wanted to make him Ellory's intellectual equal. She is humble and playful; he is arrogant and cutting. She is hardworking and unlucky; he is privileged and wealthy. I wanted someone who would challenge her without belittling her, who respected her even when he condescended to her. And, on the other hand, there is an entire world of thought and emotion inside of Hudson that only Ellory is capable of teasing out.

Why did you choose the name *Warren* for the fictional university?

Without too many spoilers, a key part of the school's history is that it was founded by members of the New England Society for Psychic Research, founded by Ed and Lorraine Warren of *The Conjuring* fame. There's even a deleted scene where Ellory goes to the museum they used to have! However, I also chose the name *Warren* because of one of the meanings of the word: "a maze of passageways or small rooms." My protagonists certainly explore several mazes of passageways and small rooms.

Despite taking place in our world, queerness is treated as casually mundane. Why did you make that narrative choice?

Whether writing a contemporary fantasy or a high fantasy, I like to write queernormative worlds. There are so many incredible authors who tackle the issues and discrimination facing the queer community head-on, and I highly suggest checking out those books, too, for a comprehensive and well-rounded reading experience. But queernormative worlds are what I prefer to write for my own healing journey.

Were any of the events in the book based on your real college experience?

Almost everything that was said to Ellory during the salon—you know the one—was said to me at some point during my four years at college. I also very much learned about American culture from media, though for me it was older stuff like *Looney Tunes*, *The Brady Bunch*, and *I Love Lucy*.

Was there any media that helped inspire this book?

Eventually, I will discuss at length how this story was largely shaped by a *Riverdale* fanfiction that I imprinted on, but today is not that day. I would say that this book is perfect for fans of *The Conjuring*, due to the Ed and Lorraine Warren connection; *Inception*, due to the constant questioning of reality; and Beyoncé's *Renaissance* album.

ACKNOWLEDGMENTS

As it turns out, writing your acknowledgments never gets any less stressful, so bear with me as I try to be brief.

One day, on the bus home from the Bronx Zoo, a girl sat down next to me and asked me about my favorite anime. Twenty-two years later, I am publishing books because that girl, Lauren, became my best friend and believed in me before anyone else did. If I only get one great love in this life, I'm glad it was you. Who needs romance when I have the best friend in the world?

Speaking of the best, I want to thank my agent, Emily Forney. Despite being my sworn enemy, there is no one in this world I could imagine navigating the publishing world with. You are my biggest bully and cheerleader, and I'm constantly in awe of you as a business partner and as a human being. I can't wait to see what we do next.

I want to thank my editor, Mary Altman, who saw the potential in this book when it was only a proposal and pushed me—and my story—to become stronger with every edit. I look forward to every midnight email and every Zoom conversation derailed by our mutual love of video games and horror movies.

I want to thank the entire team at Sourcebooks and Poisoned Pen Press: Emily Engwall, Mandy Chahal, Hartley Christensen, Nia Saxon, Ash Jon, Erin Fitzsimmons, Stephanie Rocha, Jessica Thelander, Kirsten Clawson, Tara Jaggers, Milly McKinnish, Diane Cunningham, Holli Roach, Manu Velasco, and Aimee Alker.

Chelsea, my love, my light. Thank you for listening to me cry, complain, and otherwise whine about how I couldn't get this book right, and then about how terrified I was to put it out into the world. Your opinion is always the most important to me when it comes to every story, and it especially means the world to me that you like this one.

Tyler, Jane, and Ebony, this book is dedicated to you three because you were not only my cheerleaders but my reference points to what people wear and drink at those college parties I never went to. I've never met three more loyal and inspirational people, and I'm made better just by being in your orbit.

Nadia, Ysa, and Maddie, thank you for contributing your knowledge of political science and what classes that major entails. A second thank-you to Ysa for reading an entire bad draft of this book in, like, two weeks and asking for more Boone.

Thank you to my cat, Sora, who is asleep on my arm as I write this. I will forever be grateful that you joined our family. Thank you to my sister, Dashá; my parents, Colin and Daisy; and my family across the globe. You shaped me into the person I am today, and I like to think that person's pretty cool.

Thank you to Britt, Riley, Maura, Zach, Mel Karibian, Gina Orlando, Grace Varley, Laura R. Samotin, Taylor Grothe, Terry J. Benton-Walker, Kelly Andrew, Betty Hawk, Page Powars, Tashie Bhuiyan, Chloe Gong, Christina Li, Zoe Hana Mikuta, Margaret Owen, Pascale Lacelle, the entire Debut Chat, Alaa Al-Barkawi,

Arzu Bayraktar, Ryan Ram, Amani Salahudeen, Ale Massenbürg, Audris Candra, Nadirah Ashim, and Marwa Sarraj. I just think you're all neat.

Thank you to the authors who blurbed my book, to the people who hyped my book, and to the readers who bought my book. I couldn't do any of this without this support, and I'll never take it for granted.

Finally, thank you to myself. There was a time when finishing even one book felt impossible, and now I've published several! Thank you, young me, for never giving up on yourself. I'm so proud to be you.

ABOUT THE AUTHOR

Kamilah Cole is a bestselling Jamaican American author, who has been nominated for a Lodestar Award, a Lambda Award, and a Dragon Award. Her previous work includes *So Let Them Burn* and *This Ends in Embers*, the Divine Traitors duology. A graduate of New York University, Kamilah is usually playing *Kingdom Hearts* for the hundredth time, quoting early *SpongeBob SquarePants* episodes, or crying her way through Zuko's redemption arc in *Avatar: The Last Airbender*.